I0757621

ELLEN JACOBSON

Smitten with Travel Romantic Comedy Collection

Books 1–3

First published by Ellen Jacobson 2022

Copyright © 2022 by Ellen Jacobson

All rights reserved. No part of this publication may be reproduced, stored or transmitted in any form or by any means, electronic, mechanical, photocopying, recording, scanning, or otherwise without written permission from the publisher. It is illegal to copy this book, post it to a website, or distribute it by any other means without permission.

This novel is entirely a work of fiction. The names, characters and incidents portrayed in it are the work of the author's imagination. Any resemblance to actual persons, living or dead, events or localities is entirely coincidental.

Find out more at ellenjacobsonauthor.com

First edition

Editing by By the Book Editing
Cover art by Melody Jeffries Design

This book was professionally typeset on Reedsy.
Find out more at reedsy.com

Contents

III   Smitten with Strudel

I

Smitten with Ravioli

1 - Parkaphobia

Is it weird to be jealous of other people's phobias?

One of my friends has omphalophobia—belly buttons freak her out. It doesn't matter whether it's an innie or an outie; she hyperventilates at the mere sight of one. Once, when I managed to drag her to the pool, she reached into her tote bag, pulled out a roll of duct tape, and slapped a large piece on my navel. Ripping that sucker off hurt worse than getting waxed. Note to self—be careful who you wear bikinis around.

My aunt has pogonophobia. Men with beards cause her to break out in a cold sweat. That's probably one of the reasons why she became a nun. Not a lot of guys hanging around the convent. Although, the last time I saw her, she was sprouting a few of those chin hairs that older ladies sometimes get. I'm not sure who the saint of unwanted facial hair is, but I'd bet my bottom dollar that my aunt is offering up a lot of prayers to him.

Then there's my neighbor. She has hylophobia. Wood makes her extremely uncomfortable. And we're not just talking about the large trees you see when you go for a hike in the forest. No, she's been known to faint at the mere sight of a toothpick. Show her some wooden chopsticks and she develops an unpleasant rash all over her body. Needless to say, whenever she comes over for dinner, we order pizza, not Chinese.

My phobia is utterly dull in comparison. I have aerophobia. Yep, I'm scared of airplanes. Boring, right? Whenever I tell people that I'm afraid to fly, they yawn and change the subject. But, I bet you if I told them I have anatidaephobia (the fear that ducks are watching me) or feretrophobia (the fear of coffins and being buried alive), they'd perk right up. Because those are interesting phobias. Phobias that are hard to spell. Phobias that make for scintillating cocktail party conversations. Phobias that get featured on daytime television.

Although, the more I think about this, maybe my phobia isn't all that bad in the scheme of things. It doesn't impact my daily life. I can go to the beach, look indifferently at the belly buttons on display, admire the surfer dudes sporting facial hair, all while eating ice cream with one of those little wooden spoons.

The only thing I have to worry about is avoiding flying. Piece of cake—there are cars, buses, trains, and even unicycles that can get you around.

Of course, a car, bus, train, or unicycle won't really cut it if you're trying to get from the States to Europe. For that you need a boat. A big boat. A boat so big it comes with fine dining, shopping, and Broadway shows. Yes, that's right, we're talking about a cruise ship. Just like the one I was about to embark on for my transatlantic crossing from Miami to Rome.

* * *

"Did you remember your passport, Ginny?" my mom asks as she makes a right turn into the parking lot at the cruise ship terminal.

"Of course I remembered," I say as I unfasten my seatbelt.

"Hey, buckle back up, Ginny," she says, gripping the steering wheel tightly. "I haven't stopped the car yet."

"Mom, relax. We're almost there."

She turns her head sharply and gives me her patented "listen-here-missy" look. "My car, my rules, young lady. Now fasten that seatbelt until I've found a spot and turned off the engine."

I'm pretty sure my mom has some sort of parking phobia. She can pass people on the highway going ninety miles an hour without batting an eye, but she's a nervous wreck when it comes to positioning her car between two other vehicles. There have been times when she's made me get out of the car with a ruler to take measurements. I've never been able to find an official name for her particular brand of irrational fear, so I call it "parkophobia." Not to be confused with parkaphobia—a fear of puffy jackets.

While we circle the lot for the fifth time in search of the perfect spot, I try to lighten the mood by changing the subject. "You know that I'm not a 'young lady' anymore."

"Please," she says between clenched teeth. "You're twenty-five. That's young. And I raised you to be a lady, so that makes you a young lady."

Having learned over the years not to question her particular brand of logic, I simply nod in response.

She leans forward and points at the far end of the lot. "Does it look like they're leaving? That spot would be perfect. It's right next to a loading zone so no one can park next to me."

I check the time on my phone. We're running late. Probably better not to mention that a truck might park in the loading zone. The thought of a large vehicle pulling in next to hers would freak her out and send her in search of another spot, which could take ages. There's no way I'm going to miss boarding this ship. It's my ticket out of here and, hopefully, the start of my brand new life. A new life guaranteed to make me forget all about what's-his-name.

Oh, wow, I can't believe I said "what's-his-name." That is huge progress. Just one look at the cruise ship and I can't even remember the jerk's name. I rub my hands together and smile. This selective amnesia feels awesome.

My mom finally parks the car, turns off the engine, and we walk toward the terminal entrance.

"Has Joel apologized yet?" my mom asks, totally spoiling my good mood.

I lift my suitcase over the curb and set it down. "Who?" I ask innocently.

"Joel."

"I don't know who you're talking about," I say, furrowing my brow.

"Sweetheart, you can't pretend the last two years of your life didn't happen." She squeezes my hand. "What he did to you was horrible, but you have to make peace with it so that you can move on with your life."

I snatch my hand away. "Whose side are you on?"

"I'm on your side, of course," she says as she hugs me. "But did you ever think that maybe what happened is for the best? I never was convinced that getting your PhD and becoming a professor was the right path for you." I try to pull away, but she squeezes me tighter. "And it's not because you're not smart enough or talented enough."

My eyes well up with tears as she releases me. "Of course it is. Why else did they side with him and not me?"

I bite my lip as I remember that fateful day when my thesis advisor called me into his office to tell me that I had been charged with plagiarism. The jerk—who I had wasted two years of my life dating—stole my research paper, presented it as his, then had the nerve to accuse me of being the cheater. The worst part of it was that everyone believed him, not me. Obviously no one thought I was smart enough or talented enough to have written it on my own.

My thesis advisor gave me a choice—drop out of graduate school or face the humiliation of going through a formal hearing. I chose the former. After moving back to my mom's house in Florida, I spent the next couple of months eating ice cream and potato chips on her couch while watching Spanish-language soap operas. Those shows can really suck you in, even if you don't understand a word they're saying.

One day, as I was flicking through the channels, I stumbled across an Italian cooking show and that's when it hit me. I knew how to get my life back on track—go to Italy, learn how to make pasta, then come back home and open a restaurant.

My mom wasn't quite sure that it was a well thought through plan, but she agreed that a change of scenery would do me good, even offering to help me pay for the trip.

I give my mom another hug, then say, "Dad would be so disappointed if he could see me now. A grad school dropout who can't even get a job teaching high school history. He always wanted me to go into academia and become a professor like him."

"Young lady, that is simply not true. If your father were alive, he'd tell you the same thing." She cups my face in her hands. "Virginia Morgan

Maarschalkerweerd, you listen to me, you hear? All he ever wanted was for you to be happy. He didn't care what kind of career path you took. You put that pressure on yourself, not him."

I straighten my shoulders at the sound of my full name. She only wheels that out when she means business.

"See those girls over there?" My mom indicates two women about my age. The taller one pushes her long, dark-brown hair behind her ears and smiles as her petite, blonde friend points at a large, colorful sign festooned with balloons that says, "Welcome Aboard the *Ocean Queen*!"

"See how happy they look?"

I nod.

"I bet that's because they're following their own paths, not doing what they think everyone else expects of them."

I raise my eyebrows. "That's kind of a stretch, mom. Who knows what their back stories are?"

She shakes her head. "Fine, but you get what I'm trying to say. Consider what happened with Joel and grad school to be a blessing in disguise. Take this time on the crossing over to Europe and then in Italy to figure out what will truly make you happy."

After giving me one last squeeze, we say goodbye and I set off on my new adventure. An adventure full of lots of pasta and free of backstabbing, nerdy historians.

* * *

Later that night, after settling into my cabin, I get ready for dinner. It will take over a week to get to our first port of call, Tenerife, the largest of the Canary Islands, which lie off the coast of West Africa. We'll be there for less than twenty-four hours before departing for Rome, where I'll disembark and begin my new adventure.

Because we have so much time at sea and people are likely to get stir-crazy, the crew has organized all sorts of activities, including themed events to keep everyone occupied. Tonight is a 1950s-style barbecue on the lido deck.

I came prepared for the occasion, having packed a tea-length skirt complete with a petticoat to give it fullness. I pair it with an ecru scoop-necked cashmere sweater, white gloves, and a strand of pearls. After putting a wide-brimmed hat atop my auburn curls, I check out my appearance in the mirror. Sure, the fifties were a fashionable era, but if they'd had any idea that yoga pants awaited them in the future they would have worked harder at building a time travel machine, turned the dial to take them forward in time to the twenty-first century, and scooped up a bunch of the stretchy garments on sale at Walmart. If you're going to chow down at a barbecue, clothes made of Lycra are the way to go.

My stomach grumbles, telling me it's time to stop gazing at my reflection. I grab my phone, then frown. I'm going to a 1950s event. They didn't have cell phones back then, so if I want to be true to the time I should leave it behind. Besides, that will keep me from re-reading the texts I sent to what's-his-name.

The texts demanding an explanation.

The texts demanding an apology.

The unanswered texts.

The texts that bring tears to my eyes one minute then leave me clenching my fists in anger the next.

Yes, I know, I should delete them. But I can never bring myself to do it.

I take a deep breath, smooth down my skirt, and remind myself that what's-his-name is firmly in the past. Then I chuck my phone into my dresser drawer and head to the barbecue.

Walking out onto the deck, I could swear I've been transported back in time. The tables are covered in red-and-white gingham tablecloths, people are playing croquet and horseshoes, kids are attempting to hula hoop, and there are a lot of poodle skirts, saddle shoes, and letterman sweaters on display.

As I stand in line at the buffet, I spot the two women my mom pointed out to me earlier. They're both dressed similarly to me—full skirts, gloves, pearls, and hats.

The brunette smiles at me. "Looks like we shop at the same place." She holds out her hand. "I'm Isabelle."

"Ginny," I say, shaking her hand.

"And this is my friend, Mia," she says, pointing at the blonde.

"Nice to meet you," Mia says as she grabs a plate from the stack at the end of the buffet table. Before she can pass it to Isabelle, it slips out of her hand. One of the waiters rushes over, says something in French to us, then cleans up the broken pieces from the floor. Was it my imagination or did he wink at Mia?

"It's these stupid gloves. They're slippery," Mia says, yanking them off. "How did anyone manage to get anything done back in the fifties wearing these things?"

"They probably are a safety hazard," I say, taking mine off as well. "Now what do I do with them? I don't have any pockets, and I didn't bring a purse."

Mia grins, then sticks her gloves down the front of her sweater. "That's what bras are for," she says. "They're great for holding your phone and money, along with gloves when you don't have any other way to carry them."

I giggle at the sight of the fingertips of Mia's gloves peeking out from her neckline. It looks like Thing from *The Addams Family* has taken up residence. Then I tuck my own down my sweater. Who cares how stupid I look? It's not like I'm trying to attract anyone. The last thing I need is another backstabber in my life.

Isabelle shrugs, then follows suit and joins the bra-stuffing brigade.

As we load up our plates with hamburgers, hot dogs, corn on the cob, coleslaw, and deviled eggs, Isabelle asks me if I'm traveling on my own. When I tell her I am, she insists that I join them at their table.

"Oh, yes, join us," Mia says. "But only on one condition. No talking about guys."

"Mia just had a bad break-up," Isabelle says.

"Bad?" Mia scowls. "Bad is what you say when you're describing the taste of beetroots. My mother would wash my mouth out with soap if I used a word that really describes what happened, so I won't. You'll just have to trust me, it was a lot worse than eating beetroots."

I set my plate down. "You won't get any argument from me. The last thing I want to talk about is guys. Besides, I hate beetroots too."

"Cool," Mia says as she scratches her leg. "Let's talk about why these petticoats itch so much instead. What I wouldn't give for a pair of yoga pants right now."

"Me too. I could live in my yoga pants twenty-four seven," Isabelle says. "But despite the gloves and the petticoats, you have to admit traveling to Europe on a cruise ship is heavenly. It sure beats flying."

Mia shudders. "I hate flying."

"That makes two of us," I say.

"Make that three," Isabelle adds.

I smile as I spread butter on my corn. I think I've found my tribe.

* * *

After polishing off our hamburgers and hot dogs, Mia, Isabelle, and I are enjoying angel food cake topped with strawberries. Mia informs us that because angel food cake isn't made with butter or oil, it's a healthy, guilt-free dessert option.

Isabelle raises her eyebrows and points at the chocolate milkshake her friend is slurping down. "How many calories does that have?"

Mia cocks her head to one side. "Does what have?"

"That shake, silly."

After taking another sip, Mia waves her hand in front of Isabelle's face as though she's hypnotizing her. "This isn't the shake you're looking for."

Isabelle snorts. "Your Jedi mind tricks aren't going to work on me. Or on your hips. That shake is real, sweetie." Then she turns to me and says,

"Mia is obsessed with *Star Wars*. She even has a light saber. Fortunately, I was able to convince her to leave it at home."

"Yeah, I could never really get into those movies," I say.

Mia gasps. "You don't like *Star Wars*?"

"No, I'm more into documentaries. You know, stuff that's real."

Mia shakes her head, mutters something about the force being real, then tips the glass to her lips and drains its contents.

"Is anyone sitting here, girls?"

I turn and see an elegant older woman standing by an empty chair. She's wearing a blue sheath dress paired with lavender gloves. Like us, she's wearing a wide-brimmed hat, but hers is accented with a ribbon that matches her dress.

"It's free," I say. "Please have a seat, ma'am."

She wags her finger at me. "We'll have none of that 'ma'am' nonsense. That makes me feel positively ancient. The name's Celeste." After we introduce ourselves, she sits with a flourish, removes her high heels, and rubs her feet. "I'll tell you, the 'Boogie Woogie' will really take it out of you. But it was worth it. He's dreamy, don't you think?"

"Who?" Isabelle asks.

Celeste nods at a man with salt-and-pepper hair twirling another woman around the dance floor.

"Is that your husband?" I ask.

The older woman's smile fades. "No, my Ernie passed away."

I lean forward and squeeze her hand. "I'm sorry. Did you lose him recently?"

"Yes," she says. "He's only been gone for five hundred and thirty-six days now." She glances at her watch. "Or is that five hundred and thirty-seven days? I get all mixed up with the time changes when I'm traveling."

"Do you travel a lot?" Mia asks.

"Oh, yes," she says, her eyes brightening. "This is day four hundred and ninety-eight of my world travels. Or is that four hundred and ninety-nine days?" She shakes her head. "Anyway, I'm headed to Greece next. What about you girls? Where are you going?"

"I'm disembarking in Rome and taking a train from there to Ravenna," I say.

"Where's that?" Celeste asks.

"It's in northern Italy near the Adriatic sea," I say. "About an hour away from Bologna. It used to be the capitol city of the Western Roman Empire from..." I frown as my voice trails off. "Sorry, you don't want to hear about all that."

"You sound like a history buff," Celeste says.

I chew on my lower lip. "I used to be. Now I'm a, um, a..."

"A what?" Celeste prompts.

"I'm not sure," I say, wrinkling my brow. "But I do know that I'm not a historian anymore." I take a deep breath. "But enough about me. Where are you two headed?" I ask Mia and Isabelle, realizing we haven't discussed this.

Celeste points at the three of us. "You mean you girls aren't traveling together?"

"No," I say. "I'm on my own. I just met Isabelle and Mia tonight."

She pats my hand. "Good for you. I wish I had had half the confidence you do when I was your age. But I'm making up for lost time now. Look at me, traveling solo and dancing with handsome strangers." She looks wistfully at the dance floor, then turns back to us. "So where are you two going?" she asks my new friends.

"We're getting off in Rome too," Isabelle says. "After that, it's all up in the air. The only thing I know is that I have to be in Cologne by the beginning of July. I've got a job working on one of those German river cruise boats lined up."

Mia looks forlornly at her empty shake glass, then adds, "Once we get to Cologne, I'm going to head to Paris and try to get a job at an art gallery."

"Mia is a really talented artist," Isabelle says.

"Oh, I'd love to see your paintings," Celeste says. "What do you work in? Oils? Acrylics? Watercolors?"

"Ink," Mia says.

"That sounds fascinating. I have a friend who does these wonderful pen and ink drawings of her cats. What kind of paper do you use?"

"Uh, the kind made of human cells."

Celeste looks alarmed. "Human cells?"

"She's a tattoo artist," Isabelle explains. "Emphasis on artist. She does replicas of the great masters' work. You should see the tattoo she recently did of one of Van Gogh's sunflower paintings on this guy's back."

Mia shrugs. "It would have worked better if he hadn't kept squirming. One of the sunflowers turned out looking more like a turnip."

"So what kind of tattoos do you have yourself?" I ask.

Mia laughs. "Me? Are you kidding? I would never get a tattoo. I'm scared of needles."

"Ah, aichmophobia," I say. "That's more common than you'd think."

"Ach-a-what?" Mia asks.

Before I can explain, the dapper man with salt-and-pepper hair walks to our table. "Would any of you ladies care to dance?"

Isabelle, Mia, and I all exchange glances, then point at Celeste and say in unison, "She would."

"Are you sure, girls?" the older woman asks as she slips her shoes back on.

"Definitely," I say.

As Celeste walks toward the dance floor, she says over her shoulder, "Don't go anywhere. After this dance, I want to talk with Mia about getting a tattoo."

2 - Bacon Perfume

I try to ignore the sunlight pouring through the window of my cabin. Normally, I'm an early riser, but this morning all I want to do is stay in bed and snuggle up next to Giuseppe for just a few more hours.

We arrive in Rome today; something I should be looking forward to, but I've had so much fun on this cruise that I don't want it to end. I rub Giuseppe's soft belly and think about how the week whizzed by.

Isabelle, Mia, and I became good friends, hanging out together for the entire cruise. Much of our time was spent eating. The food was delicious. A little too delicious, if you know what I mean. Thankfully, we all packed yoga pants to accommodate the extra pounds we somehow accumulated. When we weren't getting dressed up for dinner, you could find us wearing them.

After the fourth day at sea, we ran out of clean yoga pants. Isabelle suggested we start doing laps around the promenade deck to shed the unwanted weight.

It seemed like a good idea at the time. Then I tried it. Turns out it was not a good idea. Not at all. Isabelle's idea of laps involve hardcore running, not casually strolling around the deck while having a good gossip with your girlfriends. I managed to keep up with her for exactly ten seconds before I tripped and flew headlong into Mia. She had been lounging on a deckchair reading a magazine when I knocked her down to the ground with me.

The cute French waiter was walking by when the incident happened. He helped Mia up, whispering something in her ear that caused her to blush. After a good five minutes of flirting, they finally realized I was still sprawled on the deck clutching my ankle.

While Mia helped me hobble to the doctor's office, she told me she was surprised that I agreed to go running with Isabelle. Apparently, she had set all sorts of track and field records when she was in the Air Force.

Needless to say, from then on my only laps consisted of walking back and forth to the soft serve ice cream machine. By the end of the cruise, I could do one of those laps in under three minutes. I probably deserve some sort of gold medal for always beating my rivals to the soft serve despite my injury.

"I could really go for some ice cream," I say to Giuseppe. "Do you think that's an odd thing to eat for breakfast?"

As usual, Giuseppe doesn't respond. He's the strong, silent type. Well, actually, he isn't all that strong. I could probably snap him in two with one hand while holding an ice cream cone in the other.

I stretch my arms over my head and yawn. Time to get a move on. I shower and get dressed, then look at Giuseppe lounging in bed. "All right, lazy bones, time for you to get going too." I scoop him up, kiss the top of his head, and stick him in my suitcase.

Hey, wait a minute, you didn't think Giuseppe was a random stranger I picked up in the bar last night, did you? Get your mind out of the gutter. I'm not that kind of girl. No, Giuseppe is a teddy bear. A super adorable teddy bear who sports a tiny t-shirt that says "Italia" on it.

Yes, I know, I'm in my twenties and I shouldn't be sleeping with stuffed animals, let alone traveling with them, but who made up that silly rule, anyway? Probably a disgruntled elf at Santa's workshop who wanted to cut down on the number of teddy bears he had to sew during the Christmas rush.

My mom was surprised that I decided to bring Giuseppe with me because of who gave him to me. My eyes get a little misty as I think about how Joel— I mean, what's-his-name—presented the teddy bear to me when we began dating during our first year of graduate school. We'd spent hours together leafing through dusty, old documents in the archives section of the library, followed by passionate debates about the history of the Roman Empire over spaghetti in a hole-in-the-wall Italian restaurant near campus.

One night, when I was making a point about the Roman emperor Augustus, he leaned across the table and kissed me. I never could think about Augustus, the month of August, or the number six after that night without remembering the shivers that went down my spine when he pressed his lips against mine.

Are you wondering what the number six has to do with Roman emperors? August—which was named after Augustus—wasn't always the eighth month in the calendar. In ancient Roman times, it was the sixth month. So, Augustus, August, six...makes total sense, right? Well, it makes sense if you're a historian whose mind likes to go off on weird tangents.

But enough of all this reminiscing. Italy awaits.

I smile at Giuseppe. "You're the only good thing that came out of that relationship." I snap my suitcase shut and place it by the door for the porter to collect, then head to the dining room to meet the girls for our last breakfast together before we head our separate ways.

* * *

After we disembark the cruise ship, the girls and I share a taxi to the train station with Celeste. Celeste had become a bit of a mother figure to us during our transatlantic crossing, offering us advice about our love lives.

We'd point out that none of us currently had a love life and didn't want boyfriends, but she'd wave her hands in the air and tell us that the perfect guy was out there for each of us. Just like her Ernie had been for her. Then she'd launch into more of her dating tips. Some of them were a bit odd, especially after her third margarita, like put the toilet seat up when you're finished to keep him off balance, and wear perfume that smells like bacon, because no one can resist bacon.

As we pull up to the station, I smile as I remember one of Celeste's other pieces of advice—when you're riding public transportation, wear something unusual, like scuba gear. That way, if you're sitting next to a cute guy, it'll be a great conversation starter.

Seriously, she said scuba gear. She swore that it worked for a friend of hers on the subway in New York City. It was love at first sight when he stepped on one of her friend's flippers.

I look down at what I'm wearing. Faded jeans, black flats, and a gray t-shirt that reads, "Don't make me repeat myself. -History." It's nondescript enough that no guy—cute or otherwise—will want to start up a conversation with me.

"Well, I guess this is goodbye," I say as we approach the ticket booth. "We're all headed in different directions from here."

Celeste gives me a hug. Fortunately, she doesn't smell like pork products, bacon or otherwise. "Now, you stay in touch, you hear?" As she rushes off to catch the train that will take her to Brindisi, a port in the heel of Italy, where she'll catch a ferry to Greece, she yells over her shoulder, "Come visit me when you're done with your cooking school, Ginny. The food's fabulous in Greece, especially the baklava."

I turn to Isabelle and Mia to say goodbye, but they're both holding up their train tickets and grinning ear to ear. "Surprise! We decided to go to Ravenna with you," Mia says.

"What? I thought you were headed to Germany and Mia was heading to Paris," I say.

"Eventually," Isabelle says. "But first we want to spend some time in Ravenna and see these mosaics you've been raving about."

"Oh, my gosh, you guys, this is fabulous! We'll have so much fun together." I furrow my brow. "You know I'll be busy during the days, right?"

"Don't worry, we can amuse ourselves," Mia says. "Then at night, you can make us the recipes you learn in your class. I'll even do the dishes."

"It's a deal." I look at the departures board. "Looks like our train is boarding now. Anyone see where Platform B is?"

"Over there." Isabelle points at a sign on the other side of the station. "It leaves in two minutes. We'll need to run to make it."

She tears off, yelling, "excuse me" as she dodges between people. Mia and I follow, panting as we try to keep up. We dart down the stairs leading to the platform and reach the train just as the doors are beginning to close.

Isabelle manages to slip through, then wedges the doors open with her suitcase. The conductor spots us and blows his whistle repeatedly while gesticulating wildly at us. I try to placate him while Mia climbs over Isabelle's suitcase, pulling her own behind her.

"Hand me your bag," Mia says.

As I start to pass it to her, I'm knocked to the ground when someone barrels into me. I sit up in a daze and find myself staring at a man with piercing blue eyes. He's crouched over me, saying something in Italian. I think he's asking me if the fish is fresh.

I feel a spark as he touches my shoulder lightly, then repeats himself.

What is with this guy and fish? What an odd conversation to have with someone in a train station.

I look at his hand, and he pulls it away. I find myself wishing he would put his hand back on my shoulder. Then I shake my head and rub my temples. What is wrong with me? Do I have a concussion? Why am I thinking about this stranger's hand?

"Oh, you're American," the blue-eyed stranger says in English.

I feel my face grow warm. How did he know I'm American? How much of that did I say out loud? Oh, no, did I just say that out loud?

My thoughts—or my spoken dialogue, I'm not sure which—are interrupted by the conductor's whistle.

"I think he wants us to board the train," the man says. "Here, let me help you up."

As I try to stand, I collapse back on the platform, wincing in pain. "Not my ankle again," I say. Yes, I'm pretty sure I said that out loud.

"Did you sprain it?" he asks, placing his hand gently on my ankle. He pushes my jeans up slightly and I feel that sparking sensation again as his fingers brush my bare skin.

"They're not going to hold the train much longer," Isabelle says.

"Maybe we should stay here and get you to a doctor," Mia adds.

I look up in surprise. They're standing right next to me holding their bags. How did I not notice them walking over from the train to where I'm lying on the ground? Was I so mesmerized by this stranger's presence?

"I'll be fine," I say. "I just twisted it."

As Isabelle and Mia help me to my feet, I notice the blue-eyed man picking up books from the platform. They must have fallen when he collided into me. As he puts them into a scuffed leather satchel that looks like it might have belonged to Indiana Jones in a previous life, I see the title of one of them—*The History of the Roman Empire in Ravenna*. I sigh. I read that same book for a seminar in graduate school. Yet another reminder of what's-his-name.

He looks down at the books in his hands, then points at my t-shirt and smiles. "Do you like reading about history?"

"Nope," I say. "I'm more of a sci-fi kind of girl."

Mia looks at me with surprise. I shoot her a meaningful glance.

"Oh, yeah. Ginny is a huge sci-fi geek," she says. "She's seen all the *Star Wars* movies."

The guy shrugs and steps back so that I can hobble onto the train. As we make our way to our seats, I remind myself of what my t-shirt says about not letting history repeat itself. The last thing I need is to be attracted to a history nerd, even if he has amazing blue eyes.

If I ever date again—and that's a big maybe—it'll be with a guy who is as far away from academia as you can get. Perhaps a construction worker. Maybe even a used car salesman. Anything but a dweeby nerd.

* * *

"Here it is," Mia says as she reaches the end of the train compartment. "Let's see, I have 32-A." She points at a window seat. "What do you guys have?"

"I'm 32-B," Isabelle says. "Right across from you on the other side of the table. Ginny must be in one of the seats next to us, 32-C or 32-D."

I clutch the back of the seat in front of me as the train lurches forward, trying not to put my weight on my injured ankle. I glance at my ticket and frown. "No, I'm in 32-G. It's across the aisle."

Mia scoots into her seat. "Sit next to us. No one's sitting there."

"Okay," I say. As I set my purse on the table, the door to the next compartment slides open and a young boy runs through screaming at the top of his lungs in Italian. I'm not exactly sure what he is saying, but I think it has something to do with a Martian invasion.

A harried-looking woman pushes past me and grabs the boy by his arm. She marches him back to where I'm standing and points at the seat next to Mia. He reluctantly sits while she settles in next to Isabelle.

I exchange glances with the girls. Isabelle rolls her eyes. Mia says, "I guess they're not free after all."

I reach down for my purse, then sigh. The little boy is in the process of pulling everything out of my bag and arranging it on the table. His mother is tapping away at her phone, oblivious to the Jenga tower he's creating out of my wallet, make-up bag, and hairbrush. Hopefully, she's doing a search for tips on how to teach children to respect other people's property. I snatch my belongings back and stuff them in my purse.

"Excuse me, miss. Is this yours? I found it on the floor."

I turn and see the man who crashed into me on the platform. He's dressed exactly how you'd expect a history nerd to dress—tweed jacket, a button-down shirt, jeans, and sneakers. After gazing into his blue eyes for a moment too long, I look down to see what he's holding in his hand and groan.

Now would be a good time for the Martians to invade. I'd much rather die from one of their ray guns than from the embarrassment I feel as he hands me a...hmm, how should I put this? Let's just say that it was a particular product that men don't need to buy on a monthly basis.

I glare at the little boy. He giggles. His mother continues to stare at her phone.

"Thanks," I mumble, stowing it in my purse. I keep my eyes averted as I slip into my seat across the aisle from the girls and the mother and son. I sense someone sitting down in the seat across from me. Please let it be a little green man holding a ray gun. I look up. Nope. No such luck. It's the blue-eyed stranger, and he's holding out his hand. The same hand that just a minute ago was holding...well, you know what it was holding.

"I'm Preston," he says.

I reluctantly shake his hand. "Ginny."

"Guess we're going to be seatmates," he says. "Where are you getting off?"

"Bologna," I say. What I don't say is that we'll be transferring there to another train to Ravenna. He already knows what the contents of my purse are. I'm not sure I want to share any other information with him, like my final travel destination.

"Me too." He opens his leather satchel and pulls out a bottle of water. "Want one?"

"No, thanks." I lean my head back and close my eyes, hoping to end the conversation.

He doesn't get the hint.

"Hey, is your suitcase the vintage one that has all those old travel stickers on it?" he asks.

I nod without opening my eyes.

"I love its old-fashioned vibe."

That isn't a question, is it? No need to respond, right?

"It must be heavy to carry though."

This man really can't take a hint. I take a deep breath and open my eyes. If he wants conversation, I'll give him conversation.

Fortunately, Mia pipes up before I can say something I might regret. "It has wheels that are hidden in the bottom," she says from across the aisle. "It looks old, but it's a reproduction. Ginny's mom got it for her."

Preston doesn't even glance at Mia. Instead, he looks directly at me as though I was the one who spoke to him. "That's a nice present," he says.

"She helped pay for Ginny's trip over on the cruise ship too," Mia adds. "This guy betrayed her, and her mom thought—"

Isabelle leans forward in her seat and whispers something to Mia.

"Uh, so where did you say you were from?" Mia asks Preston in an all too obvious attempt to change the subject. "You sound American."

"I'm from Massachusetts," he says, still not making eye contact with Mia. He rests his elbows on the table and locks eyes with me. "Where are you from?"

"Ouch!" I yelp, then bend down to rub my ankle.

"Oh, I'm sorry, did I kick you?" Preston asks with concern. "It was an accident, I swear. Are you okay?"

"I'm fine." I eye the empty seat next to me. "Why don't I move over here? You're a tall guy. You could use the space to stretch out those long legs of yours."

When did I notice that Preston has long legs? I mentally shake myself. Get a grip, Ginny.

As I start to shift into the neighboring seat, two young guys plop down next to us. They reek of cologne. Unfortunately, it doesn't smell like bacon.

"Guess you're not going anywhere," Preston says with a smile.

3 - The Worst Smell Ever

Whoever invented body spray for men has a lot to answer for. I don't mind when a guy dabs a little bit of cologne on his wrists or splashes on some aftershave. In fact, it can be kind of nice, especially if he wears something that makes him smell like he just went for a romantic walk in a pine forest wearing a leather coat.

But, for some reason, there are guys who don't understand less is more when it comes to body spray. They spray and spray and spray until the can is empty, take a quick sniff of their armpits and call it good. Then they head out to slay the ladies.

What they don't realize is that the ladies aren't speechless in their presence because they're so enraptured by their charm and rugged good looks. No, the ladies are speechless because they're choking on the aroma cloud the guys have swirling around them. It's kind of hard to talk when a girl can't breathe.

Maybe I'm not being fair. Some men don't know their own strength. Maybe when they press down on the button on the canister with their big thumbs, it breaks and they inadvertently get every last drop of the fragrance inside the can all over them.

I check out the two guys sitting next to us. There's not an awful lot of upper body strength going on with these two. I'm pretty sure I could take them in an arm wrestling competition. And their thumbs seem smaller than mine. Thumb wrestling would be a breeze.

Nope, there's no excuse for their overwhelming smell—this was not a case of overpowering thumb strength. What makes it even worse is that they don't smell like sandalwood or citrus fruit. That might have been bearable. But this...I don't even know how to describe it.

Wait. I've got it. Imagine a cross between bubblegum and doggy doo-doo. Yep, that about sums it up.

I'm desperate for fresh air. I pinch my nose shut and try to open the window, but the latch is jammed. I start coughing and collapse back in my seat.

"Here, let me get that," Preston offers. I watch as he effortlessly lowers the window, using his normal-sized thumbs to depress the latches.

"Thanks," I say before leaning out the window and taking several deep breaths.

He glances at our neighbors and gives me a conspiratorial look. "Better?" he asks.

"Much." The breeze coming through the window blows the offending odor away from us.

Of course, "away from us" means that it's blowing directly at where my friends are sitting. I chuckle as Mia wrinkles her nose and scowls. I'm impressed with how quickly she lowers her window.

The bubblegum doggy doo-doo guys say something to each other in Italian.

I cup my hand near my face to shield my lips and whisper to Preston, "They're talking about how cold it is in here. You don't think they're going to want us to close the window, do you?"

He furrows his brow. "They didn't say anything about the temperature. They're talking about soccer."

"No, they're not. They're talking about the weather. It's basic Italian 101 stuff." I reach into my purse. "I've got a grammar book in here somewhere. You can look it up."

"That's okay," he says. "My Italian is pretty good."

"Uh, I hate to break it to you, but when you ran into me on the platform, you kept asking me if the fish was fresh. That's the kind of thing you say at the market, not after you've knocked someone to the ground."

"Maybe you should be the one studying that book of yours. I was asking if you were okay, not about fish."

I shake my head. "Nope, it was fish."

"Did you hit your head when you fell?" he asks, biting back a smile. "I think you might have a screw loose. I didn't say anything about cod, haddock, flounder, or any other kind of seafood."

I hold up my hands and shrug. "Fine, have it your way."

"This isn't about my way versus your way." He holds my gaze for what seems like an eternity, those blue eyes of his momentarily hypnotizing me again.

Then he abruptly turns and says something in rapid-fire Italian to the nasally impaired guys. They laugh, then proceed to engage him in a conversation about model airplanes.

At least I think that's what they're talking about. To be honest—and promise you won't tell Preston this—I don't understand everything they're saying. I blame it on the bubblegum doggy doo-doo body spray. If you breathe too much of it in, it can cause your cognitive processes to be impaired. That's just basic science for you.

I pull a novel out of my purse and try to ignore their chattering. The book is far from riveting, but it will be better than listening to the guys prattle on about balsa wood and glue. I flip through the pages, trying to find where I left off.

"What are you reading?" Preston asks as he grabs the book from my hands. "Hmm...a mystery. I thought you would have been reading something sci-fi."

I pull the book back. "I'm broadening my horizons."

"Fair enough," he says as he pulls a familiar-looking hardback book out of his backpack and holds it in front of him. "I had an ex who was always trying to get me to read fiction, but I could never really get into it. I prefer to read about stuff that's real, not stuff that's make-believe."

I tilt my head and try to read the title on the spine of the book. He turns the book around so I can see it—*Sanitation in the Roman Empire*. "Probably not your cup of tea."

"You know, Witmer's theory about the cultural importance of aqueducts is wrong," I say.

He taps the cover of the book. "You've read this?"

"Uh, no...of course not," I splutter before adding, "Only a dweeb would read something like that."

Total lie. Not only have I read it, I wrote a research paper on the subject of how the Romans piped water into their latrines.

"Well, then how do you know about it?" he asks with a quizzical look on his face.

"Oh, um, some guy mentioned it."

"Some guy mentioned it? Seems like an oddly specific conversation."

"Well, it wasn't so much a conversation as it was a pickup line."

"That was his pickup line—Witmer is wrong about the cultural significance of aqueducts?"

I nod.

"Did it work?"

I take a deep breath and look out the window. Something like that worked once. The first time I met what's-his-name, he dazzled me with his insights about the sewage systems at the Roman forts along Hadrian's Wall. But now I can see that it was a load of, um...how should I put this? It was a load of doggy doo-doo.

"No, not at all," I say, turning back to Preston. "I don't go for history buffs."

* * *

I do a fist pump when the conductor announces that Bologna will be the next stop. I am so ready to get off this train, and not just because of the body spray stench. Preston is getting on my nerves. He keeps trying to engage me in conversation, asking all sorts of intrusive questions like, "Where are you from?"

That one's an easy one. I go with the truth—Florida. Then I ramble on for a few minutes about the best way to make orange juice, going into great detail about how to hold the oranges when you squeeze them.

He follows up with a more complicated question. "What do you do for a living?"

I toy with my charm bracelet while I try to think up an answer to give Preston that won't cause me to burst out sobbing. Technically, I'm unemployed. I mean, I used to be a graduate student, but that's not a real job and you certainly don't get rich doing it. In fact, you get poorer as student loans mount up. Now I'm a nothing. A big fat nothing whose only employable skill involves squeezing oranges.

He runs his fingers through his wavy brown hair while he waits for my answer.

Finally, I blurt out, "I'm a chef."

Which is kind of true. Or at least it will be in the future once I finish cooking school. Isn't that what all those self-help books tell you to do? Fake it until you make it? Faking it is my new mantra.

Then he asks what kind of cuisine I make. I tell him my specialty is jus d'orange, which is French for orange juice. Mia taught me that while we were on the cruise ship.

Apparently, Preston doesn't speak French because he looks suitably impressed. Or he has heartburn. Sometimes, it's hard to tell the difference.

"So, what are your travel plans? Where are you going after Bologna?" he asks next.

I opt for an evasive answer. No need for him to know that I'm catching a train to Ravenna once we get to Bologna. I shrug and say, "I'm footloose and fancy free."

Then I laugh. A nervous kind of laugh. I've never been footloose or fancy free in my life. I went straight from high school (straight As, thank you very much) to college (graduated with an honors degree in history), then on to graduate school. My plan was so clear—get a doctorate in history, then become a professor. I never questioned it. I never thought of doing anything else.

Then my plan fell apart.

Preston leans across the table, interrupting my thoughts. "Do you have a b—?"

I can't hear the rest of his question because the conductor makes another announcement.

"Two minutes to Bologna. Two minutes," he says in English and Italian over the crackling loudspeaker.

What was Preston going to ask? Do I have a ball? A balloon? A book? A banana?

Before I can find out, the train comes to a halt and we're busy collecting our belongings.

Preston and I follow the two body spray guys down the aisle to the end of the car. When we reach the luggage rack, I put my weight on my good foot, then grab hold of the handle of my suitcase. It's wedged between a duffel bag and a large cardboard box. As I try to yank it out, I lose my balance and stumble backward.

"Here, let me help you with that," I hear Preston say as he grabs my waist to steady me. I gasp as I feel the heat of his hands burning through my t-shirt. Then I feel my face redden. Does he think I gasped because of his touch?

"You okay?" he asks, and I feel his right thumb press into my back, right above the waistband of my jeans.

I inhale sharply, then close my eyes and let my breath out slowly. "It's just my foot. It still hurts from earlier." I spin around to face him while hopping on one leg.

He leans down and says softly, "I'm sorry to have caused you so much pain."

He's managed to make me forget all about my ankle. Instead, all I can think about is the fact that he smells like he just came back from a long walk in a pine forest wearing a leather jacket. We've been sitting on a train for the past five hours. If anything, he should be smelling like bubblegum and doggy doo-doo by now.

And just like that, the spell is broken. Amazing how the thought of bubblegum and doggy doo-doo will do that.

"No worries," I say, pulling back. "It'll be fine."

"Well, the least I can do is help you with your bag."

He lifts it down from the rack and carries it off the train. After he sets it down on the platform, I hold out my hand. "Thanks for your help."

Preston shakes my hand, a bemused smile on his face. I notice that he holds my hand a bit longer than you normally do when you've just met someone.

"I can take it from here," I say.

He releases my hand. "Your suitcase is too heavy for you to carry with your bad ankle."

"No, it's got wheels, remember?" I pull it back and forth a few times to demonstrate how easy it is to operate. "Besides, my friends can help if I need it. Where are they, by the way?" I was so distracted by Preston that I almost forgot I wasn't traveling alone.

"I think they got trapped behind that little boy and his mom," he says. "It was taking a while for the mom to pack up all of their belongings."

I hear Isabelle's voice before I see her. "Excuse me, excuse me," she says as she pushes her way through the crowd, Mia trailing behind her.

"There you are! We thought we'd lost you," Mia says when she catches up.

Isabelle nudges me. "Or that you'd run off with the hot guy you were sitting across from."

My eyes widen. Why are they embarrassing me in front of Preston?

"What did you do with him?" Mia asks.

"What do you mean? He's right here," I say, looking to my left. But all I see are the bubblegum doggy doo-doo guys. I bite my lip. "I don't know where he went."

"I see him over there," Isabelle says. "It looks like he's pointing something out on a map to that woman." She looks at me slyly. "You seem disappointed that he's talking to another girl."

"Nope, not at all. He may be cute, but he's definitely not my type."

* * *

We catch our next train without another injury being inflicted on my ankle. After an hour rolling through the pretty countryside, the train pulls into Ravenna. We hail a taxi, then head to the apartment Isabelle and Mia got a last-minute rental deal on. As we pull up in front of a rustic three-story brick building, Isabelle's phone beeps.

"That was the owner," she says, reading the text. "He's running late. We're supposed to wait for him in the courtyard and he'll be here soon to give us the keys." She pushes open a green wooden gate and peeks her head through. "This must be it." Isabelle grabs her suitcase and leads the way inside.

"This is so pretty," I say, inhaling the scent of flowers overflowing from terracotta containers. A large cat lying on a black wrought-iron table looks at us and meows softly before closing his eyes. Water bubbles in a marble fountain in the center of the brick patio. The smell of roasting meat wafts down from a window on the second floor. I wrap my arms around myself and sigh contentedly. This is exactly what I was hoping my Italian vacation would be like—beautiful, charming, and relaxing.

"*Buona sera,*" a deep voice says behind me.

I turn and see a man who looks like he just came from a fashion shoot—dark hair swept back into a ponytail, smoldering eyes, and a shirt unbuttoned just far enough so that you know you want to see what else is underneath.

He sets a bottle of wine on the table, then smacks his fingers to his lips before saying, "*Che belle signore.*"

"Oh, I know this one," Mia says. "He called us beautiful ladies."

I frown. Mia really needs to work on her Italian skills. I'm pretty sure he was talking about the price of gas.

"Which one of you is Isabelle?" he asks, his Italian accent making each word sound utterly delicious.

"That's me," she says. "You must be Lorenzo."

He steps toward her and kisses her on both her cheeks in that way Europeans do. "Welcome to Ravenna," he says.

After Isabelle introduces him to Mia, and he does that kissing thing again, he turns to me. "And who is this lovely lady?"

"Ginny." I turn my head slightly so that he can plant his lips on my cheek, but instead he grabs my hand and kisses it passionately.

"What do you Americans call the color of your hair?" he asks as he caresses one of my curls.

I can't speak. I move my lips and try to form words, but nothing comes out. I don't know what kind of body spray Lorenzo is wearing, but it's really intoxicating. Intoxicating in a good way.

Isabelle pipes up. "Auburn."

"Auburn," he slowly repeats, holding my gaze. "It is very pretty." Then he breaks eye contact with me and turns to Isabelle. "The reservation was for only two, but I can arrange for an extra cot."

"Ginny isn't staying with us," Isabelle says. "She's attending a cooking program."

Lorenzo smiles at me. "Ah, you're a chef."

"No," I say. "I'm a novice cook. The program is for beginners."

He rubs his hand across the stubble on his chin. "Where is this program?"

"It's being held at the Villa Romano-Ricci. Do you know it?"

"Yes. It's on the outskirts of Ravenna. They've converted it into a retreat center. They run programs during the summer months for American tourists." He cocks his head to one side. "You don't seem like their typical participant. They're usually, how do you say...ma...ma...mature? Is that the right word?"

I look down at my faded jeans and t-shirt, my typical type of outfit when I was a grad student. I guess a t-shirt with a slogan does look a little immature. Maybe I should have worn something dressier.

"Come," Lorenzo says, motioning us toward the table. He holds up the bottle of wine. "Let's have a toast to your stay in Ravenna before I show you your apartment."

The cat stretches, then paws at the corkscrew lying on the table, trying to knock it to the ground. Lorenzo scoops up the cat and places him in my arms. "Bad cat," he says as he scratches the top of his head.

I hold out the cat at arm's length from my body and scowl. "Can someone take this from me, please?"

Lorenzo chuckles as he opens the bottle of wine. "You don't like cats?"

"No, it's not that," I say as the cat squirms in my arms. "They're fine…at a distance."

He looks at me sympathetically. "Oh, I see. You're allergic to them."

"No, it's not that either." I shudder. "They always drool on me. Cat drool freaks me out."

Mia and Isabelle break out into laughter.

"You're afraid of cat drool?" Mia asks. "That sounds like one of those phobias you're always talking about."

"It's not a phobia," I say. "Phobias are irrational fears. Being afraid of cat drool is perfectly rational. It's gross. Simple as that."

Isabelle takes pity on me and grabs the cat. He purrs loudly as she cuddles him against her neck.

"Freaks out," Lorenzo says. "This is a new expression for me."

He pours a glass of the sparkling red wine for each of us and explains that the Emilia-Romagna region, where Ravenna is located, is known for its Lambrusco. When I take a sip, the bubbles tickle my nose. Naturally that makes me think about how Preston's breath tickled my neck when he leaned in to steady me on the train.

What is wrong with me? Why am I thinking about that nerdy guy when I could be thinking about the hunky Italian standing in front of me?

I take another sip of wine and listen as Lorenzo tells Mia and Isabelle about the West Byzantine mosaics that decorate the fifteen-hundred-year-old churches in Ravenna.

Great, another history buff. Why are the cute ones always obsessed with history?

"Are you a tour guide?" Isabelle asks. "Maybe we could hire you for a private tour of the city."

"No, I, uh, how do you say it…" He makes a hammering motion. "I make the houses."

"You're a construction worker," Mia says brightly.

He beams at her. "Yes. I am a construction worker. It is the family business. My grandfather started it."

"So, not a historian?" I ask. He shakes his head. "You don't like to read books about the Roman Empire or watch documentaries?"

"No, not really," he says.

"Ooh. Do you like sci-fi?" Mia asks.

Lorenzo pulls out his phone, presses the screen a few times and shows it to her. "This is what I like."

"Love the costumes," she says before she hands the phone to me.

I watch the video, then grin. "I can't believe it. You're into *lucha libre*. I used to watch this all the time in between Spanish-language soap operas."

"*Lucha* what?" Isabelle asks, grabbing the phone from me.

"Mexican wrestling," I say, sizing Lorenzo up with interest. A construction worker who spends his time watching wrestlers in outlandish costumes toss each other around a ring. You can't get much further from a history professor than that.

4 - Terms and Conditions Apply

After enjoying another glass of wine in the picturesque courtyard, I say my goodbyes, giving Mia and Isabelle quick hugs and promising to catch up with them the following evening. "*Ciao, bella,*" Lorenzo says while kissing me on each cheek. Is it my imagination or do his kisses last longer than one would expect from a recent acquaintance? Maybe that's just how it's done in Italy.

I make my way to the retreat center where my program is being held. As the taxi pulls up the long circular drive, I admire the large, imposing villa. The building is flanked by several smaller modern buildings, their wood cladding and large picture windows a stark contrast to the villa's ornate brickwork and architectural detail.

I walk up the marble steps, gulping as I approach the entrance to the villa.

What was I thinking, enrolling in cooking school? Sure, I've watched a lot of cooking shows and I've eaten in a lot of restaurants, but the most complex recipe I've ever made involved marshmallows. I'm completely out of my depth. The minute they hand me a chef's knife, they're going to know I'm a fraud.

I pause and take a deep breath. You can do this, Ginny. So what if you end up amputating your finger while you're chopping something? I'm sure they have a well-stocked first aid kit.

While I'm thinking about the merits of butterfly stitches versus traditional stitches, one of the heavy, intricately carved doors creaks open. Two silver-haired women walk out and pause on the top step. One of them looks just like my aunt, Sister Mary Margaret, right down to the exact placement of her chin hairs. She's even wearing all black. The other woman is attired in a bright yellow tunic with a daisy pattern bedazzled on it. She grips the handrail tightly with one hand while clutching a cane with the other.

"Lovely evening, isn't it, dear?" the lady in need of some facial waxing says to me.

Her friend pokes her in the rear with her cane. "Get a move on, Loretta," she says. "I want to get back to our room before the sun goes down."

Loretta rolls her eyes. "Don't mind Mabel," she says to me. "It's the jet lag. Makes her cranky."

"I am not cranky," Mabel says, jabbing Loretta again, this time in her leg.

"You are too."

"Am not."

"Are too."

"Am not."

While the two continue to bicker about whether Mabel is cranky or not, I slip past them into the foyer. My eyes are drawn to the mosaic floor with its pattern of Roman gods and goddesses. Even though I know that it's relatively modern compared with the ancient mosaics you can find in the historic sites in Ravenna, it still takes my breath away.

I look up and see a grand staircase leading to the second floor. Along the left side of the corridor are a series of paneled doors with marble statues set between them. To my right, I spot a sign that says "Silver Fox Registration," its arrow pointing at an arched entryway. I peek my head inside and see a large reception room. An older couple sits on one of the leather couches in front of the tiled fireplace. Despite it being the beginning of June, there's a chill in the air.

"Can I help you?"

I turn and see a woman sitting at a large table at the back of the room.

She beckons me to her. "The staff entrance is at the rear of the building," she says as I approach her.

"Staff?"

"Correct." She peers at me over her reading glasses. "Just go back out the front door, make a right, go around the building, and you'll see a portico. The entrance is through there."

I shake my head. I knew I should have worn something dressier. With my t-shirt and jeans, she thinks I'm here to wash dishes or something. I stand up straight and say firmly, "I'm not staff."

"Of course, you're not," she says. "That's just where the graduate students are meeting Professor Whitaker."

"I'm not a student." I dig my fingernails into the palms of my hands to keep from losing my cool. I've had enough reminders of graduate school and professors already today.

"Sorry, my mistake," she says, adjusting her glasses. "You must be here to see your grandparents."

"Huh?"

She pulls a clipboard toward her and flips through the pages. "I saw a note about that somewhere. Oh, yes, here it is. Maggie MacDonald." She looks back up at me. "Their room is in the Dante Annex. It's the building to the right of the villa. They're in room number six."

I flinch at the sound of the number six. The unlucky number six, a reminder of what's-his-name.

"But I'm not Maggie," I say. "My name is Ginny."

The woman studies her clipboard. "I don't see a Ginny listed. Why don't we try this another way? What are your grandparents' names?"

"My grandparents? What do they have to do with anything?"

She points at her clipboard as though that explains it.

After a long pause, I tell her that they've passed away.

She looks crestfallen. "I'm so sorry." Her expression turns into one of puzzlement. "Then what are you doing here?"

"I signed up for the cooking program." I pull a paper out of my bag. "It says to register here on arrival."

"There must be some mistake. You can't possibly be enrolled in the cooking school."

I place the paper in front of her and tap it with my finger. "It says right there—Ginny Morgan Maarschalkerweerd. Paid in full."

"But, um…" Her voice trails off. She removes her glasses and rubs her temples. Then she leans forward and stares at me intently. "Exactly how old are you?"

I roll my eyes. Oh, come on. I know that sometimes I've been told that I look young for my age, but this is ridiculous. Clearly I'm over eighteen. I point at the form. "My date of birth is right here."

She puts her reading glasses back on and picks the paper up. "You're seventy-eight?"

"No, I'm twenty-five."

"But according to the birth date on this form, you're seventy-eight." She chuckles. "You must have an amazing plastic surgeon."

"There must be some mistake." I grab the paper out of her hands and examine it. "Oh, I see what I did. I transposed the numbers. Anyway, what does it matter? Can I just go ahead and register? It's been a long day and I'm exhausted."

"I'm not sure that this program would be a good fit for you."

I raise my eyebrows. "This is a beginners' course, right?"

"It is, but—"

"Then what's the problem?"

"Well, it's just…" She flings her hands in the air. "The Silver Fox Summer Academy is for seniors. And you're not a senior. Just look around you."

I turn and survey the reception area again. Every single person has white hair. At least those with hair do. "You have got to be kidding me. I signed up for an old folks' class?"

"Obviously, you can still participate in the program if you want. We don't discriminate based on age, but wouldn't you rather hang out with people your own age?"

I put my face in my hands and try to figure out what to do. While I'm considering my options, the unmistakable scent of leather and pine fills the air.

"Oh, hello Professor Whitaker," the woman says. "Your graduate students are waiting for you."

I turn and find myself looking straight into Preston's piercing blue eyes.

* * *

"What are you doing here?" I splutter.

"I could ask you the same thing," he says, a faint smile playing on his lips. "I thought you were staying in Bologna."

"I never said that."

"Yes, you did."

"No, I didn't."

"Yes, you did."

I shake my head. We sound like Mabel and Loretta, the two ladies I met outside. If only I had my own cane—I'd jab Preston in the leg with it.

"I said I was getting off in Bologna. Then I caught a train to Ravenna." I tap my ear. "You have to listen more carefully. Maybe you have some wax buildup going on."

"I was probably too mesmerized by the dimples you get when you smile to have paid attention to what you were saying."

"My dimples?"

"Uh-huh." He turns to set his leather satchel on a chair, then looks back at me. "Yep, there they are. One on each cheek."

I bite my lower lip in an effort to stop smiling. He has no right to look at my dimples. I shouldn't be showing him my dimples.

The woman at the registration desk coughs. "Ahem, Professor. Your students are meeting you by the staff entrance."

"Thank you, Evelyn," he says with a smile.

"I can't believe you're a professor," I mutter.

"Did you think I was lugging all those history books around on the train for fun?" he asks.

"They make nice paperweights."

"That's true." He grins. "I could have been carrying my collection of paperweights, cleverly disguised as books, around with me."

Evelyn stands and pats Preston's hand. "Professor Whitaker is leading the history program here in August. We're honored that he agreed to be part of the Silver Fox Summer Academy."

"Not at all. It's my honor to be here, Evelyn," he says, glancing at her. Then he looks back at me and scratches his head. "So what exactly are you doing here?"

"It's a terrible mix-up," Evelyn says. "She signed up for the cooking program, but didn't realize it was for seniors."

He furrows his brow. "Cooking? But you told me you were a chef."

I clear my throat. "I'm sure I said that I want to become a chef, not that I am one."

"Uh-huh."

I put my hands on my hips. "Are you saying you don't believe me?"

Preston's phone beeps. "I'm running late." He looks at Evelyn. "Did you say they're out back?"

"Yes, by the staff entrance."

He thanks her, then shakes my hand like he did at the train station. A long handshake that's more like a caress. It sends shivers down my spine. "Well, I guess this is goodbye again."

I nod slowly, not trusting myself to speak.

As he walks out of the reception room, he looks back at me and adds, "For now."

For now?

What does that mean?

Evelyn taps her pen on the table, interrupting my thoughts. "So, what did you decide? Do you want to stay in the program?"

I shrug. "Sure. It's not like I have a better plan."

She prints off a stack of forms, staples them together, then places them in front of me. She points at the bottom of the first page. "Sign here." Then she flips through the other pages. "Initial here, here, and here. While you're doing that, I'll get your name badge, room key, and program materials together."

My father always told me to read the fine print before I sign anything, but it's late and I'm exhausted. So I quickly scrawl my signature and initials, then pass the forms back to Evelyn.

"Great," she says, handing me a key card. "Your room is in the Pavarotti Annex. Go back out front and turn left. Walk down the path and you'll see the building." Then she points at a thick folder on the table. "Here are the course materials. Be sure to familiarize yourself with the orientation sheet before tomorrow. Class starts promptly at nine."

As I gather everything up, the key card falls on the floor. I bend down to grab it and spot Preston's leather satchel.

When I show it to Evelyn, she says, "Oh, dear. He forgot it. You know what they say about absent-minded professors."

"I can take it to him if you want," I offer before I realize what I've done. Hopefully, she refuses my offer so that I don't have to see that pompous man again.

"Would you? That would be great. I'm not really supposed to leave the registration desk. He'll be at the staff entrance."

Great. Guess I'm stuck with delivery duty.

My phone rings as I walk toward the rear of the villa. "Hey, Mia. How's the new place?"

"It's fabulous. You should ditch cooking school and come hang out with us."

"You'd be surprised how tempting that sounds right now."

"Does that have anything to do with Lorenzo?"

"Lorenzo? The guy renting the apartment to you? No."

"Come on, I saw the way he looked at you and the way you looked back."

"Sure, he's cute, but...hey, wait a minute, you're the one with the 'no talking about guys' rule. Why are you bringing up Lorenzo?"

"That rule is for me, not you. Maybe you need a holiday romance to get over Jo—"

"Mia," I say in a warning tone. "We don't say that jerk's name out loud."

"Sorry, I mean what's-his-name."

"The last thing I need is any guy," I say. "Whether it's Lorenzo or Preston."

"Preston? The guy from the train?"

I look at the satchel in my hand. "I just ran into him."

"You did?"

"Yeah. He's teaching the history program in August. Just my luck that he's meeting some grad students here today."

"Maybe the universe is trying to tell you something."

I press the phone between my shoulder and ear so that I can shift Preston's bag to my other hand. All those books weigh a ton. "It's trying to tell me to focus on cooking, not romance. Why else would I have signed up for a program with a bunch of senior citizens? There won't be any temptation here."

"Senior citizens?"

Before I can tell her about the mix-up, I see Mabel on the ground with her cane beside her. Preston is kneeling next to her.

"Gotta go," I tell Mia, then rush over to help. "Are you okay?"

Mabel's only response is a grimace.

I glare at Preston. "What is wrong with you? Do you knock every woman you meet onto the ground?"

He helps Mabel to her feet, then guides her to a bench. "Why don't you sit here, ma'am?"

She pats his hand. "Thank you, dear."

"How do you feel?" he asks.

"No worse than usual," she says sweetly.

"Do you want us to call a doctor?" I ask.

"What do I look like? An invalid?" she snaps.

I take a step back and hold my hands up. "Sorry, just trying to help."

"Well, you can help by handing me my cane." When I don't move quickly enough, she shouts, "Any day now, missy."

Before I can hand it to her, Preston grabs it. "I didn't knock her down," he says to me before presenting the cane to the older woman. "Here you go, ma'am."

"Thank you, dear. You're such a nice boy."

Preston looks back at me. "What are you doing with my bag?"

"You left it at the registration desk. I offered to bring it to you." I thrust it in his hands. "Mission accomplished," I say before storming off. This better be the last time I ever set eyes on that man again.

* * *

After a restless night, I wake early the next morning. Giuseppe is perched on the pillow next to me. He looks well rested, as usual. Teddy bears are kind of like cats—they spend their days lounging around napping. Minus the drool, of course, which is a huge selling point. Not to mention eliminating the need for a litter box. Why would anyone have a cat when they could have a stuffed animal to cuddle up with instead?

"I wish I could bring you to class with me," I say. "But I don't want to get flour and tomato sauce on you. Remember the last time I had to put you in the washing machine? I learned an important lesson that day—leftover Chinese food and teddy bears don't mix."

I hit the breakfast buffet before class starts. Italians typically start their mornings simply, usually a coffee drink, like a latte or a cappuccino, accompanied by some bread, butter, and jam, or a pastry. But for the Silver Fox participants, the staff has gone all out with a huge array of baked goods, cold cuts, cheeses, hard-boiled eggs, yogurt, and fresh fruit.

Although I should probably eat lightly considering all the food we'll be sampling in class today, I pile a bit of everything onto my plate. As they say, when in Rome, or in my case, when in Ravenna. As I sip the last of my coffee, I think about my encounter with Preston yesterday. He was definitely flirting with me at the registration desk, but when I returned his satchel to him later, he wasn't nearly as friendly. What was that all about?

I glance at my phone and see the time. Crap, I'm going to be late. I deposit my dirty dishes at the service station, then rush through the gardens to the kitchen annex, which is located at the rear of the grounds. As I push open the door, I nearly collide into a walker belonging to one of the Silver Foxes. I skirt around it and look at the large room in front of me. It has an industrial feel with exposed ductwork and pipes. Sunlight pours in through the large windows on either side of the room. At the front is a large cooking station on an elevated platform. There are smaller stations positioned throughout the room—each with a butcher block counter, sink, stove, oven, and two stools. All the stools are occupied, except for the ones at the station at the rear of the room.

I set my purse on the counter, then slip onto one of the vacant stools. The silver-haired woman in front of me turns and smiles. "Well, hello, dear," Loretta says. "Nice to see you again. Looks like we're neighbors."

Mabel is sitting next to her, her cane leaning against the counter. "Shush," she says. "The instructor is talking."

"No, she isn't," Loretta says. "She's writing something on the white-board. The class hasn't started yet."

"Yes, it has," Mabel retorts.

"No, it hasn't."

"Yes—"

Loretta cuts off Mabel and points at the empty stool next to me. "You can always move, you know."

Mabel narrows her eyes. "Maybe I will."

Great, just what I need, Mabel sitting next to me. I can't imagine anything worse.

While the older woman reaches for her cane, I hear a deep voice behind me. "Is anyone sitting here?"

I don't have to turn to see who it is. The scent is unmistakable—leather and pine.

"Oh, it's Professor Whitaker," Mabel says brightly. She nudges Loretta. "This is the nice young man who helped me last night."

He sits next to me. "Good morning, ladies," he says, oozing charm. "How did everyone sleep?"

"Soundly," Loretta says.

"I woke up alive," Mabel says. "That's always reassuring."

Preston turns to me, his eyes crinkling with amusement. "And how about you? How was your night?"

"Just swell," I say, hoping he can't see the dark circles under my eyes.

Dark circles caused by tossing and turning while thinking about him. What is he doing here, anyway?

The woman at the front of the room clears her throat. She has a Sophia Loren look about her—glossy dark hair, stunning eyes, and a voluptuous figure that her white chef's coat can't hide. "Welcome, everyone," she says with a soft Italian accent. "My name is Maria and I'll be your instructor for the next four weeks. It looks like you've all found places to sit. If you don't already know the person sitting next to you, go ahead and introduce yourselves. You'll be cooking partners for the rest of the program."

I glance at Preston. Surely, he isn't here for the program. This has got to be some sort of mistake.

He holds out his hand as though we haven't met before. "Allow me to introduce myself. Preston Whitaker."

I look at his hand, then back up at his piercing blue eyes, then back to his hand. There's no way I'm going to clasp his hand. Handshakes shouldn't make you tingle. These handshakes of his are dangerous.

He chuckles while still holding out his hand. "This is where you tell me your name."

"You already know it—Ginny."

"Nice to meet you," he says, grabbing my hand and giving it one of his patented, tingle-inducing handshakes, before whispering in my ear, "I think I have the prettiest cooking partner in the room."

I pull my hand back. "Cooking partner? You?"

He nods. "Yes. I'm sitting in on this course. It was one of the reasons why I agreed to teach the history program later in the summer. I've always wanted to learn to cook Italian food. This is the perfect opportunity." He hands me an apron. "Blue's a good color for you."

I look at the apron. It's the exact shade of Preston's eyes. I shake my head. Must stop thinking about his eyes. I place the apron back on the counter. "Will you excuse me for a moment?" I say, grabbing my purse.

"Where are you going?"

"To get a refund."

I practically run back to the villa, wincing in pain as my ankle reminds me that it's still recovering from its injury.

Evelyn is sitting at the table tapping away at her computer.

"I changed my mind," I say. "You were right. The cooking program isn't for me."

She frowns. "I'm sorry, but there's nothing I can do. The program has already started."

"It only started fifteen minutes ago. I haven't even tried on my apron." I pull my wallet out of my purse. "Do you need my credit card to issue the refund?"

Instead of answering, she opens a file folder and pulls out the registration form I signed last night. She turns to the last page and points at my initials. "Unfortunately, we can't issue refunds after the program has started. It's in the terms and conditions here."

I take a deep breath, then smile. "Are you sure there isn't anything you can do? Like you said, the program is better suited for seniors."

She shakes her head. "Sorry."

I stuff my wallet back in my purse and spin around without another word. As I slowly walk back to the kitchen annex, I try to cool down. How am I going to get through the next four weeks with Preston as my cooking partner?

When I walk back in the room, Maria is demonstrating how a pasta machine works. I set my purse on the counter and grab my apron.

"Couldn't get a refund?" Preston whispers.

I tie the apron around my waist without responding.

He grins. "Guess you're stuck with me for the next four weeks."

5 - Salmonella

After Maria demonstrates how to roll dough through the pasta maker, making it thinner and thinner with each pass, she holds up a laminated piece of paper. "You should have one of these on your workstation. It's a simple recipe for making pasta dough. All you'll need is flour, eggs, olive oil, and salt, which you can find on the shelf underneath your workstation. Why don't you go ahead and grab those now, then I'll walk you through how to make the dough."

Mabel gasps as Loretta places their ingredients on their workstation. "These eggs aren't refrigerated. If we eat them, we'll get salmonella poisoning." She raises her cane in the air and waves it back and forth, nearly decapitating her friend in the process. "Watch out," she warns everyone within earshot. "They're trying to kill us!"

I lean forward. "The eggs are fine. They haven't been refrigerated previously, so they're safe to eat."

Mabel spins around on her stool and pokes me with her cane. "No, they're not."

I grab the end of her cane. "They're fine, really."

She tries to yank it back, but I hold on firmly, worried that she'll inadvertently knock our bag of flour over.

"Listen, missy, if I say we're going to get salmonella, then we're going to get salmonella. End of story."

She tugs at her cane again. Boy, the woman can play a fierce game of tug-of-war.

"Why don't you give me the cane?" Preston places his hand on top of mine. "I don't want you to get hurt," he says with a wink. I'm not sure who the wink is directed at. Probably Mabel, because she smiles brightly at him. I let go of the cane and he guides it safely across our workstation back to her.

"Thank you, young man."

Preston smiles at her. "Did you know that if you don't wash fresh eggs after you collect them, you can safely leave them unrefrigerated? When you wash them, you remove the protective coating that prevents contamination from getting through the tiny pores in the shells."

"No, I didn't know that," she says, giving him an incredulous look.

"In the States, factory eggs are washed so they have to be refrigerated afterwards to ensure that they're safe. But these are unwashed farm eggs, so they're safe to leave out at room temperature. You'll find lots of eggs sold in Italy this way."

She furrows her brow. "So, no salmonella?"

"Nope."

She beams at him. "You're so smart." Then she looks at Loretta and me. "He's smart, isn't he? We're lucky to have a distinguished professor in our class."

"He's a history professor," I say. "Not an egg professor. Besides, I told you the same thing about the eggs being safe to eat two minutes ago. How come you believe him and not me?"

"You have to study a lot to become a professor," Mabel says, looking at me like I'm stupid.

Preston bites back a smile.

"Are you a professor?" she asks me.

I shake my head.

"Are you a rocket scientist?"

"No," I say, wondering what rockets have to do with eggs.

Preston snorts. I glare at him.

"Well then, there you go," Mabel says, as though that explains it.

Preston scoots his stool toward me. "So what exactly do you do for a living? On the train you told me you were a chef, but clearly you aren't."

"I told you that I *want* to become a chef."

"Yeah, that's right." He looks bemused. "You claimed it was my earwax that caused that little misunderstanding. I should probably see a doctor about that."

I nod crisply. "You should."

"You still haven't answered my question—what is it you do?"

I blurt out the first thing that pops into my mind. "I'm a manicurist."

He glances at my hands. They don't exactly look like the hands of a manicurist—short, unvarnished nails, and ragged cuticles. "Really?"

"Really," I say, pulling the recipe toward me. "Now, shall we get started making our pasta dough?"

* * *

I congratulate myself on making it through an entire week of cooking side-by-side with Preston without killing him. You want to know why I want to kill him? I'll tell you why.

Mabel thinks he walks on water. Everything he does is right, even if he cracks an egg and it ends up on the floor. Me, even if I make the perfect cannoli, she finds at least ten things wrong with it. And at least twice a day she whacks me in the shin with her cane. Sure, she claims it's always an accident, but with that devilish gleam in her eyes, of course, I don't believe her.

It's not just the Mabel thing that drives me batty. That I can deal with, although I'd prefer not to have all those bruises on my legs. What it comes down to is that the man is a show-off. He's constantly spitting out factoids, like he's some sort of human encyclopedia. For example, just this afternoon, he's been regaling me with an endless stream of pasta-related trivia.

"Ginny, did you know that the average Italian eats fifty-one pounds of pasta a year?"

"No, I didn't know that, Preston." I roll my eyes. "How fascinating. You must have the book, *Making Pasta for Dummies*, in your extensive library."

He smiles brightly. My sarcasm appears to be lost on him, so he continues. "Did you know that there are more than six hundred shapes of pasta?"

"Really? I was sure it was only five hundred and ninety-seven."

He wipes his hands on a dishtowel while he ponders this. "Well, I guess it's possible they rounded up." Undeterred, he continues, "Did you know that Thomas Jefferson first brought pasta to America in 1789?"

"Are you sure? I thought it was Chef Boyardee."

Preston shudders. "Chef Boyardee. I ate way too much of that stuff as a grad student."

"Yeah, I know what you mean. Cheap and quick food is the way to go when you're a grad student. I ate a lot of ramen."

He cocks his head to one side. "You were a grad student?"

"I was a student," I say evasively.

"Oh, sure. You have to go to cosmetology school to be a manicurist, don't you?"

"Uh-huh."

"What kinds of things do you study in cosmetology school?"

"Oh, you know. The usual."

"The usual?"

"Cuticle cream, nail clippers...um, the usual." Drawing a blank on manicure-related topics, I quickly say, "But I don't want to bore you. You know what I'd rather hear more about? Pasta." I lean forward and get Mabel and Loretta's attention. "You guys have to hear this." I nudge Preston. "Go on, tell them what you told me about Thomas Jefferson."

While the ladies look at him expectantly, I slip back to the pantry to grab some fresh herbs for the marinade we're making. When I get back to the workstation, practically all of the Silver Foxes are gathered around Preston.

"Go on, tell us another one," a man in the back of the crowd shouts.

"Well, if you insist," Preston says. "Italians eat the most pasta in the world, which I'm sure you all already know. But what you might not know is that if the pasta they ate was all spaghetti, as opposed to other shapes—"

Loretta waves her hand in the air like she's back in school. "How many shapes of pasta were there again?"

"Six hundred," Preston says.

I snort.

He catches my eye and smiles. "Actually, I've been informed by a reliable source that it's five hundred and ninety-seven."

One of the ladies standing next to me says, "He's so smart, isn't he? Do you think he's single? I should fix him up with my granddaughter. They'd be perfect for each other."

"I'm sure they would," I say dryly. "You should tell him all about her once he finishes boring us with pasta facts."

She tugs at her ear. "I think my hearing aid is acting up. It sounds like you said he was boring."

"Sorry, I must have misspoken." I force a laugh. "What he said about pasta meaning 'dough pastry cake' in Latin was fascinating."

"It was, wasn't it?"

The enthusiasm in her voice makes me feel guilty. I really need to try to tone down the sarcasm. The Silver Foxes are enjoying hearing what Preston has to say. Just because I don't like know-it-all history nerds like him, doesn't mean that I should rain on this lady's parade. She thinks he'll be perfect for her granddaughter. I wish them all the happiness in the world.

When class ends that afternoon, Preston asks me what I'm doing over the weekend. I tell him that I'm spending it with Mia and Isabelle since they're leaving bright and early on Monday morning.

Is it my imagination or does he look crestfallen that I already have plans?

I shake my head. Why would he be interested in me? After all, he thinks I'm a manicurist. He'd assume we have nothing in common. No, he's probably looking forward to spending his free time cuddled up with his history books.

* * *

After getting changed into clean clothes back in my room, I head to Mia and Isabelle's apartment building. When I walk into the courtyard, I see Lorenzo talking on his cell phone. He motions at me to hang on, then continues to pace back and forth, talking in rapid-fire Italian.

While I wait, I watch the cat perched on the edge of the fountain, sticking his paw into the water and terrorizing the fish. I can see drool dripping from his mouth. Must be because of all the excitement of stalking his prey. I worry that the creature is going to become dehydrated from the rapid rate of saliva he's producing, but not enough to pick him up and try to intervene. The thought of getting cat drool on my clothes makes me shudder.

Lorenzo doesn't share my fear. After hanging up, he scoops up the cat and kisses the top of his head, totally oblivious to the fact that saliva is spattering everywhere.

After setting the cat back down so that he can get back to terrorizing the fish again, Lorenzo starts to lean down to kiss my cheek. I pull back and dig into my purse. I hand him a tissue and point at his neck. "Here, you've got a little, um, cat drool there."

"Drool," he says slowly. "What is this drool?"

I tap my lips. "You know, moisture from your mouth."

He dabs his neck while repeating the word drool a few more times. Strangely, the word drool sounds sexy when spoken with an Italian accent.

"Um, I think you missed it," I say when he crumples the tissue and puts it in his pocket. I pass him another one. He dabs his neck, again in the wrong spot. "No, higher up." He tries again, this time on the other side of his neck. The side free of feline saliva. I demonstrate on my own neck with another tissue. "Like this."

He takes a step toward me and hands me his tissue. "Why don't you do it?"

As he positions his neck so that I can reach it, I recoil in horror. Not only does the saliva glisten on his neck in a very disturbing manner, but he's also wearing body spray. Doggy doo-doo and bubblegum body spray. Is this stuff all the rage in Italy now? Thankfully, he didn't spray the entire can on himself, but still, even the tiny amount he applied has managed to turn this sexy Italian guy into someone I want to avoid like the plague.

I grab a wad of tissues out of my purse, hold one up to my nose, and briefly press the rest of them against his neck. Then I release my hand, causing the tissues to fall to the ground.

For a moment I think about leaving them there. The thought of picking up tissues contaminated by feline saliva horrifies me. But, littering isn't my thing so I gingerly collect them off the ground using a clean tissue to protect my fingers.

After a quick inspection of Lorenzo's neck, I determine that the cat drool has been eradicated. If only I could say the same about his scent.

While I'm applying hand sanitizer, Mia and Isabelle breeze into the courtyard. They're looking adorable as usual. Mia is wearing a red sweater and white capri pants that accentuate her curves, while Isabelle's ruffled sundress highlights her long legs. I'm wearing my usual boring ensemble of jeans and a t-shirt.

"*Ciao*," Lorenzo says, greeting both of them with kisses on their cheeks. I'm amazed neither of them seems phased by his odor. "Are you ready?"

"Ready?" I ask.

"Didn't we tell you?" Isabelle says. "Lorenzo offered to drive us to the beach tonight. His cousin owns a restaurant there."

Lorenzo smacks his fingers to his mouth. "They make the best seafood pasta. You will love it."

As we follow Lorenzo to his car, Isabelle pulls me aside. "You don't mind, do you? He's a sweet guy. You guys can get to know each other better. Since we'll be leaving on Sunday, it will be good for you to have someone to keep you company when we're gone."

"It sounds fun," I tell her. "Assuming the windows on his car roll down, though."

"The windows?"

"Bubblegum and doggy doo-doo," I say. "Not a good combination in an enclosed space. Trust me on this one."

* * *

The drive to the beach is a bit nerve-wracking, mostly because Lorenzo turns around periodically to show us videos on his phone of his favorite *lucha libre* tag teams. Sure, he keeps one hand on the steering wheel at all times, but his eyes spend more time checking out the moves the masked wrestlers are making than on the road. On the plus side, the terror I feel as we come precariously close to crashing into oncoming traffic makes me completely forget about Lorenzo's body spray.

When he starts to demonstrate *la plancha*, a move where one guy lies flat on his back in the ring while another guy jumps down on him—a demonstration that involves reclining his seat while shifting gears—Mia grabs Lorenzo's phone and threatens to throw it out the window.

We finally arrive safely at the quaint seaside resort. Mia returns the phone, and we all enjoy a delicious dinner of pasta di frutti di mare—spaghetti with mussels, shrimp, squid, and clams in a spicy red sauce—at Lorenzo's cousin's restaurant. After we have some espresso and split a large slice of tiramisu, the girls and I go for a stroll on the beach, leaving Lorenzo and his cousin to continue arguing over who the greatest *luchador* of all time is.

As we walk across the soft, white sand, I fill Mia and Isabelle in on the highlights of the first week of my cooking program, including the scare we had the previous day when one of the Silver Foxes misplaced his dentures. Thankfully, they didn't end up in the lasagna. As I'm describing how we made our own ricotta cheese, Mia interrupts me.

"How come you haven't said anything about Preston?" she asks.

"Sure I have."

"Nope, you haven't uttered his name once in the past twenty minutes. He's your cooking partner. You'd think he'd come up once in one of your anecdotes." She bumps me with her shoulder. "I think you're deliberately not talking about him."

I stop and stare at her. "Why would you think that?"

"Well, remember how you sent those texts to me and Isabelle a couple of nights ago after you had one too many glasses of wine?"

Isabelle snorts. "They were hysterical. Let's see, how did they go?" She pulls out her phone and starts reading them off.

Preston smells like pine trees.

Preston doesn't smell like dog doo-doo and bubblegum.

I don't like dog doo-doo and bubblegum.

Wait, I like bubblegum, but only grape flavor.

Preston smells like an old leather coat.

Isabelle slaps her legs and chortles. "Wait, this is my favorite one—'I want to wrap Preston in grape bubblegum and snuggle with him.'"

I grab her phone and press the delete button while she and Mia continue to laugh.

"I knew I shouldn't have had that third glass of wine, especially on an empty stomach," I say. "It doesn't mean anything."

Isabelle puts her hands on my shoulders. "That was your subconscious talking. It means something. Now spill."

"Well, he is cute and..." My voice trails off as I think about how closely he stood next to me while I strained curdled milk through cheesecloth to make ricotta cheese.

"And what?" Isabelle prompts.

"He smells like pine trees and leather," I say with a smile.

"Pine trees and leather are nice," she says.

"They are, but that's all he has going for him."

"Are you sure?" Mia asks as she plops down on the sand.

I sit next to her and ponder the question. "Well, he is really good with the Silver Foxes. He's very respectful and patient with them. Even with Mabel."

"She's the crotchety lady with the cane, right?" Mia asks.

"Yeah. Preston told me that she reminds him of his grandmother."

"So, that's a point in his favor," Isabelle says. "He treats senior citizens well. What else?"

I shrug. "That's it, really. Most of the time he gets on my nerves with his constant mini-lectures on Italian food and Roman history. So boring. Just yesterday, he droned on for ten minutes about the chemical properties of yeast."

Isabelle cocks her head to one side. "Pot calling the kettle black."

I look indignant. "Me? I'm nothing like Preston."

"Oh, I think you're an awful lot like Preston. Who was the one who spent most of dinner telling us all about how Roman gladiator bouts were originally part of funerary rites?"

I run my fingers through my hair. "Sorry. That must have been really boring."

"Not at all," Mia says. "It was interesting. I think you would have made a great history professor. The two of you actually have a lot in common—you both love history."

"Well, it's not like I can tell him that, can I?" I chew on my bottom lip for a moment. "He thinks I'm a manicurist who likes sci-fi. Thankfully, he hasn't asked me any in-depth questions about either of those topics. I'd be caught out in seconds."

"Maybe I should give you a crash course in *Star Wars*," Mia offers.

"Thanks, but no thanks," I say with a smile. "I think I'll just change the subject if it comes up." I look at my hands. "But I might go get a manicure next week."

"You only have three weeks left of the course, right?" Isabelle asks.

I nod.

"So just enjoy your time with him. Nothing serious has to happen. He might be someone to have fun with at night and on the weekends. Although there's always Lorenzo."

"Lorenzo is sweet," I say.

"Pretty easy on the eyes too," Mia says.

"I can't disagree with that. But there's no spark. Not to mention that horrible body spray he's wearing now."

"Well, then, if there's no spark, I agree with Isabelle," Mia says. "Give Preston a chance."

"I guess," I say. "But I have to make sure he never finds out my last name."

"Why's that?" Mia asks.

"Well, it's not very common. How many Maarschalkerweerds do you know? My father was a well-known ancient history professor. Preston is sure to know of him and his work. He probably has all of his books too." I shiver in the cool breeze and wrap my arms around me. "Fortunately, my name was too long to fit on the name badge, so the lady at the registration used my middle name instead. Preston only knows me as Ginny Morgan and I plan on keeping it that way."

I stand and brush sand off my jeans. "We should probably head back before Lorenzo and his cousin decide to catch a plane to Mexico City and start their own *lucha libre* tag team."

"Oh, by the way," Mia says as we walk back to the restaurant. "I totally get what you mean about doggy doo-doo and bubblegum after sitting next to Lorenzo at dinner. It gets a bit overpowering after a while."

6 - Tweed Jackets

The rest of the weekend was fabulous. On Saturday, the girls and I took the train to Bologna to check out the archaeological museum. While they loved the display of an Egyptian cat mummy, their eyes glazed over when I explained how the Romans shaped bronze using clay forms. It made me almost wish that Preston had joined us. He would have understood why I found old coins, spoons, and glass tableware so fascinating.

The girls had a much better time on Sunday when Lorenzo took us to Venice for the day. It was a much more pleasant drive this time around as Mia confiscated his phone before he started the car. On the way we stopped at Porto Corsini where the cruise ships dock. Then we headed to the more upscale Marina di Ravenna. Isabelle was in awe of all the sailboats moored there. We chatted for a while with some of the crew of the larger boats who gave Isabelle tips on what to expect when she started her job on the river cruise boat in Germany. We capped off the day back at Lorenzo's cousin's restaurant with another delicious dinner and discussion of wrestling.

By the time Monday morning rolled around, I was exhausted and already missing the girls. One of the great things about travel is meeting wonderful people. One of the worst things is saying goodbye to them.

After three cups of coffee, I shuffle into the kitchen annex.

"Is everyone excited for week two of class?" Maria asks cheerfully.

The Silver Foxes let out a resounding cheer.

I groan.

"Today, we're going to make tortelloni burro e salvia," Maria says. "Let's see how everyone's Italian is. Who knows what that means in English?"

My coffee finally kicks in, and I raise my hand. I know the answer to this one.

Maria points at me.

"Tortellini," I say, mentally patting myself on my back.

"Good," Maria says. "Tortelloni means tortellini in English. They're spelled almost identically. But what does burro e salvia mean?"

Okay, maybe I didn't have enough coffee after all because I don't have a clue. "Uh, maybe you should let someone else have a chance."

Preston nudges me. "Go on. You've got this."

"I do?"

He nods, so I take a stab. "Um, tortellini made with salivating burros?"

Maria laughs. "Not exactly, but good try. Fortunately, there won't be any burros, salivating or otherwise, in our dish today." She holds up some herbs. "Salvia means sage and burro means butter. We'll be sautéing ricotta-stuffed tortellini in sage butter."

While she passes out laminated recipe cards, Preston grins. "Salivating burros. Where exactly did you say you studied Italian?"

"You should be giving me points for creativity."

"I was thinking more along the lines of deducting points."

I playfully punch him in the arm. "Keep it up and you're on dish-washing duty."

Maria walks back to the front. "Let's start with making the pasta dough. This should be simple for you now. You had a lot of practice with this last week. Like riding a tricycle. Is that the expression? Riding a tricycle?"

One of the Silver Foxes corrects her. "Bicycle, not tricycle."

"Ah, yes. Riding a bicycle. Learning another language isn't easy, is it?"

The class murmurs their agreement.

"Ginny understands this," Maria says. "Salivating burros instead of sage butter. Like my tricycle and bicycle, no?"

My face grows warm as the Silver Foxes look at me and chuckle.

Preston starts to say something to me, but I put my fingers on his lips. "Not another word. Let's focus on the pasta."

He nods, then starts to measure out the flour and salt onto a marble cutting board. I shape the mixture into a mound, then dig a well in the center of it. Preston cracks eggs into the well. Using a fork, I beat the eggs, gradually mixing in flour from the sides of the well until a soft dough forms.

"How was your weekend?" Preston asks.

"Great. Lorenzo took us to Venice on Sunday. Did you know that it's only about two and half hours away from here?"

"Lorenzo?"

"Uh-huh. He rented the apartment to Mia and Isabelle. Anyway, did you know that Venice came into being after the fall of the Roman Empire? The original population of Venice was made up of refugees from the mainland who were fleeing from Germanic and Hun invaders. And, this is the part that's really fascinating." I wave the fork in the air for emphasis. "There were only two to three miles of water separating Venice from the mainland, but that was enough to keep them isolated from the rest of Italy, living in relative peace for 1400 years."

"They were isolated for 1400 years by water. Was that one of Lorenzo's pickup lines?"

"Pickup lines?"

"You know, like the guy in the bar who tried to schmooze you with that line about Roman sanitation." He fiddles with the rolling pin. "But I'm sure it didn't work because you said that you don't like history nerds."

"I never said that."

"I should start tape recording you. You said, and I quote, 'I don't go for history buffs."

"See, just like I told you. I didn't say that I don't go for history *nerds*, I said history *buffs*."

"What's the difference between a history buff and a history nerd?"

"What kind of tweed jacket they wear."

"I wear a tweed jacket."

"Exactly." I set the fork aside and start to knead the dough.

"Exactly what?"

"Could you sprinkle more flour on the cutting board?"

"I will after you answer my question."

"What question?"

"What did you mean about my tweed jacket?"

I tap the edge of the cutting board. "Flour right there, please."

I look up and see Preston's blue eyes twinkling. "You want more flour?"

"Uh-huh."

"Here you go," he says, tossing some flour at me.

I put my hands to my face to wipe it off, but instead get sticky dough all over me.

"You," I say threateningly, trying to grab the bag of flour from him.

He laughs and darts around to the opposite side of the workstation. "Excuse me, ladies," he says to Mabel and Loretta as he scoots past them. He tosses more flour at me. I chase him around in a circle, pausing long enough to grab Mabel and Loretta's flour. I throw some at Preston. He throws more at me.

By this point, I'm laughing so hard that I'm crying. As I raise my hand to wipe the tears off my face, I knock a bowl of eggs over. I manage to right the bowl, but not before three of the eggs land on the ground.

"Watch out," I say to Preston, but my warning comes too late.

He tries to skid to a stop, but slips and ends up on his back on the floor. I rush over to help him, but trip over Mabel's cane, landing on top of him, just like they do in *lucha libre*.

I lay there for a moment, my head resting on his chest. His strong, muscular chest. How did a professor end up with these muscles? I can hear his heart beating. Or is that my heart?

"Ginny, are you okay?" Preston whispers, his breath hot against my neck.

"Yes. How about you?" I ask without moving.

"Fine." He shifts slightly, wrapping his arms around my back. "Although I think I have egg in my ears."

"Better than egg up your nose," I say.

He laughs. "I think there's some there too."

"Maybe we should get up," I say reluctantly.

"We probably should," he says. "If we stay down here too long a herd of stampeding, drooling burros might run over us."

I sit up and giggle. He looks like one of the Three Stooges after one of their food fights. But cuter. Way cuter. After getting to my feet, I extend my hand and help him up. He pulls me toward him.

"Good thing I wasn't wearing my tweed jacket," he says. "It would have been a nightmare to wash this out of that."

* * *

"Look at the mess you made," Mabel says as she points at the flour and eggs on the floor. She glares at me, then looks at Preston, her eyebrows drawn together. "Are you okay, dear? Did you hurt your head when you fell?" She puts her hand to the side of her mouth and stage whispers. "Do you want to see if we can find you a new cooking partner?"

"You know I can hear you, right?" I say as I pick eggshells out of my hair.

Preston smiles. "I'm very happy with my cooking partner. But I appreciate the concern."

I realize the entire room is staring at us. Everyone seems amused, except Mabel.

Maria walks toward us, stepping over the mess on the floor. "There are cleaning supplies in the cupboard over there. I'll get you some clean aprons while you mop this up." She looks back and forth between Preston and me with a bemused expression. "*Ogni vite vuole il suo palo*," she says before going to assist one of the Silver Foxes with their pasta machine.

Preston opens the cupboard and I grab a bucket and some rags. "Why do you think Maria was talking about driving a stake through a vampire's heart?" I ask.

He bursts out laughing. "Well, at least you got one word right in that sentence—*palo*. It means stake, but the rest of the sentence didn't have anything to do with vampires."

"Are you sure? You might still have some egg clogging your ears. I'm sure she was talking about vampires," I say.

Preston shakes his head as we carry the cleaning supplies back to our workstation. While he cleans the floor, I tackle the counter. After he rinses a rag in the sink, he looks at me, a serious expression on his face. "So you really don't like historians—buffs, dweebs, nerds, or otherwise?"

"I try to avoid them at all costs." I squeeze soap onto a sponge. After a beat, I add, "I was betrayed by one."

"Do you think you have enough soap on that sponge?" he asks gently.

I look down. Thinking about how what's-his-name ruined my life makes me so angry. I seem to have taken my anger out on the poor dish soap bottle, squeezing most of its contents out.

"He cheated on you, didn't he?" Preston asks softly.

I shake my head. "No, worse."

He furrows his brow. "What's worse than cheating?"

I press my lips together. That gives me pause. Is plagiarism worse than cheating, worse than infidelity? Finally, I say, "I don't want to talk about it." What I leave unspoken is that I don't want to talk about what's-his-name with Preston.

He stands quietly at the sink, not saying a word.

"I'm guessing someone cheated on you," I say after a moment.

He nods. "My ex. We had been together for three years. I thought we were happy and things were going great. Then I found her with another guy."

"How long ago was that?"

"We broke up a few months ago," he says, clenching the rag in his hands before letting it drop into the sink. "How about you? How long have you been single?"

"About the same."

"Seems like we have a few things in common."

"Single people with trust issues?"

He nods, then smiles faintly. "And we're both smitten with ravioli."

"Smitten? I love that word. It's so cute."

He frowns. "I'm not trying to be cute."

"Well, you are."

He arches his eyebrows. "You think I'm cute?"

"In an old-fashioned, nerdy sort of way."

"I guess that's a compliment."

I shrug. "If you want to take it that way, sure." Then I busy myself with wiping down the counter, trying to avoid eye contact with him.

Preston taps me on my shoulder. "I think you secretly like history."

"Nope. I'm one hundred percent sci-fi geek."

After a few minutes, we finish cleaning up and walk back to the cupboard to return the cleaning supplies. Preston sets the pail on the shelf, then looks at me sideways. "You know how Maria said, '*Ogni vite vuole il suo palo?*'"

"Uh-huh."

"Well, it's not a phrase you hear all the time. It's kind of—"

"Old-fashioned?"

"Nothing wrong with old-fashioned," he says with a smile. "Do you want to know what it means?"

"Sure."

"It means that every vine needs its stake."

"I don't get it. Does that mean we should drink wine? I sure can get on board with that."

"Not exactly," he says. "Vines need a support system, just like people."

"That involves trust," I say.

"It does." When I don't respond, he says. "Maybe I got the translation wrong. Maybe it's just about drinking wine."

"Maybe."

"So let's grab some wine one night next week."

"Okay," I say. A glass of wine with Preston won't be a problem, right?

7 - Blue vs. Green Milk

We never did get that glass of wine. Preston ended up having to work on a grant application. Every night after class, he made a quick exit and headed to Bologna to confer with colleagues at the university. At least that's what he said he was doing. Who knows what he was really getting up to. Most likely he regretted the conversation we had after the food fight. Some things are probably better left unsaid, like talking about your exes and how they betrayed you.

On Friday morning, Maria claps her hands together to get our attention. "I have a special treat for you today. As you know, Ravenna is home to eight UNESCO World Heritage sites. Professor Whitaker has kindly agreed to give us a guided tour of two of them this afternoon—the Basilica of San Vitale and the Mausoleum of Gallo Placida."

As the room bursts into applause, Mabel turns and beams at Preston. "We're so lucky to have such a distinguished professor in our class."

"I can't wait to tell the gals in my bridge group that a famous historian is giving us a personal tour," Loretta adds.

Some of the other Silver Foxes approach our workstation to express their gratitude that the professor would deign to share his precious knowledge with us commoners. Okay, that isn't exactly how they put it, but you get what I mean. A couple of the ladies even take selfies with Preston, pushing me aside to get a better angle. I wouldn't be surprised if they use the pictures on their annual holiday cards.

Preston soaks it up. He reminds me of you-know-who, cocky, with a know-it-all attitude. Another reminder of why I took a vow not to date historians and why I'm glad we never had that glass of wine together.

"If everyone could take their seats, please," Maria says over the din. "I have a few more announcements." Once everyone settles back at their workstations, she continues, "Before Professor Whitaker's tour, we're going to visit the *mercato coperto*. It's a historic covered market on the Piazza Andrea Costa. They sell all sorts of fresh produce—juicy tomatoes, beautiful fruits, gorgeous salamis, and best of all, the finest cheeses. My nephew has a stall there. He's going to do a cheese tasting for us. After that, we'll go to the Piazza del Popolo in the center of town. I think some of you have been there already?" A few people nod. "It's very popular with tourists. There are all sorts of shops, cafes, bars—"

"What about gelato?" one of the men in the front asks. "Can we get some of that there? My guidebook says that we can't leave Italy without trying some of that Italian ice cream of yours."

She nods. "Yes, there are several gelato shops there."

Finally, after several more questions (are there bathrooms available, will Professor Whitaker sign autographs, what's the best flavor of gelato), we finally get underway. Maria has organized a small tour bus to drive us to our first stop—the covered market.

As we walk through the arched entryway, Maria informs us that the building was recently renovated. "This spot has been a market area since the Middle Ages. The old indoor market first opened in 1922." We walk through the bustling food hall, past stalls with tempting treats, and take the escalator up to the second floor.

"Ah, there he is," she says, pointing at a man standing behind a long table overflowing with cheeses. "That is my nephew, Giorgio."

Whereas Maria resembles Sofia Loren, Giorgio doesn't share in her movie-star looks. He's short, has a potbelly, and is sporting a comb-over 'do that you don't often see on a guy in his twenties. But his warm smile and enthusiastic greeting makes you forget all about how he looks. This is the type of guy I should be attracted to—he spends his days making and selling cheese, not giving history lectures. People need cheese. It's practical and useful, not to mention delicious.

Maria's nephew explains the different types of popular Italian cheeses, then passes around samples for each of us to try. I can't decide if my favorite is the fontina or the pecorino romano. The fontina has an earthy, mushroomy taste that makes me want to rush out and buy a fondue pot, but the sharp and salty flavor of the pecorino has my taste buds dancing with joy.

As I grab another morsel of the fontina, Giorgio holds up a glass bowl filled with a white creamy cheese. "This is squacquerone," he says. He repeats the name of the cheese, then asks us all to try to say it after him.

Everyone giggles as we try to imitate Giorgio's pronunciation. It doesn't come easily to us English speakers. Preston, of course, says it nearly perfectly, then winks at me.

"Given your fluent Italian," he says, making air quotes around the word 'fluent,' "I bet you think squacquerone is the Italian word for Sasquatch."

"Sasquatch?"

"You know, the large, hairy, humanlike creature that walks upright."

I furrow my brow.

"Sasquatch. Come on, you have to know what I'm talking about. This is the kind of thing that is right up your sci-fi alley." He rubs his chin. "Bigfoot? That ring a bell?"

"Oh, Bigfoot. Sure, I know what you're talking about. But the man is holding a bowl of cheese, not an imaginary creature wandering around the forests in North America. Clearly, he's talking about cheese."

He smirks. "Clearly."

"Pipe down. I want to hear what he has to say about squa...swa...sac—"

"You mean squacquerone," Preston says effortlessly.

I put my fingers to his lips to shush him, then turn my attention to Giorgio.

"This cheese is a specialty of the region," he says. "It's made from cow's milk. It is a soft cheese with the consistency of yogurt. We like to spread it on piadina—a flatbread that you'll also find in this region. It is delicious."

"We'll be making piadina next week," Maria interjects.

"There are claims that this cheese goes back to Roman times," Preston says quietly.

I elbow him. "For a professor, you'd think you'd know how to be quiet when someone is speaking."

He smiles, then bends down and whispers in my ear. His breath tickles my neck. "During the papal conclave of 1799, Cardinal Carlo Bellisomi was going through withdrawal for squacquerone. He wrote a letter complaining about how much he missed it. His secretary sent him some, but it came two days before Lent, when he wouldn't have been able to eat it. Do you think he cheated and ate it during Lent or do you think he finished it all up beforehand?"

When I don't respond, he adds, "Anyway, that letter is the first proof of the cheese. Historians love that kind of thing."

"I'll tell you what historians like," I say, turning and jabbing my finger in his chest. "They like..." My voice trails off. Touching him like this is reminding me of what it felt like to be laying on top of him after our food fight, my head pressed on his chest, listening to his heartbeat. I step back and shake my head.

"What do historians like?" Preston asks.

"Never mind," I mutter. "It's not important." Then I grab another hunk of fontina and shove it in my mouth before I say anything stupid.

* * *

After we finish our cheese tasting and have some free time to explore the market, we walk to the first historical site—the Basilica di San Vitale. It's an octagonal-shaped building that combines Roman features such as a dome and stepped towers with Byzantine ones such as narrow bricks, flying buttresses, and a polygonal apse, Preston tells the group as we gather by the entrance. It's something I knew already, but I act like it's the first time I've heard it. Gotta keep up my pretense that I'm just a sci-fi loving manicurist who couldn't care less about history.

When we walk inside, Preston ushers us toward the center of the basilica.

Light streaming in through the arched windows illuminates the labyrinth mosaic pattern laid out on the marble floor. The three hundred and eighty-four marble triangles lead walkers from the center of the labyrinth to the exit on the west side. I have to admit I didn't know about the labyrinth until Preston mentioned it, so I'll give him points for that one.

However, when it comes to the mosaics that adorn the walls and ceiling, I could have repeated Preston's lecture word for word. While he drones on about how the mosaics in the altar area illustrate events and people from the Old Testament, I walk over to examine the mosaic on the southern side of the apse more closely. It depicts Teodora, one of the most powerful women in the Roman era, wearing Byzantine court clothes and adorned in jewels.

I feel my eyes start to well up as I think about how much my father would have enjoyed touring the basilica and how much fun it would have been to experience it together.

"Did you hear what Professor Whitaker said about these mosaics being the largest and best-preserved Byzantine mosaics outside of Istanbul?" Loretta asks.

I surreptitiously wipe my eyes. Then, once I'm sure I can speak without my voice cracking, I respond, "They are incredible, aren't they?"

"They are," she says, looking around the basilica, her eyes wide with wonder.

Preston walks up to us. He tilts his head and looks at me intently. "Are you bored?"

"Bored? How could anyone be bored here?" Loretta asks.

"Ginny doesn't like history," he says to her. "She's into sci-fi. She'd probably rather be at the Galaxy's Edge at Disney World. Didn't you say you've been there four times?"

Loretta puts her hand to her chest and gasps. "Four times? You're so lucky. The grandkids keep begging me to take them there." She smiles. "They know grandma is a sucker for *Star Wars*."

"You like *Star Wars*?" I ask in astonishment.

"Sure, I do. Doesn't everyone?" She puts her hand on my arm and leans forward. "Now tell me, what was your favorite part?" Before I can answer, she adds, "Did you drink green milk while you were there?"

"Green milk?" I splutter.

"You know, like Luke drank in *The Last Jedi*."

I'm not entirely sure if this is a trick question, but I nod slowly and take a stab at the right answer. "Sure, green milk. Yep, did it."

"Oh, my gosh, you're so lucky." She squeezes my arm and asks earnestly, "Did you try any of the blue milk? You know to compare?"

I raise my eyebrows. "Blue?"

"Of course, blue. Don't you remember when Luke had it in *A New Hope*?"

"Of course," I say in my most convincing voice. "Who could forget that scene when Mike chugged down a gallon of blue milk."

Preston frowns. "Mike? You mean Luke, right?"

"Luke. That's what I said." I point at his ear. "You might still have some egg stuck in there. Or maybe it's that earwax problem you've been having. Whatever it is, it's interfering with your hearing." Then I smile at Loretta. "Would you excuse me for a minute?"

Good thing I have Mia on speed dial. I send her a text.

Quick. What do you know about the Galaxy's Edge?

OMG. I'd love to go there!

I need facts. I'm getting grilled about it. I don't want Preston to find out I don't have a clue.

Don't you think you should fess up?

No!

Okay, fine. Tell him how much you loved the Millennium Falcon Smuggler's Run ride.

Millennium Falcon?

It's a ship.

Got it. Thanks.

Loretta taps me on my shoulder. "Ginny, are you ready to go? We're going to walk over to the Mausoleum of Gallo Placida now. Professor Whitaker says that it's the earliest and best-preserved mosaic monument. I can't wait to see it."

I tuck my phone in my purse. "Sure thing."

As we walk to join the rest of the group, I casually toss out, "Be careful if you go on the Millennium Falcon ride, Loretta. I got so seasick on it."

"You got seasick?" She blinks rapidly. "That's odd. I can't see how that could happen."

"Well, it's a ship, right?"

"Yes, a spaceship. You'd get space sickness on the Millennium Falcon, not seasickness."

"Oh, a spaceship." I frown. Mia could have been a little more precise in her texts. I was imagining some sort of pirate ship with her mention of smugglers.

"Are you feeling okay, dear? You look a bit dazed."

Truth be told, I am feeling a bit dazed. *Star Wars* and sci-fi is more complicated than I thought it would be. But I plaster a smile on my face. "All good. Nothing a good old glass of blue milk wouldn't sort out."

* * *

When we get back to the retreat center later that afternoon, I hear a familiar, sexy baritone voice call my name as I step off the bus. I turn and see Lorenzo carrying a ladder under his arm. He sets it on the ground, then strolls toward me as though he's on the set of a men's fragrance commercial. He pulls his long, dark hair out of its ponytail holder, flicking it from side to side while licking his lips and fixing me with a sultry gaze.

As he nears, I pray that he isn't wearing that overpowering doggy doo-doo and bubblegum body spray again.

When he reaches me, he leans down and kisses my cheeks. "Ah, my *bellissima*, Ginny."

I breathe a sigh of relief. The only thing he smells like is a guy who's been doing manual labor all day in the hot sun. Slightly stinky, but a million times better than how he smelled the last time I saw him.

He steps back and looks me up and down. I feel my face redden. It's the kind of look that should make my heart go pitter-patter and send shivers up and down my body. The guy is drop-dead gorgeous. But I feel nothing. My pulse rate is normal. No shivers happening here.

"I have missed you," he says, taking my hand in his and kissing the back of it. "I don't see you anymore now that your friends have left." He continues to hold my hand, gently caressing it. "We must repair this situation."

"I think you mean 'remedy' the situation, not 'repair,'" I say.

"Remedy, yes," he says, staring deeply into my eyes. "We must remedy."

I sense Preston walking up behind me before I hear his voice. "Aren't you going to introduce me to your friend?" he asks.

I pull my hand away from Lorenzo and take a step back, giving Preston a sheepish smile. "Uh, sure. Lorenzo, this is Preston. Preston, this is Lorenzo."

Lorenzo narrows his eyes as he sizes Preston up. Preston doesn't flinch, staring straight back at Lorenzo. All I can think of is the macho guys in the *lucha libre* videos Lorenzo showed me and the girls. I start to giggle as I picture Preston wearing one of the masks that the Mexican wrestlers wear along with his tweed jacket.

Preston gives me a sideways look, then turns back to Lorenzo. "How do you know Ginny?"

"Ginny and I have spent a romantic evening at the beach."

Preston tenses, and I quickly intervene. "Lorenzo rented that apartment to Mia and Isabelle. I've told you about him before. We all went to the beach one night and ate at his cousin's restaurant."

Why am I explaining myself? Why do I care what Preston thinks my relationship with Lorenzo is?

Before I can sort out my feelings, Lorenzo turns to me. "You must be lonely now that your friends are gone. We should go back to the beach on Saturday. My cousin will make zuppa di pesche for us."

Preston puts his arm around my shoulders. "She can't. She has plans with me."

I turn my head and look up at him. "I do? Since when?"

"Remember on the bus ride back Maria was telling us about that restaurant that serves ravioli with spinach and artichokes?"

"Yeah."

"And you said that you wanted to try it"

"Uh-huh."

"Well, your wish is my command. I'm taking you there on Saturday."

Lorenzo smiles. "No, she is coming to the beach with me."

I remove Preston's arm from my shoulder and hold my hands up in the air. "Sorry, guys, but I think I'm going to stay in on Saturday and give myself a pedicure."

Lorenzo starts to protest, but an older man carrying a tool bag waves at him, shouting something in Italian. "Sorry, I must go. We're doing some renovations and Pietro needs my help. I'll call you later."

"Lorenzo has your phone number?" Preston asks. "How come I don't have your phone number?"

"I see you every day in class. Why would you need my phone number?"

"So I can call and invite you to dinner." He pulls his phone out of his pocket and looks at me expectantly. "So, what's your number?"

Before I can decide whether to give it to him, Maria comes up and thanks Preston for leading the tour. I use that as my opportunity to slip away.

As I walk to my room, I think about what just happened.

Was Preston asking me out on a date?

I shake my head. No, probably not. It was probably a testosterone thing. He saw Lorenzo making a move and had to make one too. For all I know, he'd be just as happy taking Loretta and Mabel to dinner as he would me.

* * *

Later that night, I go down to the reception room to get an herbal tea. Preston is sitting on one of the leather couches by the fireplace. When he sees me, his face lights up. "Come join me," he says, holding up a bottle of wine. "Maria gave this to me as a thank you, but I can't drink it by myself."

I shrug. "Okay. That sounds better than a cup of chamomile."

He pats the couch next to him and I sit. After he opens the wine, he pours a small amount into a glass. "Do you want to try it first to make sure it isn't corked?"

"I don't know anything about wine," I say. "I don't think I'd know the difference."

"I don't know much either," he says, swirling the wine around in the glass. "Except if I like it or not."

"Really? That surprises me. You seem like one of those guys who knows something about everything."

He looks at me quizzically. "I'm not sure how to take that. Either you think I could win a fortune on *Jeopardy* or you think I'm an obnoxious know-it-all."

I simply smile in response.

He scratches his chin, then takes a sip of the wine and nods approvingly. "It's delicious."

After filling both glasses, he hands one to me. I take a sip and sink back into the couch. "It is good."

Preston takes another sip, then turns his body to face me. "So which is it—a *Jeopardy* contestant or a know-it-all?"

I toy with my wineglass. "I guess it's a hazard of your occupation. You're a professor. You like sharing information."

"That's true. I get excited about history and want to share it with other people." He leans forward. "Teaching classes and seeing students engaged with the subject matter is my favorite part of being a professor."

"Well, you did a good job today," I say. "The Silver Foxes were enraptured. They can't stop talking about how much they enjoyed having you lead the tour."

He can't contain his grin. "Really? You think I did a good job?"

"I do. You actually reminded me of my father."

"Your father? Is he a professor?"

"A professor, uh…" My voice trails off. My eyes are welling up for the second time today.

"What's wrong, Ginny?"

After setting my glass on the coffee table, I put my hands over my mouth and try to control my breathing. After a few moments, I compose myself. "He died. My father died."

"Oh, Ginny, I'm so sorry," Preston says softly.

"It was an accident," I say, twisting my charm bracelet around my wrist. "I miss him."

Preston sets his glass next to mine on the coffee table. "Tell me about him."

"He was the kindest man. A bit absent-minded at times." I smile. "One time he went to work in his pajamas. He didn't even notice until someone pointed it out to him."

I continue to share memories about my father, while Preston listens intently.

After I point out the charm that my father gave me on my sixteenth birthday, Preston takes my hand in his and strokes it gently.

The sensation is so different from when Lorenzo caressed my hand earlier that afternoon. My heart goes pitter-patter, I feel shivers up and down my body, and, most of all, I feel a deep sense of caring from Preston. I feel like if I spent enough time with him holding my hand, my pain would go away.

I look into his blue eyes and smile. "Is that offer for dinner still open?"

8 - Smitten with Ravioli

I fidget with my charm bracelet while I wait for Preston. I'm early. Normally, I like being early. However, tonight, I'm not thrilled with my punctuality. What if he thinks I'm so eager to go to dinner with him that I've been standing here waiting for hours for him to arrive?

Nope. Can't have that happen. The only solution is to sneak outside and hide behind the bushes by the entrance. Once I see him go inside, I'll wait for ten minutes, then casually stroll into the reception room as though I've completely lost track of time.

I grin. This is a good plan. I scurry out of the room and into the hallway. Darn. I forgot my purse. I scurry back, grab my cute little clutch, then scurry back into the hallway.

I look down at what I'm holding. Wait a minute. This isn't my cute little clutch. This isn't cute at all. Unless you happen to think that having a purse bedazzled with a likeness of Elvis on it is cute, then this is just the ticket.

I'm pretty sure it belongs to Mabel—the reigning queen of bedazzling among the Silver Foxes. Scared that she might whack me with her cane because she'll be convinced that I stole it, I scurry back to the lounge.

As I look around the room for my purse, I think about the word "scurry." Did you ever find that the more times you say a word to yourself, the less it makes sense? Maybe it's the wrong word? Maybe the word I'm looking for is "scurvy" or "surly" or possibly "scurrly"? Is "scurrly" even a word?

Whatever it is I'm doing, I pick up the pace. I need to switch purses and get behind those bushes pronto. After finding my clutch and switching it out with Mabel's, I scurrly—let's pretend it's a real word—back into the hall and straight into Preston. I startle, dropping my purse on the floor, then look up.

"Sorry, I'm late," he says before bending down to pick up my purse. He starts to hand it to me, then takes a step back. His gaze slowly travels from my face down to my toes, then back up again. After a beat, he locks eyes with me. "Wow. You look amazing."

I bite my lip, then return the compliment. "You're wearing a bow tie."

Okay, I'm not sure if that was a compliment or more of an observation, but the grin on his face seems to suggest that he's taken it as a form of praise.

He moves closer to me. "I am."

"It has polka dots on it," I say, tossing out more of my keen observations.

His smile fades a little. "Don't you like polka dots?"

"Who doesn't like polka dots?" I say in a reassuring tone.

"And you're wearing a dress," he says, a full grin back on display.

"I am."

"It has straps."

I bite back a smile. "Don't you like straps?"

"Straps are good."

Neither of us says a word. He looks at my straps, and I look at his bow tie. Then the silence is broken.

"Where are you two off to?" Loretta asks as she walks toward us.

"Wait up," Mabel calls, her cane tapping on the marble floor as she scurries—see, there's that word again—down the hall.

Preston hands me my purse. "We're going to dinner at that restaurant that Maria recommended."

"The place that serves the ravioli with spinach and artichokes?" Loretta asks.

"That's the one."

Mabel's eyes light up. "Ooh. I love artichokes. We should join you."

"You don't like artichokes," Loretta says.

Mabel scowls. "Yes, I do."

"No, you don't."

"I most certainly do."

Loretta takes a deep breath. "No, you like arugula, not artichokes."

"They're the same thing."

"No, they're not."

"Yes, they are."

Preston and I exchange glances while the two ladies continue to bicker. I'm actually torn. On one hand, I'm not sure I can handle listening to them argue about whether arugula and artichokes are the same thing during the entire meal. On the other hand, they might be a good distraction from Preston.

Not that I need to be distracted from Preston. Or that Preston is distracting. Sure, the color of his eyes match the blue polka dots on his bow tie, and that nerdy smile of his makes my stomach do flips, but he isn't distracting.

Not one bit.

Not distracting at all.

Seriously. Not distracting.

"Earth to Ginny," Loretta says.

"Weren't you listening?" Mabel purses her lips. "You seem distracted."

"Sorry," I say, stepping back a safe distance from Mabel's cane. "What did you say?"

"Preston doesn't think we'll be able to get seats at the restaurant," Mabel says. "He only booked a table for two. But I can't see how they can turn two old ladies away, can you?"

A horn sounds outside.

"I think that's our taxi." Preston smiles as he grabs my hand. "Tell you what, ladies," he says to Mabel and Loretta. "Why don't I take the two of you there next weekend instead of tonight so that I can give you my undivided attention?"

"Good idea," I say. "That will also give the two of you time to figure out if Mabel likes artichokes or not."

Then we scurry to the door and make our escape.

* * *

The restaurant is everything that Maria promised—a small, family-run establishment tucked away in a non-touristy part of town. The kind of place you'd only find if a local told you about it.

As Preston holds the door open for me, his hand brushes my shoulder. I've never been more conscious of the fact that I'm wearing a dress with straps until tonight. I glance back at him. I have to restrain myself from turning around and untying that polka-dot bow tie of his.

"*Buona sera*," an older woman says as we enter. She's wearing a floral dress with a lace collar, her silver hair is pulled back into a neat bun, and her hazel eyes sparkle in the candlelight. When Preston tells her that Maria sent us, she pulls us into a warm embrace. "Ah, that makes you family."

She taps her chest. "You must call me Mama Leoni." She grabs our hands and pulls us toward the kitchen. She pushes the door open and points at the three men inside. "That is Papa Leoni and those are our two sons—Luigi and Pepe." Papa Leoni nods as he drains some pasta. Luigi smiles as he stirs a pot on the stove, while Pepe gives us a cheerful wave before turning back to chop vegetables.

"They will make you the most delicious ravioli," Mama Leoni says as she leads us to a table in the back of the restaurant. After we're seated, she furrows her brow. "You do like artichokes, don't you?" After we reassure her that we do, she says, "Good, good. Some people don't."

"I've heard some people even confuse it with arugula," I say.

"Very odd. They're nothing alike," she says, raising her eyebrows. "Ah, never mind. People who can't tell the difference between arugula and artichokes generally don't come here."

As she bustles off to seat another couple, I admire our rustic surroundings. Tables are covered in white tablecloths, red candles are set in old wine bottles with wax dripping down their sides, classical music is playing in the background, and dark-paneled walls add to the ambiance.

Mama Leoni returns with a bottle of the local Lambrusco and a plate of bruschetta. "We grow the tomatoes and basil ourselves," she says pointing at the bread, which has been grilled, then rubbed with garlic and drizzled with olive oil. "Enjoy," she says, beaming at us before returning to the kitchen.

Preston and I raise our glasses. "Here's to ravioli," he says.

"And tiramisu," I add. "Did you see it in the kitchen? Is there any better dessert in the world?"

"I'll drink to that," he says, then takes a sip of wine.

For some reason, the way he's looking at me makes me flustered. I feel all those first date anxieties—is anything stuck in my teeth, do we have anything in common, does he think I'm interesting, is he interesting—you know, the types of things you worry about when you're out to dinner with a stranger.

But Preston isn't a stranger. We've spent two weeks side by side in cooking class. And this isn't a date. So why am I nervous? Or is it a date? Is that why I'm nervous?

"This is awkward, isn't it?" he says after a long pause.

"So, it isn't just me," I say, leaning forward.

He cocks his head to one side. "Should we pretend we just met?"

"Sure."

"Okay, I'll go first." He adjusts his bow tie. "So, miss, is this your first time in Italy?"

"No, I've been here several times. But this is my first time in Ravenna."

"Really?" he asks. "You've been to Italy before?"

"Can't you tell from my flawless Italian?" I grab a piece of bruschetta. The juicy homegrown tomato is bursting with flavor. I push the plate toward Preston. "You have to try this."

He takes a bite, smiles appreciatively, then quickly devours the rest of his slice. "You know, I could always teach you Italian," he says as he picks up another piece of the grilled bread. "I'm a good teacher. My students always give me great evaluations."

I roll my eyes. "You realize they're just sucking up to you, right?"

He smiles. "I guess I don't have to worry about that with you, do I?"

"Never," I say. "I'll always tell you the truth."

We're silent for a few minutes as we finish the rest of the bruschetta. Preston refills my wineglass, then asks me where I've traveled in Italy.

"All the usual spots—Rome, Florence, Milan, and Pisa."

"Did you get a selfie with the Leaning Tower of Pisa?"

"Of course," I say. "What self-respecting tourist doesn't? I've also spent a bit of time in Sicily."

"Sicily? That's off the beaten track for most tourists. What made you go there?"

"Oh, it was for my father's work. We spent a few summers there."

"What did he do?"

"Oh, uh..." I stare at the flickering candle and try to figure out how to respond. I can't tell Preston that my father was a professor. That would lead to too many follow-up questions. Finally, I blurt out, "He was an animal trainer."

"He trained animals? Like for the circus?"

"Uh, no, cats. He trained house cats."

"Is that even possible?" He picks up a stray piece of tomato from the plate and pops it in his mouth. "I thought cats were untrainable."

I avert my eyes. "Only if you don't know the secret."

"Does it have something to do with treats?"

"Not exactly." I focus on rearranging my silverware, continuing to avoid eye contact. "But I can't tell what it is because it's a...you know...secret."

"So let me see if I get this straight," Preston says, leaning back in his chair. "Your father took you and your family to Sicily in the summers to train cats."

"Yeah, that about sums it up."

"Are there a lot of cats in Sicily that need training?"

Fortunately, Mama Leoni appears, causing Preston to forget about his line of questioning. Which is a good thing, because my knowledge of the Sicilian feline population is a bit lacking.

"Passatelli del noni," she says proudly, setting bowls down. "Bread and parmigiano reggiano cheese soup. It's a secret family recipe."

After sampling the soup, we both agree that it's delicious.

"It's a shame that the recipe is a secret," I say.

"Another family secret," Preston says. "There seems to be a lot of secrets tonight—how to train cats and how to make this wonderful soup."

"Surely, you have a secret or two."

He doesn't respond until he finishes his soup. After he sets his spoon down, he says, "Don't we all?"

"Tell me one of your secrets," I say playfully.

"No, I can't. It's too embarrassing."

"Go on, you can trust me."

"Do you promise you won't tell anyone?"

"Pinky promise."

"Frogs freak me out. I break out into a cold sweat whenever I see one."

"Just frogs or all amphibians?"

"Frogs are the worse, but salamanders come a close second."

"Sounds like batrachophobia. Fear of amphibians."

Preston rubs his hand across his forehead. "See? Cold sweat. Just talking about it does it to me."

"Well, let's change the subject then." I reach across the table and squeeze his hand. "What would you like to talk about?"

"Tell me more about how your dad wrangled cats. I bet you have some funny stories."

I bite my lip and stare down at the table. There are funny stories about my father that I could share, but none of them have to do with cats. But it's not just that. There's another reason that I don't want to talk about him, especially not today. Today of all days.

"Ginny, are you okay? You haven't said a word for five minutes."

I look up at Preston.

He frowns when he sees my expression. "What is it?"

"I shouldn't have come tonight," I say. "I thought this would be a good distraction, but..."

"A distraction from what?"

"Remember how I told you that my father passed away?" He nods, staring at me intently with those blue eyes of his. "Well, today is the one-year anniversary of his death."

"Oh, my gosh. I'm so sorry. I didn't know."

I smile faintly. "It's not your fault. I thought I could pretend today was a day just like any other, but it isn't."

"Do you want me to take you back to the retreat center?"

"No," I say, shaking my head. "I don't think I could stand being alone right now."

"Well, I'm not going anywhere."

"Thanks," I say, looking off into the distance. My body feels cold. I take a sip of wine, hoping it will warm me up, but it doesn't. "He died in a plane crash. I was at school when my mom called to tell me."

His eyes widen. "Wow, a plane crash. No wonder you're afraid to fly."

"Yeah, I'll never set foot on a plane ever again." I straighten my shoulders and look directly at Preston. "Ever."

* * *

Bless Mama Leoni's timing. She always seems to come by with a new course at the exact moment when we need an interruption. She sets a shallow bowl down in front of each of us with a flourish. "Our famous ravioli with spinach and artichokes." After grating some parmigiano reggiano cheese on top of our pasta, she gives a slight bow and retreats back to the kitchen.

"I hope no salivating burros were involved in the making of this," Preston jokes.

I grin. "No, you only find them in tortellini dishes, not ravioli."

I appreciate Preston's efforts to keep the conversation light-hearted, and we continue to banter back and forth as we polish off our pasta. After two more courses—piccata di pollo and a generous slice of tiramisu—I lean back in my chair.

"I'm stuffed."

"Me too," Preston says, scraping the last bit of sweetened marscapone cheese off his plate.

My phone beeps. "Sorry, I need to check this. It might be my mom." I feel my eyes start to water. "It's been a tough day for her."

"And you too," he says softly, reaching across the table to squeeze my hand.

I squeeze his hand back, then pull my phone out of my purse.

"Was it your mom?" Preston asks. "You're smiling."

"No. It's just a silly text from Mia and Isabelle."

"What'd they say?"

"Um...they want to know how the food was." I feel my face grow warm as another lie escapes my lips. Of course they didn't want to know if we enjoyed our meal. They want to know if Preston is a good kisser. I quickly type a reply—*For the millionth time, it's not a date*—then tuck the phone back in my purse.

When I look up, he cocks his head to one side. "Why don't I believe you?"

"It's true. I'd show you the text to prove it to you, but I accidentally deleted it." My face is burning by this point as the lies tumble out.

"Uh-huh."

I look around for Mama Leoni. "It's getting late. Maybe we should get the check."

"You know what I think?" he says, leaning back in his chair with his arms behind his head. "I think your friends were texting about how you're smitten with me."

"Smitten? With you? Arrogant much?" I say with a smirk. "I think you have yourself confused with the ravioli. If I'm smitten with anything, I'm smitten with those little babies. What has you so smitten with the word 'smitten' anyway? It's kind of an old-fashioned word."

"I'm an old fashioned kind of guy."

I grab the last piece of bread and tear off a piece. "How so?" I ask before I pop it in my mouth.

"Well, I respect my elders, I try not to swear, and I wear bow ties occasionally." Preston pauses as Mama Leoni places the check on the table, then pulls it toward him. "I also pay for dinner when I take a lady out on a date."

"When did this become a date?"

"The minute I saw you in that dress."

My mouth goes dry. I push back my chair from the table and mumble something about going to the ladies' room. After checking my make-up, I make a few origami birds out of paper towels while I wait for my heart to stop beating so fast. Why did he have to say that about my dress? It's not like I wore it for him.

My face grows warm again. Now, I'm even fibbing to myself. Of course, I was thinking about him when I chose my outfit. I wanted him to see me in something other than jeans and t-shirts.

I close my eyes and take a deep breath. Time to nip this flirtation in the bud.

When I return to the table, Preston stands. "Ready to go?"

"Did you pay the check?"

He nods.

I reach for my purse. "How much do I owe?"

He smiles that nerdy smile of his, and my heart melts. "Nothing. Remember, I'm old-fashioned."

I place my purse back on the table. "This isn't a date," I say firmly.

"Yes, it is," he says, taking a step toward me.

"No, it isn't."

"Yes, it is."

I take a step toward him, closing the rest of the gap between us before jabbing a finger in his muscular chest. "No, it isn't"

He grabs my hand and pulls me toward him. "You always have to be right, don't you?"

"No, I don't."

"Yes, you do." Then he laughs. "Look at us. We're bickering just like Loretta and Mabel."

I smile. "No, we're not."

"Yes, we are," he says.

I tilt my head up and say softly, "No, we aren't"

"Yes, we..." His voice trails off as he locks eyes with me. "I'm going to kiss you now, okay?"

I start to contradict him, but as his face nears mine, I whisper, "Yes, you are."

He lightly kisses each side of my mouth before softly pressing his lips to mine. I moan as his gentle kiss turns more urgent. Running my fingers through his hair, I draw him closer to me and press my body against his. The rational part of my brain tries to remind me that we're in public, but the other side of my brain tells it to be quiet. It wants these kisses to keep coming. It wants this tingling sensation coursing throughout my body to continue. It wants this sharp stabbing pain in my right calf to...

Hang on, what's going on? Stabbing pain? Why does my leg hurt?

"I told you it's them," I hear a familiar voice say behind me. Then I feel a sharp stabbing pain in my other calf.

Preston pulls back, the glazed look in his eyes turning sheepish. He raises his head to look at the person behind me. "Good evening, ladies."

I spin around, put my hands on my hips and glare at the silver-haired woman in front of me. "Mabel, would you mind not jabbing me with your cane?"

9 - Calorie Bombs

Preston demonstrated his old-fashioned gentleman credentials after dinner on Saturday night. Once we got back to the retreat center, he escorted me to the residential annex where I was staying and paused at the entryway. After kissing me so thoroughly that I thought my knees were going to buckle underneath me, he stepped back, stroked my cheek, then bid me goodnight.

We didn't see each other again until Monday morning. During the rest of the week we only saw each other in class as he continued to be swamped with his grant proposal, spending most of his free time in Bologna at the university. But by the time Friday rolled around, he told me he was now able to spend all of his spare time with me.

"I have a surprise for you tomorrow morning," Preston says as he dices celery for the ragù a la rumagnôla we're making, a meat sauce that's a specialty of the region.

I grab an onion out of the basket on our workstation and place it on my cutting board. "What is it?"

"It wouldn't be a surprise if I told you," he says with a twinkle in his eye. "Just make sure you eat a hearty breakfast. You're going to be working off some serious calories."

"How many calories?"

"Plenty."

"So I can have two bombolones?" My mouth waters as I think about the delicious Italian donuts crammed full of apricot jam that they serve in the mornings. I'm pretty sure the translation of bombolone into English is calorie bomb. I usually try to go for a healthier option, like a yogurt, but those donuts are awfully tempting.

"You better have three."

"Three. That does sound serious. What exactly are we going to be doing that warrants three donuts?"

"You're having a hard time understanding the concept of a surprise, aren't you? You just have to trust me." He scrapes the chopped celery off his cutting board into a bowl, then casually asks, "You trust me, don't you?"

While I peel my onion, I think about his question. Do I trust him? Can I trust him?

I shake my head. The better question is, do I *want* to trust Preston? I trusted what's-his-name and look where that got me. When he offered to review my research paper before I turned it in, I eagerly agreed. I valued his expertise. His feedback would be a huge help. My paper would be ten times better with his input.

What a fool I was.

My hand trembles as I recall the day my thesis advisor called me into his office. I had turned my paper in the previous day, five minutes before the deadline. Normally, I liked to turn them in at least twenty-four hours before the cut-off, but I had been waiting for what's-his-name to send me his feedback. Usually we grabbed lunch between classes, met up at the library at night to study, and hung out over the weekends. But after I gave him my paper the previous week to review, he had become scarce, coming up with all sorts of excuses from his parents being in town (they weren't), being sick (a hangnail doesn't require bed rest), to having to walk his neighbor's dog (she has a hamster).

When I didn't hear back from him about my paper, I turned the original version in and hoped for the best.

I should have hoped for the worst, then I wouldn't have been disappointed. Because I can't imagine anything worse than having my thesis advisor show me a copy of the paper what's-his-name turned in three days prior to mine. A paper that was exactly the same as mine, except for the name on the front.

Even when I pulled out my laptop and showed him the date stamps of the original paper on my hard drive, I was met with disbelief. Those things can be faked, I was told. You're not smart enough to have written this. You've been coasting along on your father's coattails. That's the only reason you were accepted into this program.

I was devastated by his assessment of my intellectual capability. But my devastation turned to anger when my thesis advisor stood by what's-his-name, despite all evidence to the contrary. When I demanded a formal hearing, he pulled out the trump card—my father. My dead father. Did I want to ruin my father's reputation with a formal hearing? It would get out that his daughter had been accused of plagiarism and, whether or not my name was cleared, the damage would be done. Wouldn't it be better to drop quietly out of grad school?

It wasn't until later that I found out why my thesis advisor didn't support me. Turns out he had lost out on a prestigious research grant to my father. My mother said that he had never really had a shot—my father's academic credentials were far superior—but that didn't stop him from blaming my father and finally taking his revenge out on me years later.

When I asked my mom why my father hadn't told me about this professor's feud with him when I was accepted into the grad school where he taught, she shrugged. "It would have never occurred to him that he held a grudge," she said. "He always believed in the best of people. Just like you do."

"Like I used to," I told her. "Now I know better."

"Hey, you didn't answer me," Preston says, resting his hand lightly on my shoulder and snapping me back to the present. "Do you trust me?"

I plaster a smile on my face. "Of course I do."

No, I don't.

He smiles back, then reaches across me for the carrots.

I breathe in his scent of pine and leather. My fingers itch to touch his skin, to leave a trail of kisses down his neck, to press myself...

Get a grip, I tell myself. You're in public, surrounded by twenty senior citizens. If you start making out with Preston, there's a good chance more than one of them will have a heart attack from the shock of seeing the heat between the two of you. The retreat center only has one defibrillator. Do the math. It would not be a good outcome.

"That onion's not going to chop itself," he says, pointing at my cutting board.

As he busies himself peeling the carrots, I bite my lip. Who cares if I trust Preston or not? Cooking school will be over at the end of next week. This is just a short-term fling, right?

* * *

"Did you get enough calories at breakfast?" Preston asks the next morning as I walk down the marble steps of the villa.

I nod and rub my stomach, wishing I was wearing my yoga pants.

"Good. Are you ready?"

"Yes," I say warily. "But ready for what? What are you hiding behind your back?"

He grins and hands me a bike helmet.

"So your surprise is something that's going to give me bad hair?"

He places the helmet on my head, gives me a quick kiss on the cheek, then fastens the strap underneath my chin. "You're cute no matter what your hair looks like."

"I'm not entirely sure if that's a compliment. Are you saying my hair normally doesn't look nice?"

Instead of answering, he grabs my hand and leads me around the corner. "Ta da!" he says as he points at two bikes—one black and one pink.

I walk over to the black one. "I'll take this one, thanks."

He frowns. "I thought you'd prefer the other one."

"Why do people always assume girls like pink?" I ask, putting my hands on my hips.

"Is it pink?" He shrugs. "I didn't really pay attention. I picked it out for you because of the bell."

89

"The bell?"

"Yeah, come have a look."

I squint at the bell attached to the handlebar. There's a woman on it in a white gown holding some sort of sword. She looks vaguely familiar.

"It's right up your alley, isn't it?"

I look at him blankly.

"Princess Leia. I thought everyone liked her. Oh, wait, do you prefer Luke? Sorry, this is the only *Star Wars* bell they had. It was either this or one with a dinosaur on it."

"Luke...wait, I remember. He's the one who drinks the funny-colored milk."

"Yeah, and Leia is his sister."

"Sure, of course, I knew that." I ring the bell. "Love her sword."

"You mean light saber."

"Sword, light saber, same thing."

"I guess. Except one has a—"

"Light," I say, finishing his sentence. I hop onto my pink Princess Leia-themed bike. "Well, should we get going?"

"Yep, we'll bike around town for a while, then it's about four miles to our destination."

"And where's that exactly?"

"The Basilica of Sant' Apollinare in Classe. It's one of the UNESCO sites in the area. But it's not visited as much as the other sites because it's outside of Ravenna. I know you're not crazy about history, but I thought it would be a fun outing. Plus, I packed a picnic lunch with plenty of calories to replenish the ones we'll be working off."

After exploring Ravenna by bike, we pedal out of town mid-morning. I think about how Preston has planned the perfect romantic date, from picking out a bike he thought I would like to organizing a picnic. What's-his-name used to do things like that. All guys all start out sweet, like bombolones, but then you end up being betrayed. Don't get too close to Preston, I remind myself, unless you want to go through that heartache again.

When we arrive at the basilica, we park our bikes. I remove my helmet and stow it in my basket. Running my fingers through my curls, I try to get them to fluff up after being squashed under my helmet. Preston rings the bell on my bike to get my attention. He points at the church. "This way."

As we walk up the cobbled path toward the entrance, he goes into professor mode. "For five hundred years, the city of Classe was an important military port for the Roman Empire. Did you know that when the basilica was built 1500 years ago, it was on the seashore?"

Yes, I want to shout out. I do know that. I studied ancient history in grad school.

But he doesn't wait to hear my answer, assuming I don't have a clue about the history of the area. Assuming it was just a rhetorical question, he continues with his lecture. "But with all the accumulation of silt over the years, the coastline is more than five miles to the east now. Octavian probably chose this spot because of its strategic location."

He pauses for a moment to let a group of nuns pass by, then leans down and smiles. "You might know Octavian better by the name Augustus, which he took when he became emperor."

I clench my fists. The last thing I want to be reminded of is Emperor Augustus given his association with what's-his-name.

Oblivious to the effect that his history lesson is having on me, he carries on. "It was a great site in many respects, but it didn't have easy access to fresh water. That all changed when Emperor Trajen built an aqueduct to Ravenna, which some say also served Classe." He smiles. "But, hey you probably already know that."

Yes, I do know that, but I pretend to be surprised. "Why would I know that?"

"You told me about that guy trying to pick you up by talking about Witmer's theory about the cultural importance of aqueducts, remember?"

"Yeah, he was a jerk."

"He didn't deserve you," Preston says, ruffling my hair. "Anyway, 'classe' comes from the Latin word—"

I hold up my hand, impatient with his ongoing lecture. Any ancient history grad student worth their salt knows this. "Yes, yes, I know, it comes from the Latin word, *classis*, which means fleet."

He stops walking. "How did you know that?"

"Lucky guess?"

"No seriously, how did you know that?"

Think quick. How do I explain the fact that my father started teaching me Latin before I could walk?

"I went to Catholic school. We had to study it."

"Oh," he says. "Most people forget the Latin they learned in school. I'm impressed."

"That's all I remember, really," I say with a slight shrug. Then I look down at the ground and chew my lip. Why did I lie to Preston? Sure, it was only a partial lie. I did go to Catholic school, and I did study Latin, but that's not the real explanation as to why I know what *classis* means. But it's not like I want a boyfriend, especially not one who is a history professor, so it doesn't matter if I wasn't exactly honest with him, right? Or does it?

He runs his fingers up my arm, interrupting my thoughts. "Maybe this was a bad idea, coming here. You don't like history. You're going to be bored. Sometimes, I forget that not everyone is as passionate about history as I am."

"No, it'll be fine," I say. "They have mosaics, right?"

He nods.

"I like those. They're pretty."

"Well, if you're sure..."

"I'm sure," I say, tugging on his arm. "Let's go inside."

We walk through the nave, past marble columns and faded frescoes. When we reach the triumphal arch, my jaw drops. Even though I've seen the mosaics in pictures before, they're a million times more impressive in person.

"Do you like it?"

"I love it."

I want nothing more than to talk with Preston about the historical significance of the basilica. But I can't. I can't let on that not only do I love history, but that I've spent years studying it. If only I was here with someone else, someone other than Preston, someone I could be my real self around.

No, that's a lie. The only person I want to be with right now is Preston. I love being with him. I love spending time with him. I wish I could be honest about who I really am. But I can't. Because if I did, he'd never speak to me again.

* * *

Just when things couldn't get worse, I see someone I know—Professor Ratcliffe. Normally, I'd be delighted to see him. He and my father were good friends and co-authored several research papers together. But the last thing I need is for him to recognize me and come over and say hi. The game would definitely be up then.

I tug at Preston's sleeve. "Actually, do you mind if we go? I'm probably mosaiced out for the day."

"Of course," he says. "History in small doses is probably best."

I keep my head down as we walk out of the basilica and pray that Professor Ratcliffe doesn't turn around.

"Hungry?" Preston asks once we're outside.

"Yep," I say. "As long as lunch doesn't involve bombolones. I think I've had my fill of donuts for the year."

"You might change your mind tomorrow morning," he says dryly.

"Probably." I chuckle. "My willpower is less of a power and more of an aspiration."

He walks toward a large tree, pulls a blanket out of his backpack, and lays it on the ground.

"Shouldn't we picnic somewhere else?" I ask, feeling anxiety course through me. The last place I want to linger at is the basilica for fear that Professor Ratcliffe will see us.

93

"I think we're allowed to picnic on the grounds, and it's a romantic spot, don't you think?"

"Uh-huh," I say, wishing I had a hat to hide my face from being spotted.

"I thought being in the shade would be good. It's getting kind of warm. But we can move to over there, if you want," he says, pointing at a bench by the entrance.

"No, this is good," I say. "But maybe we should move the blanket to the other side of the tree. It has a better view." By better view, I mean one that's out of the way, out of view of people passing by.

"You want a view of a trash can?" he asks, perplexed.

"Uh-huh. It's an Italian trash can," I say, as though that explains it.

He furrows his brow, apparently confused by my interest in foreign garbage receptacles. Then he shrugs and moves the blanket. He probably figures it's no less bizarre than my father's supposed cat training business. I really need to make my lies a bit more realistic. Or maybe stop lying.

Preston has thought of everything. It's amazing what he managed to stow in his backpack—crusty bread, cheese, meat, olives, and sodas.

As we sip on our drinks and take in the romantic view of our garbage can, Preston gives me a sideways look. "So, what are your plans after the cooking program is finished?"

I chew on my lip while I consider this. Then I answer honestly. "I don't know. I guess I'll head back home. I was thinking about booking passage on a freighter ship. Or trying to get a job on a cruise ship."

"Will it be hard to find another manicurist job?" he asks.

"I have no idea." Another honest answer, since I'm not actually a manicurist. I decide to go for a trifecta of lies. "I'm thinking about making a career change." Completely true. Since I don't have a future as a history professor to look forward to, I'll need to figure out what else to do with my life. My money will run out in a few months, and I can't imagine my mom will let me live on her couch for the rest of my life without chipping in.

"Really? What did you have in mind?"

"I have no idea." I sigh. "But enough about me. Why don't you tell me about you? Did you always want to be a professor?"

He shakes his head. "When I was growing up, everyone assumed I'd take over my dad's business. He has a car repair shop. I worked there in the summers and over the weekends, but I hated it. It took me a while, but I finally worked up the courage to tell him that I wanted to go to college."

"How did he take it?"

"Not well. I think he thought that I betrayed him."

"Funny how we think we need to follow in our father's footsteps," I muse.

"Did everyone expect you to become a cat trainer?"

"No, if I'm honest, I put that pressure on myself." I'm actually talking about being a professor, not a cat trainer, but Preston doesn't know that, so again, I'm not lying to him. "Maybe that's why I don't know what I want to do with my life. I never opened myself up to the possibility of being anything other than a..."

"A manicurist?"

"Exactly." Oh, well. I guess my run on the truth was going to end sooner or later.

He looks at my short, unvarnished nails. "How come you never give yourself a manicure?"

"Oh, just taking a break," I say breezily. "It's good to let your nails have a breather from nail polish."

He leans back against the tree trunk. "You know, we've never talked about us."

"I'm surprised you don't have a string of girlfriends back home."

His eyes widen. "First of all, I would never have a string of girlfriends. I'm a one-woman kind of guy. And second, do you really think I would have kissed you if I did have a girlfriend?" Then his face darkens. "I would never cheat on anyone."

"I'm sorry," I say, putting my hand on his. "I didn't think you would. I guess I just thought someone as cute as you would already be taken."

"You think I'm cute?"

"A little bit," I say, holding up my fingers. "This much."

"That sure is a little bit."

I spread my fingers farther apart. "Okay, this much."

"Still not a lot to write home about."

"This much?" I ask, increasing the distance by another inch or two.

"Okay, that'll do...for now." He grins. "Ready for our next stop?"

"Where's that?"

"The archaeological park. We passed it on our way here. I have a friend who is going to give us a guided tour."

"Super. Just let me hit the ladies' room and I'll be right back."

I take a very circuitous route to and from the restroom, ducking occasionally to avoid Professor Ratcliffe. As I near our picnic spot, I think I hear the professor's voice. I go to dive behind a tree, but I startle as a squirrel darts in front of me, and I end up tripping on a rock and landing on the ground.

10 - Bad Dad Jokes

Preston rushes over. "Oh, my gosh, are you okay?"

"I'm fine," I say. "Just embarrassed."

He grins as he helps me to my feet. "You get knocked down a lot."

"At least it was on soft grass this time." I press my hands against his chest to steady myself. I feel his heart beating through the thin material of his shirt. It's beating fast. Or is that my heartbeat pitter-pattering?

His hands travel up my arms to my shoulders, lightly squeezing along the way. "Anything hurt?"

"I don't think so." Not that I would know if I was in pain. All I can feel right now is pure pleasure as his fingers graze my neck.

He cups my face in his hands. "How about here?" he asks as he lightly brushes his lips against mine.

"I'm not sure. You better check again." I slide my hands around his back and tilt my head sideways. He nips my bottom lip, then runs his hands through my hair, drawing me toward him as he deepens the kiss.

It seems like forever before he finally pulls back. My breath catches in my throat at the sight of those blue eyes of his.

"How was that?" he asks softly.

He's looking at me with such intensity that I can barely speak. "It was..." My voice trails off. I don't know how to express what I'm feeling. What I wouldn't give for a dictionary right now so I could do a search for just the right word. I rack my brain.

Oh, wait, I've got it.

Smitten.

That's what I feel.

I'm smitten. Smitten with this gorgeous man in front of me whose kisses make me tingle from head to toe.

But instead of telling him how I feel, I tug on his shirt, pulling him toward me. "Kiss me again," I whisper.

And he does.

Slowly and thoroughly.

It's torture. Torture in a good way. A really, really good way.

"Wait a minute, what happened to my purse?" I ask, breaking free from his embrace.

"Your purse?" Preston smiles. "All you can think about after that kiss is your purse?"

I turn and look around me. "When I fell, I must have dropped it. Do you see it anywhere?"

"Relax. It's over there." He points at the garbage can. My purse is lying next to it, its contents strewn in the grass. A squirrel is sniffing at my belongings, presumably looking for acorns. Or maybe breath mints. I imagine even wild animals get stinky breath from time to time.

"Come on, I'll help you pick everything up," he says.

I feel my face grow warm as I remember the last time Preston helped me collect the contents of my purse. I thought I was going to die of embarrassment when he handed me those feminine products that men don't have a need of. There's no way I can let that happen again.

"No, I can do it," I say, rushing in front of him. I shove everything back in my purse, then make a quick inventory. Hairbrush—check. Phone—check. Wallet—check. Breath mints untouched by squirrels—check. Everything seems to be there except my passport. I frantically dig through my belongings again.

"Looking for this?" Preston asks, playfully waving my passport at me.

I breathe a sigh of relief and hold out my hand.

"Not quite yet," he says. "I want to see your picture first."

"Please, don't. It's awful. I look like I got into a fight with an orangutan and the orangutan won."

"How awful can it be? You're adorable." He gives me a quick kiss, holding my passport over his head so that I can't grab it. Then he darts a few feet away and flips it open. "Well, you're definitely cuter than an orangutan. Similar hair color, though."

"Hmm. I'm not quite sure how to take that."

"Virginia," he reads out loud, then glances at me. "So Ginny is short for Virginia. It suits you. Virginia is far too serious of a name."

I feel a cold pit in my stomach as he looks back at my passport and purses his lips.

"Virginia Morgan Maarschalkerweerd." He says my full name slowly, stumbling slightly as he tries to pronounce my last name. The last name that I never wanted him to know. The last name that will connect me to my father. The last name that will let him know that I'm not who I said I was.

His blue eyes turn steely. "Why did you tell me your last name was Morgan?"

* * *

Preston furrows his brow as he reexamines my passport. "I don't understand. You said your name was Ginny Morgan, not Ginny Maarschalkerweerd." When he looks back up at me, his expression is cold. "Is Morgan your maiden name? Are you married? Were you married?"

I feel a weight lift off my shoulders. He hasn't made the connection to my father. "Nope," I say with a smile. "I'm not married. Never have been. I'm happily single."

"You're single?"

I nod.

"Happily single?"

"Yep."

"Single?"

I nod again.

"Happily?"

I chew on my lip. Where is he going with this?

He snaps my passport shut, then fixes his gaze on me. "So, if you're single, then what's this between us?"

I'm not sure how to answer. I know how I feel about him, but I also know that we don't have a future. After a beat, I say, "It's nice."

"It is," he says, nodding slowly.

I look down at the ground. "The cooking program will be over at the end of next week and I'll be leaving then, so—"

"So, it's nothing serious," he says, finishing my sentence. "Two single people enjoying some time together. Right?"

"Right," I force myself to say.

He hands my passport back to me. "So what's with using Morgan, then?"

"Morgan is my middle name. Like the horses. My mom was a big horse person. She was so disappointed that I didn't love them too, but, you know, allergies." I sneeze to make a point. Then I sneeze two more times. For some reason, I can't help but sneeze three times in a row. Never two, never four. Always three.

"Bless you," Preston says. "Good thing my surprise was a bike ride, not horse riding."

"For sure. If you think I looked bad in my passport photo, imagine what I look like when my eyes are bloodshot and swollen, and my nose is runny from allergies."

"I never said you looked bad." A faint smile plays on his lips. "I said you looked cute."

"Cuter than an orangutan," I remind him. "Hardly a glowing endorsement."

His smile grows wider, then quickly fades. "Hey, why are you using the name Morgan in class if that isn't your last name?"

"That must be a clerical mix-up," I say evasively as I shove my passport into my purse. I need to distract Preston from continuing to focus on my last name. "What's your middle name?" I ask him brightly.

"George. I'm named after my father."

"Preston George," I say. "That has a nice ring to it."

He rubs his face with his hand. "I generally don't tell people what my middle name is. It's a reminder of how much I disappointed him by not taking over the family business. George was my grandfather's name. My dad wanted my first name to be George, but my mom put her foot down, insisting on Preston instead. She thought it would be confusing to have more than one George in the house."

"My father would be disappointed with me too," I say.

"Because you're a manicurist?"

I feel a lump forming in my throat as I think about all the lies I've told Preston. I remind myself that it will all be over at the end of next week and I'll never see him again. "We better get going to this archaeological park of yours."

"Okay." He hands me my bike helmet, then straps his on. "So, do you think you would change your name when you get married?"

"It depends on the last name. If it's easier to spell, then sure." I laugh. I can't imagine any last name harder to spell than mine.

"Ready?" Preston asks.

"Yep, I'll follow you."

As we head onto the bicycle path, I frown. Why was Preston asking if I'd change my name when I got married? Didn't we just agree we were just two happily single people simply enjoying a holiday romance in Italy?

* * *

During the short ride to the archaeological park, I think about Preston's mixed signals. One minute he's going on about how he's happily single. The next minute, he's asking me if I'd change my last name if I get married.

Was he thinking about me when he mentioned marriage?

No, he couldn't be.

Could he be?

I mean, sure, Whitaker is a lot easier to spell than Maarschalkerweerd. If we got married, I'd change my name in a heartbeat. Virginia Morgan Whitaker. That has a nice ring to it. Ginny Whitaker. That sounds good too.

Then I slam on the brakes. And not just the brakes on my bike because we've arrived at the park, but the brakes in my stupid head. Stop thinking about getting married. Especially to Preston.

This is just a summer fling. This is just a summer fling. This is just a summer fling.

I squeeze my eyes shut and repeat this mantra over and over silently to myself.

"What's that, Ginny?"

I open my eyes and look sideways.

Preston is next to me, leaning over his handlebars. "I didn't catch what you said."

My eyes widen. I really need to learn not to say my thoughts out loud, especially any mantras about how Preston doesn't mean anything to me. "You didn't hear what I said?"

"No, you were mumbling." He smiles. "It was kind of cute, with your eyes all scrunched up, and your hands clasped together, kind of like you were saying a prayer."

I seize on what he says. "That's exactly what I was doing, praying to the patron saint of bicyclists."

"Oh? Who's that?"

I dig deep into the recesses of my mind. My aunt, the nun, used to quiz me on patron saints when I was a child.

Saint Barbara? No, she's the patron saint of fireworks. I definitely don't need to pray to her. There's enough fireworks when Preston kisses me as it is. Although, that's probably not the kind of fireworks Saint Barbara is all about.

Saint Isidore of Seville? Nope, he's the guy that looks out for users of the internet. I consider pulling out my phone and doing a quick Google search, but that would kind of give away that fact that I don't have a clue about who bikers pray to.

After a few more moments, I ring my Princess Leia bell and shout out, "Madonna del Ghisallo! She'll protect us on the rest of our bike ride."

"That's good. Given how often you fall down when you're simply walking, the last thing we need is for you to have a bike accident." He taps the side of my helmet. "Maybe you should wear this at all times, not just on your bike."

I quickly remove my helmet and fluff up my hair with my fingers. "Hah. Very funny."

We stow our bikes, then Preston grabs my hand and we walk into the visitor center. As I take in my surroundings, a stocky man with a goatee bounds over to us. After shaking his hand, Preston introduces us. "This is Matteo—"

"Call me Matt," he says as he extends his hand to me. "It's easier for English speakers to pronounce."

Preston nudges me. "Ginny is fluent in Italian."

"I never said I was fluent," I protest.

"That's fine," Matteo says. "I will be conducting the tour in English, in any case. It is good practice for me." He checks his phone and frowns. "Apologies, the other person joining us is running late. We wait inside the park for him, okay?"

We exit the visitor center onto a raised, glassed-in platform that over-looks the archaeological park. Matteo points out the ruins of the original warehouses, briefly explaining how they were constructed and how they housed goods to support the ancient Roman naval port located at Classe. After he informs us that the cobbled streets are called *basolata*, he asks us if we know why archaeologists go bankrupt.

"Because it's not a very high-paying job," I venture.

Matteo nods. "Yes, that is true. But the correct answer is because their careers are in ruins."

"Ba dum," Preston says, mimicking someone playing the drums.

"See if you know the answer to this one," Matteo says with a grin. "Why did the archaeologist's wife divorce him?"

Preston and I both shrug.

"Because he was carbon dating behind her back." Matteo slaps his hands on his thighs and guffaws. "Okay, one more. A Roman goes into a bar and holds up two fingers. 'Give me five beers,' he says." Matteo holds up his right hand, his index and middle finger making a V-shape. "Get it? The letter V stands for the number five in Roman numerals."

I put my head in my hands and groan. "Just when I think they couldn't get any worse."

"Hey, I've got one," Preston says. "A historian joke."

"Oh, good. I am always looking for new jokes for my children." Matteo pulls up a photo on his phone and shows it to me. "Lucia is seven and Leonardo is five."

"They're adorable," I say before handing the phone to Preston.

"They are cute," he says, putting his arm around my shoulder and giving it a squeeze.

"Your joke," Matteo reminds Preston.

"Right. If your name is Victor, you would have to become a historian. Why? Because history is written by the victors."

I roll my eyes. "These are the worst bad dad jokes ever."

"My kids love them," Matteo says.

"I think they're just humoring you," Preston says.

Matteo smiles. "Wait until it is your turn, my friend. You will be telling plenty of bad jokes. Hopefully, your children take after the *bellissima* Ginny instead of you."

My eyes widen, and I take a step back from Preston. "We, uh, we're not, um—"

"But, you two are engaged, no?" Matteo says to Preston. "Surely, you will have children after you are married."

Preston clears his throat. "Ginny isn't my fiancée."

I hold up my left hand, highlighting the absence of an engagement ring.

There's a long, uncomfortable silence. I even think about sharing a bad dad joke to break the tension, but I can't think of any. Matteo's phone buzzes. He glances at it. "Ah, the other member of our party is here."

He waves at someone standing behind me. I turn, and my jaw drops. It's

Professor Ratcliffe, my father's friend. What are the chances that he would be the person we were waiting for? My stomach clenches—how am I going to get out of this jam?

The professor walks toward us, surprise on his face. "Ginny? Ginny Maarschalkerweerd? Is that you? What are the chances that I would run into you here? At an archaeological park in Ravenna?"

My question exactly. What are the odds? Apparently, they are very good ones.

"I just came from the basilica. The mosaics there are stunning. Have you seen them yet?" he asks me. After I nod, his expression softens. "They made me think of your father."

"You knew Ginny's father?" Preston asks.

"Yes, we worked together on—"

I quickly jump in before he reveals too much about my father. "Yes, my dad helped Professor Ratcliffe with his cat. It was a tricky situation." I put my hand on the professor's arm, hoping he'll get the hint. "What was her name again?"

"My cat? Esmeralda, but your father didn't—"

Before he can say any more, I do what anyone would do in my situation. I pretend to stumble, fall into the professor's arms, and whisper in his ear. "Just play along and I'll explain later."

11 - Happy Birthday!

When I wake the next morning, I ignore my hunger pains. There's no way that I'm going to go down to the breakfast buffet and risk running into Preston after yesterday's debacle.

After my fake stumble into Professor Ratcliffe the day before, I managed to convince him to go along with my story that his wife had been a regular customer at my fictitious nail salon. I told Preston and Matteo that she and I had become friendly, bonding over a shared love of acrylic nails. That had led me to inviting her and the professor to a barbecue at my house one weekend, which was where they met my father.

Over a couple of beers, the professor and his wife told my father about the problems they had been having getting their cat, Esmerelda, to stop sharpening her claws on their furniture. My father offered his cat training services and in no time Esmerelda was happily restricting her claw-sharpening activity to the designated cat scratching post.

It was a pretty elaborate story. I even described in great detail the correct way to file your nails—only go in one direction and never file your nails when they're wet. The guys' eyes started to glaze over, which was exactly the reaction I was looking for. I went in for the kill, explaining the differences between acrylic and gel nails. My reasoning was that they'd want to change the subject and talk about anything other than how I knew Professor Ratcliffe and the condition of his fake wife's cuticles.

No such luck. For some reason, Matteo wanted to know more about the professor's wife. You'd think that wouldn't be a problem, but it was a huge problem. You see, Professor Ratcliffe isn't married. Never has been. So when pressed for details about his non-existent wife, he froze. Naturally, I jumped in to fill the silence. Ten minutes later, even I was starting to believe that Mrs. Ratcliffe was real. Once I finished describing their twenty-fifth wedding anniversary celebration, we finally started our tour of the archaeological park.

Normally, I would have been fascinated to have the opportunity to explore the historic site, but my nerves were frayed by this point. I managed to make it through the rest of the afternoon, and when Preston and I finally got back to the retreat center, I feigned a migraine. Before rushing off to my room, I explained that my migraines usually last for a good twenty-four hours, then wipe me out afterward so he shouldn't expect to see me until Monday. After a gentle kiss on my forehead and making me promise to call him if I needed anything, Preston said goodbye, and I began my self-enforced isolation in my room.

The previous night was fine—I hadn't been hungry, but this morning is a whole different story. I remind myself that besides avoiding Preston, there are other benefits to missing a meal or two. Lately, the only thing that has been comfortable to wear are my yoga pants. With all the delicious food we prepare and eat during class, the pounds have been piling on. I dread having to put on regular clothes every morning.

I remind myself that I have a clear plan that needs to be followed—stay in bed all day, snuggled up with Giuseppe, reading, and ignore my growling stomach.

By noon, I'm starving and I can't stand what I'm reading. It's a *Star Wars* book that Loretta lent me because she thinks I'm a huge fan of the franchise. Now I have to read it because she's sure to want to discuss it with me. But the plot is so ridiculous. Seriously, shaggy seven-foot creatures called Wookies who fly around in spaceships?

My phone buzzes, giving me an excuse to put my book down. After checking to make sure it isn't Preston calling me, I grin. It's Mia and Isabelle wanting to video chat.

"Hey, guys," I say, propping my phone up against the pillow and turning on my side.

"Are you still in bed?" Mia asks.

"Uh-huh."

Isabelle pops into view. "Are you sick?" she asks with concern.

"Only as far as Preston knows. I told him I have a migraine."

"You're faking it?" Mia asks. "Why?"

I groan—partly from the agony of having to tell them how deep in doo-doo I've gotten myself with my fake manicurist backstory and partly because of hunger pains. After I explain about running into Professor Ratcliffe and inventing a wife for him, Mia surprises me. "You should tell Preston the truth. You two so belong together."

"What? I thought you were the one who didn't think we should get serious about guys."

Isabelle laughs. "That was until she met Pierre."

"Pierre. That's a French name. Aren't you guys in Germany?"

"We are," Mia says, turning the phone so that I can see a classic Bavarian town in the background. "You remember Pierre from the cruise ship, don't you?"

"Pierre?" The only men we really spoke with on our transatlantic crossing were Celeste's suitors—there hadn't been many guys our age. I furrow my brow. "Oh, wait a minute. Is he that waiter?"

Isabelle says, "Bingo. The two of them have been in constant contact since we disembarked."

"He's calling you from the cruise ship? Isn't that expensive?"

"No, he's in Paris," Mia says. "He finished up his contract. I'm going to meet up with him when I get there. He said he'll help me find a job at an art gallery through his connections."

"She's in love," Isabelle coos.

"No, I'm not," Mia says. "But he is cute, and nice, and—"

Isabelle interrupts. "Enough about Pierre. That's all I hear about these days. Tell us more about Preston."

"There's nothing to report," I say.

"Liar," Mia says. "You're turning bright red. Something's going on."

"It is not." I put my hand on my cheek and remember how Preston caressed it at the basilica on Saturday.

"Oh, that's right," Mia says. "You're not in love with him, you're smitten with him. That's what he always says, right? Smitten?"

"Uh-huh." I roll over on my back and hold the phone in front of me. "He does have some old-fashioned quirks."

"Just tell him how you feel and why you thought you had to hide who you really are from him," Mia urges. "He'll understand."

"But what if he doesn't? He's a bigwig in the ancient history community. Once he finds out I've been accused of plagiarism, he won't want anything to do with me."

"He won't believe that you're actually guilty," Mia says.

"That's exactly what he'll believe. I dropped out of graduate school. It's like an admission of guilt."

Isabelle's face fills the screen. "Or he might just think you're not a fighter. That you gave up without a fight."

"I couldn't fight it," I say. "I didn't want to ruin my father's reputation."

"You'll regret that for the rest of your life," Isabelle says bitterly. "Trust me. I know from my own experience." Then she shakes her head. "Sorry. That's my baggage, not yours. Let's look at this logically—"

"Love isn't logical," Mia says, pulling the phone back so that she's on screen.

Isabelle ignores her. "You have two options, really—continue with your story and enjoy the last of this holiday fling, or come clean and see if there's something more. Something long-term. It really comes down to how you feel about him. Do you want him enough to fight for him? To fight for your relationship?"

"It's not worth it," I say. "He won't believe me, and I'll have to show for it is more humiliation. I can't go through that again. I've already cut off everyone I know from the academic world. People told me they believe me, but I could see in their eyes that they had doubts. I don't want to go through that with Preston too. And then when you add in the fact that I've lied about pretty much everything to him, there's no way things will ever work out with him."

"Well, there's your answer then," Isabelle says. "You don't feel strongly enough about him to risk telling him the truth."

I take a deep breath, then let it out slowly. "You're right. I have to accept that this is just a holiday fling. Now all I have to do is survive the last week of cooking school without him making the connection between my last name and my father."

* * *

When I wake on Monday morning, I have a headache. I'm not sure if it's some sort of cosmic payback for faking a migraine to get out of seeing Preston or if it's due to the fact that I haven't eaten since Saturday night.

I get dressed and brave the breakfast buffet, bracing myself in case Preston is there. Mercifully, the only people dining are the Silver Foxes. No young professors in sight. After three cups of coffee and several bombolones, my head starts to feel better. My stomach, on the other hand, is twisted into knots. Sooner or later, I'm going to have to face him. Checking the time on my phone, I realize class is going to start in a few minutes. I guess it's going to be sooner, not later. I take a deep breath and head to the kitchen annex.

"How do you feel?" Preston asks when I set my purse down on our workstation.

"Not great." Which is true. Just not for the reasons he thinks.

"Should you be here? Why don't you go back to bed?"

"No, I'll be fine," I say. "Besides, there's no way I'm missing today—we're making Teodora cake."

Always looking for an opportunity to turn any conversation into a history lecture, Preston asks, "Did you know it was named after Teodora, the wife of Justinian the Great? She was the empress of Byzantium."

"I did know that," I say. "We saw a mosaic of her at the basilica."

"You remembered that?" He beams at me. "See, we'll make a historian out of you yet."

Great. Now, not only does my stomach ache, my heart does as well. Heartache over the fact that I won't see Preston ever again after this week. Heartache that he doesn't know the real me.

My musings are interrupted by Maria, who claps her hands to get our attention. "*Buongiorno*, class. Did everyone have a nice weekend?"

Everyone nods except me. My weekend was not the greatest.

"Wonderful," she says. "Today, we have a special guest instructor who is going to demonstrate how to make Teodora cake."

Preston nudges me and then points at the older woman standing at the front of the room. "Check out the guest instructor. Isn't that Mama Leoni from the restaurant we went to?"

"I think you're right." My face grows warm as I remember our first kiss after dinner that night.

While Maria hands out recipe cards to each workstation, Mama Leoni explains the cake that we're going to make. "This was invented in 2002 by a group of bakers in Ravenna. It uses pine nuts and cornmeal, which are traditional local ingredients, along with cinnamon, almonds, flour, eggs, and powdered sugar. *Deliziosa*!"

Maria rejoins Mama Leoni at the front. "Teodora cake is delicious," she says. "And it's not the only dessert we're making today. This afternoon we'll be making zuppa inglese which is a cross between a tiramisu and a trifle."

I tug at the waistband of my jeans. I'm not sure I'll be able to zip these back up with all the rich food we'll be eating today, not to mention all the donuts I ate at breakfast.

"It is especially fitting that today is a dessert day, because it's someone's birthday today," Maria says with a twinkle in her eye.

Mabel spins around on her stool to get a three hundred and sixty degree view of the room. "Whose birthday is it?" If I didn't know better, I'd think she was jealous that someone was going to get more attention than her today.

"Is it your birthday?" Preston asks me.

"Nope. Mine was a few months ago. Is it yours?"

"No. Mine is in August."

I feel a premonition wash over me. "August what?"

"August sixth."

I rub my temples and groan.

"What's wrong? Is it your head again?"

"No, my head's fine."

"You look faint." He pulls a stool over. "Here, sit down."

"Thanks, but I'm okay." I tap the side of my head and smile at Preston. A smile that doesn't quite reach my eyes. "All better now."

But I'm not better. I'm worse. Preston's birthday is August sixth. Guess who he shares a birthday with? Yep, that's right—what's-his-name. Surely, it's a sign from the universe. Preston and my ex have the same birthday. Clearly, this wasn't meant to work out.

I manage to get through the rest of the morning, working side by side with Preston. I even manage to smile when Mama Leoni stops by our workstation to check on our progress.

"How are the lovebirds today?" she asks us.

"We're great," Preston says. "It's so nice to see you again. I can't stop thinking about that ravioli we ate at your restaurant."

"You must come again," Mama Leoni says.

"We'd like that." Preston glances at me. "How about Friday?"

"Maybe," I say. "Why don't we play it by ear?"

Mabel turns and says loudly, "If you don't want to go with the handsome professor, then I will."

Loretta tugs her friend's arm. "Stop interfering."

"I'm not interfering."

"Yes, you are."

"No, I'm not."

I roll my eyes at the ladies' bickering. Mama Leoni seems amused by it. Eventually, they stop arguing, but only because Maria reminds them that they're supposed to be mixing their batter.

"Do you think you'll be well enough to catch up tonight?" Preston asks me.

"I'm not sure." I hand him the eggs. "It might be better if I have an early night."

He looks crestfallen. "Hopefully, you'll be up for it tomorrow."

"Hopefully," I say.

After we finish baking our Teodora cakes, we break for lunch. I excuse myself and escape to my room for an hour. When I return to the kitchen, Maria announces that she has another surprise for us. The Silver Foxes are beside themselves with anticipation. Fueled by the coffee they had at lunch, they shout out their guesses.

"Is it gelato?" asks the man who is obsessed with the Italian ice cream.

"No, it's not gelato," Maria says.

"Is it another field trip with Professor Whitaker?" Mabel asks.

The entire room turns and smiles at Preston. He smiles back as a blush slowly creeps over his face. "I don't think you want to hear another history lecture from me."

"Yes, we do," Mabel says.

Everyone murmurs in agreement.

"Unfortunately, the surprise isn't a field trip with Professor Whitaker," Maria says. "However, it does involve him."

Preston raises his eyebrows. "It does?"

"Yes," Maria says. "And Ginny."

"Me?" I ask in a squeaky voice.

"The tourist board has asked us to do a cooking demonstration on Thursday. We're going to make several of the dishes we've already prepared in class." Maria points at a couple at the front of the room. "Frank and Jeannie, I thought you could demonstrate minestrone soup." Frank and Jeannie look thrilled to have been chosen, giving each other high fives.

Then she indicates two women at the back. "Sylvia and Lois, can you demonstrate the Teodoro cake?" They jump up and down like they've just been selected as contestants on *The Price is Right*.

Finally, Maria turns and looks at us. "And, Ginny and Preston, I would like you to make tortelloni burro e salvia. Tortellini with butter and sage."

She grins. "Or, as Ginny likes to call it, toretellini with salivating burros."

Everyone chuckles except Mabel. Instead, she grumbles that she and Loretta weren't selected.

"There's a lot to do to get ready for the demonstration. Each pair will need to work closely with each other over the next couple of days."

Preston grins at me. "Looks like we'll be spending a lot of time together."

Great. Just when I was hoping to spend less time with Preston, now I'll be spending more time with him.

12 - The Patron Saint of Shoes

"Are you ready?" Preston asks me.

We're standing backstage waiting to be announced for our segment of the cooking demonstration. I peek around the curtain and take a deep breath. The place is packed. Public speaking isn't really my thing, let alone public cooking demonstrations. Truth be told, part of me never wanted to become a history professor because I would have had to give lectures in front of lots of people. Maybe my mom was right. Maybe I had been on the wrong career track all along.

But this is not the time for introspection about the choices I've made. I have to focus on what's in front of me—cooking. I take a deep breath and smooth down my skirt. Why did I wear white? My hands are shaking with nerves. I'm sure I'll end up splattering the sage and butter sauce all over me.

"Maybe you should go on by yourself," I say. "There really isn't room up there for more than one person."

He laughs. "The stage is huge. There's plenty of room for both of us."

"I think I forgot something back in my room. I'll be right back."

Before I can flee, he pulls me into his arms and kisses me lightly. "You'll be fine. I'll be right by your side the entire time." He steps back and looks me up and down. "You look gorgeous, Ginny. It'd be a shame to deprive the audience of such a beautiful cook."

"I don't know about that. I think everyone's attention is going to be focused on that bow tie of yours."

He grins. "Is not."

"Is too," I say.

"Is not."

"Is too."

"Is—"

Maria peeks her head around the curtain. "Are you ready? They're about to introduce you."

"We're ready." Preston holds out his arm. I tuck my arm through his and take a deep breath. Conscious of Preston's leather and pine scent, I tremble as he escorts me up the steps to the stage.

The emcee smiles at us, then turns to the audience. "Please welcome Preston Whitaker and Ginny…" He pauses, adjusts his reading glasses, and peers at his notes.

I bite my lip. I've been here before. When confronted with my last name for the first time, it's hard for people to figure out how to pronounce it. As much as I love the fact that it links me to my father and his Dutch ancestry, there are times when I wish it had a lot less letters in it. Something like Smith or Jones would be ideal.

I glance at Preston. He's frowning. Why is he frowning?

After a pause, the emcee says slowly, "Ginny Morgan."

I breathe a sigh of relief when I remember that when I registered, Evelyn used my middle name instead of my last name on the class forms. But my relief doesn't last long. Preston is still frowning.

"Morgan," he mumbles to himself. "Virginia Morgan Maarschalker-weerd," he says as though he's reading my passport out loud again. He looks at me. "That's a very uncommon last name, but I've heard it before."

My eyes widen. He's figured it out. He's made the connection. But before Preston can say anything else, the emcee summons us over to the center of the stage.

While Preston and I prepare the tortelloni burro e salvia, Maria explains what we're doing to the audience. It's almost like we're on one of those cooking shows that I used to watch at my mom's house.

We work smoothly together, in a rhythm that we've developed over the past month. But despite the harmony we have when it comes to cooking, it's obvious that there's tension between us on a personal level. At one point, Maria even encourages Preston to smile more.

As we're preparing the sauce, his smile fades. "Maarschalkerweerd. You're not any relation to Nicholas Maarschalkerweerd, are you?" he whispers.

"I think the sage is burning," I say to distract him.

He lowers the heat, stirs the butter and sage sauce, then points at me with the spoon. "Wait a minute," he says. "You know a lot about Roman sanitation, you know Latin, and, from what Loretta says, you're clueless about *Star Wars*." He takes a step back. "Oh, my gosh. I know who you are. You're Virginia Maarschalkerweerd."

I nod slowly. "Uh-huh. It's a common name."

"Maarschalkerweerd? No it's not. I've only known of three people with that name. One is a renowned ancient history professor, Nicholas Maarschalkerweerd. I met him once at a conference. The second person is you. And the third person is someone I've only heard about from some colleagues. She has the same name as you—Virginia Maarschalkerweerd. But she was involved in a plagiarism scandal at—"

Maria pushes her way between the two of us. "What's going on here?" she asks under her breath. "Why aren't you cooking?"

"Sorry," I say. "We were just debating how long to cook the tortellini. Right, Preston?"

"Sure," he says flatly. "But I think I've figured it out." He looks at me meaningfully. "Yes, I've definitely figured it out."

"Good," Maria says. "I was worried for a moment there."

"Just nerves," I say, then turn my attention back to our dish.

I'm not sure how I do it, but I make it through the rest of the presentation without fainting or throwing up. After the emcee and Maria thank us, and the audience claps, I rush off stage, nearly tripping flat on my face as I race down the steps.

Preston catches up with me and grabs my elbow. "We need to talk."

I pull away. "Later."

"No, now."

"No, later."

"No, now," he says firmly.

It feels good slipping back into our cute little bickering routine, but then I realize that he isn't finding this cute. Not one bit. I can see anger in his eyes. I can't blame him. Not only have I lied to him, he thinks I committed the ultimate academic sin—plagiarism. It's not just anger in his eyes. It's condemnation.

"Later," I say softly, then spin on my heels and barrel straight into someone. The only reason I don't end up on the ground again is because Preston grabs me and steadies me on my feet.

I look up and see an elegantly dressed woman. For a moment, I think it's Celeste. She has the same hairstyle, eye color, and dress sense, but when she opens her mouth, her Italian accent makes me realize my mistake. Oh, how I wish it had been Celeste, or Mia, or Isabelle standing there. I could really use a friend right now.

"That was a wonderful demonstration," she says. "You two did a great job. Tortelloni burro e salvia is one of my favorite dishes."

Neither Preston nor I respond. He's staring at the floor, and I don't trust myself to say anything.

The woman looks back and forth between the two of us, then extends her hand to me. "Allow me to introduce myself. Gabriela DiRusso. I taught for a semester at Preston's university last year. You must be his fiancée. I've heard so much about you."

Preston looks up sharply. "No, she's not my fiancée, she's my..." he starts to say before his voice trails off.

What was he going to say?

His girlfriend.

His ex-girlfriend.

His brief holiday fling.

The cheater.

The plagiarizer.

The woman he regrets meeting.

The woman he never wants to see again.

I have no desire to find out how he'd finish this sentence. So I run, faster than I've ever run before, pushing my way through the crowd, only stopping once I get outside. Then I sink onto a bench and start sobbing.

* * *

After a good cry, I wipe away my tears and push myself up off the bench. It's going to be a long walk back to the retreat center, but I figure it will help clear my head. Dodging tourists searching for the perfect souvenirs and local families out for a stroll, I wander through the pedestrian-only zone in the center of Ravenna before turning onto Via di Roma. After walking through the Porta Serrata, one of the old gates leading into the city, a car honks its horn behind me. I ignore it, but the driver continues to lay on the horn.

I turn and see Preston leaning out of the window of a taxi, waving at me. He gets out and strides toward me.

"I've been looking for you everywhere," he says.

I cross my arms across my chest. "Lucky me."

"You ran off before I could explain."

"Explain what? That you lied to me? That you have a fiancée?" I jab my finger into his chest. "All this time, you've been cheating on her with me."

He grabs my hand and pushes it away from him. "I would never cheat on a woman. Never."

"You're lying. You have a fiancée. Gabriela said so. Are you saying she's a liar?"

"No, I'm not saying that."

"Hah!" I say, throwing my hands up in the air. "You just admitted it. Gabriela didn't lie. You did."

Preston runs his fingers through his hair and exhales slowly. He looks intently at me, his normally bright blue eyes dull and lifeless. "When Gabriela was a guest professor at the university, I was engaged. She never met my fiancée, but she knew that I had one. Operative word being 'had.'"

"Had?"

"Yes, had. We broke up. I told you about it."

"No, you didn't. I think I would remember if you told me you were engaged."

"Do you remember when we had that food fight?" I nod. "You told me that someone betrayed you and I told you that I caught my ex with another guy."

Memories of that day flood back. Some happy ones, like how cute Preston looked with flour smeared across his nose. Some not so happy, like the pain in his eyes when he told me about his ex cheating on him. He was so vulnerable that day, sharing the hurt he had experienced.

"So, you see, I didn't lie to you," he says.

"In all fairness, I didn't know your ex had been your fiancée." Even as I utter those words, I realize how lame they sound. He seizes on them.

"You're playing semantics now. I'm not the liar, Ginny. I never was. You are." He thrusts his hands in his pockets. His gaze hardens. "You've lied from the first minute I met you. You lied about being a manicurist. You lied about not liking history—you were an ancient history graduate student, for goodness' sake. You were using a fake last name. You pretended you could speak Italian. You lied about what your father did. A cat trainer? How could I be so stupid to fall for that? And I'm pretty sure you've never even seen *Star Wars*."

I press my fingers along the bridge of my nose, willing myself not to cry.

"I can't believe I let myself get involved with someone like you." Preston shakes his head. "I'm surprised you aren't trying to spin more lies. Go on, you're going to try to deny everything now, aren't you?"

"No, I'm not. It's true. I lied about everything." I clench my hands. "And I can see by your reaction that I was right to. If you had known who I really was, you would have looked at me with disdain and condemnation, like you are now. The only mistake I made was..." I put my hand over my mouth before I can finish what I was going to say.

"Only one mistake? You made a lot of mistakes."

I straighten my shoulders and take a deep breath. I'm glad I didn't tell this pompous jerk what that *one* fundamental mistake was. Oh, how he would gloat if he knew that I had made the ultimate mistake—falling for the wrong guy. Someone I could never be with, not in a million years.

Cocking my head to one side, I say, "Look, we just have to get through class tomorrow. I'm sure we can manage to be civil to each other for a few hours, then we never have to see each other ever again."

"Fine by me, Virginia Morgan Maarschalkerweerd," he says, his eyes hard and unforgiving.

I turn, but before I can resume walking, I feel Preston's hand on my shoulder.

"Get in the taxi, Ginny," he says. "You can't walk all the way back to the retreat center."

I spin around to face him. "Can too."

"Can not." When I don't respond, he scowls. "Just get in."

"No," I say, putting my hands on my hips.

"Fine. Have it your way."

I watch as he gets back in the taxi and slams the door shut. So this is how a holiday fling ends—slamming car doors on his part and lots of tears on mine.

* * *

Preston's taxi follows me all the way back to the retreat center. Periodically, he leans out of the window and tells me to get in. Each time, I refuse. My feet are killing me—high heels and cobblestones are not a stellar combination— but there's no way that I'll let him know that.

By the time I reach the marble steps leading up to the villa's entryway, I've made a solemn vow to Saint Crispin—the patron saint of shoes—to wear sneakers and flats for the rest of my life. I pause for a moment, expecting Preston to tell me to wait for him, but when I turn around, I see the taxi pulling away down the circular drive and Preston's retreating back as he walks across the grounds toward one of the annex buildings.

Fine, I didn't want to talk with him anyway.

I slip off my heels and slowly walk to the residential annex, occasionally wincing in pain. After entering my room, I scoop Giuseppe off the bed and slump to the floor.

I only have myself to blame for this mess I'm in. The minute I found out that Preston was in my cooking class, I should have dropped out. So what if I would have lost all the money I paid? That would have been far better than losing my heart.

My heart.

How could I lose something I never gave to him? It was a summer fling, right? It wasn't serious. Just a bit of fun.

Except it wasn't.

It was more than that.

A whole lot more.

I press my back against the door and snuggle my teddy bear against my face. I wait for ages, expecting Preston to knock on my door. He doesn't.

You'd think I would be relieved that I didn't have to deal with another confrontation with him. Instead, I feel disappointed.

I pull my phone out of my purse and scroll through the pictures like a masochist. There's one of Preston kneading pasta dough. And another one of him sautéing sage leaves in butter. The next one is one I took of him the night we had dinner at Mama Leoni's restaurant. I smile at how nerdy he looks wearing that polka dot bow tie of his. Then I sigh as I remember how blue his eyes are.

My phone rings. My first instinct is to fling it across the room. The last thing I want to do now is talk to Preston. But I restrain myself and glance at the screen. It's Celeste. We've kept in touch, mostly through emails and text, but for her to call me out of the blue seems strange. It's even stranger when I recall how I initially thought Gabriela was Celeste.

"Is everything okay?" I quickly ask.

"Everything is just dandy," she says. "My niece flew over to Greece to stay with me for a bit. It's so much fun to have a young person around that it made me think of you and the other girls. We sure did have a good time on the cruise ship, didn't we?"

"We did," I say, my voice cracking slightly.

"What's wrong, dear?"

"Nothing."

"Sweetheart, don't you nothing me. I can tell that there's something wrong. Now, go ahead and tell me what's going on."

I spill my guts, pausing several times to wipe away my tears and blow my nose.

"You know what you need? Some of Celeste's TLC. Pack your bags and come to Greece. The change of scenery will do you good."

"No, I couldn't impose on you like that," I say, standing up and placing Giuseppe back on my pillow.

"It's not an imposition at all."

"But your niece is there. I don't want to crowd you."

"Goodness, don't be silly. The house I'm renting is huge. The more, the merrier."

"Well, if you're sure. A change of scenery would be nice." I pace back and forth, thinking through the logistics. "We have our last day of class tomorrow, so I could leave here on Saturday." I stop and look out the window. Several of the Silver Foxes are gathered in the courtyard below me, their attention completely focused on a man wearing a very familiar tweed coat. I shake my head. There's no need to stick around here. Having to see Preston again tomorrow would be torture. "You know what, Celeste. Why wait? I'm going to skip class and head to Greece in the morning."

13 - Cat Burglars

After an insanely long journey involving four trains, five taxis, and three ferries, I finally make it to Celeste's place. You'd think that an ordeal like that would help me get over my aerophobia. Hopping on a plane would have been so much easier. But there was no way that was going to happen. The very thought of it still makes me break out in hives and hyperventilate.

The house Celeste is renting is beautiful. I stand in the courtyard and look around in awe. Sunlight bounces off its whitewashed walls, and the bright blue paint on the door and shutters is the same color as the waters surrounding the island. Flowering vines clamber over a pergola, providing much needed shade in the middle of the day, and the infinity pool is large and inviting. I bet even people with aquaphobia would be tempted by this pool with its views of the sailboats anchored in the bay below.

Celeste welcomes me with open arms. "How long has it been since you broke up with Preston?" she asks after she embraces me.

"Um...I'm not sure." I start to count the days on my fingers, but stop as it's too painful. My hand is aching from hauling my luggage up the steep path that leads from the ferry dock to the top of the hill where Celeste's rental house is located. The wheels on my suitcase were pretty much useless on the cobblestone path, and the steep incline meant I had to keep a tight grip for fear my bag would slip and end up back at the bottom of the hill.

I chew on my lip as I remember when I first met Preston and how he helped me with my bags at the train station. He had loved my suitcase's retro vibe. It suited his old-fashioned personality perfectly. When I rub my fingers, trying to get the circulation back, memories of Preston kissing the back of my hand come flooding back.

I purse my lips. Too many memories of my time with Preston. I'm here in Greece to get over him and erase those memories from my mind.

"I'm not sure," I finally say. "It's somewhere between not long enough and too long."

She envelops me in another hug. "Don't worry, the perfect guy is out there for you. I remember before I met my Ernie, I had been going steady with another fellow. He broke up with me and I was devastated, but it turned out to be for the best."

"Did you know it was for the best right away?"

"No. I cried my eyes out for weeks. But then I found out that he had been hiding something from me."

"What was that?"

Celeste's eyes dart around to make sure that we're alone, then satisfied that no one is eavesdropping, she leans forward and says, "He was a cat burglar."

"Why would anyone steal a cat?"

She laughs. "No, he didn't steal cats. He stole jewelry. He broke into rich people's homes in the middle of the night and stole their rings, bracelets, earrings, and watches. One time, he even made off with a ruby and emerald tiara."

"I'm still not getting the connection to cats."

"It's how he did it—he'd climb over roofs, through windows, even jump from balcony to balcony. He was agile, like a cat."

"Yet another reason why I don't like cats. They're sneaky. They—" I yelp and jump backward as a streak of black fur flies past me. "What was that?"

"That's Midnight, the resident cat. He has free rein of the house so keep your door closed if you don't want him in there."

"Duly noted." I glare at the black cat. He's casually washing behind his ears while plotting how to sneak into my room in the middle of the night and cough up a hairball on my suitcase.

"Have you seen *To Catch a Thief*?" Celeste asks. I shake my head. "It's wonderful. We'll have to watch it while you're here. Cary Grant's character reminds me of my old beau. Sure, he could have gotten me wonderful diamond jewelry, but it would have been awfully lonely when he was in jail. So, you see, he wasn't the perfect guy for me. Things definitely turned out for the best."

I take a deep breath. "Yep, this is for the best."

She cups my chin in her hand and looks me in the eye. "Are you sure?"

"I think so."

"You *think* so? You don't *know* so? That doesn't sound very sure. Could it have all been a misunderstanding?"

I stiffen. "I'm pretty sure I didn't misunderstand him. He called me a cheater."

"Are you sure that's what he said?"

I think back to what transpired after the cooking demonstration. I've tried so hard to block the memories of that day out of my mind, that things are a bit blurry. What exactly did he say? I accused him of being a cheater, then he called me a cheater. Or did he?

I shake my head. Of course he did. That's what everyone assumed. I was accused of plagiarism, so I must have committed plagiarism. No one believed me. Why would he be any different?

"Honestly, it doesn't matter what he said. We were never meant to be. I'm glad it's over."

"Well, as long as you're sure. Now, come and meet my niece." Celeste leads me to the kitchen. A young woman with a tousled bob turns and beams at me. Standing next to her is a man who looks like a marble Greek statue come to life—tall and muscular. Except instead of holding a spear or a bow and arrow, he's holding a spatula and a jar of honey.

"You must be Ginny," the woman says. "I'm Olivia and this is my friend, Xander. You're just in time. He's going to teach us how to make baklava."

"He owns the taverna by the ferry dock," Celeste says. "You must have seen it when you arrived."

"We ate dinner there when I first arrived," Olivia says. "Xander is the best cook on the island."

He sets the spatula and honey on the counter, then brushes a lock of hair off her face. "I think you might be a bit biased."

She smiles at him. "Not at all. I know what I like and I like your cooking."

It's obvious that they adore each other.

Celeste puts her arm through mine and whispers, "Isn't he a doll? I think he's taken a fancy to her."

"He's smitten with her," I mumble under my breath.

"What's that, dear?" she asks.

I don't think I can take watching how cute they are together for much longer. It reminds me too much of Preston. "I was asking if it would be okay if I skipped the baklava right now. I'm exhausted from the travel. I think I might go lie down for a bit, if that's okay."

"Of course, dear," Celeste says. "Your room is at the end of the hall. Don't forget to keep the door closed unless you want Midnight to keep you company."

* * *

Greece is beautiful. At least, that's what I've heard. To be honest, I wouldn't know. I haven't stepped foot outside of Celeste's house since I got here. And that was a week ago.

I spend most of my time sleeping. When I'm not sleeping, I wish I could fall asleep. It's only when I'm sleeping that I can forget about Preston and, even then, half the time I end up dreaming about him. The other half of the time I dream about yoga pants.

Why yoga pants? Well, that's probably because I had a tragedy on my first day here. I opened my suitcase, rustled through its contents, and discovered that I hadn't packed those delightfully stretchy garments. I could see in my mind's eye the drawer where I kept them, but in my rush to get packed and flee the retreat center, I completely forgot to grab them.

Celeste suggested that we go in search of some at a local shop, but I couldn't be bothered. Instead, I lounged around her living room in my pajamas. Pajamas are almost as good as yoga pants. Almost.

I wish that I had forgotten to pack my phone instead. There are countless texts, emails, and voice mails from Preston, more each day. I ignore them all. The last thing I need is to hear how little he thinks of me. Deleting them immediately is one of my key coping strategies.

Celeste peeks her head into my room. "Honey, don't you think it's time you got up? You've moped around enough. One hundred and seventy-two hours, to be exact. Now, go take a shower and put on a pretty dress. We're going for dinner at Xander's taverna. He's going to make his specialty— moussaka. You can't disappoint him."

After a few more minutes of her trying to cajole me, I give in to Celeste and shuffle off to the shower. When I emerge in the living room an hour later, Celeste smiles at me brightly. "You look lovely, dear."

"That color really suits you," Olivia says. "And the way the straps cross in the back is super cute."

I smooth down the front of my dress, remembering how Preston complimented me when I wore it. As we walk down the path to the dock, I'm determined to enjoy the evening. I've been a terrible houseguest and an even worse friend. Celeste has gone out of her way to take me in and try to cheer me up, but I've resisted her every step of the way.

Xander's moussaka is wonderful—the layers of eggplant, minced lamb, and bechemal sauce explode with flavor in my mouth. I gobble down two helpings, practically licking my plate clean. After a week of not having an appetite and picking at my food, I'm ravenous.

"You like it?" Xander asks.

"I love it," I say. "I should have gone to a Greek cooking school instead. You'll have to give me the recipe."

Xander wags a finger at me playfully. "Fine, but I'll want a favor in return."

"Sure. I'm happy to do the dishes."

"No, not the dishes." He looks at Olivia, who is walking back to the table from the restroom. "I'll fill you in later," he says quietly. After pulling Olivia's chair out for her, he claps his hands. "Who wants baklava?"

We all raise our hands, me more enthusiastically than the others. After I eat my last gooey bite of the flaky, cinnamon-flavored phyllo pastry oozing with honey and nuts, Xander tells us that he has a surprise for us. He summons a teen-aged boy from the kitchen. "This is Demetrius."

The boy nods shyly at us, then hands each of us a woven leather bracelet.

"Demetrius made these," Xander explains. He points at the blue and white glass charm dangling from the bracelets. "That is an evil eye. It will protect you from harm."

"It's very pretty," Olivia says. "Thank you, Demetrius."

While Xander helps Olivia fasten the bracelet on her wrist, Celeste turns to me and glances at my bare wrist. "I haven't seen you wear that lovely charm bracelet of yours since you've been here."

"When you're attired in pajamas every day, you don't really need to wear a lot of accessories," I say wryly. I rub my wrist and try to recall the last time I wore the bracelet my parents gave me. I had it on at the cooking demonstration. I remember Preston warning me not to let the charms dangle in the ricotta cheese. I also remember seeing it on my wrist when I jabbed my finger at him during our argument later that afternoon. But I don't remember seeing it after that.

My good mood vanishes in a flash. The moussaka and baklava sit heavy in my stomach, and my eyes start to tear up. Not only have I lost Preston, I've lost my charm bracelet as well. The bracelet that was one of my last links to my father.

I look at the bracelet Demetrius gave me. If only I had been wearing an evil eye during my time in Ravenna, it might have protected me from all this heartbreak.

14 - Hairballs

Later that night, I lie in bed alternating between twirling my new evil eye bracelet around my wrist and glaring at Midnight. The cat is perched inside my suitcase, having sneaked into my room when we were out to dinner. When I tried to shoo him away earlier, he growled at me until I backed off and kept my distance. Now he looks content, purring and kneading his paws, making a cozy nest in my clothes. I shudder as tiny droplets of drool form at the side of his mouth.

My phone buzzes repeatedly. I grab it off the nightstand and gulp when I read the texts from my mom.

Preston called me.

Why is Preston calling my mom? I never even told her about him.

Your boyfriend seems like a sweet guy.

My boyfriend? What did Preston say to her? Did he tell her he was my boyfriend?

He seems hurt that you haven't spoken or texted him.

I shake my head. My mom doesn't understand. Preston isn't hurt, he's angry. He hates me. The only reason he's been trying to get a hold of me is so that he can tell me what an awful person I am. Before I can text her back and set the record straight, she sends me another message.

He thinks you have pistanthrophobia, which is why you're avoiding him.

What? He thinks I have pistanthrophobia? He's so wrong. I'm not avoiding him because I have trust issues after my experiences with what's-his-name. I'm avoiding him because he's a jerk. Just like what's-his-name. Even if I had told Preston the truth about who I am and why I dropped out of graduate school, and even if he had told me that he believed me, he would have ended up betraying me eventually.

So I told him about Joel and how I thought he was never the right guy for you.

I sit up straight in bed and throw the covers off me. She told him about my ex-boyfriend? What? Why? My hand shakes as I dial her number.

"Mom, why did you tell Preston about what's-his-name," I blurt out once she answers.

"Hi, honey. It's so nice to hear your voice. I thought you'd be asleep by now. What time is it there now?"

"It's eleven."

"Eleven? Really? I thought it was one in the morning. I never can figure out the time difference between Florida and Europe. Did you get my texts?"

I grit my teeth. "Yes, Mom. That's why I'm calling."

"That Preston of yours is so sweet."

"He's not my Preston," I say.

"Did you know that he's going to be awarded with the Herodotus Prize for excellence in teaching? The award ceremony is taking place in Boston. He's there now for a couple of weeks before he heads back to Ravenna to teach at the Silver Fox Summer Academy."

"Mom," I say, trying to get a word in edgewise.

She continues without stopping to take a breath. "Did I mention that your father received the same award before you were born. Isn't that an amazing coincidence?"

"Amazing," I say dryly.

"You must be so proud of him. Your father dedicated the award to me in his acceptance speech. Maybe Preston will do the same."

"Dedicate the award to you?"

"No, silly. Dedicate it to you."

"Mom, I don't know what Preston told you, but I think you have the wrong end of the stick. He isn't my boyfriend."

"He isn't? But I assumed—"

"Exactly, you assumed. But your assumption was wrong. He isn't my boyfriend. He isn't my anything." When she doesn't respond, I add, "Mom, are you still there?"

"I'm here, honey. I'm just confused. When I spoke with Preston, it was obvious that he's in love with you. He went on for an hour gushing about what an amazing woman you are."

"Gushing about me? Are you sure that was Preston you spoke with? The Preston I know isn't in love with me. He detests me."

"Why would he detest you? No one could detest you."

A smile plays across my lips. "Well, you have to say that. You're my mother."

"I would say that even if I wasn't your mother."

"That's sweet, but..." I chew on my bottom lip for a moment. "But Preston doesn't see things that way. For one thing, I lied to him about who I am."

"He told me about that. I certainly didn't raise you to be a liar, young lady," my mom says sternly. Then she laughs. "I can't believe you said your father was a cat trainer."

"It's not just that. I lied about all sorts of things." I sigh. "It started off small when I first met him on the train. I led him to believe I was staying in Bologna, not going on to Ravenna. I also told him I was a chef. But that was when I thought I wouldn't see him ever again. Then he showed up in class, and I was stuck with him as my cooking partner. When I found out that he was a professor of ancient history, I couldn't tell him the truth, that I had been a graduate student, and the lies started snowballing from there."

"But, honey, I don't understand why you didn't tell him about grad school in the first place."

I'm dumbfounded. Of course, I understand why my mom wouldn't approve of me lying to Preston. I'm ashamed about it myself. But surely she sees why I felt compelled to. "Mom, don't you get it? There's no way I could have faced his scorn."

"Scorn? Scorn for what?"

"For plagiarizing."

"But you didn't plagiarize."

"I know that," I snap. "But he doesn't. Apparently, I'm all the talk in the ancient history academic circles. Everyone is talking about how Ginny

Maarschalkerweerd, the daughter of the great Nicholas Maarschalkerweerd, was a cheat. That she's so stupid that she had to copy someone else's research paper. That she couldn't make it on her own. That she doesn't hold a candle to her father."

I hear my mother sigh. "How many times do I have to tell you that you're not stupid before you'll believe me?"

"But I am stupid. I was stupid to drop out of grad school. I only did it because my thesis advisor told me that unless I did, he'd smear Dad's reputation. But he broke his promise and did it anyway. He's behind all the stories swirling around about me." I take a deep breath. "Maybe Isabelle was right. I should have fought the charges. I should have stood up for myself."

"Don't be so hard on yourself. You did what you thought was right at the time. Besides, from what Preston told me, his plan backfired. No one thinks any less of your father."

"That's good," I say. "But they do think less of me."

"Oh, honey, only the people who don't know you think less of you. Anyone who knows you doesn't. They're on your side."

"I wish that was true, but it isn't."

"Preston's on your side."

I furrow my brow. "He is?"

"He is."

"He believes I'm innocent?"

"He does."

"No, that can't be right," I say, shaking my head. "Why would he believe me?"

"Because he loves you." My mom chuckles. "Despite the ridiculous stories you told him. Did you really try to pass yourself off as a *Star Wars* fan?"

"Yeah, not my finest moment. In fact, I haven't had a lot of fine moments lately."

"Well, it's time you pick yourself back up and make things right. The first thing you need to do is apologize to Preston. Next, you should think about what really makes you happy. Then you should—"

"Mom, can you hold that thought? I need to go. The cat is hacking up a hairball on my favorite sweatshirt."

* * *

I pick Midnight up and plop him on the tiled floor, then take a few steps to the side to get out of the way. Instead of coughing up a hairball as I expected, he pads over to me and rubs his body against my legs. I take a few more steps away from the cat, but end up tripping over my sneakers and tumbling backward onto my bed.

Midnight yowls, then leaps into the air, landing directly on my chest with a thud. He snuggles up against my face, purring loudly. "Don't you dare get that drool on me," I warn the feline. He responds by licking me, leaving a trail of cat saliva on my neck. Oddly, it feels comforting. I gently stroke the back of his head while I think about the conversation I had with my mom.

Yes, she's right, I should apologize to Preston. But I'm going to have to work up my courage for that conversation. It won't be easy. I push that thought out of my mind for now. Instead, I ponder my mom's second suggestion—think about what really makes me happy. I don't think she was just talking about my love life. Ever since I dropped out of graduate school, she's been trying to get me to reassess what I really want out of life, career-wise.

This trip to Italy has made me realize that being a professor isn't it. I smile as I think about how enraptured the Silver Foxes were during the tour Preston led of the Basilica di San Vitale and the Mausoleum of Gallo Placida. They loved hearing him tell them about this history of the two sites. Even during class, when he'd share a snippet or two about the history of the Roman Empire, they ate it up.

I have to admit that he's a great teacher—engaging and knowledgeable about his subject matter. Not to mention patient. Even when someone would ask what I would consider to be a silly question, he didn't make them feel dumb. He was never condescending or full of himself, like I thought he was. He's simply passionate about what he loves. Just like my father was.

As for me, I do love ancient history, but the thought of teaching it leaves me cold. Nor do I want to go back to graduate school. Academia isn't really for me. Sure, I thought it was, but over the past few weeks, I realize that I haven't missed it one bit. I have no idea what the future holds for me, but I do know one thing for sure. It'll involve something I'm passionate about, not just what I think I'm supposed to do.

While I'm scratching Midnight's belly, I realize that I never asked my mom why Preston called her. I send a quick text and she responds saying that he has my charm bracelet and wants to return it to me. It fell into the pocket of his jacket during our fight after the cooking demonstration. He's offered to mail it to my mom if that's what I'd prefer since I don't seem to want to see him, let alone talk to him. I tell her that I have a better plan—I'm going to pick it up from him in person.

My mom mentioned he was going to be awarded the Herodotus Prize. That would be the perfect time to get my bracelet from Preston and apologize to him. After doing a quick search online, I break out into a cold sweat, hives erupt all over my body, and I begin to hyperventilate. The award ceremony is in two days' time. The only way I can get there in time would be to fly.

An airplane? No way, no how.

15 - Drooling Cats vs. Teddy Bears

The next evening I find myself at the airport in Athens, a plane ticket and my passport clutched in my hand. When I reach the end of the jet bridge, my feet turn to clay. A cheerful flight attendant beckons me forward, but I can't budge. Thoughts of my father dying in a fiery plane crash overwhelm me. My pulse rate doubles, my breathing is shallow. I feel my backpack slip out of my hand. It hits the floor with a thud, startling me.

You can do it, I tell myself.

No, I can't.

Yes, you can.

No, I can't.

Ginny, knock it off. You can do it.

You're not the boss of me!

Hysterical laughter bubbles up inside me. This ridiculous back and forth I'm having with myself reminds me of all the disagreements Preston and I have.

Not *have.* It's *had.* Past tense. I don't have disagreements with him anymore. I ended things and for good reason. He's a jerk. I can't trust him. He'll end up breaking my heart, just like what's-his-name did. Now, turn around and march back up that jet bridge. He's not worth getting on this plane for.

But Mom said that he's on your side. He thinks you're innocent of the plagiarism charges.

No, he doesn't. He thinks I did it.

You think that she made that up? Are you saying that she's a liar?

Of course, Mom isn't a liar. She misheard what he said. That's all.

Hmm...I don't think she misheard him at all. I think you just don't want to believe it. Preston was right. You have pistanthrophobia. Admit it—you have trust issues.

What I have is issues with you. Did anyone ever tell you how annoying you are?

Stop trying to change the subject. You wouldn't be getting on this plane if you didn't think there was a chance for something between you and Preston.

"Come on, lady, get a move on." I turn and see the man behind me holding my backpack. He thrusts it in my hands and jerks his finger at the airplane door. "We don't have all day."

I take a deep breath, tell my inner voice to be quiet, and take a cautious step forward. The flight attendant's expression is no longer cheerful. "Seat 46-L," she says crisply, looking at my boarding pass. "Cross through the galley, then turn right."

"Do you have to pay for air sickness bags or are they complimentary?" I ask.

"No, they're free," she says. "You'll find one in the pocket in front of your seat."

"How many are there?"

"Bags? Just the one." Her eyes widen and she takes a step back. "Why? Do you feel sick?"

"No, I just like to be prepared."

Clenching my backpack tightly, I make my way down the aisle and look at my fellow passengers. They all seem so calm. Don't they realize that this silver tube is a death trap? Don't they realize we're all going to die? Don't they realize—?

Hey, inner voice, knock it off!

You can't tell me what to do!

Yes, I can!

No, you can't!

If you promise to be quiet, I'll buy you an overpriced cocktail once they start the drinks service.

That seems to do the trick. There's nothing my inner voice loves more than an overpriced drink.

As I near my seat, an overpowering stench overtakes me. Three men are seated in the row in front of mine and they all reek of body spray. What makes it worse is that they're all wearing different scents. One smells like the guys from the train—that intoxicating blend of doggy doo-doo and bubblegum. Another is sporting a fragrance that was probably inspired by a landfill. The third man is the least offensive, with an odor reminiscent of a teen-aged boy's gym shoes.

I pull my scarf over my nose and scoot into my spot by the window. After tucking my backpack under the seat in front of me—the one occupied by Mr. Landfill—I grab the aircraft safety card and familiarize myself with what to do in case of an emergency. The two seats next to me are empty. I breathe a sigh of relief. That will make it so much easier to dash to the rear of the airplane, where the nearest exit is located, should it be required.

"Excuse me, excuse me, coming through," a nasally voice says loudly. I pop my head up and see a middle-aged woman wearing a colorful mumu slowly pushing a roller bag in front of her. A soft-sided case is perched on top of her suitcase. A large purse is slung over one shoulder and an overstuffed tote bag is dangling from the other.

"Sorry about that," she says as her tote bag smacks Mr. Smelly Gym Shoes in the face. She looks at her boarding pass, looks at the seat next to me, then smiles brightly.

My inner voice groans at the thought of spending the next ten hours seated next to Mrs. Mumu. At last, I'm in agreement with my inner voice for once.

She hands the soft-sided case to Mr. Smelly Gym Shoe. "Hang onto this for a moment, hon, while I get settled." Then she passes her purse and tote bag to me. "Do you mind?"

She peers at the overhead storage bin. "Humph. It looks full."

"Please take your seats quickly so that we can have an on-time departure," the flight attendant says over the loudspeaker.

The woman continues to stare at the overhead storage bin as though it's a puzzle to be solved. Then she shrugs, pushes her suitcase further down the aisle toward the rear of the aircraft and leaves it there.

The flight attendant announces over the intercom, "All luggage must be stowed before takeoff." After a beat, she adds, "That means you in the back, ma'am."

Mrs. Mumu puts her hands on her hips, then screeches, "There isn't any room, hon. How about if I set it on its side so it doesn't roll down the aisle?"

"If you can't find a spot to stow it, bring it back to the front of the aircraft and we'll check it in for you to your final destination."

"Don't worry, hon, there's a spot right here." She opens the door to the lavatory and shoves her bag inside. "Problem solved."

The flight attendant marches down the aisle. "Ma'am, you cannot stow your suitcase in there."

"That's okay. I don't need anything during the flight from it. I have everything I need in these," she says as she pats her tote bag and purse.

The flight attendant shakes her head, grabs the suitcase out of the lavatory, and wheels it down the aisle, muttering something about making a poor career choice.

The woman shrugs and slides into the aisle seat. Then she lifts up the armrest between the aisle and middle seat and scoots next to me.

"Ladies and gentlemen, we're ready to get underway. Flight attendants, prepare doors for departure and cross-check."

I feel the airplane move backwards. "It looks like the aisle seat is empty," I say. "If you move over there, then we'll have more room."

She shows me her boarding pass. "No can do. It says 46-K right here. This is my assigned seat."

"Oh, I'm sure it will be fine if you take the aisle seat," I say confidently.

"No, if the plane crashes, they use the seat map to identify the survivors."

I grip the armrest tightly and try to calm my breathing. I do not need talk of plane crashes right now. From my personal, painful experience, people don't survive.

Mrs. Mumu taps the seat in front of her. "Sonny, want to hand me that bag?"

He passes it over the seat back and she sets it in her lap. Then she coos, "It's okay, Pookie. Mama's got you." She unzips the front of the bag an inch or two and a paw snakes out. A cat's paw. It manages to sink its claws into my arm, before her owner turns the bag to face her, forcing the creature to detach itself from my body.

As I inspect the scratch marks on my arm, I reassure myself that things could be worse. Instead of only having to put up with a loud, obnoxious woman and her vicious cat for the entire flight, I could have been seated next to a crying baby.

Then the cat starts yowling, a sound so intense and piercing that I think my eardrums are bleeding. A crying baby—heck, even crying triplets— would be heaven in comparison.

* * *

"You can't have a cat on board the plane," I say as the plane taxis to the runway.

"Of course, I can," she says. "Pookie is my support animal. She can sense when I'm going to have a panic attack."

The flight attendant walks down the aisle. When she nears the guys sitting in front of me, she gags, then unties the scarf around her neck and holds it over her nose. After telling them to fasten their seatbelts, she turns to Mrs. Mumu. "Ma'am, please stow your bags under the seat in front of you for takeoff."

"No problem, hon," she says cheerfully. After stowing the cat carrier and other bags, she taps my arm. "It's nice having this unoccupied seat, isn't it? It gives me plenty of room for Pookie and my other bags."

I try again to convince her to move into the aisle seat, but after she rattles off statistics about aviation safety and refuses to budge, I give up and begin praying in earnest to Saint Joseph of Cupertino to protect us during our journey.

About an hour into the flight, the drinks service still hasn't started. But that doesn't appear to faze my neighbor. Turns out that despite the fact that Mrs. Mumu won't break rules when it comes to sitting in an unassigned seat, she has no qualms about breaking open a bottle of her duty-free booze.

After taking a slug of vodka, she burps, then leans down to speak with her cat. "Do you need to use the litter box, Pookie?"

"You brought a litter box on board?" Part of me is horrified, while the other part thinks that the smell of a litter box might cover up the disgusting odors emanating from the body spray brigade seated in front of me.

"No, don't be silly," she says, waving her bottle wildly in the air. I duck just in time to avoid getting clobbered in the head. "Pookie uses human toilets. When she's done, she even flushes it all by herself. Isn't that clever of her?"

"Very clever," I say wryly. "Sounds like something you should post on YouTube."

"Oh, I already have. When I get back, I'll show it to you." Mrs. Mumu passes the bottle to me. "Here hold this." Then she reaches down, pulls the cat carrier out from under the seat, and trots off toward the lavatory.

I do what anyone would do in my situation, stuck on a plane with a toilet-trained cat, three smelly men, and a crazy lady. I put the bottle to my lips and take a tiny sip. As I'm screwing the cap back on, the flight attendant taps me on my shoulder. "Miss, what do you think you're doing? It's against regulations to drink anything on board that isn't sold by us."

"It's not mine, I swear."

"I can smell the vodka on you from here." She scowls at me and holds out her hand. "Give the bottle to me." I meekly give it to her, then blanch when she mentions that she's going to have to report me to the authorities. Visions of police officers storming on board the plane, yanking me out of my seat, handcuffing me, and marching me off to jail flash through my head. I knew I should have stayed in Greece instead of flying across the Atlantic Ocean to see Preston.

A half hour elapses before Mrs. Mumu returns. I'm not sure what took so long, but it's probably better that I don't ask. She stows the cat carrier back under the seat. "Wait until you see this video I got of Pookie washing her paws in the sink." She hands me her phone, then looks around her. "Where's my vodka?"

"It got confiscated."

"Confiscated?" She arches her eyebrows. "We'll see about that. No one confiscates my booze without a fight."

"Does this sort of thing happen often to you?"

"Well, I am a frequent flyer," she informs me before sashaying down the aisle, her mumu swinging back and forth. I watch as she has an animated conversation with the flight attendant. A few minutes later, she returns with a blanket in her arms. She winks at me as she sits back down. Once she fastens her seatbelt, she pulls a bottle out from under the blanket.

"Where did you get that?" I ask.

"It's better if you don't know all the details." She holds the bottle in one hand, then pulls the blanket over her head, hiding under it like it's some sort of fort. I hear her uncap the bottle. From the movements under the blanket, I'm pretty sure she's taking a few sips. The hiccupping noise afterward confirms my hunch. After a few moments, she peeks her head out. "Want some?"

"No, thanks. I think I'll pass."

Eventually, her hiccups turn into a soft snoring sound. While she sleeps, I stare out the window. It seems so peaceful here above the clouds. Maybe I could get used to flying again. Maybe it isn't so bad.

That feeling is short-lived. The plane starts shaking violently. Then it bounces up and down sharply like it's on the end of a yo-yo string. People start screaming.

Okay, from the way everyone is looking at me, I think I'm the only one screaming.

The flight attendant makes an announcement. "Attention, ladies and gentleman. The captain has advised that we're going to have some turbulence for the next twenty minutes. Please return to your seats and fasten your seatbelts."

I thought she might have gone for a soothing tone in her voice. Instead, she sounds bored, like this sort of thing happens every day. While I still don't have any idea what career direction I want to take, I can tell you one thing for sure—it won't involve becoming a flight attendant.

Mrs. Mumu stirs. She pulls her blanket down and yawns. "What's going on?"

I grab her hand and squeeze it tightly. "We're going to die."

"Oh, is that all?" She pulls her hand away, then tucks the blanket around her. "Wake me when it's over."

The turbulence shows no sign of letting up. I spend the next twenty minutes clutching my airsickness bag in readiness.

Finally, the captain addresses us. Instead of using the calming tone I'm hoping for, he sounds jovial, like he's having the best time of this life. "This is the captain speaking. Sorry about the turbulence, folks. Looks like it's going to be rough for a while. So sit back and enjoy the onscreen entertainment. Make sure to keep those seatbelts fastened. And thank you for flying with us."

I look at my hands. They're shaking so violently that I drop my airsickness bag on the floor. As I bend down to try to retrieve it, Pookie starts yowling. I startle and jostle Mrs. Mumu's legs with my head.

"What's going on? What are you doing down there?"

I sit back up, clutching my airsickness bag. "Retrieving this."

"Oh, no, don't tell me you're going to be sick." She holds her bottle up and examines it. "Did you drink some of this while I was sleeping?"

"No, of course not."

She raises her eyebrows. "Hmm. Well, someone's been drinking it."

"It wasn't me."

The cat meows again, distracting Mrs. Mumu from the mystery of the missing vodka. "What's wrong, Pookie? Do you need the litter box again?" She thrusts the bottle at me. "Here, hold this while I check on my princess."

I hold my hands up. "No way. I'm not getting in trouble again."

"Humph." She frowns at me, then taps the seat in front of her. "Boys, can you watch this for me?" After she passes the bottle to them, she lifts the cat carrier onto the seat next to her and unzips it. "You can come out now, Pookie."

I don't know what kind of cat I was expecting—maybe a fluffy Persian or a sleek Siamese—but what I am confronted with completely creeps me out. Have you ever seen a cat without fur? Well, I never have until now. Fortunately, Mrs. Mumu pulls a tiny sweater out of her purse. After putting it on Pookie, she coos, "Is that better? Were you cold?"

The cat does look much better, its hairless body now covered in a cute multi-colored pattern. The polka dots on it remind me of Preston and his bow ties.

The plane does a sudden dive. I forget all about Preston's neck attire and get my airsickness bag ready. It's quite possible I scream again.

"Shush, dear. You're bothering Pookie."

I glare at Pookie. Pookie glares back.

Mrs. Mumu looks at me with concern. "You look terrible. Do you need a drink?"

"No, I need my teddy bear." The plane finally levels out, and I grab Giuseppe out of my backpack and clutch him to my chest, tears welling in my eyes. I say a few more prayers to Saint Joseph. After a few minutes, I start to feel calm. I set Giuseppe on my lap and dry my eyes. As I'm crumpling up my tissue, I hear a low growl, then a flash of polka dots as Pookie flies out of Mrs. Mumu's arms, grabs Giuseppe in his mouth, and snatches him away from me.

"Hey, your cat stole my teddy bear!"

"Oh, isn't that cute?" Mrs. Mumu beams at the evil feline who is now perched on the empty aisle seat, chewing on Giuseppe's ear. "He has a bear just like that at home. Every night, he pounces on it, pretends to kill it, then brings it up to bed and presents it to me like a little love offering."

I unfasten my seatbelt, reach across Mrs. Mumu and try to yank my teddy bear back. The cat puts up a good fight, but I eventually win the tug-of-war contest. I sit back in my seat triumphantly and press Giuseppe against my face. He feels soft and fluffy and...wait a minute, he feels wet.

"Your cat drooled on my teddy bear!"

Mrs. Mumu smiles and scratches Pookie behind his ears. "I know. He always does that when he gets overexcited. Isn't it adorable?"

16 - Ladies Seldom Eat Cheese

Thankfully, the flight from Athens to Boston is a direct one. I really doubt I could have convinced myself to get on a connecting flight after the ordeal I just experienced. And I'm not sure what the worst part of it was—fearing that I was going to die in a plane crash or having a hairless cat drool all over my teddy bear.

Fortunately, there's no one waiting to arrest me when we land. The flight attendant tells me that she's going to let me off with a stern warning, but that an incident like that better not happen again or else the airline will bar me for life. It wasn't much of a scare tactic. I have no plans to board another plane ever again.

As I wait in line for a taxi, I turn my phone on. After a few moments, it beeps repeatedly, letting me know that I missed a number of texts while I was in the air. The first one is from Mia.

Arrived in Paris. Eating croissants with Pierre. Next stop—the Louvre to see the Mona Lisa.

I'll have to call her later and get the scoop about what exactly is going on with Pierre. It seems like things have gotten serious, fast. I scroll down to the next text. This one is from Isabelle.

Call me when you get a sec. Have to tell you about the mysterious guy I met last night.

Ooh, that sounds intriguing. Isabelle started working aboard the riverboat cruise ship in Germany. I wonder if the mysterious guy is someone who is part of the crew or a passenger.

Next up is my mom asking if I've done the three things yet that she told me to do. Three things? I remember her telling me to apologize to Preston, which I'm planning on doing. She also told me to consider what would really make me happy. I did give it some serious thought on the plane when there wasn't any turbulence. I have some ideas, but still not completely sure what to do in the career department. As for the third thing, I have no idea what it is. She had started to tell me, but then I had to hang up to save my clothes from a hairball.

The last few texts are from Celeste. I laugh out loud when I read them. They're so typical of her—bizarre dating advice coupled with motherly concern.

If you go to a reception at the university with Preston, remember that ladies seldom eat cheese in public.

That sounds like good advice if you're lactose-intolerant. But I love me some lactose, especially in the form of cheese. If there's any on offer— cheddar, provolone, pepper jack, any kind, really—you can be sure that I'm going to gobble it up.

Don't chew gum, especially grape-flavored gum.

I smile. No problem there. Chewing gum interferes with cheese eating. Why it matters if it's grape or another flavor is beyond me. When I get to her last text, it makes me a bit teary-eyed.

Don't let Preston slip away. I almost did that with my Ernie. Imagine if I had, I would have missed out on 14,632 of the best days of my life.

I feel something poking me in my back. I turn, half expecting to see Mabel behind me, brandishing her cane. Instead, it's a pleasant-looking man trying to get my attention. He points at the taxi pulling up to the curb. "Excuse me, miss, but you're next."

As I slip into the back seat, I look at my phone. Should I text Preston and let him know that I'm in the States and coming to see him, or let it be a surprise? A surprise, I think. That way, I'll know from the look on his face when he sees me, how he really feels about us.

* * *

Walking through the campus reminds me of my time in graduate school. The park-like setting, old ivy-covered brick buildings, students chatting to each other as they make their way to their next class, and members of the rowing team rushing to practice.

I approach the auditorium where the awards ceremony is taking place. My stomach is in knots. My heart is beating rapidly. My hands are clammy. Facing Preston is more anxiety inducing than flying across an ocean was. After taking several deep breaths, I slowly push the door open. I step over the threshold and into the large room. Standing at the back, I look down over the rows of seats. The place is jam-packed—it's standing room only.

The chair of the history department approaches the podium. After some introductory remarks, she begins with the first award of the evening. "I have the honor of presenting the Hubert Robinson Prize. As you know, this prize recognizes promising graduate students in ancient history. Students from around the country submit research papers for consideration. This year, the standard of submissions was incredibly high. It was a real challenge to narrow the field down to a short-list of four finalists."

She pauses and takes a sip of water before reading off the names of the finalists. I gasp when she reaches the final name. The name I've tried to forget. My ex. The jerk who stole my research and presented it as his. The man who accused me of plagiarism. How is it possible that Joel is in contention for this prestigious prize?

I clench my fists and narrow my eyes. My nervousness at seeing Preston again has been replaced with a different emotion—red-hot anger. I scan the auditorium. Where is he? Where's that coward, Joel?

While I'm searching for my nemesis, a young man rushes onto the stage, covers the microphone with his hand, and whispers something in the woman's ear. She raises her eyebrows, then pulls him to the side to confer with him. The crowd murmurs among themselves, wondering what's going on.

When she returns to the podium, she holds up her hands for silence. "I have just been advised that one of the finalists has been disqualified for plagiarism." When she says Joel's name with disdain, I do a fist pump.

Finally, the truth has come out. The world now knows him for what he is—a cheater.

She waits for the audience to quiet down, then continues. "Evidence has been brought to the committee's attention that proves without a doubt that the paper he submitted was authored by someone else. Due to these circumstances, we will need to reconvene the panel of judges at a later date to consider how best to proceed. In the meantime, we will continue with the remainder of the awards on the program."

I'm completely distracted during the next presentations. It's only when she reaches the final award of the evening—the Herodotus Prize—that my ears perk up. This is the one that Preston is going to be awarded. When he walks on stage, I'm grinning ear to ear. A tweed jacket and bow tie never looked so good. Even from this distance, I can see his blue eyes sparkling in the overhead lights. Oh, how I want to see those blue eyes up close and personal.

After his acceptance speech, the ceremony draws to a close. Preston remains on stage, chatting with the history department chair and some other professors. I sling my backpack over my shoulder and grab my suitcase. The crowd is walking up the aisles to the exits. I'm going the opposite way, pushing my way through people as I try to get to the stage before Preston leaves.

As I near the front of the auditorium, I wave and call out his name. He turns. His eyes lock with mine, his eyebrows raised in surprise. I wait anxiously for some sort of reaction, any reaction. Then he breaks his gaze, turns, and says something to the person next to him. My heart sinks. That's his reaction? Ignoring me?

I chew on my bottom lip, my eyes welling up with tears, then I turn to make my way back up the steps, toward the exit, and out of the auditorium alone. All alone.

"Excuse me," I say to the cluster of men in front of me, blocking my way.

They're so caught up in discussing the plagiarism scandal that they don't hear me.

"Excuse me," I say again. "Trying to get through."

They're still oblivious, so I try to slip around the side of them, but as I take a step forward, one of the guys takes a step backward. I stumble and end up on the ground, splayed across the bottom step, my belongings scattered about.

I turn my head sideways and see the top of Giuseppe's head with its half-eaten ear sticking out of my backpack. I smile. No matter what ends up happening with Preston, at least I know there will always be one guy in my life who will stand by my side.

"Are the two of you okay?" someone asks.

I glance back at Giuseppe, then look up and see the man who tripped me.

"He'll be fine," I say. "I know it looks bad, but I can stitch up his ear later."

"His ear?" He turns, looking to the left of me. "Did you hurt your ear?"

"No, my ear's fine," a familiar voice says.

I turn over on my side, wincing in pain. I look down at my ankle. Probably sprained. Then I allow my gaze to look at the man lying on the ground next to me who must have been taken down with me when I fell. It travels up from his sneakers, to his jeans, to his tweed jacket, to his adorable bow tie, then up to his eyes. His gorgeous blue eyes.

He's grinning ear to ear. "We have to stop meeting like this."

* * *

An hour later, we're sitting in the cafeteria, sipping on coffee, my leg propped up on a chair with an ice pack on my ankle. After telling Preston about my journey and getting him to promise that he'll never wear body spray or adopt a hairless cat, he leans across the table and grabs my hand.

"I can't believe you did that. Getting on a plane must have been so terrifying."

"It was." I look down at the charm bracelet on my wrist. "But it was worth it."

He frowns. "Is that why you came back? For your bracelet?"

I squeeze his hand. "That's not the only reason. There's another one."

"What's that?"

"My mom gave me some advice. She said that there were three things I needed to do. One of them was to think about what would really make me happy in terms of my career direction."

"Ah, so that's why you came back." He releases my hand. "Are you going back to grad school? You can do that now. Your name has been cleared. Everyone knows that you're the one who wrote that paper."

"Nope. Grad school isn't for me. I'm not sure what my future holds, but that isn't it." I cock my head to one side. "Do you know how they found out about Joel stealing my paper?"

He bites back a smile. "No idea."

"Oh, my gosh. It was you. You found the evidence proving my innocence." I run my fingers through my hair. "All this time, I thought you wouldn't believe me. But not only did you believe me, you set out to restore my academic reputation."

"I can't take all the credit," he says. "There were other people looking out for you. You just didn't have enough faith that folks would be on your side."

"But why? Why did you do that for me?"

He pulls his chair closer to mine, leans forward and strokes my cheek. "Don't you know?" I tremble as he lightly kisses my neck, working his way up from my collarbone to my ear. He runs his fingers through my hair, turning my face toward his. After gently nipping my bottom lip, he whispers, "It's because I love you."

I pull back, my eyes wide. "You...you...?" I can't say the rest of the sentence out loud. It can't be true. There's no way he could love someone like me, especially after what I did to him.

"I love you," he repeats.

"No, you don't."

"Yes, I do."

"No, you don't."

He grins, then pulls me back toward him and silences me with a kiss.

When we come up for air, I take a deep breath. "Hang on for a moment." I look around the cafeteria. Fortunately, it's empty at this time of night so no one saw that kiss. Because, wow, that was some kiss. "There's something I need to do before my mom sends me another text about it."

"What's that?"

"Apologize to you."

"You don't have to—"

I put my fingers on his lips. "Shush. Let me do this. I owe you an apology. A big, fat apology for lying to you. Once I started, I didn't know how to stop." I shake my head. "No, that's another lie. I didn't want to stop. I didn't want you to find out who I really was."

"Ginny, it's okay."

"No, it's not."

"Actually, you're right. It's not okay. But I understand why you did it." I sit back in my chair. "You do?"

"I do." He looks down at the table. "Remember how I was engaged?" I nod. "Well, when I discovered that she was cheating on me, I was angry. Really, really angry."

"That's understandable."

"But I was also mortified." He runs his hand across his chin and smiles wryly. "I was worried what people would think if they knew that my fiancée cheated on me. Even though I didn't do anything wrong, I was embarrassed. So embarrassed that I pretended we were still engaged for a couple of months after we broke up."

Preston pauses to take a sip of coffee. "She had moved to another town to be with him. She was a business consultant, always traveling around the country for work. So, for a while, it was easy enough to just pretend that we were doing the long-distance relationship thing."

"What happened?" I ask, leaning forward and putting my elbows on the table.

He shrugs. "I got caught. She came back to town to visit some friends for the weekend with him in tow. Word got out that she was with another guy, and I ended up looking like even more of a fool than I already was."

"Wow." I can't think of what else to say that could ease the hurt I see in his eyes, so I simply repeat myself. "Wow."

He points at my cup. "Finished?" I nod and he scoops it up, along with his, and walks over to a garbage can to deposit them. When he sits back down, he looks at me intently. "So as you can see, we both have a lot in common. We've both lied because we were too embarrassed to tell the truth."

My phone buzzes. "Hold that thought," I say. "It's a text from my mom."

"What does it say?"

A smile slowly creeps across my face. "She's reminding me of what the third thing is that I need to do."

"Oh, and what's that?"

"Tell you how I feel about you." I tug on the sleeve of his tweed jacket, pull him toward me and whisper in his ear, "I love you."

I pause, expecting him to engage in silly banter with me saying, "No, you don't," but instead he simply says, "Yes, yes you do."

Epilogue – Preston

As the ship's horn blasts, Ginny leans over the railing and waves at the crowd on shore watching us leave port. She turns back toward me, a huge grin plastered on her face. Her smile is so infectious that before I know it, I'm grinning from ear to ear as well. How did I get so lucky? I still can't believe she said yes.

Of course, the way I proposed to her might have had something to do with it. I made her a special ravioli dish from scratch, then served it to her during a candlelit dinner. If there's one thing she's smitten with, it's ravioli. I think I come in a close second—probably tied with her favorite cake, tiramisu—because when I asked her to marry me at the end of the meal, she jumped up from the table and squealed with delight.

She's squealing with delight now, too. "Look, I think those are dolphins escorting us out to sea."

"I can't imagine a more wonderful birthday than this." I tuck a stray auburn curl behind her ear, then trace my fingers down her cheek. "Going on a honeymoon cruise with my beautiful wife to the Caribbean and dolphins—it doesn't get any better than that."

"Happy birthday, Preston," she says. "I think August sixth might just be my new favorite day of the year. Right after the day we got married."

"It doesn't make you think about sanitation in the Roman Empire and what's-his-name?"

"Who? What?" She cocks her head to one side. "I've never heard of either of those things. The only thing I know is that the most wonderful man in the world was born on this day."

"Oh, who's that?"

"My husband." She looks from side to side mischievously, then lowers her voice. "He's a really adorable nerd. But don't tell him I said that. It might go to his head."

"I bet he's a historian. They're the worst."

"They are, aren't they? Can't stop talking about the past."

"I suppose you want to talk about the future instead?"

She bites her lip and looks off into the distance for a moment, then says, "I have an idea about the future. More specifically, my future."

I squeeze her shoulder. "Go on. Tell me."

"I think I've finally figured out what I want to do with my life." She takes a deep breath, then the words rush out of her. "You know how I love history, right? But I don't like academia and professors." She glances at me. "Present company excluded."

"Obviously," I say wryly.

"And you know how I love food and travel."

"I'm well aware of that."

"Well, I got a call from a friend who's the editor of an online magazine. She wants me to write a weekly column for them featuring recipes from around the world, tying them in with the history of the various regions. I might even get to travel to do research." She twirls around like a little kid. "Me! Can you believe they want me?"

When she stops spinning, I kiss her on the forehead. "Of course, I can believe it. It's the perfect job for you."

She leans against the railing and holds up her left hand. The emerald-cut diamond on her ring finger sparkles in the sunlight. "Are you admiring your ring?"

"I am," she says. "I really love the art deco setting."

I furrow my brow. "Is it too old-fashioned for you? We can exchange it if you don't like it."

She laughs. "Not on your life. I like old-fashioned things. After all, I married you."

"I'm one lucky guy."

She reaches up and tugs at my bow tie, then raises herself on her toes and lightly brushes her lips against mine. "I'm one lucky girl."

I put my hands around her waist and pull her toward me, kissing her slowly and thoroughly. The horn blasts again, and she breaks our embrace. She leans over the railing and watches the dolphins for a few moments. Then she turns back toward me and runs her fingers along my collar. "I like your bow tie."

Slipping my fingers underneath the straps of her sundress, I say, "Your straps are pretty nifty."

She slowly unties my bow tie. "But I think I like you better without it."

I slip one of the straps off her shoulders. "Ditto."

As the horn blasts one last time, she grabs me by the hand. "Shall we continue this in our cabin, Professor Whitaker?"

"With pleasure, Mrs. Maarschalkerweerd-Whitaker."

II

Smitten with Croissants

1 - Smoochy Face

"For crying out loud, this is a buffet line, not some nightclub," I mutter under my breath. "Go play smoochy face someplace else."

My friend, Isabelle, glances at me. "Smoochy face? What are you talking about, Mia?"

I point at a young couple engaged in a full-on make-out session and pull a face. "No one wants to see that while they're waiting to eat. Why did they even bother coming on a cruise if all they're going to do is grope each other? They should have stayed home. Or, at the very least, inside their cabin."

Isabelle laughs. "You really aren't a fan of public displays of affection, are you?"

"That's not true," I protest.

She arches an eyebrow. "Hmm . . . I seem to remember the time your boyfriend tried to hold your hand in public. You almost decapitated him with that sword of yours."

"First of all, he wasn't my boyfriend. I only went on a few dates with him. A few too many, I might add." I put my hands on my hips. "Second, it's a *lightsaber*, not a sword. And third, his hand was all gross and sweaty."

"Gross and sweaty, huh? So that's why you stabbed him?"

"I did not stab him . . . At least not on purpose. Listen, all I did was try to pull my hand away. But then I lost my balance and tripped, and that's when my lightsaber accidentally smacked into his neck."

"Good thing it's made of plastic, otherwise you could have done some serious damage to his carotid artery."

"I guess." I purse my lips. "Unfortunately, I can't afford one of those custom-made steel lightsabers with a titanium handle."

Isabelle rolls her eyes. "Did you ever think that perhaps you're a tad bit over obsessed with *Star Wars*?"

I ignore her jibe, instead nodding toward the couple holding up the line. "Geez, look at where his hands are now. If he moves them any more, we're going to find out what color her underwear is any second now."

"Hmm, you might be right. Her skirt is pretty short. Doesn't really fit the 1950s theme for tonight's dinner. Miniskirts weren't a thing until the sixties." Isabelle toys with her pearl necklace. "But I guess it's pretty hard to pack for all the themed events they have planned for the cruise."

"Well, if I managed it, anyone can."

Isabelle snorts. "That's true. You are one of the most disorganized people I've ever met."

"I'm not disorganized. I'm creative. Completely different." I shake my head as the couple continues to hold up the line. Standing on my tiptoes, I wave my hands over my head at them. "Hey, knock it off or get a room. Some of us want to eat tonight."

Isabelle grabs my arm and pulls me back. "Shush. They'll hear you."

"That's the point."

"The line's moving now. You can cool your jets."

"My jets are just fine, thank you very much."

Isabelle scoffs, then turns and smiles at the girl in line behind us. It's one of those smiles that says, "Please ignore my friend. She's constantly embarrassing me."

The girl smiles back. I'm pretty sure her smile means, "Your friend is totally right about that couple. I admire her for saying out loud what the rest of us were thinking." At least, I'd like to think that's what it means. Who knows, maybe she was just smiling about the fact that they're serving two kinds of coleslaw tonight. People can get excited about that kind of thing.

"Looks like we shop at the same place," Isabelle says to the girl.

It's true. She's dressed similarly to us with a full skirt, gloves, and pearls. As I admire her auburn curls, which are tucked underneath a broad-brimmed hat, I toy with a strand of my long blonde hair, trying to decide if I would look good as a redhead.

After we introduce ourselves—the other girl's name is Ginny—I turn my attention back to the line in front of me. It still hasn't moved an inch while the lovebirds continue to express their desire for each other for all the world to see.

Oh, by the way, Miss Lovebird's underwear is pink. Way more information than you or the rest of us waiting in line probably want to know.

"Excuse me." An older woman standing behind the couple taps the man on his shoulder.

They pull back from each other, just now seeming to notice where they are—on the lido deck of a cruise ship making a transatlantic crossing from Miami to Europe.

"You must be newlyweds," the woman says to them. "I remember when my Ernie and I got married forty years ago. We couldn't keep our hands off each other either."

After some inane chitchat between the three of them about flower girls and ring bearers, the line finally moves forward.

I grab a plate, but as I turn to pass it to Isabelle, it slips out of my hands and crashes on the floor, shattering into pieces.

A waiter rushes over. As he bends down to clean up the mess, the collar of his white shirt pulls back, and I can see something that looks like a tattoo at the base of his neck. I lean forward to get a closer look, when he suddenly shifts position, bumping his head against my arm.

I startle as I realize that my fingers are lightly brushing his hair. His impossibly soft, sandy-brown hair. The dude has some great conditioning products going on.

He stands and I quickly take a step backward, putting my hands behind my back.

"Sorry about the plate."

"*Ne soyez pas désolée*," he says, his hazel eyes twinkling. "*Je voulais vous rencontrer depuis que vous êtes montée à bord du navire.*"

My jaw drops as I watch him walk away. I know that my French is rusty, but did he just say that he had been looking for an excuse to meet me since I boarded the ship? And did he wink at me?

"You're kind of a klutz today," Isabelle jokes, snapping me back to reality. "First you spilled perfume in our cabin and now this."

"It's these stupid gloves. They're slippery," I say as I yank them off. "How did anyone manage to get anything done back in the fifties wearing these things?"

"They probably are a safety hazard." Ginny pulls her gloves off as well then looks at them. "Now what do I do with them? I don't have any pockets, and I didn't bring a purse."

I grin and stick my gloves down the front of my sweater. "That's what bras are for," I say. "They're great for holding your phone and money, along with gloves when you don't have any other way to carry them."

Ginny grins back and stuffs her gloves down her sweater. Isabelle frowns. I wonder if she's going to join in—drawing attention to herself is something she generally avoids. But after a moment, she joins the bra-stuffing brigade.

The three of us giggle about our lopsided cleavage as we pile hamburgers, hot dogs, corn on the cob, two kinds of coleslaw, and deviled eggs on our plates.

"Are you traveling on your own?" Isabelle asks Ginny.

"I am," she says.

"Come sit with us," Isabelle says.

"Oh, yes, join us," I say. "But only on one condition. No talking about guys."

"Mia just had a bad break-up," Isabelle says.

"Bad?" I scowl. "Bad is what you say when you're describing the taste of beetroots. My mother would wash my mouth out with soap if I use a word that really describes what happened, so I won't. You'll just have to trust me, it was a lot worse than eating beetroots."

Ginny sets her plate down. "You won't get any argument from me. The last thing I want to talk about is guys. Besides, I hate beetroots too."

"Cool. Let's talk about why these petticoats itch so much instead. What I wouldn't give for a pair of yoga pants right now."

"Me too. I could live in my yoga pants twenty-four seven," Isabelle says. "But despite the gloves and the petticoats, you have to admit traveling to Europe on a cruise ship is heavenly. It sure beats flying."

I shudder. "I hate flying."

"That makes two of us," Ginny says.

"Make that three," Isabelle adds. "I couldn't believe my luck when I won two free tickets on this cruise ship. Mia and I were just about to book flights to Europe when it happened."

"It sure beats flying," I say. "But I would have sucked it up and gotten on a plane if I had to. Nothing is going to get in the way of what I want to achieve."

"What do you want to achieve?" Ginny asks before taking a sip of her milkshake.

"World domination," I say. "Isn't that every girl's dream?"

* * *

"World domination?" Ginny chuckles. "I'm not sure I could handle managing an entire planet. I'd be happy just knowing what I want to do with my life."

"Really? I've known what I want to do with my life since I was a little girl," I say.

"Mia is very goal oriented," Isabelle says.

"I used to be goal oriented too," Ginny says. "But then my world got turned upside down by a jerk. Now, I'm rethinking everything."

I lean forward. "Same. Except the rethinking part. I still know what I want to do, but after a guy screwed up my life, it kind of threw a monkey in the wrench."

"That doesn't make sense," Isabelle says. "How can you throw a monkey in the wrench? Why would you throw a monkey in the first place?"

"It's an expression," I say. "You know, from the movie *Die Hard*. Don't you remember the scene where Bruce Willis' character said, 'Just a fly in the ointment, a monkey in the wrench, a pain in the—"

Isabelle holds up her hand. "Please, no more Bruce Willis quotes." She turns to Ginny. "She's obsessed with Bruce Willis. It's almost as bad as her obsession with *Star Wars*."

"Am not," I say.

"Are too," Isabelle retorts.

Fortunately, Ginny intervenes and changes the subject, telling us that the original expression, "throw a monkey wrench in the works," dates back to the early 1900s when people threw tools inside industrial machinery as an act of sabotage.

During dinner, she shares other historical trivia, including the fact that ancient Romans used to eat while reclining on couches. Totally my kind of people. It's good to know that there's a historical precedent for all the times I lie on my sofa in my yoga pants while eating pizza.

After we polish off our hamburgers and hot dogs, I bring back dessert for everyone at the table.

"We can eat this without feeling guilty," I say, setting the tray down. "Angel food cake isn't made with butter or oil."

Isabelle shakes her head. "How many calories does that have?"

"Does what have?" I ask.

"That shake, silly."

I wave my hand hypnotically in front of Isabelle's face. "This isn't the shake you're looking for."

She snorts. "Your Jedi mind tricks aren't going to work on me. Or on your hips. That shake is real, sweetie."

I roll my eyes while Isabelle tells Ginny about how she convinced me to leave my lightsaber at home. Little does she know that I packed a Princess Leia costume. I'm positive it will come in handy at some point.

When Ginny says that she doesn't really like *Star Wars* movies, I gasp.

"I'm more into documentaries," she says. "You know, stuff that's real."

I gulp down the rest of my milkshake, astonished that anyone would think that the Force isn't real.

"Is anyone sitting here, girls?"

I look up and see the older woman who intervened and got the annoying couple to stop playing smoochy face at the buffet long enough for the rest of us to get our dinner.

"It's free," Ginny says. "Please have a seat, ma'am."

"We'll have none of that 'ma'am' nonsense," she says, wagging a finger. "That makes me feel positively ancient. The name's Celeste."

After we introduce ourselves, I get teary-eyed as Celeste toys with her wedding ring and tells us about her late husband, Ernie. Marriage suits some people. Not me, though. Not gonna happen. Not ever. Never ever . . . again.

Yeah, that's right. I was married once. And trust me, once is enough.

I surreptitiously wipe my eyes, then change the subject, asking Celeste if she travels a lot.

"Oh, yes," she says. "This is day four hundred and ninety-eight of my world travels. Or is that four hundred and ninety-nine days?" She shakes her head, trying to do the math involved with changing time zones. "Anyway, I'm headed to Greece next. What about you girls? Where are you going?"

Ginny tells us that she's disembarking in Rome, then taking a train to Ravenna.

"We're getting off in Rome too," Isabelle says. "After that, it's all up in the air. The only thing I know is that I have to be in Cologne by the beginning of July. I've got a job working on one of those German river cruise boats lined up."

Celeste nods, then looks at me.

"I'm going to head to Paris and get a job at an art gallery," I say with more confidence than I feel.

"Mia is a really talented artist," Isabelle says.

"Oh, I'd love to see your paintings," Celeste says. "What do you work in? Oils? Acrylics? Watercolors?"

"Ink," I say.

"That sounds fascinating. I have a friend who does these wonderful pen and ink drawings of her cats. What kind of paper do you use?"

"Uh, the kind made of human cells."

Celeste looks alarmed. "Human cells?"

"She's a tattoo artist," Isabelle explains. "Emphasis on artist. She does replicas of the great masters' work. You should see the tattoo she recently did of one of Van Gogh's sunflower paintings on this guy's back."

"It would have worked better if he hadn't kept squirming. One of the sunflowers turned out looking more like a turnip."

When Ginny asks me about my own tattoos, I laugh. "Me? Are you kidding? I would never get a tattoo. I'm scared of needles."

"Ah, aichmophobia," she says. "That's more common than you'd think."

I furrow my brow. "Ach-a-what?"

An older gentleman interrupts before Ginny can explain. He asks if any of us would care to dance, but it's obvious he only has eyes for Celeste. As he escorts her to the dance floor, she says over her shoulder, "Don't go anywhere. After this dance, I want to talk with Mia about getting a tattoo."

"What kind of tattoo do you think she wants?" Ginny asks.

"Maybe something that reminds her of her husband," Isabelle says.

I watch as Celeste's dance partner twirls her around. "I'm not so sure about that. He's been gone for over a year. Maybe it's time for her to move on."

Isabelle looks at me thoughtfully. "Maybe it's time for you to move on too."

* * *

After dinner, Isabelle and Ginny went to watch a Broadway revue. I begged off. I'd rather get a tattoo then listen to chirpy performers sing show tunes.

Instead, I go out on deck and lean over the railing, looking at the moonlight reflecting on the water. How in the world am I going to find a job at an art gallery in Paris? The French have a reputation for being aloof, especially in the art world. It's doubtful they're going to welcome an American girl like me into their fold.

I run my fingers through my hair and admonish myself. "Stop with the negative thoughts, Mia. Just because your family doesn't believe in you, doesn't mean you won't succeed."

When I announced my plans to my parents, they'd scoffed. They couldn't understand why anyone would want to leave the small town that I had grown up in, let alone go abroad.

"They eat snails in France," my mother said, wrinkling her nose.

"You mean *escargot*?" I asked.

"Es ... es ..." My father scowled as he struggled with the pronunciation. "Why can't they just say snails like normal people? Why can't they eat normal food like pot roast?"

"*Escargot* is French for snails," I explained. "They're served in garlic butter. You like garlic bread, Dad. Maybe you'd like *escargot* too."

He folded his arms across his chest. "Only an idiot would eat a common garden pest, garlic butter or no garlic butter. I bet they serve those es... es ... snails at that fancy country club where you used to be a waitress. It's exactly the type of thing rich people would pay top dollar for."

"Well, then I must be an idiot because I plan on ordering a big plate of them when I get to Paris." While I sounded defiant when I uttered this, inwardly I was shuddering. The thought of eating snails makes me queasy, but there was no way I was going to let my parents know that.

The sound of high heels clicking on the deck interrupts my thoughts. "There you are," Celeste says as she walks toward me. "I've been looking for you everywhere."

I cock my head to one side. "What's up?"

"Let's talk tattoos," she says. "It's on my bucket list, but I can't decide what to get, let alone where to get it. At my age, I have my fair share of wrinkles. Can you tattoo over wrinkles? What about saggy skin? Am I too old to get a tat? That's what you say, right? Tats?"

"You're never to old to get a tat," I say with a smile. "Did you know that

Judi Dench got her first one at eighty-one? And you're way younger than she is."

"Ooh . . . I love Judi Dench." Celeste squeezes my arm. "You've convinced me. Let's do it."

"What? Here on the cruise ship?"

"Sure, why not?"

"Uh . . . well . . . you probably need some sort of special license."

"If the captain can marry people at sea, I'm sure a little old tattoo wouldn't be a problem. Come on, we can get set up back in my suite."

I grin at her enthusiasm. "Unfortunately, I didn't bring my equipment with me. You need a special machine and needles, not to mention ink. Besides, you should really think about it carefully before you go ahead. It's not something you can undo easily."

"Nope, my mind is made up. When I know what I want, I go for it. Just like I did with my Ernie when I first laid eyes on him." Celeste rests her hands on the railing, closes her eyes, and breathes in the sea air deeply. "I wish he could be here now. He would have loved to go on a cruise."

"Why didn't you ever take one with him?"

"Well, when we first got married, we were completely broke. Besides, cruises weren't really a thing back then like they are now. Later, when we had more money, we didn't have the time. Or rather, we didn't make the time. That's what's nice about seeing you young people having adventures now before you get married and settle down."

I chew my lip. "It almost didn't work out that way for me."

Celeste turns her head and looks at me. "What do you mean?"

"When I was twenty, I almost settled down. Thankfully, it didn't work out."

"You were engaged?"

"More than engaged. I was married."

"Really? For how long?"

"Less than twenty-four hours."

She raises her eyebrows. "That's a short marriage. What happened?"

"His parents happened," I say bitterly. "They were dead set against me from day one. I wasn't good enough for their precious boy."

"But they must have come around in the end. The two of you got married."

"No, they completely freaked out when he told them that he wanted to propose to me, so we ended up eloping. When they found out what we had done, they hit the roof. They threatened to disown him."

"Were they serious?" Celeste asks. "I can't imagine any parents wanting to cut off contact with their child."

"They had threatened to disown him before, when we were dating, but we never thought they would go through with it . . ." My voice cracks as I recall the phone conversation with them. Then I straighten my shoulders and continue. "The family lawyer tracked us down hours after our wedding ceremony and insisted on a private conversation with my husband. After about an hour, the lawyer handed me a letter."

"The lawyer? What happened to your husband?"

"He left." I snap my fingers. "One minute we were happy newlyweds, looking forward to our honeymoon. The next minute, he had vanished, and I was all alone."

"What did the letter say?"

"A whole bunch of legal mumbo-jumbo which boiled down to one thing—my marriage was over. My husband chose his family fortune over me."

"Oh, sweetie, you poor thing." Celeste squeezes my hand. "I can't imagine why anyone would choose money over you. Why wouldn't his parents have approved of you? It makes no sense."

I take a deep breath. "Oh, it's the usual story—a girl from the wrong side of the tracks. They assumed I was a gold digger, just out for their son's money. What they didn't realize was that I was marrying him *despite* his money, and his parents, and all of their country club connections."

"It sounds like you're better off without him and his family. Money isn't everything." Celeste gets a faraway look in her eyes. "There was a guy who was sweet on me once. He was loaded, but I never could have been with him."

"Because he was rich?"

She laughs. "No, I didn't mind the money. It was *how* he made his money.

Not exactly on the up-and-up, if you know what I mean. But it all worked out in the end. I met my Ernie a few years later, and he turned out to be the love of my life. He was the guy I was meant to be with all along. You'll see. The same thing will happen to you. You'll meet a good man who will stand up for you against anything, and anyone."

I shake my head firmly. "I don't ever plan on falling in love again, let alone getting married. Once was enough."

"Was your marriage annulled? If so, it's like you get a do-over."

"Just because you get an annulment doesn't mean it didn't happen." I clench my fists. "What kind of stupid rule is that, anyway? If you're going to put on a white dress and have a minister marry you, you're married. Even if it only lasts for less than twenty-four hours. If I ever get a tattoo, it would say..." My voice trails off as I feel my nails digging into the palms of my hands.

"Say what?" Celeste asks.

"Never mind," I say, slowly unclenching my fists. "It's not like I'm going to get a tattoo, anyway. They're too permanent."

Celeste furrows her brow. "That's odd, considering you're a tattoo artist."

I grin. "That's me . . . odd. Anyway, let's talk about your tattoo. There are all different kinds of styles to choose from. I can show you some pictures."

She nods. "That sounds like a good idea. I know that I want it to say 'floss' but I'm not sure what style to do it in."

"Floss? That's cute. Is it a nickname? What Ernie called you?"

Celeste looks at me blankly. "Nickname? No, 'floss' as in 'floss your teeth.' I figure it would be a good reminder."

"You want to tattoo a reminder about...dental hygiene on your body?" I stammer. "Wouldn't it be easier to tape a note on the mirror?"

"No, don't be silly. I'd never notice that. But something tattooed, well, I'd see that every day when I get out of the shower."

"You sure you don't want something like a flower or a rose, maybe? Or a cat? Cats are really popular."

"No, dear. I'm going to go with 'floss.' It's far more practical than a tattoo of a cat."

I rub my temples. This is possibly the strangest tattoo that I've ever heard, and I've heard some real doozies. "Did you have any other ideas?"

"Well, sometimes I forget to take my blood pressure pills and there's the issue with my dishwasher—"

Before she can tell me what kind of dishwasher-related tattoo she's considering, we're interrupted by a commotion on the deck below us. I lean over the railing and see a woman jabbing her finger at a waiter while complaining at the top of her lungs about the fact that her strawberry daiquiri tastes like . . . wait for it . . . strawberries.

I've dealt with her type before when I was a waitress at the country club. I'm impressed with how the waiter is managing to keep his cool. If this happened to me, I would have told the obnoxious lady exactly where to go. The kind of place that's hot all year round, if you get my drift. Keeping my mouth shut was never my strong suit. Probably explains why my waitressing gig only lasted three days. Longer than my marriage, so there is that.

The woman shoves the glass into the waiter's hands, sloshing its contents everywhere. As she storms off, I call out, "Hey, aren't you going to clean that up, lady?"

I gasp as the waiter looks up. It's the same guy from earlier in the evening. The one with the sandy-brown hair that's softer than kitten fur. I feel my face grow warm as he locks his hazel eyes with mine.

"Who's that?" Celeste whispers. "He's cute."

"I have no idea," I say softly.

"I think you better find out," she says. "Because I'm pretty sure he just winked at you."

2 - Sweaty Hands and Rutabagas

A few days later, I'm lounging in a deck chair, a stack of glossy magazines and an iced tea on the table next to me. We're about a third of the way through our transatlantic crossing, and I'm already bored out of my mind. Not being able to see anything on the horizon other than endless water isn't helping my mood either. I almost wish I had flown instead . . . almost.

"I'm fed up with magazines trying to tell me what to do and what I should look like," I mutter, flipping through an article dedicated to the latest weight loss fads. "Rutamentals? A diet based on rutabagas, guaranteed to help you lose those unwanted pounds? That sounds disgusting. I'm happy with my curves, thank you very much."

After flinging that magazine on the deck, I pick up another one and thumb through it. "Five steps to getting a boyfriend...ridiculous. How about five steps to making sure you *don't* get a boyfriend? That would be more far more useful."

I take a sip of my tea while I ponder what my anti-boyfriend steps would be. "Let's see, first, you have to avoid eye contact at all costs. Guys have been known to hypnotize you with their eyes. It's like a superpower. Whether they're baby blues, or deep, dark eyes framed with long eyelashes, or a pair of hazel eyes which are mischievously winking at you—"

I pause as a woman walking past looks sharply at me. Oops. I guess I've been talking out loud to myself. I do that sometimes. Sure, it might be a little weird, but I don't care what anyone thinks of me, least of all some snobby lady whose first word as a child was probably "tsk-tsk."

After a few moments, I realize that I'm not talking out loud anymore.

Instead, all I'm doing is thinking about hazel eyes. Hazel eyes with a twinkle in them. Or, to be more specific, a cute French waiter with broad shoulders, hair you want to run your fingers through, and mesmerizing hazel eyes that just happen to be winking at me.

I mentally shake myself. Why in the world am I thinking about *him?* I haven't even seen the guy since the first night of the cruise. I don't even know his name. I don't want to know his name. I don't want to know anything about him.

This brings me to step number two—when you find yourself thinking about a guy, distract yourself with . . . well, with anything. I tend to think about the state of my cuticles.

After deciding I should apply some cuticle remover later, I grab the health and fitness magazine back off the deck and try to engross myself in diet recipes. Who knew you could puree cooked rutabaga and tofu, put it in the freezer for a few hours, and then pass it off as ice cream to unsuspecting dinner guests?

I glance up and see Isabelle effortlessly jogging toward me like a gazelle, her long ponytail swinging back and forth. She's smiling blissfully—the endorphins from her runner's high have clearly kicked in. Ginny is trailing behind her, shuffling from side to side like a duck waddling toward a pond. She's grimacing while she gasps for breath. Definitely no endorphins happening there.

Isabelle gives me a quick wave as she passes. Ginny tries to do likewise, but as she reaches her arm out, her hand gets caught in a life ring mounted on the railing. While trying to extract it, she trips over the stack of magazines on the deck, flies into me, and knocks me to the ground.

"*Permettez-moi, mademoiselle.*"

I look up and see Mr. Hazel Eyes holding out his hand to help me up.

I'm torn. What if his hands are sweaty and gross? How disappointing would that be? Cute guys shouldn't have gross, sweaty hands—although in my experience they usually do. I'm confident that statistics will back me up on this. But, on the other hand, what if his hands are pleasantly dry? Don't I owe it to science to find out if he's a statistical anomaly?

"*Mademoiselle?*"

Science wins. I place my hand in his and gasp. Not only are they dry, they're emitting some sort of weird energy particles that are causing my entire body to tingle from the tips of my fingers—which he's lightly caressing—down to the soles of my feet. The whole tingling thing is another one of those superpowers that the opposite sex use on us to make us swoon.

As he helps me to my feet, I wonder what these energy particles are. Could this be related to the legendary Force from *Star Wars*?

I quickly pull my hand away, avert my eyes, and try to distract myself by thinking about rutabaga and tofu ice cream.

The waiter furrows his brow. "*Vous allez bien?*"

"I'm fine, thanks," I say.

"I am very glad to hear that," he responds in perfect English, spoken with a swoon-worthy British accent. He scoops up the magazines strewn across the deck. As he hands the stack to me, he points at the headline promising five easy steps to get a man in your life. "Is this how you got your boyfriend?"

"Me? Boyfriend?" I stammer, clutching the magazines against my chest. "What boyfriend?"

His only response is a lazy grin.

"I don't have a boyfriend."

He nods slowly. "Hmm . . . no boyfriend. Interesting."

I scowl. This topic of conversation is *far* from interesting. Time to set Mr. Hazel Eyes straight. I shuffle through the magazines, find the article I'm looking for, then thrust it at him. "This is why I bought this—because of this photo shoot."

He cocks his head to one side. "Wedding dresses? That *is* interesting."

I feel my face grow warm. "No, it's not about the dresses. It's about the tattoos. See how each of the brides has a tattoo? They were done by Dominic de Santis. He's the go-to guy when celebrities are looking to get some ink. He's an incredible artist."

"I'd love to get something like that one day." He points at a close-up picture of one of the brides' hands.

I quirk an eyebrow and say with a slight smirk, "A bouquet or a diamond solitaire engagement ring?"

"No, the tribal tattoo on her wrist. But, I'm afraid my employer wouldn't approve."

"But you already have a tattoo?"

He frowns. "How do you know that?"

"Um . . . I saw it the other night when you were cleaning up the plate I dropped."

He rubs his hand on the back of his neck, worry creasing his brow. "I didn't think anyone could see it."

"I don't think anyone can normally," I say. "It was the way you were positioned underneath me. Your shirt was pulled back and I could see some black ink."

I feel flustered as I remember that tantalizing bit of ink. What does the rest of his tattoo look like? How far down his back does it go? What does his back look like?

I mentally shake myself and continue, "Most people wouldn't have noticed. If they did, they probably thought it was dirt. Not that anyone would think you have dirt on your neck. I mean, that would be strange. Why would you have dirt on your neck? No, I'm sure no one could see it. The only reason I noticed was because—"

Someone clears their throat, interrupting my train of thought, which is probably a good thing because I was starting to babble.

"Uh, excuse me. I could use a little help down here."

I glance down and see Ginny lying on the deck, her hand pressed against her ankle.

"Oh, my gosh. I'm so sorry," I quickly say as I bend down next to her. "Are you okay?"

"I think I twisted my ankle."

"I'll summon the doctor," Mr. Hazel Eyes says in a smooth, professional tone.

"No, that's not necessary," Ginny says firmly. "Just help me up. I'm sure I'll be fine."

After the two of us assist her to her feet, and she reassures us that she's fine, the waiter—whose name I still don't know—excuses himself to take a drink order from a nearby couple.

Ginny nearly collapses as she tries to put her weight on her ankle.

"Maybe we should see that doctor," I say.

"I think you're right," Ginny says. "Where did your friend go?"

"My friend?" I say. "He's not my friend. He's just a . . . a . . . um . . . waiter."

Ginny smiles. "Okay, maybe he's not your friend. But he's definitely not *just* a waiter. Unless, waiters usually wink at you like that."

* * *

Ginny slings her arm around my shoulders, and I help her hobble to the doctor's office. Actually, I'm not sure that I'm any help given how much shorter I am than her. Because Ginny has to lean down at an awkward angle for me to support her, I worry that the two of us are going to topple over again and land on the floor.

Fortunately, we reach the elevator without an incident and the doors glide open as soon as I press the button. Unfortunately, Mr. and Mrs. Smoochy Face are inside the elevator car, locked in a tight embrace while they make gooey eyes at each other, and completely blocking our way.

I clear my throat to get their attention, but they're oblivious.

"Excuse me," Ginny says.

There's no response to her polite request.

"Hey, we're trying to get on," I say more forcefully.

Still no response.

As the elevator doors start to close, I hurl my stack of magazines in their direction. That finally gets their attention. They shuffle over a few steps, still glued together, and Ginny and I manage to squeeze in behind them.

"Give us some sugar, my little petunia," the guy says, leaning down to kiss his bride.

"Petunia?" She giggles. At least I think it's a giggle. The sound reminds me of my childhood pet guinea pig when he was demanding a carrot.

"You don't like petunia?" He pulls her closer to him. "Okay, how about my little mother of dragons?"

She giggles again as he nuzzles her neck.

I groan. They've completely ruined *Game of Thrones* for me. How can I ever watch that again without thinking of squeaky guinea pigs engaging in way too much PDA?

"My little banana muffin?" he suggests, turning his body so that we have a close-up view of their lips locking. "My little baby cake?"

I gag while saying a prayer to the elevator gods. *Please, please don't let the elevator break down.* Someone is going to get hurt if I'm stuck in here with these two.

Finally, we reach our floor and the doors open.

After I help Ginny out, I turn to them. "If you want my opinion, I think you should go with 'my little guinea pig.'"

"Oh, that's cute," the girl squeaks.

As the doors shut behind us, I look at Ginny. "Some people just don't seem to get sarcasm."

She looks at me quizzically.

"I'll explain later," I say. "First, let's get you to the clinic."

While we wait for the doctor, Ginny chews on her lip as she scrolls through old texts from her ex-boyfriend.

"Why do you keep torturing yourself?" I ask. "You need to forget about him."

"Easier said than done." She shoves her phone back into the pocket of her sweatshirt. "It seems like everywhere I look there are reminders of him. My mom thinks I should start dating again. Casual dates with nice guys to help take my mind off what happened."

"Hmm . . . I'm not sure that works. My friends are constantly trying to set me up, but I feel like I'm wasting my time. All guys are the same—focused on money."

"How so?"

"They're either rich already—you know, stuck-up country club types—or they're obsessed with climbing the career ladder so that they can buy a big house and expensive car. They can't understand how I can be happy working at a tattoo parlor and why I'd rather talk about art than designer purses. Even worse, most of them have sweaty hands."

"Sounds like you're not dating the right kind of guys. Maybe you should go for something different. Someone who doesn't have a corporate job. What about that waiter you were flirting with earlier?"

I raise my eyebrows. "Flirting? Me? No way. Never."

Ginny rubs her ankle and smiles. "Uh-huh."

"I'm serious. I'm not one of those girls who bats her eyelashes, makes gooey eyes at a guy, or, worse yet, giggles when he calls her a silly pet name."

The nurse interrupts us. "The doctor is ready for you now."

"You sure about those gooey eyes?" Ginny says over her shoulder as she limps into the doctor's office. "I saw how you were looking at that waiter—positively gooey."

"Was not," I mutter at her retreating back.

* * *

While I wait for Ginny, I pass the time reading magazines. They're full of ridiculous articles—like how to sculpt your glutes while mopping the floor, melting down crayons to make the ultimate hostess gifts, and decorating your hamster's cage for Halloween. It's a relief when Ginny finally appears in the reception area, leaning on a cane.

I jump up to help her. "What did the doctor say?"

"He thinks I just twisted it. Should be okay in a day or two with some rest. I need to ice it to bring down the swelling."

"Let's get you back to your cabin."

As we walk toward the elevators, Isabelle rushes up to us.

"Are you okay, Ginny? I had no idea you were hurt until Pierre told me."

"Who's Pierre?" I ask.

"You know Pierre." Isabelle turns and points at a guy standing at the end of the hallway.

"Hey, it's the winking waiter," Ginny says under her breath, giving me a sideways glance.

Pierre gives Isabelle a small wave. She motions him toward us. "Don't be shy. Come join us."

Ginny grins. "Shy? He's not shy. At least not with Mia."

"Shush," I say, giving her a nudge.

As Pierre approaches us, he smiles at me, his eyes twinkling. Worried that this twinkle might turn into a wink, I avert my eyes and carefully study the carpeted floor. It's not helpful. The plaid pattern is made up of slate blue, dark green, and deep brown colors—the exact hues in Pierre's hazel eyes. Why couldn't the cruise line have picked something in pinks and purples instead?

"How is your ankle, *mademoiselle*?" I hear Pierre asking Ginny.

"It's okay. Mia's helping me back to my cabin so that I can elevate my leg."

I look up sharply. Why did she have to tell him my name?

"May I be of any assistance?" he offers.

Ginny gives me a mischievous glance, then says brightly, "Maybe you can walk with us and make sure we get there okay?"

"I think we can find our way back by ourselves," I say. "It's not like we need help pushing elevator buttons."

"Oh, I'm an excellent button pusher," Pierre says. "I would be happy to escort you ladies."

"Great," Ginny says.

She and Isabelle take the lead, with Pierre and I trailing behind. When we reach the elevator bank, I bite back a smile as Pierre dramatically presses the button.

"How do you girls know each other?" he asks while we wait for the elevator car.

"Mia and I have been friends forever," Isabelle says. "We met at the—"

I hold up my hand and give her a warning look. "I'm sure he doesn't want *all* the details."

"I can't believe you're still embarrassed about what happened," she says to me. Before I can protest, she continues. "Anyway, never mind how we met. The important thing is that she saved me from making a fool out of myself. She's always been there for me. I couldn't ask for a better friend."

My first instinct is to roll my eyes at Isabelle's sappiness. But when she puts her arm around my shoulders and gives me a sideways hug, I get misty-eyed.

Thankfully, the elevator arrives, and everyone is distracted while I dab my eyes.

"It's pretty full," Isabelle says. "Should we wait for the next one?"

Ginny shakes her head. "Nah. We'll take this one. Pierre and Mia can grab the next one."

"Good idea," Isabelle chimes in.

For someone with a twisted ankle, Ginny seems pretty spry as she hops into the elevator car before I can. She and Isabelle give us a cheeky wave as the doors close, pleased with their scheme to stick me with Pierre.

I scowl at them, then study the carpet again. For some unknown reason, the stupid hazel-colored plaid reminds me of what Pierre said to me on the first night of the cruise. Studiously avoiding eye contact with him, I casually ask, "That night at the buffet, what did you mean when you said you had been looking for an excuse to meet me? At least that's what I think you said. My French is pretty rusty."

"No, you got it right. That's what I said."

"Uh, okay, but what did you mean by it?"

"Oh, it was your *Star Wars* backpack. I wanted to know where you got it."

I give Pierre a sideways glance. "You're a *Star Wars* fan?"

"Guilty."

I look back down at the carpet, feeling oddly conflicted. On one hand, I'm glad the only reason he wanted to meet me was to geek out about *Star Wars*.

But, on the other hand, I'm kind of disappointed that it was my backpack he was interested in . . . not me.

After a few moments, Pierre suggests that we take the stairs. "The elevators are busy this time of day."

I shrug. "I can find my own way. You probably need to go do waiter stuff."

"It's no problem. I'm off duty." He cups my elbow with his hand and guides me toward the stairwell. "Besides, it's a good chance for me to get you alone."

My stomach flutters. "Alone?"

"Uh-huh. Isabelle told me that you're a tattoo artist. I want to get your opinion on a tattoo I'm thinking of getting."

When I realize that it's my professional opinion he wants, the stomach-fluttering stops. "The tribal one from the magazine? I thought you couldn't have one on your wrist?"

He holds the door to the stairwell open for me. "No, this would be on my back. Easier to hide."

As I walk down the stairs, I say over my shoulder, "I guess you can't take your shirt off then if you want to keep it a secret."

He doesn't respond until we reach the landing. "I suppose I can take my shirt off in front of people who can keep a secret," he says softly, his breath warm against the back of my neck. "Can you keep a secret, Mia?"

I spin around to face him. "Uh, sure. Secrets. Great at them."

"Good to hear. Is that why you're trying to unbutton my shirt?"

"Huh?"

"Your hands," he says simply.

Somehow, my hands are pressed against his chest, my fingers toying with the buttons on his crisp, white shirt. The crisp, white shirt covering a hard, muscular chest. A chest that would look amazing with a tattoo on it . . . Whoa. What is going on here? Why am I thinking about Pierre's chest? Why am I thinking about tattoos on his chest?

I pull my hands away. "Um, I gotta go. I forgot something at the doctor's office."

As I dart up the stairs, Pierre calls out, "I'll catch you later, okay? I still want to get your opinion on that tattoo."

I mutter something non-committal, continuing to run up the stairs. Isabelle would be proud of the pace I'm setting.

When I reach the next level, I slump on the floor and put my head in my hands. Then I cringe. My hands are covered in sweat. Me, of all people, with gross, sweaty hands. I groan as I grapple with two horrifying questions— Did I leave sweat prints all over Pierre's shirt? And what is it about this guy that caused me to break out into a nervous sweat?

3 - Cornettos vs. Croissants

A week later, Isabelle and I are sipping cappuccinos in Italy. This was not the original plan, as Isabelle likes to remind me.

When the cruise ship docked in near Rome, we had planned to make our way directly to Germany. But we had been having so much fun with Ginny on the transatlantic crossing to Europe, I suggested that we join her in Ravenna, a quaint city near the Adriatic Sea. While Ginny was in cooking school during the day, Isabelle and I could explore the city. Then, in the evenings, we'd all hang out and eat delicious Italian food.

After a quick search online, I snagged a last-minute deal on an adorable vacation rental in the heart of the city, and we hopped on the train with Ginny. Now here we are, sitting in a picturesque courtyard, surrounded by terracotta planters overflowing with flowers, and listening to the sound of water bubbling in a marble fountain.

"Admit it," I say to Isabelle. "Spending a week in Italy was a great idea of mine."

She furrows her brow. "Well, I suppose."

"You're just upset because you didn't have time to do hours and hours of extensive research, make a detailed itinerary, and—"

Isabelle holds up her hand. "There's nothing wrong with being organized."

"There's organized, then there's *organized.* No wonder you loved being in the Air Force so much. All that structure. You knew exactly what you were supposed to do every minute of the day." I shudder. "I couldn't have ever handled it."

Isabelle laughs so hard, she almost snorts coffee out of her nose. "No kidding. You wouldn't have lasted a minute in the military." Then her face grows serious. "Actually, that's one of the things I love about you—you're so impetuous."

"Impetuous?" I ask. "Is that one of your Scrabble words?"

"You have *Star Wars*. I have Scrabble," she says with a smile.

I shrug. "I guess they both start with the letter 'S.'"

"You know what I mean. You're carefree. You make decisions on the spur of the moment. You're not afraid to try new things."

I squeeze her hand. "You're perfect as you are. And besides, we make a good team."

"Yeah, kind of like *The Odd Couple*."

"Which one was that one again?"

"We just saw it on the cruise ship. How is it that you can only remember movies that have Bruce Willis in them or are part of the *Star Wars* franchise?" Isabelle rolls her eyes. "It was the one starring Jack Lemmon and Walter Matthau as Felix and Oscar. You're Oscar, the fun-loving slob—"

"Oh, yeah, I remember now. You're Felix, the neurotic control freak."

"I don't know about freak," she says with a smile. Then her expression sobers. "I'm going to miss you."

"I'm going to miss you too, but you'll meet lots of fun people at your new job."

She fidgets with her bracelet. "You know how much I hate meeting new people. I get so shy."

"But you did great making friends with Ginny and Celeste on the cruise. In fact, you were the one who introduced yourself to Ginny."

"That was hard, but I'm trying to force myself out of my comfort zone. Working with my new therapist has made me realize that I need to take more chances." She gulps. "But I may have gone too far accepting this job in Germany."

Before I can reassure her that everything is going to be okay, a baritone voice behind me says, "*Buongiorno, signore.*"

I turn and see Lorenzo, the owner of the apartment we're renting. He sets a pastry box on the wrought-iron table, then leans down and greets us European-style with kisses on our cheeks.

"I brought some Italian delicacies for you to try." He looks around the courtyard. "Where is your *bellissimo* friend, Ginny?"

"She's at her cooking class," Isabelle says.

Lorenzo's shoulders slump. "That is a shame."

"But she'll be back here tonight," Isabelle says. "She's going to meet us for dinner."

His face brightens. "Good. Perhaps I will see her then."

I smile, wondering if I should warn Ginny that Lorenzo has the hots for her. First, there was that American guy on the train who kept flirting with her. Now there's this Italian dude who appears to be after her.

"Try one of these," Lorenzo says, placing a crescent-shaped pastry in front of me.

"It looks like a croissant."

"A croissant?" The horrified expression on his face reminds me of the look on my mother's face when I came home from high school one day with a purple mohawk. "Croissants are French . . . how do you say it . . . they are *ripugnante.*"

Even though I don't speak Italian, I can tell that *ripugnante* is not something one should aspire to be. Especially if one is a pastry.

Lorenzo continues, "This is a *cornetto.* It means 'little horn' in English. Try it. It is delicious. Far superior to a croissant."

Isabelle takes a delicate bite of hers and murmurs appreciatively. I take a much larger bite, and groan with pleasure. Inside the soft, eggy dough is a rich custard cream. I quickly devour the rest of it.

Lorenzo smiles and hands me another one. "It is good to see a woman that has a healthy appetite."

My phone buzzes. As I lick cream off my fingers and reach for it, Isabelle says, "Is that Pierre again?"

"What do you mean *again*?"

"He's texted you a million times since we got off the cruise ship."

"That's a bit of an exaggeration," I say.

"Really. Count them up for me. I'll bet there's at least a hundred."

"Sure, but you're going to lose." Scrolling through my texts, I lose count after the thirtieth. "Okay, maybe there were a few from him," I admit.

"Who is Pierre?" Lorenzo asks. "That is a French name."

"He's Mia's boyfriend," Isabelle jokes.

"No, he's not. He's just a friend."

"Good," Lorenzo says. "The French do not understand pastry."

I laugh and take a selfie of myself eating a cornetto. I send it to Pierre along with the message, *Cornettos – 1, Croissants – 0.*

He responds immediately. *You need to get out of Italy. They're brainwashing you with inferior pastries.*

They don't taste inferior to me.

That's the brainwashing talking. Come to France so we can deprogram you.

But these have cream inside.

Wait until you try our pain au chocolat. Croissants filled with chocolate.

I smile mischievously as I type my reply. *I don't like chocolate.*

WHAT? I thought all girls liked chocolate.

But I'm not like other girls.

He sends a GIF of Princess Leia that says, "She's royalty."

Hardly, I type back. *I'm a commoner.*

There's nothing common about you.

I roll my eyes at his cheesiness, then text him a bunch of cheese emojis.

Are you saying you want a cheese croissant? That can be arranged.

I decide it's time to set the record straight. *Confession: I love chocolate.*

Phew. I don't have to return the box of chocolates I bought you.

You bought me chocolate?

To celebrate.

Celebrate what?

Your new job! Check your email.

I munch on a third cornetto while I check my inbox. These are delicious. I'm afraid Pierre's croissants are up against some stiff competition. As I read through the email Pierre sent me, I almost drop my pastry in shock.

"Did you just squeal?" Isabelle asks.

"Do I look like a guinea pig?" I say, placing my half-eaten cornetto back in the box. "That was a high-pitched yelp. Completely different from a squeal."

"Sounded like a squeal to me," she says dryly. "What happened?"

"A job at a small art gallery located at a boutique hotel in Paris. Pierre knows the manager." I scroll back through the email. "They're looking for someone who speaks English."

"You speak English."

"Yeah, but there are a million people who speak English. Why would they be interested in me? There has to be something Pierre isn't telling me."

* * *

While Lorenzo tells Isabelle all about *lucha libre*—apparently he has aspirations to move to Mexico and become a huge wrestling star—I stare at my phone, trying to figure out how to respond to Pierre's offer to help me land my dream job.

A large gray cat saunters across the courtyard, then jumps into my lap. He sniffs at my half-eaten cornetto before I pull him back.

"Sorry, bub. That one has my name on it. Not to mention my teeth marks." While I savor the buttery pastry, the cat nestles in my lap, purring loudly. "Pierre is off his rocker. There's no way a croissant can compete with this. So delicious."

After popping the last bit into my mouth, I stroke the cat's fur. "So, what do you think I should do? If I take this job, it would be because some guy helped me, not because I earned it on my own. You remember the last time that happened, don't you?"

The cat rolls over on his side and looks at me quizzically. Then he nudges my hand with his head, indicating exactly where he wants to be scratched.

"Well, of course you don't remember the last time that happened. I just met you." As I scratch behind his ears, I fill him in. "You see, when I worked at the country club, there was this guy. This really rich guy. You know, one of those CEO-types. Some sort of tech start-up . . . or was it an IT firm? Maybe a lingerie company?"

The cat meows sharply, giving me an impatient look, apparently uninterested in how the guy had made his money and more interested in a distraction-free petting.

"Okay, I guess that's not important. Well, anyway, I always wanted to go to art school, but I couldn't afford it. And it's not like my parents were in any position to help out. Just when I thought I was going to be a waitress for the rest of my life, this guy says that he can get me a scholarship. I couldn't believe my luck."

I pause and check the pastry box to see if there are any more cornettos left. Nope, just boring, dry, crunchy biscotti. I break off a piece and offer it to the cat. He spits it out. I can't say that I blame him. Biscotti definitely don't make my top-ten cookie list. Maybe Italians should stick to making cornettos.

"So, where was I? Oh, yeah, the rich dude and his scholarship. You'd think I would have learned my lesson the first time I got involved with a rich guy, but I didn't. He suggested that I come to his house for drinks so that he could help me fill out the application. I assumed his wife would be there. She wasn't. And you can imagine what happened next. He expected something in return for his generous offer. I told him where he could shove it. The next day when I showed up to work at the country club, the manager pulled me aside and told me one of the members had filed a complaint against me and that they had to let me go. You seem like a smart kitty. I bet you can guess who that was."

Isabelle glances at me. "Are you talking to yourself again?"

"No, I'm talking to the cat," I say. "He's a good listener."

"His name is Bacio," Lorenzo says.

"Can you hand me a napkin?" I ask. "He's drooling."

"That means he is happy," Lorenzo says. "What were you telling him? It must be a good story."

"Not so much a good story as an age-old story," I say. "Rich guy offers to help, but the offer comes with strings."

"That is what this Pierre is?" Lorenzo asks. "A rich guy with stringy job offer?"

I laugh, thinking this is probably what it sounds like when I speak French. "Not stringy job offer. Job offer with strings."

Lorenzo furrows his brow. "Strings? Like a violin?"

"It doesn't matter," Isabelle says. "Pierre isn't rich. He's a waiter. There aren't any strings."

"Actually, he was a waiter," I say. "Now he's a bellboy."

"Really? When did that happen?" she asks.

"It just happened. His contract with the cruise ship ended, and he got a job at the hotel where the art gallery is located."

"Honestly, I don't see what the big deal is. Pierre is just a nice guy trying to help you out. So what if he knows the manager? That's probably how he got his job too. It's just good luck, that's all."

"You're the one with good luck," I tell her. "After all, you won the tickets for our transatlantic cruise. But when it comes to me, there's no such thing as good luck. Only bad luck initially disguised as good luck."

Lorenzo gives me a bemused look as he pulls his long hair back into a ponytail. "Ah, I understand now."

"You mean the string thing?" I ask.

"No. I understand why you hesitate to accept the job offer. You have romantic feelings for this Pierre."

I scoff. "Pierre? Romantic feelings? Hardly."

"I see it in your eyes. Italian men have romantic sixth sense."

I fold my arms across my chest. "I think your romance sensor is broken. The only feelings I have for Pierre are as a friend."

Lorenzo considers my response. After a few moments, he shrugs. "Okay. Then I set you up with my cousin. He also wants to be a *lucha libre* wrestler."

4 - Grammatical Confusion

Okay, I ended up saying yes. Not to Lorenzo's offer to set me up with his cousin—a wrestler wearing spandex, a cape, and a mask isn't really my idea of a dream guy—but to Pierre. Maybe Isabelle is right. Maybe my luck has changed for the better. I'd be a fool not to take him up on his offer to help me get a job at a Parisian art gallery. He doesn't have a hidden agenda. He's just an ordinary guy looking to help out a friend.

Although, if I'm honest, my bank account helped make the decision for me. Whenever I log on to check my balance, there's a lot of red on the screen. At first, I thought it was some sort of decorative thing for the holidays, like a Rudolph the Reindeer or candy-cane themed web design.

Isabelle put a damper on that idea, pointing out that: (a) Christmas is a long way off; (b) banks aren't known for taking a festive approach to accounting; and (c) at the rate I'm spending money, I'd be lucky to be able to afford a candy cane.

She explained to me that red is bad and black is good. That only made sense to me after she pointed out that, when it comes to clothes, black is slimming. Looking slimmer is good. Therefore, numbers that are black are good. Then she helped me put together a budget. When we got done, I realized how much I needed a paying job. And that's when I sent a text to Pierre saying, "*Oui.*"

He sent back a picture of a flaky croissant and a link to a timer counting down the days until I arrive in France and try the best pastry the world has ever known.

Finally, the moment has come. After traveling around Europe for a few weeks, I'm at Gare de Lyon in the heart of Paris, stepping off the overnight train from Italy. I sling my *Star Wars* backpack over my shoulder and wheel my suitcase toward the end of the platform.

My breath catches when I glimpse Pierre standing on the other side of the ticket barrier holding a bouquet of flowers. The color seems odd—they have kind of a brownish hue to them—but maybe wilted flowers were all that he could afford on a bellboy's salary. It's the thought that counts, right?

As I elbow my way through the throng of travelers, I chew on my lip. Why did Pierre get me flowers? That's not something you normally do for someone you're just friends with. Maybe it's a Parisian thing, like eating snails.

Once I pass through the barrier, Pierre saunters toward me. No lazy grin this time. The man is full on beaming at me. For some reason, I can't move my feet. They're stuck to the tiled floor. I must have stepped in some bubblegum. A rather large wad of incredibly sticky bubblegum because no matter how much I will my feet to walk in Pierre's direction, they refuse to obey.

When Mr. Hazel Eyes reaches me, he cups my face with one hand and plants a soft, lingering kiss on my cheek. Then he slowly turns my head and kisses the other cheek. I'm used to these European-style kisses from my time in Italy, but this seems different. Really different. Instead of the casual "hello" vibe I usually get when someone greets me, these kisses seem to promise something more.

I take a deep breath, inhaling the scent of his cologne. It's a blend of sandalwood, bergamot, and something else I can't quite put my finger on. Wait a minute. Is that bread I'm smelling?

I glance down at the bouquet of flowers, except they're not flowers— they're croissants, each one fastened on a "stem" made out of a green bamboo skewer adorned with paper leaves. I burst out laughing. I love this guy's sense of humor. And this totally makes sense now. You get a girl that you're just friends with a bouquet of pastries, not flowers.

"*Bienvenue en France*," Pierre says softly, in a silky French accent. It reminds me of the rich chocolate mousse filling you find in a French silk pie. It's my mom's go-to dessert when the ladies from church come over for lunch. It's a time-consuming recipe, but so worth it. Although, I'm pretty sure there's nothing French about it since the pie crust she uses is made from Oreo cookies. But the ladies sure do drool over it.

While I'm surreptitiously wiping drool from the corner of my mouth—just thinking about my mom's pie will cause that to happen—Pierre switches to English. His British accent reminds me of crème brûlée. There's a smoothness to it that evokes the creamy, vanilla-flavored custard base, but there's also a crisp overtone, like crunchy burnt caramel topping which is the hallmark of crème brûlée.

I can't decide which accent I prefer. Come to think of it, I can't decide which dessert I prefer either.

"I hope you're hungry," Pierre says. "My friend at the bakery made these especially for you."

"Really? That was sweet. I don't even know him."

"Her," Pierre clarifies.

"Her?" I ask, my voice cracking slightly.

The corners of his mouth twitch. "Yes, her. *Elle.* I have female friends. Does that bother you?"

"Of course not. I'm female, and we're friends." I gesture at the bouquet. "That's a lot of croissants."

"One for each day you were in Italy eating those awful cornettos."

"I count more than seven."

"Maths never was my strong suit."

I smile at his British use of *maths* rather than the American *math.* I have to confess that it sounds sexy. His accent, not any reference to mathematics. Math is definitely not sexy. All that addition and subtraction. No wonder my bank account is looking so bleak.

"I wasn't great at math either," I say. "I barely passed algebra in high school."

"How did your parents react?"

"Well, I didn't flunk."

"And that was enough for them?"

"Sure. They had other things to worry about."

"Like what?"

"You know, the usual—paying the mortgage, making sure there was food on the table, that kind of thing."

Pierre looks off into the distance. "People shouldn't have to worry about that kind of thing."

"No, they shouldn't. But when your dad gets laid off, well . . ." My voice trails off as I think about how hard my parents worked to take care of our family. I take a deep breath, then exhale slowly. "But enough about that. Let's talk pastries. The smell of these is driving me crazy."

"If you think the smell is good, wait until you try them." Pierre tears a piece off one of the croissants. I reach my hand up to take the morsel from him, but he pops it in my mouth before I have a chance. He watches me intently as I chew, waiting for my verdict. "Well?"

"Well what?" I ask innocently.

"Did you like the croissant?"

I brush flakes of buttery pastry off my shirt. "It's okay."

He reacts with mock horror. "Okay? Just okay? What did they do to your taste buds in Italy?"

"The food was delicious in Italy—zuppa di pesche, ravioli, bombolones, and, of course, the cornettos were to die for."

Pierre narrows his eyes as I smack my fingers to my lips. He selects another croissant from the bouquet. Instead of tearing off a small piece for me to sample, he presents it to me as if it is a single, exquisite rose. "Try this one. It's a pain au chocolat."

"Ooh, a chocolate croissant," I say.

"Exactly. If you don't fall in love with French pastries after eating this one, well, then, I'll just have you deported."

"Yeah, right," I scoff. "Like a bellboy has so much pull with the government."

He grins. "Never underestimate bellboys."

After I take a bite of the chocolate croissant, I groan with pleasure. There's no way I can keep up this pretense that French croissants are mediocre.

"This is absolutely delicious."

Pierre brushes my lips lightly, wiping off a morsel of chocolate and popping it into his mouth. "*Oui, elle est délicieuse.*"

I simultaneously shiver and furrow my brow. A weird physical reaction. But what just happened was weird. The shiver I can write off as some sort of sugar high reaction to the chocolate filling, certainly not Pierre's touch.

The furrowed brow, on the other hand...that's because I'm utterly confused by what he said.

See, here's the problem with the French language—instead of "it" like we use in English, they use masculine and feminine pronouns. *Il* for masculine and *elle* for feminine. So, if we were talking about how a croissant tastes, we'd say, "It is delicious." The French would say, "*Il est délicieux,*" using *il* instead of *elle* because croissants are masculine.

But I could swear Pierre said, "*Elle est délicieuse.*" There was a whole ton of feminine going on in that sentence—the feminine pronoun, *elle*, and the feminine ending to the word 'delicious.'

There are four explanations that I can think of. Number one is that I didn't pay enough attention in French class, and croissants are feminine after all. That's actually a pretty plausible theory, considering my grades in high school. The second explanation is I misheard Pierre, and he really said, "*It est délicieux.*" Also pretty plausible. I was distracted at the time by his fingers brushing against my lips. The third possibility is that Pierre made a mistake, confusing *elle* with *il.* Not very likely, though. He was born and raised in Paris.

I take another bite of the chocolate croissant, pondering the final explanation. Is it possible that Pierre wasn't talking about the croissant, but instead was talking about me? Was he saying that *she* is delicious? *She* meaning me? Does he think I'm delicious?

No, I tell myself firmly. That is the *least* likely explanation. People don't describe other people as delicious. That's just weird. Sure, I can see that gooey-eyed couple from the cruise ship—the ones who couldn't keep their hands to themselves in public—calling each other delicious, but normal people don't say things like that.

I shake my head. What was I thinking? Pierre would never be interested in me in that way. Polishing off the rest of the croissant, I make a vow to brush up on my French. The last thing I need is a grammatical mishap with Pierre, especially a grammatical mishap of the romantic kind.

* * *

I clutch my half-eaten croissant bouquet while Pierre and I wait at the taxi stand outside the train station.

"First stop, your apartment to drop off the luggage," he says. "Then, I thought we'd swing by the Louvre before I take you to the hotel to meet your new boss."

At the mention of the world's largest art gallery, I clap my hands together in glee, inadvertently squashing a few of the pastries in the process. "I have wanted to go to the Louvre ever since I was seven years old."

"Don't most seven-year-old girls want to have tea parties with their dolls instead of going to museums?"

"I didn't have dolls," I say archly. "I had stuffed animals."

"Is there a difference?"

"A big difference," I say as we get into the taxi.

As we drive toward the *quatrieme arrondissement*, the area in Paris where the apartment I've rented is located, I tell Pierre about my second-grade teacher. "Mrs. Murphy loved art and wanted her students to appreciate it as well. She would show us pictures of famous paintings and ask us what we thought. I fell in love with *The Lacemaker* by the Dutch artist, Johannes Vermeer. I was blown away by the detail, especially on the yellow shawl the lacemaker is wearing. Then Mrs. Murphy told me about this magical place in France—the Louvre—full of even more amazing artwork. That's when I decided that one day I would find a way to get to Paris and see it for myself."

"Well, we only have time for a quick visit today," Pierre says. "But I have a friend who works at the Louvre who can arrange for a private tour at a later date."

"You seem to have a lot of connections. The friend at the bakery, the manager of the art gallery who agreed to hire me sight unseen, your friend at the Louvre—"

Pierre interrupts as we turn down a dark alley. "Are you sure you have the correct address?"

I check my email. "Yep, this is the right street."

The taxi comes to a halt in front of a dilapidated building. The exterior brickwork is cracked in a way that would probably make a structural engineer nervous. The front door is hanging off the hinges. Most of the windows are boarded up. Those that aren't have cracked window panes, which I suppose are good for ventilation. I hear it gets hot in Paris during the summer.

I open the taxi door, but before I can get out, Pierre pulls me back in. "You can't possibly be serious about staying here."

"I'm sure it's fine inside," I say. "The landlord did warn me that they were doing renovations to the building. That's why the rent is so cheap."

As I scoot out of the taxi, I hear Pierre telling the driver to wait for us. When I try to open the trunk to get my bag, Pierre puts his hand on top of mine and shakes his head. "No, you're not staying here."

I snatch my hand away. "Of course I am. Do you know how hard it is to find an apartment in Paris that I can afford? Do you expect me to sleep on the street?"

"The street would be better than this place."

I spin around and flounce up the stairs, avoiding the piles of garbage in my path. When I try to pull the front door open, it won't budge. Pierre comes up behind me and yanks forcefully on the handle, his biceps bulging underneath his t-shirt. The door pulls free from the hinges, and Pierre sets it to the side.

"After you, my lady," he says, bowing at the waist.

I cautiously walk inside, gagging at the stench, which I suspect is coming from the black mold peeking out from behind the peeling wallpaper.

Pierre looks at me, his hazel eyes steely. "Seen enough?"

"No. I haven't seen my apartment yet. It's on the fourth floor. They're probably doing renovations from the top floor downward." I dash up the stairs, calling out behind me. "Come on. I bet you twenty euros that it's really charming."

By the time I make it to my floor, I'm gasping for breath. I had forgotten that the French number their floors differently. What we call the first floor, they call the ground floor. Our second floor is their first floor, and so on. So when I got to what I thought was the fourth floor, it turns out it was only the third floor. It was a struggle to climb that final set of stairs, let me tell you.

When we reach my apartment, Pierre pokes his head inside. "This is charming?"

"Well, at least I don't need your help to open the door."

"That's because there isn't a door," he says dryly.

"Technicalities," I say, following him into the main living area.

"There aren't any windows either. Is that another one of your technicalities?" Pierre folds his arms across his chest. "This is definitely not *charmant.*"

Before I can argue with him, a rat scurries across the floor and stops in front of me. He raises himself on his hind legs, sniffs the air, then starts to climb up my jeans. I scream and drop my bouquet. Fortunately, the rat jumps off my leg. Unfortunately, he begins feasting on one of the almond filled croissants.

"Tell you what," Pierre says. "You can forget about the twenty euros you owe me if you agree that you're not going to stay here."

"Agreed. But where am I going to stay?" I put my head in my hands.

He pulls his phone out of his pocket. "Don't worry about it. I'll take care of it."

By the time we're back at the taxi, he's arranged accommodations for me. "It's perfect for you. No commute to work."

"What do you mean 'no commute'?"

"I got you a room at the Hôtel de la Marmotte."

I gulp. Hôtel de la Marmotte is where the art gallery I'm going to be working at is located. It's also one of the trendiest hotels in Paris. "There's no way I can afford that."

"The concierge is a buddy of mine. He's arranged for you to stay in it for free for as long as you need. It's a spare room that the hotel normally keeps vacant." Pierre puts his arm around my shoulders and gives me a squeeze. "It's all taken care of. I'll have the taxi drop off your luggage at the hotel and you and I can walk to the Louvre."

My jaw tightens. Pierre is starting to sound like my ex-husband. Swooping in and saving the damsel in distress. Taking care of things. Calling in favors from his buddies for the little woman. I want so desperately to refuse Pierre's offer, but what choice do I have? Finding another apartment is going to take some time. I'm too exhausted from the train ride to tackle that now. And, besides, the Louvre awaits.

* * *

"I can't believe I finally got to see the *Mona Lisa*," I say to Pierre as we leave the Louvre. Pausing to take a picture of the glass pyramid structure that towers over the museum courtyard, I try to decide whether I like the juxtaposition of I.M. Pei's modern design with the classic French Renaissance architecture of the original building.

I decide that I do like it. In a way it's like what I do—taking classic oil paintings and transforming them into something new using tattoo needles and ink.

"Did you have any other favorites?" Pierre asks as he hails a taxi.

"Oh, yes. The one by Georges le Tour."

"Which one was that again?"

"*The Card Sharp with the Ace of Diamonds*," I say. "It was the one depicting a card game."

"Oh, yeah. That poor guy. Oblivious to the fact that he's being cheated."

"Serves him right, don't you think? Wealthy people think they're so entitled. It's nice to see them get their comeuppance, even if it's only in an oil painting from the 1600s."

Pierre furrows his brow. "That's not really what you think about rich people, is it?"

"Maybe they're not all like that," I concede.

Pierre is quiet during the ride to the hotel. Occasionally, he points out landmarks, like the Jardin des Tuilieres and the Place de la Concorde, but for the most part, he stares at his phone, a pained expression in his eyes. I wonder if it's a touch of indigestion. We did eat a lot of the croissants before I sacrificed the rest of the bouquet to the rat.

"We're here," he announces. "Notice the panes in the windows and the absence of rodents?"

"Ha-ha." I've come to terms with staying at this luxury hotel while I look for another apartment to rent. Sure, I don't like that Pierre had to come to my rescue, and he probably could have done with less of a take-charge attitude, but he's a nice guy who's just trying to come to my aid.

As one of the bellboys opens the door and helps me out of the taxi, I stifle a laugh. I can't picture Pierre wearing this get-up—a red, double-breasted fitted jacket with a band collar, gold trim, and way too many buttons, paired with a matching pillbox hat. It looks like something an organ grinder's monkey would wear, not a grown man.

Pierre and the bellboy joke around with each other for a few moments while I stare in awe at the ornate marble facade of the hotel. This place is so fancy that even the members of the country club back home might feel uncomfortable here.

A woman wearing a gray suit rushes out. "Pierre, *la directrice de l'hôtel aimerait te voir. Bouge-toi.*"

I give him a sideways glance. "Hmm . . . The director of the hotel wants to see you. That can't be good."

He sighs. "No. I can't imagine it is."

"Don't worry," I say. "Just be your usual charming self and sweet talk her."

He gives me a wry smile, then places his hand on the small of my back and ushers me into the lobby. "Jean-Paul, can you look after Mia while I take care of something?"

A distinguished-looking older man comes round from the concierge's desk, takes my hand in his and kisses the back of it. "It would be my pleasure."

"Jean-Paul, you smooth talker, you." Pierre pulls my hand away and cups it between his. I smile at the reference to that cute scene in *The Empire Strikes Back* where Lando Calrissian flirts with Princess Leia. "Save it for your wife."

Jean-Paul holds his hands up. "Ah, do not worry. My wife is the only woman I have eyes for."

"How long have you been married?" I ask.

"Almost thirty-five years." Jean-Paul beams as he tells me how he met his wife.

The woman in the gray suit waves urgently at Pierre.

"I have to go," Pierre says to me. "Jean-Paul is the head concierge at Hôtel de la Marmotte. Any questions you have about the hotel or Paris, he can help you with."

"Go, go," Jean-Paul says. "I'll get Mia settled in her accommodations, then introduce her to Amélie."

"Amélie is the manager of the art gallery and Jean-Paul's wife," Pierre explains before he rushes off.

Jean-Paul chuckles. "It's good to have him back in Paris. I've known him since he was a baby. He's grown into a fine young man."

"Ooh, I bet you have some great stories about him as a kid."

"I certainly do. And for the right price, I'll tell you, especially the embarrassing ones." Jean-Paul hands me his business card. "Now, first things first. These are my contact details. If you need anything at all, let me know."

"Thanks, that's really sweet." I inspect the card, smiling at the hotel's quirky logo of a yellow-bellied marmot sitting in a claw-foot bathtub. I love that they've named this hotel after an adorable furry rodent. The place might be fancy, but it also has a sense of humor.

Then I frown when I read the small print underneath the hotel's name—a Toussaint property.

"Toussaint," I muse. "That's Pierre's last name."

Jean-Paul cocks his head to one side. "Yes, that's correct. Pierre Toussaint."

I chuckle. "For a minute there, I thought he was related to the owners of this hotel, but I guess it's a pretty common name."

"But he *is* related to the owners. They are his parents. Didn't you know? Pierre is the heir to the Toussaint fortune."

5 - Love is Like a Toothache

"The Toussaint fortune?" I splutter. "What are you telling me? Pierre is some sort of billionaire?"

Jean-Paul smiles. "I have no idea what his net worth is. It's not something we discuss. We talk about more important things like the rugby."

"Pierre plays rugby?" I've always been fascinated by rugby. Men in striped jerseys and shorts engaged in a full contact sport, which is similar in some ways to American football, but without the protective gear.

"He did when he was in college, but then he was injured."

Rugby explains a lot. His confidence, which borders on cockiness at times. His slightly misshapen left ear. His broad shoulders. His muscular chest. His—

Whoa. I need to stop this train of thought. Get your mind out of the gutter, Mia. Remember who Pierre is—a rich, pretentious guy who likes to dole out favors so that you'll bow down and worship him. He is not someone who you should fantasize about. Focus.

"So, Jean-Paul, tell me about Pierre's injury. What happened?" There, that should be a safe topic. Injured guys are so unsexy.

Jean-Paul's face clouds over. "That's something you should probably ask him about."

"Okay . . . well maybe you can answer this. If he's so rich, why is he working as a bellboy? Shouldn't he be wearing a suit and tie, sitting in some fancy boardroom, sipping on scotch and counting his money?"

"Pierre wants to learn all aspects of the hotel business. It's important to him to have hands-on experience. Earlier this year, he worked as a receptionist at the front desk. Before that, he was a dishwasher in the kitchen. After his rotation as a bellboy, he's going to work for me as an assistant concierge."

"Won't that be strange—you being the boss of the, well, the, um, boss?"

"Pierre has a . . . what do you call it . . . he has an egalitarian spirit. He thinks everyone is equal."

I guess I can see how people might think that. Pierre was joking around with the bellboys earlier, and the woman from the front desk spoke to him informally, telling him to hurry up. But at the end of the day, the boss is the boss.

"And don't forget. I've known Pierre since he was a baby. I've even changed his diapers. He knows who's boss."

Jean-Paul chuckles. It's infectious—a mixture of Santa Claus-style ho-ho-hos and Mr. Rogers' more sedate laughter. I find myself joining in, my grin turning to full-fledged belly laughs as I picture Pierre in a baby-sized rugby jersey and diapers.

When I catch my breath, I ask about Pierre's stint as a waiter. "Does his family own the cruise ship?"

"No, they are strictly hoteliers. The cruise ship line is owned by friends of the family. Rather than work at one of the hotel restaurants, Pierre thought it would be a good idea to get experience as a waiter elsewhere because . . ." Jean-Paul's voice trails off. He gives me a penetrating gaze, then stares at the floor. "Perhaps you should ask—"

"Ask Pierre? Got it."

Jean-Paul looks back up at me. "We're all delighted that he's back now. He seems so happy since he returned. I think you have something to do with that."

"Me?"

He grins. "Yes, you. In fact, I haven't seen him this happy since he came back from Africa."

I shake my head. "Africa?"

"Hasn't he told you about his time in Africa?"

"No," I say slowly. Now that I think about it, Pierre hasn't told me much about himself. All we seem to talk about is *Star Wars*, croissants, and tattoos. "What was he doing in Africa?"

Not surprisingly, Jean-Paul gives me an evasive answer.

"Never mind," I say. "I get it. It's something I should ask Pierre about."

"That would be best," the older man says. "Now, why don't I show you to your room? You can freshen up before you meet Amélie."

As Jean-Paul leads the way to the elevator, I ponder our conversation. In a short space of time, I've discovered there's a lot I didn't know about Pierre. He's loaded. He has a mysterious injury. He's spent time in Africa. And, for some reason, he didn't want to work as a waiter at one of his family's hotels.

What other secrets is he hiding from me?

* * *

Jean-Paul inserts the key card and opens the door to my new accommodations. After he carries my suitcase in for me, I walk into the room, my feet sinking into the plush oriental carpet.

As I set my *Star Wars* backpack on a carved wooden console table, I check out my surroundings. Oddly, there's no bed. Just living room furniture. But this isn't the kind of furniture you'd find in your average American's home. No, there is some seriously fancy stuff going on here. A large bay window is flanked by a Louis the Sixteenth settee and armchairs . . . or is that Louis the Fifteenth? Why all these old rich dudes all had to have the same name is beyond me. Anyway, the point is that this is the type of stuff royalty would sit primly on while sipping sherry or whatever it is that people drank back then, not a sectional couch from Ikea that a dude named Lou would lounge on in his boxer shorts munching on a bag of potato chips.

What really perplexes me is figuring out where I'm supposed to sleep. I'm pretty sure the settee isn't hiding a foldaway bed inside its silk, toile upholstery fabric. I turn to ask Jean-Paul about it, but he's disappeared. I peek behind the heavy brocade curtains, but he's not hiding there. He isn't on the balcony either, or behind the potted plants.

Okay, I really doubt that a distinguished-looking Parisian concierge is playing hide and seek, but it does give me a good opportunity to have a nosy.

As I'm looking in the closet, I hear someone clear their throat. Jean-Paul is standing in a doorway that I assume leads to the bathroom.

"Is everything to your satisfaction?"

"Yeah, it's great," I say.

"If you'll let me know which bedroom you prefer, I'll place your suitcase in there."

"Which bedroom? You mean there's more than one?"

"Yes," Jean-Paul says nonchalantly. "They're back this way, across from the kitchen and dining room."

I rub my temples. "Kitchen, dining room, bedrooms . . . this isn't a simple hotel room, is it?"

"Well, this is a bit simpler than some of our suites. It doesn't have a humidor or sauna."

"Considering I don't smoke cigars or like to sweat, I think I can live with that."

Jean-Paul smiles kindly at me, and I instantly regret my sarcastic tone.

"I'm sorry, it's just that this is really overwhelming. When Pierre offered me the spare hotel room to stay in temporarily, I envisioned a converted broom closet."

"You're probably tired from your trip. You took the overnight train from Italy, right? Why don't you rest for a while? I'll arrange for you to meet Amélie later." Jean-Paul looks at his watch. "Shall we say two hours from now?"

A nap does sound good. I pick the bedroom that's decorated in subdued blue tones. The only pop of color is a large oil painting of a marmot hanging above the fireplace. It makes me smile. A painting of a marmot wearing a Scottish kilt and tam isn't exactly something you expect to find in a fancy hotel suite. But that's what this place is known for—its quirky touches.

I lie down on the four-poster bed and exhale slowly. What am I going to do? I can't in good conscience stay here. Rolling over on my side, I press my face into the soft down pillow. Again, not the type of pillow you'd buy at Ikea. This thing is probably stuffed with phoenix feathers. And, yes, I know that phoenixes are mythical creatures. But, if you're wealthy, you can probably employ a team of geneticists to create your very own phoenix in a lab, just so you can pluck its feathers for your pillows.

The phoenix pillows do their job, and I feel myself drifting off to sleep. An hour later, the alarm on my phone jolts me awake. There's nothing worse than waking up abruptly when you're having a weird dream. And a dream of Pierre playing rugby while dressed in a marmot costume is pretty weird.

While I take a bath—complete with begonia-scented bubbles and rubber duckies—I consider my options. Stay at the hotel and take the art gallery job or move into the boarded-up, rat-infested apartment and try to find another paying gig.

After toweling off and getting dressed, I make up my mind. Rats and unemployment it is.

"Why do you have your suitcase?" Jean-Paul asks when I walk up to the concierge desk.

Before I can answer, a middle-aged man wearing a business suit steps in front of me and brusquely asks Jean-Paul to organize a skydiving excursion near Paris. I feel a shudder course through my body. I've had to fly a few times when car, train, or bus travel wasn't an option, but it's always involved a panic attack that not even a giant-size Toblerone chocolate bar can cure. Voluntarily getting into a plane, then choosing to jump out of it? Wow, talk about insane.

Jean-Paul asks one of the other concierges to escort me to the art gallery while he assists the businessman with his high altitude death wish.

The Galérie d'Art Animalier is located on the ground floor of the hotel. When the concierge leads me through an entrance off of the lobby, I immediately understand why the gallery has the name it does. Everywhere I look are paintings, photographs, and sculptures of various animals. The styles range from serious to whimsical. Something for every animal lover, regardless of their stylistic preferences.

I spot a woman lightly running a feather duster over a picture frame. Everything about her screams elegance. Her makeup is flawless, her silver hair is pulled back in a classic chignon, and her tailored suit looks like it came from a chic boutique. When she sees us, she sets the duster down, then gracefully walks over to us.

After the concierge makes the introductions, Amélie kisses me on each cheek. "*Enchantée.*"

I try to dredge up the correct response from my high school French days. "*Ç'est un plaisir faire votre connaissance.*"

She waves a perfectly manicured finger at me playfully. "No French, please. I need to practice English. That is one of the reasons I hired you. I would like to improve my English."

"Uh, about that. I don't think I can take the job."

She presses her hand to her chest. "What? No, I am counting on you. Madame Vernier is counting on you. All the ladies are counting on you. Not to mention the dogs. The dogs are counting on you."

I press my fingers underneath my eyes. "Who exactly are all these people and canines, and why are they counting on me?"

"Didn't Pierre tell you?" When I shake my head, she shrugs. "Ah, perhaps he wanted to surprise you."

"Yes, he's full of surprises," I mutter.

Amélie places her hand on my arm. "I knew you would be perfect for this job when I read your articles on *Art Girl Moderne*."

I'm stunned. *Art Girl Moderne* is an obscure webzine run by a friend of mine. Its readership is small. I mean, really small. You could fit all of them on a sectional couch from Ikea and still have room for Lou and his bag of potato chips. How the manager of a chic art gallery in Paris stumbled across it is beyond me.

"Your take on Rembrandt's brush strokes was . . . what is the word I am looking for?"

"Boring?"

"*Non*, not boring." She smiles at me. "I could tell from the minute I make your *conaissance* that you could never be boring. It was insightful. That is the word—insightful."

Considering I've never been called insightful in my life, I'm still pretty sure that the word she meant was "boring."

"I received your paperwork and a copy of your work visa and everything is in order. Normally, we pay employee salaries in arrears. But, you probably have many expenses settling into a new city." Amélie hands me a pad of paper and a fountain pen. "Write down your account details and I will arrange for an advance to be transferred to your account."

And just like that, I've been bulldozed into accepting the job in the most charming French way.

* * *

"Mia, Mia, are you there? I can't see you."

Celeste is on the other end of the phone, trying out her new video chat app, while I'm walking along the Seine River back to my rat-infested apartment. It's a long walk, especially with luggage in tow, but taking a taxi is out of the question. Even though Amélie is going to give me an advance on my salary, things are still tight financially.

"Turn the phone around. Good, there you go. Now I can see your face. Can you see mine?"

"I can. Don't you look pretty, dear. Paris must be agreeing with you."

"I don't know about that. I've been here less than twelve hours and my life is a mess." I slump down on a bench, being careful to avoid stepping in a pile of dog poop. It reminds me of the guys Ginny was stuck next to on the train from Rome to Bologna. Their overpowering body spray smelled like a cross between dog poop and bubblegum. Not a winning combination.

"A mess?" A crease forms on Celeste's brow. "What happened?"

I shake my head. "Oh, never mind. I'm fine, really."

"Fine is what donkeys are after they've had a carrot. You, young lady, are not fine."

"Donkeys? Carrots?"

"Haven't you ever fed a donkey a carrot?"

I chuckle. "Not that I can remember. Do guinea pigs count?"

"No, dear. Donkeys and guinea pigs are completely different when it comes to carrots."

"They are?"

"Trust me on this one. Anyway, let's get back to what's wrong."

My feet are aching and I could use a break, so I settle back against the bench and fill her in on everything that's happened with Pierre, from the bouquet of croissants he presented me with to discovering he has a secret life.

"You know what George Burns said about love, don't you?"

"Who's George Burns?"

Celeste blinks her eyes rapidly. "Did you just ask who George Burns is? He was only the funniest man in show biz. Sexy too."

"I think you mean Bruce Willis. The perfect combination of deadpan delivery and a receding hairline."

"Bruce who?"

"You know, *Die Hard*."

"Die hard? Why would I want to do that? I'd rather die soft. Like a Tootsie Roll."

I shake my head. "I think we're talking about two different things."

"I was talking about love."

"I thought you were talking about George Burns?"

"I was. Anyway, he said that love is like a toothache. It doesn't show up on x-rays, but you know it's there."

"My teeth feel fine."

"But your heart doesn't. You've grown attached to Pierre. It always hurts when we find out someone isn't who we thought they were. That's what happened to me with . . . never mind."

"Hurt seems a stretch," I say. "He's just a guy."

"He's more than that."

"Okay, I'll admit it. I thought he was my friend. But friends don't deceive each other like that."

"Did he tell you he was poor?"

"Well, no, not exactly in so many words."

"So how did he deceive you?"

"By not being . . . well, who I thought he was."

"How is he different now that you know he has money?"

"He's a stuck-up snob."

"He's the same person, dear. It's just your perception of him that's changed. Love is about seeing who someone is, despite their outer trappings."

"I'm not in love with him," I scoff. "I'm . . ."

"You're what?"

"I was attracted to him, okay? But that's it. Insta-attraction, but not insta-love. Fortunately, there are a million cute guys in Paris." I scan the area, then turn the phone so that Celeste can see. "Like that one there."

"You mean the mime, dear?"

"No, not him. The man next to him. The one putting something in the trash can."

"I hate to break it to you, but I don't think he's throwing something out. He's going through the garbage. Poor soul, I think he's homeless."

The guy I had been talking about has already walked away, but Celeste is right. There's another man standing by the trash can. I take a closer look and frown. "Oh, I think you're right. He looks like he sleeps on the street. I might end up sleeping on the street too if my apartment doesn't work out."

"But you're not homeless, dear. You have a lovely hotel suite to stay in while you get your feet on the ground. If I can offer some words of wisdom, you've been fortunate enough to have been given some unexpected blessings. Don't let your pride get in the way. Take the job. Take the offer of temporary housing. Then prove everyone wrong. That's something you like doing, right? Proving people wrong?"

After a few more minutes of motherly advice, Celeste hangs up. I've decided she's half-right. I'll keep the job at the art gallery, but staying at the hotel is a step too far.

I scrounge in my backpack to see if I have any loose change. My feet are killing me and I still have a long walk to my apartment. To my surprise, I find a twenty-euro note tucked in a zippered compartment. I have no idea how it got there, but I don't care. It's my lucky day. I can afford a subway ticket and dinner.

As I head toward the Pont Neuf Métro station, I think about my recent spate of good luck. I look down at the money in my hand, then tap the homeless man on the shoulder and hand it to him. Time to pass some of that good luck along. A little more walking won't hurt me.

After what seems like an eternity, I finally arrive at my apartment building. There have been some changes since I was here earlier. Instead of waiting for me inside, the rats are sitting on the stoop like some sort of welcoming committee. I think the price of entry is a croissant. The smell of the garbage has a more nuanced quality to it. "Nuanced" being a polite way of staying that the stench is unbearable. And there's a new front door.

I distract the rats with a roll of breath mints, then try to open the door. But it won't budge. Probably because it's not so much a door as it is a piece of plywood firmly nailed in place. And this time, I don't have Pierre to help me pry it off.

After breaking a fingernail, I notice a sign affixed to the side of the building. My heart sinks when I read it—*bâtiment condamné*.

Swell. The building is condemned, the rats have devoured the breath mints that I was going to have for dinner, and my feet are killing me. But what's even worse is that I'm going to have to swallow my pride and accept Pierre's offer to stay at the hotel.

6 - Pastry Overload

It's been a long couple weeks of hide and seek. Pierre keeps looking for me, and I keep hiding. Easier said than done when you work in the same hotel. Fortunately, he's been on the night shift while I've been working days. It also helps that both of us have been crazy busy in our spare time. He's been focused on projects related to the family business, while I've been completely absorbed helping Amélie and Madame Vernier curate an exhibition at the gallery.

I'm pretty excited about the exhibition. It's right up my alley—photographs of animal-inspired tattoos—and what's even better is that all the proceeds are going to be donated to a no-kill dog shelter. Working with the premier tattoo artists in Paris and world-renown photographers has been a dream come true. For the first time in my life, I feel like I'm doing what I'm meant to be doing and, more importantly, that I belong in the art world.

But there's a lot to get done. Everything has to be ready in time for the launch party. It's the perfect excuse for avoiding Pierre. While I had sent him a gracious text thanking him for helping me land the job and finding me a place to stay, I haven't wanted anything else to do with him. Hence, the elaborate game of hide and seek we have going on.

By the time the end of my second week at the art gallery rolls around, I've become a pro at it.

I'm in the back room on Sunday afternoon framing photographs, when I hear a familiar voice ask Amélie, "Is Mia here?" Setting aside the mat board and cutter I'm using, I crouch behind some large canvasses propped up in the corner.

Amélie rats me out. "I think she's in the back, *cheri.*"

I hear him walking toward the rear of the gallery, each of his custom-made leather shoes making a distinctive sound as he traverses the marble floor. Can footsteps be sexy? If so, his certainly are. As his firm, confident, masculine steps near my hiding spot, I inch backward and hold my breath. There are times when being as short as I am comes in handy, like today. Squeezing into tight spots has become a new specialty of mine.

After a few moments, I hear Pierre's footsteps retreating back into the gallery.

"She's not there," he says to Amélie. "Can you let her know I stopped by when you see her? I texted her last night, but she didn't respond."

I continue to stay hidden. Pierre may be trying to outfox me, leaning against the counter in the gallery, waiting patiently for me to reveal myself. After ten minutes, I decide the coast is clear. But before I can emerge from behind the canvases, I hear the sound of a pair of shoes coming into the back room. It's not Pierre. These footsteps are brisk and impatient, with a sharp staccato clicking noise that high heels make.

They're followed by two other sets of footsteps. The first is another set of high heels, but they have a more gentle quality to them. I know this sound—those heels belong to Amélie. The other set is unfamiliar to me.

My legs cramp up as Amélie and the other woman discuss a display of textile art. Apparently, it's not up to the standards that this other woman expects. Amélie handles the criticism gracefully. If I was in her place, I would have bopped the other lady in the nose by now.

But as their conversation progresses, I realize why Amélie is being so conciliatory. The other woman is *la directrice de l'hôtel.* Generally, it's not a good idea to bop your boss in the nose.

I massage my calf, willing the two of them to stop talking and go on their merry ways. As I reach down to rub my ankle, something licks my hand. Stifling a yelp, I pray that it's not an extraordinarily large rat looking for a croissant. I curl up into a tight ball and close my eyes, but the creature continues to advance toward me, panting heavily in its quest for French pastries.

"Lyonette, *ici*," the hotel director orders.

Lyonette ignores the command, instead pushing its face into mine. That's when I realize, much to my relief, that this isn't a giant rat, it's a poodle.

"Nice doggie," I whisper.

The poodle responds by growling at me. Okay, not such a nice dog after all. As the growls increase in intensity, the poodle shakes, as though it has just had a refreshing swim in the lake. With each shake of its body, the canvasses rock back and forth. I try to stroke the dog to calm it down, but as I place my hand on its fur, it barks loudly and lunges at me. The canvasses crash to the floor, my hiding spot with them.

"Mia, what are you doing down there?" Amélie asks.

I feel my face grow warm as I look up. The director is tapping her foot, her arms folded across her chest. Like Amélie, she has that effortless Parisian chic vibe to her. Her burgundy Chanel suit is accessorized with pearls, and her dark hair is pulled back into an elegant twist.

Lyonette has a similar chic vibe going on with a classic poodle cut, a pearl collar, and burgundy bows on her ears.

"Uh, I dropped something?" I make a show of searching the floor, crawling on my hands and knees and poking under shelves and tables.

"*Assis*," the *directrice* commands.

So I sit on my haunches. The dog does too.

She smiles approvingly at Lyonette, then frowns at me. Turning to Amélie, she tells her to take care of the problem.

"*Oui, madame*," Amélie says before following her back out to the main gallery.

I look at the dog, trying to decide which one of us is the problem that needs to be taken care of.

"It's me, isn't it?" I ask Lyonette.

The poodle gives me a haughty look that seems to say, "Duh, of course it's you."

A deep voice with a British accent says, "I don't think she likes you."

I raise my eyes and see Pierre leaning against the door frame, a bemused look on his face. I can't tell whether he's bemused by the ridiculous bellboy uniform he's wearing or by the fact that I'm sitting on the floor trying to interpret dog expressions.

"Who? The dog or the hotel director?"

He laughs. "Possibly both."

Amélie scoots in behind him and helps me to my feet. Then she snaps her fingers and tells Lyonette to go find her mistress. As the dog departs, she gives me a look that says, "So long, loser."

Avoiding eye contact with Pierre, I brush dust off my black high-waisted trousers and smooth down my fuchsia leopard print top. "Oh, well, it's not like it matters since I'm not going to be working here anymore."

Amélie gasps. "You cannot quit."

"I'm not quitting. You're firing me."

"Why would I fire you?"

"Well, I assumed by the way your boss told you to 'take care of the problem' that I didn't have a job here any longer."

Amélie smiles at Pierre. "If people were fired every time they displeased her, there would be no one left working at the hotel. Her bark is worse than her bite."

"Whose bite? The dog's or the director's?"

"Both," Amélie and Pierre say in unison.

"Are you sure?"

"Positive," Amélie says. "Within an hour, she will have forgotten that you were crawling on the floor. What did you drop, by the way?"

"Oh, I don't think she dropped anything," Pierre says. "I think she was hiding from me."

"Why would I hide from you?" I ask.

"I text, I call, but you never respond. Whenever I come to the gallery to speak to you, you're mysteriously on break. It's obvious. You're avoiding me. And I want to know why."

The last thing I want to do is get into this with Amélie watching us. I run my fingers through my hair. "I'm just busy, that's all."

"No, I don't think that's it." As he shakes his head emphatically, his pillbox hat slides off and rolls toward me.

When I hand it to Pierre, his fingers brush against mine, sending a jolt of electricity through my body. I had forgotten what his touch feels like. It feels good. Real good. Too good.

I step backward, shoving my hands in my pockets. "Yes, it is. I'm super busy with the exhibition. Lots to do."

"Too busy to go to the *Star Wars* convention on Saturday?"

"Tickets sold out months ago." I shrug. "Even if I had the time to go, I couldn't."

"It just so happens that I have tickets."

I lock eyes with him. "You do?"

"Uh-huh. So you'll come?"

Every fiber in my being wants to shout, "Yes!" Not because I want to spend time with Pierre, but because this is the *Star Wars* convention we're talking about. Who in their right mind passes up an opportunity to go to that?

Me, apparently. I hear myself coolly say, "Sorry, but I have to work on Saturday." Amélie starts to contradict me, but I give her a warning look. "Yep, working all next weekend."

"I'll bet you twenty euros, which you still owe me by the way, that I can get you to change your mind," Pierre says.

"Sounds like easy money to me." I straighten my shoulders. This is going to be the easiest twenty euros I've ever made. I'm going to have no problem resisting Pierre.

Then he winks at me, and I suddenly realize this is going to be a lot harder than I thought.

* * *

Pierre's campaign is relentless. Every fifteen minutes, my phone buzzes with a *Star Wars*-related text from him, each ending with a link to the convention website. For the first few hours, I'm mildly amused, but by the time midnight rolls around, I'm over it. I'm wearing out the delete button on my phone, and I've run out of ways to say no.

I finally drift off to sleep, only to be woken at two in the morning with this text: *Roses are red, violets are blue. If you love* Star Wars, *may the Force be with you.*

I send back a GIF of Darth Vader that says, "Don't make me destroy you."

My phone goes silent after that.

I should be relieved. But I'm not.

I should be able to fall peacefully back to sleep. But I don't.

I should be able to stop thinking about Pierre's hazel eyes. But I can't.

All I seem to be able to do is stare at the ceiling, waiting for the sun to rise, wishing I could get the heir to the Toussaint fortune out of my head.

* * *

The next morning, I walk into work, hiding my bleary eyes behind a large pair of sunglasses. Before I put my purse in the back room, I check my phone again. Nope, no more texts from Pierre. I guess my Darth Vader GIF did the trick.

I push my glasses up on my head and sniff the air. Something smells wonderful, and I'm not just talking about the begonia-scented body wash I used in the shower.

"You have an admirer." Amélie sets a large gift basket on the counter.

My stomach growls when I pull back the red gingham fabric covering the contents. The basket is overflowing with croissants, small jars of raspberry and strawberry preserves, and a crock full of rich, creamy butter.

Amélie points at the card tied to the handle. "Who is it from?"

"It's not signed," I say as I hand it to her.

"Something to Chewbacca on," she reads out loud, then turns to me. "What does this mean?"

"It's a *Star Wars* reference."

"I have never seen this movie. What is a Chewbacca?"

It's way too early in the morning to explain what a Wookie is. I offer her a croissant instead. While Amélie breaks off a piece and delicately spreads butter and jam on it, she asks me why I'm not having one.

"Oh, I'm not hungry," I say, lying through my teeth. But I've accepted enough from Pierre. I'm not going to add more croissants to the list, no matter how delicious they look. I snap a picture of the gift basket and send it to Ginny and Isabelle.

Can you believe the nerve of this guy? Trying to win me over with croissants!

Isabelle responds right away. *The nerve. LOL.* Then she sends me a picture of what she's having for breakfast. *I bet you wouldn't say no to this strudel.*

Depends who gave it to me. If it was from Pierre, then I would have to refuse.

Ginny responds a few minutes later with a historical tidbit. *Did you know that croissants aren't originally French? An Austrian baker, August Zang, introduced the croissant in Paris in 1838. It's an adaptation of an old Austrian pastry, the kipferl, which dates back to the 1300s.*

I file that juicy little morsel away to taunt Pierre with later.

After spending the first part of the morning helping an American couple decide between a stone sculpture by a Zimbabwean artist and an oil painting by an up-and-coming artist from the Bronx—they ended up buying both— I finally break down and devour a croissant. As I'm wiping away telltale crumbs from my blouse, Pierre walks into the gallery. Because he doesn't start his shift until the evening, he's dressed in regular clothes—jeans, a button-down shirt, and sneakers. It's a way better look for him than the organ grinder's monkey costume.

"I see you got my present," he says.

"Oh, was that from you?" I ask innocently. "The card wasn't signed."

"Do you get many pastry baskets from secret admirers?"

I shrug. "Oh, you'd be surprised."

He furrows his brow. "So I have competition?"

"Competition for what?" I ask with all the nonchalance I can muster.

"Not for what. For whom."

Now, I go in for the kill with full-on sarcasm. "For *whom* . . . look at you all fancy with your perfect grammar."

"What would you say?" he asks, his hazel eyes twinkling.

"I'd say for *who.* I'm sure that's wrong, but I didn't have all your advantages in life. How did you get that British accent, anyway? Boarding school?"

His eyes stop twinkling. "Boarding school isn't all it's cracked up to be."

I chew on my lip. There's a story there. Another secret.

But before I can ask him about it, he changes the subject. "So, what time should I pick you up on Saturday?"

I shake my head. "I told you. I can't go. I'm working all weekend."

"That's not what Amélie says."

"Sounds like a misunderstanding. You know how she's trying to improve her English."

"Our conversation was in French." He leans across the counter and plucks a croissant out of the basket. As he tears off a piece, he says, "So, that's settled. You're free to come with me this weekend."

I fold my arms across my chest. This man is infuriating. Always assuming everyone is going to do what he wants, just because he's rich. I refuse to respond. If I stand here long enough, not saying anything, eventually he'll leave, right? Pouty resistance always wins in the end.

Geez, how long does it take to eat a croissant? I want to rip the pastry out of his hand and shove it into his mouth. I want to trace my finger on the side of his mouth and wipe that stray bit of strawberry preserves away. I want to touch his lips. I want to—

Stop it, Mia. Stop thinking about him.

"So, you realize that I'm going to keep sending you croissants until you say yes," Pierre says.

I stamp my foot. "For the love of all that is flaky, no more croissants."

"Fine. Challenge accepted." He gives me a cocky grin, then walks out of the gallery.

I put my head in my hands and groan. How does he always manage to turn the tables on me? What in the world does he have in store for me next?

* * *

Turns out what he has in store for me is more pastries and more *Star Wars* texts. On Tuesday, I find a basket of palmiers. As I crunch my way through the delicious palm-leaf shaped treats made out of puff pastry, I laugh at one of Pierre's riddles. *What do you get when you cross an elephant with Darth Vader? An ele-Vader.*

I text him back one of my own. *Why did Luke Skywalker cross the road? To get to the Dark Side.*

Good one, he texts back. *Pick you up at 10:00 on Saturday?*

I send back a GIF of Princess Leia haughtily saying, "no thanks," then shove my phone into my purse for the rest of the day.

* * *

Wednesday's basket is full of éclairs. All kinds of éclairs. Chocolate éclairs so decadent that you moan with pleasure as you eat them. Éclairs filled with a vanilla-flavored crème pâtissière and topped with a salted caramel icing and chopped hazelnuts (my personal favorite; I eat two). Others are crammed full of chestnut puree (definitely not my personal favorite; I only eat one bite), fruit-flavored fillings (the fruit makes them a healthier option, or at least that's what I tell myself), and coffee-flavored whipped cream (the perfect way to get a caffeine buzz).

By the time I work my way through the basket, I have a tummy ache. I think this is Pierre's plan. Wear me down with stomach pains, then offer to take me to the doctor's office if I say yes to the *Star Wars* convention.

Hah. The joke is on him. My skirt has an elastic band and I'm wearing a loose top. A bloated stomach is not a problem for this girl.

* * *

I come into work late on Thursday. Indigestion can really interfere with one's sleep. While the basket waiting for me on the counter is tempting— it's full of macaroons—I resist.

Pierre sends plenty of texts throughout the day. I'm not sure how he does it. Since he works the night shift, he should be sleeping during the day. I ignore them all. Just like I ignore the macaroons.

The thing is, I don't really like macaroons, which makes that easy. But when it comes to Pierre, he's a little harder to resist. The Force is strong in this one.

* * *

When I come into work on Friday, I'm greeted by . . . nothing. No pastry basket. No *Star Wars* texts. Nada. Zilch. Zippo. Or *rien*, as the French would say.

Good. Pierre has finally gotten the message. I'm not interested in him or his pastries.

Amélie nudges me. "Mia, I think someone is here to see you."

Han Solo is standing in the doorway. Well, it's not Han Solo himself— he's a fictitious character, after all. No, it's Pierre dressed up as the captain of the *Millennium Falcon*. And, boy, does he look good. Ridiculously good. He sure can pull off the look of an interstellar smuggler—fitted black pants tucked into boots, a white shirt layered under a vest, and a holster slung around his hips.

Pierre winks at me, then spins around. "How do I look?"

"You know exactly how you look," I mutter. "Hot."

"What was that?" he asks.

"You're missing your blaster."

He looks down at his holster. "Oh, I must have left it back at my apartment. But don't worry, I'll have it with me tomorrow."

"Tomorrow?"

"Uh-huh. The Star Wars convention. Since you already have a Princess Leia costume, I thought I'd wear my Han Solo one." He strokes my cheek with his finger and lowers his voice. "You haven't forgotten our date tomorrow, have you, *cherie*?"

Now I know how Princess Leia felt when she was outcharmed by Han Solo. No wonder she let him kiss her on the *Millennium Falcon*.

"Our date," I say slowly.

"Yes, our date," he whispers in my ear.

Then he pulls back, giving me a cocky grin. "Ten o'clock. Don't be late, your highness."

7- The Best Lightsaber Ever

My phone buzzes, alerting me to the fact that Pierre will be here any minute now to pick me up. I smooth down my white gown and inspect myself in the full-length mirror. This is one of my favorite Princess Leia costumes. The flowing material, high collar, and bell sleeves flatter my figure, and the flat boots are comfortable.

Everything looks authentic, except for my hair. While I have it styled in the classic cinnamon bun style that Carrie Fisher wore in the original *Star Wars* movie, my hair is blonde instead of dark brown. I had considered dyeing it last night, but I ran out of time.

After adjusting my metallic belt, I pick up the lightsaber lying on the bed. Should I bring it with me or not? Princes Leia didn't wear a lightsaber with this outfit. It wouldn't be authentic. But, on the other hand, it's a lightsaber. Everything looks better with a lightsaber.

I hear a knock on the door. When I open it, Pierre lets out a low whistle. He motions for me to twirl around, and I oblige. Not because he wants me to, but because I like how my dress swirls around my ankles.

"You look fantastic," he says. "This is my favorite Princess Leia look."

"Hmm. I thought most guys preferred the metal bikini she wore in *Return of the Jedi*."

"Not me. I like it when something is left to the imagination." He winks at me. "And I have a great imagination."

I step back and examine his outfit. It's the same Han Solo costume that he had on yesterday, but somehow it looks even better today. I twirl my finger in the air. "Fair's fair. Turn around." He spins around, and I realize what's different. He's had a haircut and his shirt doesn't have a collar. The combination of those two things means that the very top of his tattoo is visible when he bends his neck at just the right angle. The black and gray ink is tantalizing. What does the rest of the tattoo look like? As I wonder what lies underneath Pierre's shirt, I realize that I have a pretty great imagination too.

* * *

I don't need a map to know when we've arrived at the convention center. The people standing in line look like they came directly from the set of a *Star Wars* movie. There are the usual costumes—multiple Princess Leias, Luke Skywalkers, and Han Solos—but there are also some fascinating alien creatures. Like the Quarren, who have four tentacles protruding from their jaws, menacing Tusken raiders, and amphibious Gungans.

"Wow, look at that," I say.

"Those guys? Don't you think they're a little tall to pull off Ewok costumes?"

"No, that lightsaber." I pull a napkin out of my backpack and wipe drool off the side of my mouth. Yes, I'm drooling. And, no, I'm not embarrassed because that's how awesome this lightsaber is. Anyone would drool over it.

"You already have one."

My eyes grow wide. "But not like that one. See the intricate carvings on the titanium hilt and the handcrafted blade? That is the ultimate in lightsabers."

"Why don't you buy one?"

"Why don't you buy one?" I say in a mocking tone. "Just like a billionaire. You see something you like and you buy it. You don't think twice about how much it costs. Whatever you want is yours for the taking."

"Who said that I'm a billionaire?"

"It's an educated guess." I tick the evidence off on my fingers. "Boarding school in Britain, custom-made shoes, a polo horse—"

"Who told you I have a polo horse?"

"Amélie."

"I think she might have meant a pool house. We have one at the place in Aruba."

"I stand corrected," I say dryly. "The pool house. Oh, yeah, and there's one other tiny giveaway—you're the heir to the Toussaint fortune."

For once he doesn't look cocky. He takes a deep breath, then exhales slowly. "You're right. I do come from money. And sometimes I forget that not everyone is as fortunate as me. It's something I'm working on. Forgive me?"

I feel his fingers wrap around mine. "You're holding my hand."

He glances down. "Oh, is that what that is? It felt rough and scaly. I thought it was some sort of tentacle."

"My hand isn't rough. I moisturize regularly."

He caresses the back of my hand. "You might need to add an anti-scaling lotion to your beauty routine."

I let out an indignant huff and try to pull my hand away, but he holds on firmly. "I'm just kidding. Your hands are smooth and silky. They feel almost humanlike. I don't think anyone here would suspect that you're really an alien in disguise."

I laugh despite myself. "I'm glad to know that I have everyone fooled. But seriously, you shouldn't be holding my hand."

He furrows his brow. "Why?"

"Because we're in public."

"I'm only holding your hand." He stares intently into my eyes. "It's not like I'm kissing you . . . or worse."

My body tingles as I imagine what he means by "worse." Then I yank my hand away. "I don't believe in public displays of affection."

"Just because you don't believe in something doesn't mean it isn't real. The Force is a prime example. Han Solo doesn't believe in it, but we both know it's real."

I put my hands on my hips. "You know what I mean."

"Fine. I'll just hold your hand and kiss you in private." He leaves the word "worse" unsaid.

***

"That panel was amazing," I say as we walk out of the auditorium. "Can you believe Yoda was almost played by a monkey?"

"A monkey could never have pulled that performance off. I'm glad they went with a puppet instead," Pierre says. "Are you hungry?"

"I could eat. Provided it's not croissants. I think I've had my fill of them for a while."

Pierre leads me to the VIP lounge. The attendant takes one look at his pass, then quickly removes the red velvet rope to let us in. As we enter the room, a waiter holds out a tray of crystal glasses.

"*C'est quoi?*" Pierre asks.

"And you call yourself a Star Wars fan," I say. "It's blue and green milk, like they drank in *A New Hope*."

"Yes, miss," the waiter says in halting English. "But it is, how do you say?"

He shoots off rapid-fire French at Pierre, half of which I follow.

"It has a kick to it," Pierre explains. "Like a white Russian."

"Oh, it has liquor in it," I say.

"Which color do you prefer?" Pierre asks.

"Green," I say. "No blue. No, I mean green. No—"

Pierre smiles and takes the tray from the waiter. "Why don't we try them both?"

As I sink into one of the couches scattered around the room, Pierre sets the tray on the coffee table. He sits next to me, then offers me a glass of blue milk. He watches me intently while I sample it. "What do you think?"

"It's good, but I think I need to sample the green to be sure." After a few more sips of each color, I say, "They're both good."

"I prefer the green. I'm surprised you don't have a favorite. You usually have an opinion about everything."

"Well, not everything."

He cocks his head to one side. "Really? What can't you make up your mind about?"

I set my glass down on the table. No more milk for me. The alcohol is going to my head and I'm afraid if I have any more, I'll babble out something I'll regret, like "You. I can't make up my mind about you. You've got a geeky quality that I love, but you're also rich. And rich guys can't be trusted."

"You seem to have a problem with my background," he says.

"What are you talking about?"

"You just said that rich guys can't be trusted."

My face grows warm. "I said that out loud?"

"Yes. Your enunciation was crystal clear. You don't trust me because of the family I was born into. But it's not like I chose my parents. Did you choose yours?"

"Well, of course not."

"Would you change your background if you could?"

"No, not at all," I say firmly. "Sure, my parents can be annoying, and they don't understand why I want to work in the art world, but they gave me the values and work ethic that I have today."

"Amélie talks about your work ethic all the time."

"All the time? How often do you see her?"

"I go to their place once a week for dinner. Jean-Paul and Amélie are like second parents to me." He strokes his chin. "You should come one night."

"You can't invite me to dinner at someone else's place."

"That's true. I should invite you to dinner at my place."

"Oh, you want me to come to your mansion?"

"I don't live in a mansion. I live in an apartment, just like normal people."

I raise my eyebrows. "Normal people? Let me ask you something. Do you have a doorman at your apartment building?" He nods, looking abashed. "Okay, then, not exactly like normal people."

The silence gets awkward and I'm glad when a waiter comes by bearing a tray of canapés.

"Oh, mousse de saumon," Pierre says. "They're my favorite. You have to try it."

He hands me a small slice of rye bread spread with a spread of smoked salmon, sour cream, and lemon juice. I devour it in two bites. He smiles and hands me another. This one I scarf down in just one bite.

Pierre's eyes light up. "Ah, I see escargot over there."

As he waves the waiter over, I gulp. It's going to take a lot of blue and green milk before I work up the courage to eat snails.

Fortunately, by the time the waiter comes over, he's out of escargot. I breathe a sigh of relief. Before Pierre can search out another waiter with a tray loaded up with slimy garden pests, I distract him by pointing out an adorable toddler dressed up as Yoda. His mother is crouched on the floor, taking pictures as he walks toward her. When he tumbles to the ground and starts bawling, she rushes over and soothes him.

"Oh, poor thing," I say.

Pierre presses his fingers against the bridge of his nose and breathes rapidly, almost as though he's hyperventilating.

"Don't worry. He'll be fine. Toddlers fall all the time. It's part of learning to walk." When the boy's mother tickles his belly, and he giggles, I say, "See, all better."

"It's not better," Pierre says, his voice cracking. "It will never be better."

I place my hand on Pierre's arm and give him a gentle squeeze. "Hey, what's going on?"

He takes a few deep breaths, then says softly, "I'm sorry. They reminded me of something, that's all."

"Who? The mom and her son? What do they remind you of?"

"They remind me of my mother." Pierre drains the contents of his glass. "Of my birth mother. Today is the anniversary of the day when she abandoned me and my father. I was that boy's age. Seeing how sweet his *maman* is with him . . ."

He picks up another glass of milk, considers it, then sets it back on the tray. He slumps back into the couch and stares vacantly into space.

I'm at a loss. What do you say when someone tells you that their mother left him? Turns out, I don't need to say anything. Pierre twists his body around to face me, then tells me everything. He barely pauses to catch a breath. I learn how devastated his father was. He didn't know how to deal with raising a small child. So there were nannies and boarding school. His father kept his distance, engrossing himself in his work, acquiring hotels across the globe.

"Things got better when my father met my mother," Pierre says.

I furrow my brow. "Met your mother? You mean she came back?"

"No, my birth mother died shortly after she left us, in a tragic accident. The woman I'm talking about is technically my stepmother, but I think of her as my mother. They got married when I was eight years old. My father refers to her as his lioness. She's fierce. She'll do anything to protect us."

"I'd love to meet her."

"Would you?" Pierre chuckles softly. "Then come with me to the charity ball on Saturday night."

I shake my head. "A charity ball? That really doesn't sound like my cup of tea."

"But it's for a good cause. We're raising money for orphanages in Africa."

"I'd rather make a donation than get dressed up and make small talk with people I don't know."

"Do it for me."

His hazel eyes are twinkling again, and I'm almost tempted to say yes. But I have too many unpleasant memories of going to charity balls at the country club with my ex. His family and friends looked at me with disdain, making it clear that they thought I came from the wrong side of the tracks.

Pierre grabs my hands and caresses them. "Please, do it for me. I have to give a speech and I'm nervous about it. If you're by my side, I'll—"

"You? Nervous? You practically reek of self-confidence."

"I guess I'm a good actor. Maybe they should cast me in the next *Star Wars* film."

I grin. "I'd love to see you wear a Wookie costume."

"I bet you would. All that fur. A total turn-on." He gives me a smile that makes my toes curl, then turns more serious. "I took a year off after college and spent it working in Africa at an orphanage. The experience was . . ." He struggles to find the words to express the impact it had on him. Finally, he says, "Actually, it doesn't matter what I got out of the experience. What matters is helping children who have lost their parents. I set up this charity to raise money for orphanages across Africa. This is our inaugural fundraiser. Hence, the speech. Hence, my nerves. Hence, I want you by my side."

"That's a lot of 'hences,'" I joke, trying to lighten the mood.

"So, *hence,* you're coming?"

"I'll be there."

He leans in, and I panic that he's going to kiss me in public. When his phone buzzes, I scoot off the couch and perch on a chair, the coffee table creating a barrier between the two of us. He laughs at my reaction.

I watch as he has a one-sided conversation with the person on the other end of the line. His responses are mostly variations of "*oui*" and "*non.*" After hanging up, he taps on his phone pensively for a moment, then turns to me. "I'm so sorry, I have to go. Some urgent family business has come up. Let me get you a taxi to take you back to the hotel."

I wave him away. "No need. I can take the Métro."

He glances at his watch. "Are you sure?"

"I'll be fine. Go."

He leans down and gives me a kiss on the cheek, then rushes off. I slouch back in the chair and sip on my blue milk. I've certainly learned a lot about Pierre this afternoon. His mother abandoning him, the charity work he does in Africa, and the fact that he thinks green milk tastes better than blue. But there are a few things I still need to find out about—the injury that meant he couldn't play rugby anymore, why he worked as a waiter on the cruise ship rather than at one of his family's hotels, and, perhaps most importantly, what the tattoo on his back looks like.

8 - Toilet Paper Mishaps

On the way to the charity ball, Pierre talks to his father on the phone. I know that he's disappointed his dad can't make it tonight, but he understands that the grand opening of a new Toussaint hotel in Thailand takes precedence.

While they chat, I amuse myself pushing buttons on the console next to me. The only other time I've been in a limousine was at my senior prom. Actually, it wasn't so much a limo as it was a converted hearse. While it did have a mini-bar, it was seriously grim compared to this sleek town car.

As he says goodbye to his dad, Pierre squeezes my hand. "I'm glad you came tonight. Isabelle thought you might try to get out of it."

"Isabelle? When did you speak to her?"

"I texted her yesterday."

I furrow my brow. "Why exactly?"

"I needed some info."

"Info about what?"

He leans over and playfully tugs my earlobe. "About you."

"Whoa. Wait, a minute. You're texting *my* friend to get information about me?" I pull out my phone and dial her number.

"That won't do you any good," Pierre says, glancing at his watch. "She just started her shift."

"How come you know her work schedule?"

"I know lots of things. For example, I know about the volunteer work you did back home, and I know all about this guy Isabelle just met. To be honest, I'm not so sure about him."

I hold up my hands, at a loss for where to start. What else has Isabelle told him, and how come I don't know about this guy she met?

"I think it's pretty amazing what you did," Pierre says. "Not everyone would volunteer to work with guys like that. That's pretty brave."

"Everyone needs a second chance," I say quietly. "Isabelle shouldn't have told you about that. It's not something I like to tell people about."

"Don't worry, it will be our little secret."

"Well, I hope you're better at keeping secrets than Isabelle is."

As we pull up to the hotel where the charity ball is being held—also a Toussaint property—I take a deep breath. I watch as a glamorous couple gets out of the car in front of us. The woman's evening dress is haute couture, the diamonds dangling from her ears are the size of golf balls, and her hair and makeup are runway ready.

My dress is off-the-rack. Seriously off-the-rack. I literally found it on the floor in a second-hand shop. After steaming the wrinkles out and strategically placing a rhinestone broach over a stain, it was as good as new. Just not as good as haute couture.

My jewelry consists of a necklace my parents gave me for my eighteenth birthday. It might not be encrusted with diamonds, but its value is priceless to me. My hair and makeup, on the other hand, might just pass muster. Amélie helped me get ready, putting my hair into an elegant updo and giving my face an evening look that's chic and timeless.

After Monsieur and Madame Glamour pose for the photographers, our car advances to the entryway. I start to open the passenger door, but Pierre tells me to wait while the chauffeur walks around to my door. I feel like I'm in a fairy tale when he helps me out of the car.

Pierre takes over after that, tucking my hand through his arm and escorting me across the red carpet to the hotel entrance. As we pause for photographs, I whisper, "The volunteer work I do is nothing compared to this."

He puts his arm around me and draws me toward him. In hushed tones, he says, "In all honesty, this is just an excuse for people to get dressed up, show off, and feel good about themselves because they donated money to a good cause. Most of them are oblivious to the harsh realities that the orphans they're supporting have to deal with."

"But you're raising money."

"Yes, but it costs a lot to put on an event like this. Besides, money isn't everything."

As we make our way inside, I think about what he's said. If push came to shove, would Pierre really think that money isn't everything? Looking around at the wealth and opulence surrounding me, I'm not so sure.

* * *

"You sure you'll be okay on your own?" Pierre asks.

We're standing at the front of the ballroom, and the hotel staff wants to test Pierre's microphone. "I'll be fine," I say. "It's not like I'm the shy, retiring type."

He grins. "No, you certainly aren't."

Actually, I am feeling a little nervous about mingling with this crowd, but there's no way I'm going to let Pierre know that. He has a speech to give, and the last thing he needs to worry about is me. "Go shake your money-maker," I say.

"I'll find you as soon as it's over," he says over his shoulder as he's whisked away.

I try talking to a few people, but not even the waiters passing out champagne will give me the time of day. Maybe I have lipstick smudged on my teeth? Maybe there's a stain on my dress that I didn't notice? Maybe they're all just a bunch of snobs.

Feeling my eyes well up, I do what women have done since the invention of modern plumbing. Rush to the ladies' room to hide.

It takes me a while to find it, not helped by the fact that everyone pretends that they can't understand me when I ask them to point in the right direction. I may not be fluent in French, but I know enough to be able to ask where *latoilette* is. I even mimed what I was looking for, pointing at the general direction of my bladder, without any success.

Eventually, I stumble across the ladies' room. Although it does take me a while to figure out that's what it is. That's because the place is bigger than my parents' entire house. I have to wander through several rooms before I find the one containing toilet stalls. I don't need to go to the bathroom, but I do need the privacy it offers to regroup and get a hold of myself.

I perch on the edge of the toilet and stare at the door. Unlike many of the restrooms I'm used to, this one doesn't have things scrawled on it, like "Mandy loves Steve," "I like writing on walls," and "Believe in yourself."

Thank goodness for cell phones. You can text your friends for moral support even while hiding out in the ladies' room in an opulent hotel in Paris. I open my evening bag and pull mine out, then utter a curse. A fancy place like this doesn't have cell phone coverage? Unbelievable.

I wipe away a tear forming at the corner of my eye. *Get a hold of yourself, Mia. You need to go out there and support Pierre. You can do it.*

Another tear threatens to fall down my cheek and ruin my makeup. As I go to pull a piece of toilet paper off to dab at it, I hear a low growl. Lyonette, the hotel director's poodle, tunnels her way under the door, then grabs the end of the toilet paper from my hand and yanks hard.

Of course, they have high-quality toilet paper at this hotel. If you yanked at the toilet paper at my apartment back home, the roll purchased on sale at the local dollar store, it'd tear off easily. No, this stuff is industrial strength, while having a soft, luxurious feel—yeah, I don't know how they do that either.

"Hey, hang on a minute," I say to Lyonette. "Toilet paper is for humans, not dogs."

The dog gives me some serious side eye. Then she barks sharply at me. Her meaning is clear. "This toilet paper isn't meant for humans like you. Your derriere isn't worthy."

She tunnels back under the door, the toilet paper unwinding behind her. I push the door open to chase after her and run straight into the woman I least want to see—Lyonette's owner. Go figure. She's surrounded by a posse of glamorous women, all staring at me like I'm an alien from one of the *Star Wars* movie.

In between giving me disdainful looks, they take turns commenting on my appearance. They're speaking in French, probably assuming that the barbarian in front of them can't understand. But I do. Let's just say their comments aren't flattering.

I bite my tongue. You have no idea how hard this is, but the last thing I need is to lose my temper in front of the director, and then lose my job. Funny how not too long ago I would have walked away from the job and Pierre, but now . . . something's changed.

The director gives me an appraising look, but says nothing. After a beat, she summons Lyonette, then turns on her heel and walks out of the room, her posse following in her wake.

Two good things have come out of this incident. First, it's reminded me not to give a hoot what other people think of me. And, second, that stupid dog pranced out of the ladies' room with toilet paper stuck to her paw. Imagine how embarrassed she's going to be when she realizes it.

* * *

As he finishes his speech, Pierre locks eyes with me. I'm standing at the back of the ballroom, but I can see him winking from here. Making a fist pump in the air, I yell, "Whoot-whoot." He did such an amazing job. Eloquent, self-effacing, and inspiring, all wrapped up in one delectable package.

As I let out another "whoot-whoot," Lyonette rushes over and alternates between growling and barking at me. If she didn't look like she was about to fly at me in a rabid rage, I'd almost think the toilet paper stuck to her paw was comical.

A woman sitting at the table in front of me turns and gives me an icy stare. She calls Lyonette over and scratches her on the head, telling her what a good doggy she is. Why this pretentious poodle deserves praise is beyond me.

I wait while Pierre makes his way toward me. It takes him a while as people stop to congratulate him. I hope they're also handing him fistfuls of euros for the orphanages. When he eventually reaches me, he brushes his fingers up my arms, across my shoulders, then cups my face in his hands.

Before he can kiss me, I turn my head. "Whoa, not here, mister. Half of France's upper crust, along with one very obnoxious poodle, are watching."

"But the French are very passionate people. They see nothing wrong with kissing a beautiful woman in public."

"This isn't about them. This is about me." I twist my body, slipping out of his grasp. Pointing at the nearest exit, I lead him out of the ballroom and into the adjacent courtyard. Looking around to make sure we're not observed, I pull him behind a large trellis of roses that hides us from view.

I smile. "Well, what are you waiting for?"

"Is this the American version of hide and seek?" He jokes as he peeks around the trellis. "Can we play tag next?"

"Yeah, tag, you're it." I punch him playfully. I feel his bicep tense as my knuckles graze him. I slowly unclench my fist, raking my fingers against his muscular arm. He shivers and his breath quickens. With my other hand, I do the same thing on his other arm. Then I trace a path with my fingernails from each of his arms to the center of his chest. When I reach the middle, I grab his lapels, pulling him toward me.

"I like how you Americans play tag."

Then he kisses me. It isn't a gentle kiss. It isn't a tentative kiss. It's the kind of kiss a man gives someone when he knows exactly what he wants. And he wants me.

He presses me against the wall, his kiss leaving me breathless.

The sensation is overwhelming.

Suddenly, he pulls back. His hazel eyes are unreadable. He holds his hands up as if he's surrendering.

I inhale sharply. Is he going to say this is a mistake? Is he going to make a hasty departure? My stomach is twisted in knots. He stares at me for a beat, then a cocky grin slowly spreads across his face.

He taps me on the arm. "Tag, you're it."

So I kiss him. It isn't a gentle kiss. It isn't a tentative kiss. It's the kind of kiss a woman gives someone when she knows exactly what she wants. And I want him.

I pull him toward me, my kiss leaving him breathless.

The sensation overwhelms me. I have no doubt that the sensation overwhelms him too.

Then a woman's sharp voice says, "Lyonette, *ici*," and I'm overwhelmed by a completely different sensation—fear. Fear of being discovered.

I send a silent prayer up to the gods of hide and seek—*Please don't let that horrible dog find us.*

The gods are apparently playing their own game of hide and seek because they're nowhere to be found. Lyonette barrels toward us, knocking down the trellis in the process.

"Pierre," the woman snaps.

Oh, no. I know that voice. It's the hotel director. Encountering her in the ladies' room was bad enough. Now she and her interfering poodle have to turn up and ruin everything.

I try to burrow into Pierre's chest. I'm short. Maybe she won't see me.

No such luck. Pierre turns, leaving me exposed. I give a half-hearted wave. She ignores me. Her dog, on the other hand, bares her teeth and growls.

Pierre smiles at the director, bending down to kiss her on each cheek. Then he turns and formally introduces me to her. "*Maman, je te présente Mia. Elle travaille à la galerie d'art.*"

You don't have to be fluent in French to understand the critical word in that sentence—*maman*. The director of the hotel is Pierre's mother. She may not have given birth to him, but she's the woman he considers to be his mom. Fluency in French isn't required to translate her response either. Her body language makes it crystal clear—she's going to do everything in her power to keep the two of us apart.

9 - Sweating in a Snowsuit

Pierre's mother crooks her perfectly manicured finger at him, then turns and walks briskly back into the ballroom. Lyonette trots along next to her, the toilet paper stuck to her paw flicking back and forth.

Pierre loosens his bowtie, then runs his fingers through his sandy-brown hair. "I better go talk to her. Wait for me here?"

He doesn't wait for my response. To be honest, I don't know how I would have replied.

I could have said something like, "Sure, no problem. I'll stay here and twiddle my thumbs while you explain to your mother why you're making out with an American girl who is clearly unsuited to your social standing."

Or maybe something along the lines of, "You don't seriously expect me to wait around while you run off with your tail between your legs like some sort of mama's boy? No way, buddy, I'm out of here."

I'm torn. Should I stay or should I go? With an old song from the punk rock band, The Clash, playing through my head, I weigh up the pros and cons.

If I go, then Pierre will know that I'm no pushover. He'll get the message that I'm a strong woman who does just fine on her own, thank you very much.

I smooth down my dress, straighten my shoulders, and inhale deeply. Yes, that's exactly what I'm going to do. I'm going to march on out of here, head held high.

But as I turn to leave, my stomach starts growling. "Hey, wait a minute, Mia," it says. "If you leave, you're going to miss a seriously good meal.

Lobster bisque to start, followed by steak au poivre, and finished off with apple tarte tatin. You don't want to skip that, do you? You can swallow your pride and stay, can't you? For little old me, please?"

I pat my tummy. "With all the pastries I've been eating, you're not all that little anymore. Besides, we don't want Pierre to assume he has me wrapped around his little finger, do we? He didn't even wait for my answer. He just assumed that I'd stay here, fixed to this spot, waiting for him to return."

"Well, I guess you do have a point," my stomach says, in between loud gurgles. "But, if we go, can we stop at that kebab place on the way back to the hotel?"

My heart decides to intervene. "Enough with this food talk. We're talking about how Mia feels, not how hungry you are." Beating rapidly, it adds, "This is exactly like what happened at that Halloween dance Mia and her ex went to."

I put my head in my hands, flashbacks to that night flooding my brain.

Naturally, the Halloween dance had been held at the country club. No surprise there. Folks like my ex don't exactly rent out the high school gym and rely on the local sub shop for catering when they have a party. Nope, they need valets to park their cars, attendants in the restrooms to hand them towels, and waiters to ensure the champagne keeps flowing.

I remember being so excited about my costume. I spent hours making a replica of the white snowsuit Princess Leia wore on the planet Hoth, keeping it a secret from my ex. When he picked me up, I twirled around, a huge grin on my face. But his only reaction was to raise his eyebrows and say, "Don't you think you're going to be hot?"

When we got to the country club, he was distant. Normally, I had to fend off his public displays of affection, but this time, he didn't even try to hold my hand. After getting me a drink, he told me to wait for me at the bar while he spoke with someone about an important business deal.

By "someone," he meant all the women in attendance. I watched as he flirted with the girls my age—all of whom were dressed up in sexy, skin-revealing costumes—fawned over the married ladies, and schmoozed the elderly widows.

I waited, and waited, and waited. Eventually, I had to remove my parka, totally ruining my Princess Leia look. He had been right. I was boiling. Boiling from how hot it was in the bar and boiling from rage as he continued to ignore me.

Eventually, his mother took pity on me. At least that's what, in my naivety, I thought it was at the time. But it really was condescension. While I wiped sweat off my brow, she suggested I go home and change into something more comfortable. She even offered to have her chauffeur take me back to my apartment, and then, once I was ready, she suggested that I text her son to come pick me up.

You can probably figure out what happened. I went home. I changed my clothes. I texted my ex to come get me. I waited for him to respond. I waited for him some more. I texted him again and waited even more. Eventually, I fell asleep on the couch, clutching my lightsaber to my chest like a security blanket.

A low growl jolts me back to the present. This time it isn't my stomach; it's Lyonette. The poodle is sniffing at the hem of my dress. Then she crouches on the ground near me, fixing her beady eyes on me, as if to say, "Have I got a little surprise for you."

I narrow my eyes. "Don't you dare pee on my dress."

Stepping back just in time, I scowl as she finishes her bio-break. When she's done, she scratches the flagstone patio, then barks sharply at me. Her meaning is clear. "Snap to it and clean this mess up, loser."

I give her the finger. Yes, that's what it's come to; I'm flipping dogs off. Realizing that the evening isn't going to get any better, I hightail it out of there, leaving Lyonette to find some other human to do her bidding.

* * *

Pierre texted me that night, asking where I had disappeared to. Rather than get into it, I told him that I had eaten one too many hors d'oeuvres and went home with an upset stomach. They say that if you're going to lie to someone, to base it on a partial truth. I *had* eaten too many hors d'oeuvres. Who can say no to crème fraîche tartlets? Or caramelized figs topped with smoky bacon? Not this girl. Plus, there was that kebab that I ate on the way back to the hotel. That didn't help matters.

The next day, it was easy to make excuses for not catching up. Pierre was busy with a board meeting for his charity during the day, then he worked the night shift. I was occupied at the art gallery with a constant stream of customers during the day, followed by spending the evening putting together promotional materials for the upcoming photography exhibition.

But now it's Monday, and I can't avoid him any longer. Probably because he's standing right in front of me holding a chocolate croissant.

"Is your stomach feeling better?" he asks, waving it under my nose.

The smell of chocolate is intoxicating. So is the smell of Pierre's cologne. I want them both. But I know that only one of these two temptations is good for me.

So I grab the high-calorie pastry from his hand.

He laughs while I cram it in my mouth. Ladylike I am not, especially when it comes to chocolate croissants.

"I guess you are feeling better. Dinner tonight?" he asks. "I know a place that serves the best cassoulet outside of Carcossonne."

I tap the glossy catalog on the counter. "Sorry, I have to proofread this so that we can get changes made in time for the opening night of the photography exhibition."

Yes, that was only partially true. I do have to review the catalog, but there's time before I have to get the final changes to the printer.

After Pierre leaves, Amélie gives me a stern look. "If you don't want to go out with him, you should just say so."

"It's not that I don't want to go out with him, it's that I don't want to . . ."

"Don't want to what, *chérie?*"

I opt for the full truth this time. "I don't want to fall for him."

She gives me a wry smile. "I think it's too late for that."

I chew on my lip. She's right. Not only am I telling fibs to Pierre, I'm lying to myself.

"Okay, I admit it," I say. "I like him. But I'm definitely not head over heels—"

"Head over heels? What does this mean?"

I scratch my head, trying to figure out how to explain the expression to her. Learning idioms in foreign languages is so hard, at least for me. Like, "*avoir un coup de foudre,*" which literally means to be struck by lightning. But its idiomatic meaning is "to fall in love at first sight." Not that I know anything about that. No, sirree. I'm not in love with Pierre. I'm just attracted to him.

"Head over heels?" Amélie prompts.

"It's when you're so madly in love with someone that it feels like you're tumbling head over heels."

Amélie still looks perplexed. "Tumbling?"

Sometimes, it's easier to demonstrate something than explain it. I look around to make sure that we're the only ones in the gallery. Then I do a somersault.

Okay, talk about a really bad decision. As my back strikes the floor, I realize that marble is really hard. There was a reason why we used padded mats back when I did gymnastics. I think I'm going to need chiropractic treatment after this. Being impetuous isn't all it's cracked up to be. If Isabelle had been in my situation, she would have thought through this carefully, decided demonstrating a somersault was extremely misguided, and figured out how to explain "head over heels" with actual words, rather than her body.

As I complete the somersault, I realize that this is actually worse than a bad decision. Pierre's mother is standing there, her jaw slack.

But, wait, it gets even worse. Lyonette is right by her side. Apparently, she interprets my gymnastic move as an invitation to play with her chew toy. And guess who her chew toy is.

* * *

I grab a wet washcloth from the bathroom in the back and sponge dog drool off my face and arms. It's going to be harder to fix the rips in my top.

Amélie knocks on the door. "It's safe to come out. They're gone."

I peek out, making sure there aren't any vicious dogs lying in wait. Who knows? Lyonette could have been holding a gun to Amélie's head, forcing her to tell me that the coast is clear. Realizing that the lack of opposable thumbs might make hostage-taking a challenge, even for the most determined poodle, I finally step out of the bathroom.

When Amélie sees me, she removes her cardigan and hands it to me. "This will hide the tears in your blouse. *La directrice d'hôtel* will have a replacement sent to your room later today."

"Pierre's mother is going to replace my top? I find that hard to believe."

"Why?" Amélie seems genuinely puzzled.

"Uh, well, she could have stopped her dog from attacking me in the first place."

"Attacking you? *Non*, the dog was playing. That means that she likes you. She does that all the time with Pierre. It is, what do you call it . . . tough-homing?"

"You mean rough-housing?"

She nods, repeating the expression slowly. "Knowing her, *la directrice* will most likely send you several new blouses. And they will all be designer labels."

"Of course, they will be," I say dryly. "That's probably why she sicced her dog on me. She thinks my off-the-rack clothes aren't good enough to work here at the hotel."

Amélie cocks her head to one side. "*Au contraire.* She appreciates people who have a unique sense of style like you do. It would not matter to her where you got your clothes."

"With people like her, that's all that matters."

"I think, perhaps, that is because you do not know her." Amélie leans in and lowers her voice. "She shows a tough exterior to the world, but there is good reason for that. She is a lioness. She protects those closest to her. Sometimes, that comes off as cold and hard, but, I promise you, that is not what she is like inside."

I don't want to get into an argument with Amélie. Ever since I came to Paris, she's taken me under her wing and given me the most amazing opportunities. "I'll have to take your word for it," I say evenly.

Her phone rings. "Ah, it is Madame Vernier. I have to take this."

While Amélie chats with Madame Vernier about catering for the opening night reception, I flip through the proof copy of the exhibition catalog. The photographs that will be displayed are amazing. It's art at multiple levels— the art created by tattooists using ink on skin and the interpretation of that art by the photographers through their camera lenses.

Amélie hangs up the phone and turns to me, a playful smile on her lips. "It is a good thing you told Pierre you are busy tonight."

I furrow my brow. A few minutes ago, Amélie was chastising me for lying to Pierre.

"I need you to go to the Voodoo Hoodoo Tattoo Parlor tonight. One of our featured tattoo artists is going to be there, and a photographer is going to be there to take pictures of him in action. I need you to be there to coordinate everything." She gives me a teasing look. "Unless you'd rather stay here and proofread the catalog?"

"No way. Visiting the Voodoo Hoodoo has been on my list of things to do in Paris. Count me in. Who's the tattoo artist?"

"Dominic de Santis."

I squeal like a guinea pig. And I'm not ashamed of it either. Dominic de Santis is my tattoo artist crush. My idol. If I could be a tenth as good as him, I'd be ecstatic.

As I twirl around in circles, squealing and clapping my hands together, Amélie laughs. Then she says more seriously, "You don't mind if Monsieur de Santis does a small tattoo on you for the photographs, do you? They want to document his process."

I gulp, realizing that I've never told Amélie that I don't have any tattoos of my own, let alone why. What would she think if I told her I'm afraid of needles? Heck, what would Dominic de Santis think? I don't know of any other tattoo artists who don't have tattoos. Is it time for me to bite the bullet and get one of my own?

* * *

When I arrive at Voodoo Hoodoo, I pause on the sidewalk and take it all in. Its quirkiness fits in with the other buildings on this uber-cool street. The building is painted black, the door is a glossy cherry apple red, and the shutters are made out of corrugated metal. But what really catches my eye are the hundreds of voodoo dolls that have been attached to the exterior.

I step closer to examine the dolls, shuddering when I see the pins stuck through some of them. It's not much different from getting inked—tiny needles being inserted into your skin. Can I really go through with getting a tattoo? Even if it's the world-renowned Dominic de Santis who would be doing it? How many people can say that they have a Dominic de Santis tat on their body? It doesn't get any more prestigious than that.

Why are you being so indecisive? Get a grip. This is a huge career opportunity for you. I take a deep breath and push open the door.

"Are you Mia?" a young woman with pink dreadlocks asks. "Madame Vernier said you would be helping out tonight."

When she holds out her hand to shake mine, I admire the watercolor-style tattoo that wraps around her forearm. Pastel flowers are interspersed with tropical birds. "The subtle shifts in color are amazing," I say.

"Thanks," she says. "One of the tattoo artists here did it for me."

"Do you work here?"

She nods. "I'm an apprentice."

"I remember my apprenticeship," I say. "Those two years just flew by."

"I'm going to start working on skin next week."

"That's so exciting." She gives me a faint smile while she fidgets with her large silver earrings. "Don't worry, you'll be fine. They wouldn't let you near skin if they didn't think you could do it."

"I hope you're right." After pulling her dreadlocks back into a colorful hair tie, she says, "Come on, let me introduce you to Dominic."

She leads me over to a small seating area at the back of the tattoo parlor. Dominic is sitting on a red velvet couch, sipping on a glass of sparkling water. After introductions, he motions for me to sit next to him.

"I was very happy when Madame Vernier arranged for you to be here," he says.

His Italian accent reminds me of Lorenzo, the guy who Isabelle and I rented an apartment from in Ravenna. But that's where the similarity ends. While Lorenzo looks like a male model, Dominic is the spitting image of my Uncle Joe. Short, balding, and wearing a polyester leisure suit straight from the 1970s. Uncle Joe wears leisure suits to all of our family gatherings. It's a look he adopted in the previous century and hasn't deviated from since. Dominic's leisure suit, on the other hand, screams quirky vintage, clearly meant to be an ironic fashion statement.

After offering me a glass of water, he gets down to business. "The photographer will be here soon. I'd like you to coordinate with him. It's essential that he understand the process of *tatouage* so that he can truly capture the essence of what we do. Because you are a tattoo artist, you will be able to explain things to him."

I bite my lip. He just called me a tattoo artist. Without a doubt tattoos are an art form, but am I an artist? Until today, I had always referred to myself as a tattoo artist. But now I'm sitting in the presence of Dominic de Santis, a man whose designs are legendary and whose skill at applying tattoos is unparalleled.

As if he can read my mind, he tells me that he's seen my portfolio. "I admire how you take paintings by the Old Masters and reinterpret them as tattoos. I was particularly intrigued by your take on Johannes Vermeer's *The Girl with the Pearl Earring*. Replacing the pearl with a skull and weaving a subtle pattern of insects into the dress the girl is wearing was genius."

"Really?" I stammer.

"You apprenticed under Henry Tusk, didn't you?" I nod. "He taught you well."

I take a sip of my water, stalling for time. I have no idea how to respond without babbling like an idiot. Dominic de Santis knows my work *and* he likes it. The bubbles tickle my nose. As I stifle a sneeze, I realize that there's only one thing I can say.

"Can I have your babies?"

I'm kidding. Of course, I don't say that. Although, the idea of plump little babies wearing polyester leisure suits makes me giggle. If I ever decide to make a career change, that's going to be it—designing retro babywear.

What I do say is, "Tattoo me."

And I mean it. I'm ready to get my first tattoo. Needles or no needles. I am going to overcome my fear.

Dominic looks taken aback. I guess it did come out like some sort of weird command.

"Madame Vernier said that you were going to do a small tattoo on me for the photographs," I say, the stammer back in my voice.

"Ah, yes, that was the original plan. But I have another model lined up. You are more valuable to me coordinating with the photographer since you know about *tatouage*." Dominic sets his glass down on the coffee table. "My assistant should be finished prepping the workstation and getting the model ready. Come, I will introduce you."

I follow Dominic into an adjacent room. A man is lying on a table face down. My eyes travel from his form-fitting jeans, up to his muscular back, and then to the sandy-brown hair on his head. While the assistant wipes the model's right shoulder blade with alcohol, I notice a tattoo on the base of the man's neck.

As I lean closer to examine it, Dominic says, "The shading of the elephant's ear is exquisite, don't you think?"

"The use of gray tones is stunning," I say. "Is it one of yours?"

"I wish I could take credit," he says. "But, alas, I cannot."

"What kind of tattoo are you doing today?" I ask.

While Dominic washes his hands, the assistant shows me the design.

My jaw drops. "Is that what I think it is? A yellow-bellied marmot?"

The man lying on the table turns his head and looks at me. His hazel eyes sparkle in the overhead lights.

"Pierre . . . you're the model?"

"I guess you don't have to work on the catalog after all tonight, Mia," he says. Then he winks at me.

10 - Planes, Trains, and Babbling Idiots

"So let me get this straight. You got Pierre to strip down for you?" Ginny asks.

Isabelle chimes in. "Exactly how naked was he?"

I'm stretched out on my bed, video chatting with my two friends. After the session at the tattoo parlor finished, I texted the two of them a picture of Pierre's back so that they could see the elephant tattoo on the base of his neck, as well as the new marmot tattoo inked by Dominic de Santis. Within seconds, they both texted back, wanting to get the full scoop.

"He wasn't naked," I say. "He only had his shirt off."

"So, half-naked," Isabelle says.

I roll my eyes. "Stop using the word 'naked.' You're making it sound dirty. It was purely professional. He was getting a tattoo and I was—"

"Drooling over his half-naked body," Isabelle says.

"I wasn't drooling," I say. "I was . . ."

"Salivating?" Isabelle suggests.

"Isn't that just another word for drooling?" I ask.

Isabelle shakes her head. "No, drooling is when saliva drips out of your mouth."

Ginny shudders. "Please don't talk about drooling. I just had a cat drool all over me. It's disgusting."

"Where are you, anyway?" I ask her. "That doesn't look like Boston in the background."

"I'm in Florida, visiting my mom," Ginny says.

"Is Preston with you?" I ask.

"Hang on a minute. We can talk about Ginny and Preston later. But first, I want to hear more about Pierre getting naked for Mia," Isabelle teases. "He looks pretty hot in that picture."

I prop up the pillow underneath my head. "Doesn't Dominic do fabulous work? I'm in awe of how he's incorporating Pierre's scar into the tattoo. See how he's turning it into the rock that the marmot is perched on? I can't wait to see how the tattoo looks once it's completed."

"How did Pierre get that scar, anyway?" Isabelle asks.

"I'm not sure," I say. "It wasn't exactly the time or place to ask him."

"But you are going to ask him, right?" Isabelle asks before taking a sip from her wineglass.

"What are you drinking?" I ask.

"Riesling." She holds up the glass so that we can get a better view. "In the Rhine and Moselle regions, this is what you traditionally serve Riesling in. It's called a Roemer glass. See the green stem and how it looks coiled?"

Ginny interrupts. "Isabelle, as much as I'd love to talk about the historical origins of the glass you're drinking out of, you do realize that Mia's trying to change the subject by getting you to talk about wine instead of Pierre, right?"

Isabelle laughs. "Very sneaky, Mia. Let's get back to your sexy Frenchman. When are you going to see him next?"

"Well, as I was leaving Voodoo Hoodoo, I got a call from Amélie. She's sending me to one of the Toussaint hotels in Carcassonne tomorrow so that I can set up an art display at their gift store."

"Where's Carcassonne?" Isabelle asks.

"It's in southwestern France, about fifty miles east of Toulouse."

Ginny gets a dreamy look in her eye. "I would love to go to Carcassonne. Did you know that the area has been occupied since Neolithic times? It was also strategically important to the Romans."

"You're such a history nerd," I joke.

"And you're a *Star Wars* nerd," she retorts.

Isabelle pipes up. "Just for the record, I don't have any nerdish qualities whatsoever."

"Yeah, that's a serious character flaw," I say.

She rolls her eyes. "I just googled Carcassonne. The place looks like it came straight out of a fairy tale. There's a castle with turrets and a drawbridge."

"That's the walled medieval city," Ginny says. "It's a UNESCO World Heritage Site."

"It's so romantic," Isabelle says. "You think you'd be happy being sent on a business trip there, Mia. All expenses paid, right?"

"Uh-huh," I say flatly.

After a beat, Isabelle says. "Oh, my gosh, I know what's going on. Pierre is going to be there too, isn't he?"

I nod. "His father asked him to attend a meeting on his behalf at the hotel."

"I thought he was a bellboy," Ginny says.

"He is. But while his father is away in Thailand, Pierre has to fill in for him at certain management events. Just my luck one of them happens to be in Carcassonne at the same exact time I'll be there."

"Good, that will give you an opportunity to ask him how he got that scar," Ginny says. "And if you're lucky, maybe he'll take off his shirt again so that you can examine it more closely."

"Do you think he has scars anyplace else?" Isabelle asks.

"Looks like I'm losing cell phone reception," I say, making a crackling sound with a crumpled up piece of paper. Then I quickly hang up before they start talking about Pierre removing any other of his clothing items.

* * *

There are times when I'm glad I'm afraid of flying, and this is one of them. Pierre needed to be in Carcassonne early, so he flew there on the company's private plane. A pretty flight attendant probably served him mimosas while he nibbled on freshly baked croissants. When he landed, a chauffeur was likely there waiting for him, ready to carry his bags to a plush town car.

Me, on the other hand, I'm currently sitting on a crowded train sipping a cup of cold coffee and eating a stale pastry. The only person who is going to be waiting for me when I arrive at the train station in Toulouse is the clerk at the car rental desk. He'll hand me the keys to a compact-size sedan, which I'll use to drive myself to Carcassonne.

The upside of my decidedly less luxurious travel arrangements is that I don't have to sit next to Pierre, look at Pierre, or speak to Pierre.

If I sit next to him, I'm going to be distracted by the smell of his sandalwood and bergamot cologne. Naturally, the smell of Pierre's cologne is going to compel me to glance at his jawline to see if he's freshly shaven or if he has a sexy five o'clock shadow going on.

Once I glance at his jawline, then my gaze will be drawn upward to his hazel eyes. But because his eyes are so mesmerizing, I'll quickly look away, and find myself staring at his suit jacket. I might glimpse one of his cufflinks. I'll probably be momentarily distracted wondering how much they cost, but then my mind will quickly turn to the shirt they're attached to. And we all know that that shirt is hiding broad shoulders, a sculpted chest, a muscular back, and two tattoos. You know exactly what will happen next. To get my mind off of what lies underneath that shirt, I'll start speaking to Pierre.

Speaking? Hah. More like babbling like an idiot. Something along the line of, "How did you get that scar on your back? Do you mind if I see it again? What's the deal with the marmot tattoo? Do you mind if I have another look at it? Can I touch it? It's purely professional interest on my part, I swear."

I shake my head, imagining his reaction to my babbling. His hazel eyes would twinkle, and he'd give me a cocky grin.

See how terribly wrong things could have gone if I had flown on the plane with Pierre? It's a good thing I'm on a crowded train, drinking cold coffee, and eating stale pastry. Better for everyone.

* * *

Pierre pokes his head into the gift shop later that afternoon. "There you are."

I set down the picture I was in the process of hanging, and watch as he walks toward me. Man, he looks so much better wearing a suit than his bellboy uniform.

As he bends down and kisses me on my cheeks, I breathe in the scent of his cologne.

"Do you have a cold?" he asks, offering me the crisp white pocket square from his suit jacket.

"No, why?"

"You're sniffling."

"Sniffling? No, I'm not sniffling. I'm sniffing."

"Sniffing what?"

Realizing how weird it would be to admit that I was sniffing his neck—that cologne of his is intoxicating—I fake sneeze. "No, you're right, I'm sniffling."

"But you said you were sniffing."

"Don't you think they should make a law against having words sound practically the same? Sniffling with the letter 'l' and 'sniffing' without one. It really makes communication complicated." Then I fake cough.

"Okay, I'm officially confused. Do you have a cold?" He grins. "Or do you have a cod? See what I did there with the missing 'l'?"

I laugh. "I most certainly do not have a fish. But I might be coming down with something."

Yeah, I'm coming down with something for sure. A serious case of falling for a guy who is all wrong for me.

"That's a shame," he says. "I have reservations at Auberge du Canard tonight and I was hoping you would join me."

I pause mid-fake sniffle. Auberge du Canard has won all sorts of awards, been featured on television, and consistently makes the top ten best restaurant lists. Not that any of that matters to me. But what does matter is that if I dine at Auberge du Canard, I can rub it in the faces of everyone at the country club back home.

One of the members—the creepy guy who tried to entice me with an art scholarship—visited southern France last year. Eating at Auberge du Canard was at the top of his list of things to do. But, despite tipping the maître d' an obscene amount of money, he couldn't get a reservation. He was furious. Imagine if I post pictures of me eating there on social media. His head would explode from envy.

"I think it's just allergies," I say.

"Great. Meet you in the lobby at seven."

I try to return his pocket square to him—I haven't needed it for my fake cold—but he tells me to keep it.

Lightly pressing it against my face, I watch as he chats with the manager of the gift shop about her twin boys. It amazes me how at ease he looks no matter what role he's playing—waiter, bellboy, or hotel executive. Then I wonder what kind of role he's playing with me—flirtatious billionaire or something more serious.

* * *

You know what they say about revenge dining—it's best served bubbling hot. Which is good, as that's exactly how the cassoulet at Auberge du Canard is served.

As the waiter places a rustic, wide-mouthed earthenware bowl on the center of the table, my mouth waters at the smell of the bean stew.

"Cassoulet is traditionally simmered for four days," Pierre informs me. "Each day, the cook slowly simmers it, then allows it to cool overnight. As it cools, a crust forms on top. The next morning, you pierce the crust, then cook it again. Let it cool overnight, pierce the crust, cool it again, and so on. This allows the beans to absorb the flavors from the meat while retaining their shape."

"Serving a four-old day dish. I wonder if you could get away with that in the States," I muse.

Pierre shakes his head. "This attitude is why fast-food restaurants are so popular in America."

"Hey, I'm not turning my nose up at cassoulet," I say. "No need to be a snob."

"You think I'm a snob?"

I hold up my hands. "No comment."

"If appreciating good food makes me a snob, then I'm happy to be one." Pierre nods at the waiter to serve the cassoulet. As he ladles it onto my plate, Pierre describes the ingredients. "Those are the finest pork sausages from Toulouse. There are also duck legs, mutton, and of course, white beans. All simmered with rosemary and thyme."

"You forgot the duck confit."

"Ah, I see you already know about cassoulet."

"You can't really go wrong when you cook something with a lot of fat. That's what duck confit is, isn't it?"

"That's true, but French fat is far superior to American fat."

"Says someone who has probably never eaten fries at McDonald's. I'm not sure why we call them French fries, cause they're one hundred percent American. We took potatoes and perfected them."

He grins, then points at my plate. "Go on, try the cassoulet, and then we can compare notes."

First, I take a picture on my phone and post it to my social media accounts, making sure to tag Auberge du Canard and adding the hashtag, "reservations required." Then I groan as I sample the rich, hearty stew. Despite the fact that it's four days old, it's utterly delicious. The beans are soft, the sausages are subtly spiced, the duck is juicy, and the mutton is tender.

Pierre dabs his mouth with a white linen napkin. "Well?"

"It's okay."

"Liar."

"I am not a liar."

"Hmm. Let's see, if I recall correctly, you told me that *Solo* was the best *Star Wars* film. That was clearly a lie. Everyone knows that *Return of the Jedi* is the best one."

"You're delusional," I say before taking another bite of the cassoulet, carefully managing to get a bit of everything onto my fork.

He leans forward, his hazel eyes flickering in the candlelight. "Admit it, you loved the scene when Luke and Leia rode speeder bikes in the forest on Endor."

"Sure," I say between mouthfuls.

"Aha!"

"Aha, nothing." I set my fork down. "Is that why you like marmots so much? Because they look like Ewoks?"

He plucks a piece of crusty baguette from the bread basket. "Hmm . . . I never thought about it that way. I think it's more that I like Ewoks because they remind me of marmots."

"What's the deal with the marmots, anyway? Your family has a hotel named after them and you have a secret tattoo of a marmot on your back."

"Secret being the operative word. There are only a few people who know about my tattoos—you, Amélie, Jean-Paul, Dominic de Santis, and, well, never mind. The important thing is that I want to keep it that way."

I chew a piece of bread thoughtfully. Who else knows about his tattoos? Who else has seen Pierre without his shirt on? Obviously the person who did his elephant tattoo. When he goes to the gym to work out—and Pierre definitely works out—the guys in the changing room would have seen them. But is there someone else? An old girlfriend, perhaps? Did he get his original elephant tattoo for her? Who is she?

I feel my jaw tightening and it isn't because I'm chewing too hard. The bread isn't that crusty. The thought of another woman seeing Pierre without his shirt on is, well, it's giving me an uncomfortable feeling inside. Something I haven't felt for a long time—jealousy.

"So what's the big deal about having tattoos?" I ask. "You're a grown man. You can do whatever you like. They don't have a stigma like they used to."

Pierre runs his hands through his hair. "It's complicated. Let's just say that my mother would be disappointed."

"It's impossible to go through life without disappointing your mom at some point," I say. "But imagine how much more disappointed she'll be when she finds out about your tattoos and the fact that you didn't tell her about them. Something like that won't stay secret forever."

"I agree," he says. "That's one of the reasons I got the marmot tattoo. When she sees that, she'll—"

I never get to find out what his mother will do because I hear a loud squeal behind me. It's so piercing that I'm surprised the crystal chandelier doesn't crack. I turn, expecting to see a very large guinea pig behind me. Instead, I'm confronted by a woman so stunning that if she isn't already a professional model, it's only because she made a conscious career choice to do voiceover work for documentaries about guinea pigs instead of modeling.

Pierre greets her, kissing one cheek, then the other. As he goes to pull away, she snakes her perfectly manicured hand through his hair and pulls him toward her, kissing him lightly on the lips. He pulls back, glances at me, and has the decency to look embarrassed.

He introduces us—apparently Pierre went to boarding school with this Giselle chick's brother—then asks who she's dining with.

Giselle points breezily at a large table by the window. I recognize several of the occupants from celebrity magazines. The men look like they played polo earlier, and the women look like they spent the afternoon shopping at exclusive boutiques. "You know, the usual crowd. You should come join us."

"I can't. I'm here with Mia," he says coolly.

I feel my jaw tightening again. *I can't?* That's his response?

Briefly allowing her eyes to graze over me, Giselle responds. "I under-stand."

I understand? What's that supposed to mean? I feel like there's all sorts of subtext going on here that only someone who has been educated in posh British boarding schools and hangs out with European aristocrats would understand.

She squeezes his arm. "You'll be back in Paris this weekend, right? We're going skydiving on Saturday. You should come. It'll be a blast."

Pierre pauses for a beat, then says, "Mia is afraid of flying."

Now, I'm utterly confused. I'm pretty sure she wasn't inviting *me* skydiving.

Giselle purses her lips for a moment, then gives me a brittle smile. "Such a shame you won't be able to join us." As if dismissing me, she turns to face Pierre. Her fingers trail down his arm. "But we'll see you there, won't we? We haven't done an accelerated free fall together in ages."

The way she says "accelerated free fall" makes me see red. She's making skydiving sound sexy. How is that even possible?

I drop my fork on my plate, and the noise startles the two of them. "Don't worry, Giselle. I'll be there too. I wouldn't miss it for the world. Jumping out of a plane? Sounds fabulous."

11 - The Countdown Timer

Friday morning rolls around and I'm pacing back and forth in the art gallery at Hôtel de la Marmotte while I periodically check my phone. I've set a timer that is counting down the hours, minutes, and seconds until I have to jump out of a plane. Right now, my appointment with death is twenty-six hours, thirteen minutes, and forty seconds away.

To be fair, that's just a guesstimate. While I know that we have to be at the airport early tomorrow morning, I have no idea how long it's going to take to strap a parachute on, get on the plane, fly up to the right altitude, and then make my leap of doom.

I stop pacing and put my hand to my chest. Jump out of a plane? What was I thinking? I'm too young to die. There's so much I still want to accomplish before my time on this planet is up—open my own combination art gallery and tattoo shop, adopt a cat, and buy a custom-made lightsaber.

My heart flutters, forcing me to acknowledge something I've been trying to suppress. "Be honest with yourself, Mia," it says. "There's one other thing you want to check off your list. You want to kiss Pierre again."

True, heart, so true. Ever since that night at the charity ball when his mother and her poodle interrupted us, we haven't so much as held hands. Initially, that was due to the fact that I had been avoiding Pierre, but things changed for me the night we went to dinner at Auberge du Canard in Carcassonne. After meeting in the lobby of his family's hotel, we strolled through the heart of the picturesque walled city, enjoying the balmy weather.

As we walked through the narrow, winding streets, Pierre regaled me with historical tidbits about the area. But his eyes really lit up when he talked about the local rugby team and how their emblem features an image of the ancient city.

Then our conversation turned to Pierre's charity work. I was surprised when he asked my advice about grassroots fundraising. He told me that he felt uneasy about hosting extravagant fundraisers, especially when a significant portion of the money raised went to putting on the fundraiser itself, rather than to the orphanages. I wondered if I had misjudged him. Maybe you could be insanely wealthy and still be a good guy.

When I stumbled on the cobblestones, Pierre briefly grabbed my elbow and steadied me. Then he abruptly dropped his hand. At the time, I chalked it up to him knowing that I didn't approve of public displays of affection.

When we were at the restaurant and he reached across the table, I thought he was going to squeeze my hand. Turns out he just wanted some salt for his appetizer of wild mushrooms sautéed in fresh herbs.

By the time our cassoulet arrived, I was itching for him to touch me, even if it was to casually brush his fingers against mine. Then, of course, you know what happened—Giselle arrived on the scene, reminding me of Pierre's true nature. A spoiled billionaire who was out on some sort of pity date with me. The rest of the evening was awkward, the conversation was stilted, and I was glad when it was over.

But still, I wanted to kiss him. And I still do. What does that say about me? That I don't care that Pierre is a rich jerk? That I care about Pierre despite the fact that he's a rich jerk? Or that I just want to put Giselle in her place?

Truthfully, it's probably the latter. Girls like Giselle deserve to know that just because you look like a supermodel doesn't mean you can have everything you want.

My heart flutters, then softly says, "Are you sure you're being honest with yourself, Mia? Is this really about Giselle? Or is this about protecting yourself?"

* * *

Twenty-one hours, twelve minutes, and two seconds until things go splat on the ground. Things being me. I need to know more about what I'm getting myself into.

I ask Amélie if I can take a break. She says yes, provided that I return with an espresso for her and a chocolate croissant for me. She's getting tired of my pacing back and forth and the constant checking of my phone. She's hoping a sugar buzz will soothe my frazzled nerves. I'm not sure she understands how sugar works on the nervous system, but a croissant does sound good.

As I walk toward the concierge desk, I pause to watch the daily parade of ducks. Bellboys, waiters, and desk clerks make a procession down the grand staircase to the large reflection pool in the center of the lobby. Each of them carries a yellow rubber ducky nestled on a small red velvet cushion. With great ceremony, they lower their ducks into the water, carefully holding onto them so that they can't drift away. Then the front desk manager strikes a gong. All the hotel guests wait in hushed anticipation while the lights on the bottom of the pool are illuminated and the fountain in the center of the pool starts to bubble. The hotel manager strikes his gong a second time, and the ducks are released to float aimlessly around the pool. Everyone applauds, chattering among themselves about how delightfully quirky Hôtel de la Marmotte is.

Pierre catches my eye as he hands his velvet cushion to a fellow bellboy. He starts to walk toward me, but his mother calls his name. Giving me an apologetic look, he turns and follows her into her office.

I watch the duckies for a few moments, trying to reconcile the odd touches at the hotel, such as the duck parade and the oil painting of a marmot on a Harley Davidson at the entrance to the restaurant, with Pierre's mother. She seems so formal, so aloof, so serious, so not fun. Yet, according to Pierre, this hotel is her baby. She purchased the building, oversaw the renovation, and turned it into one of the hottest boutique hotels in Paris, if not in all of Europe.

I shrug and continue on my way. The woman hasn't said one single solitary word to me since I started working here. It's not like we're suddenly going to become best friends and she's going to spill all her hotelier secrets to me. Everything about the Hôtel de la Marmotte is probably a dry, commercial decision on her part, carefully calculated to attract more guests and bring in more money to the Toussaint empire.

When I reach the concierge desk, Jean-Paul nods at me. While he assists a woman with tickets to the Moulin Rouge, I pick up a skydiving brochure from a rack by the hotel entrance. The pictures on the front, of people smiling while they're hurtling toward the ground, would lead you to believe that jumping out of a plane from ten thousand feet in the air is the ultimate thrill.

It's not like I read the dictionary regularly, but I'm pretty sure that the word "thrill" means a feeling of excitement and pleasure. Obviously, whoever designed this brochure has no clue about the English language. Skydiving isn't thrilling; it's terrifying. I grab a pen from the desk, cross out "ultimate thrill" and replace it with "ultimate terror." Truth in advertising is important.

"What are you doing, Mia?" Jean-Paul asks. When I show him the brochure, he smiles. "I heard you're going skydiving. I have to say that I was surprised. I thought you were afraid of flying."

"I am."

He cocks his head to one side. "I don't understand."

"Yeah, that makes two of us." I fiddle with the brochure in my hand. "What do you know about this Giselle chick?"

"Ah, now I think I understand," Jean-Paul says. "Pierre told me that Giselle was at Auberge du Canard when the two of you were there. She is very fond of skydiving. I suppose she'll be there tomorrow?"

I nod, picturing Giselle looking like a James Bond girl in a form-fitting jumpsuit, the zipper pulled down to expose a lacy bra, high-heeled boots, and designer goggles perched on her head. She'll fawn all over Pierre, then the two of them will gracefully jump out of the plane. After performing acrobatic maneuvers in the air, they'll glide to the ground, land effortlessly, then embrace passionately.

"Did the two of them used to date?" I blurt out.

"You don't need to worry about Giselle," Jean-Paul says.

"Who says I'm worried?"

He points at the brochure I'm holding. I seem to have torn it into tiny pieces. Half of them are still clenched in my hand. The other half are scattered on the desk. "You're clearly anxious about something."

"I'm worried about dying."

"Skydiving is perfectly safe," Jean-Paul says.

"But what if I forget to pull the parachute in time? What if the cord breaks? What if my parachute has a giant tear in it? What if—"

Jean-Paul holds up his hand. "You don't need to worry about any of that. For your first skydive, you'll be doing a tandem."

"A what?"

"A tandem. You'll be harnessed to someone else. All you'll have to do is enjoy the ride down."

"Harnessed to someone else? That sounds weird."

Jean-Paul pulls another brochure off the rack and opens it up. "See how this woman is wearing a full-body harness? It's connected to her instructor's harness. He has the parachute on his back."

"What if the instructor forgets to deploy the parachute?"

"Pierre won't forget. He's very experienced."

"Pierre?"

"Yes, he's planning on doing the tandem dive with you. He's a certified skydiving instructor."

Well, of course he is. In addition to running a charity for African orphanages, working as a bellboy, and filling in for his father at meetings, he also teaches people about how to hurtle themselves to death from a plane. Next, I'll find out that he also does brain surgery in his spare time.

Jean-Paul pats my hand. "I probably shouldn't tell you this, but I've never seen Pierre like this with any girl before."

"Like what?"

"Like . . ." He scratches his head, trying to think of the word in English. "Smitten. Yes, that's what it is. He's smitten with you."

I smile. Smitten is such an old-fashioned term. Cute, but old-fashioned. Then my expression sobers. "I doubt that Pierre is smitten with me."

"No, he definitely is," Jean-Paul says. "I know that he met with his lawyer yesterday to discuss a matter related to you."

My stomach clenches. "His lawyer? Why in the world would he do that?"

"I've said too much." Jean-Paul shakes his head. "It's best if Pierre explains the rest."

He refuses to divulge any more information, no matter how persistently I question him. Eventually, I give up.

After walking over to the cafe and ordering an espresso for Amélie, I glance at my phone. Nineteen hours, thirty-two minutes, and twenty seconds until I do a tandem skydive with Pierre. I've never been more terrified in my life.

* * *

It's Saturday morning. Four hours, two minutes, and thirty-six seconds to go, and I still haven't come up with a way to get out of skydiving.

While I wait outside the hotel for Pierre to pick me up, I think about my options. My best idea so far has been to buy a life-size dummy—like the ones they use in automobile crash tests—dress it up like me, sneak it aboard the plane, strap a parachute on it, then jettison it once we reach the jump altitude. But when I talked it over with Isabelle, she pointed out a few flaws with my plan.

First, a crash test dummy can't pull a ripcord. When no one sees the parachute unfurl, they'll assume the worst. An ambulance will race over, sirens blaring, expecting to find my dead body. Instead, they'll see the dummy's head with a blonde wig on it, and plastic arms and legs scattered about.

Second, Pierre and I are supposed to tandem skydive. Do I really think he won't notice when a crash test dummy is strapped to him instead of me? We've been up close and personal before, kissing at the charity ball. He's bound to notice that something isn't quite right. And, if he can't spot the difference between me and a plastic mannequin, I have bigger problems than jumping out of a plane.

Third, crash dummies don't come cheap. My credit card is already maxed out. I can barely afford to buy an espresso, let alone make a purchase that large.

I tap my foot anxiously while I wait for Pierre's car to pull up. *Think, Mia, think. There has to be a way to get out of this.*

Fake an illness? No, Pierre would probably see through that one. I've already told him how I used to pretend to have a stomachache when I wanted to get out of selling Girl Scout cookies door-to-door. I loved being a Girl Scout. Selling cookies, not so much.

My phone informs me that the hours, minutes, and seconds are ticking away. Do I have enough time to get a coffee before Pierre gets here? More importantly, do I have enough money? I rummage in my backpack, but only find sixty-five cents. That's definitely not enough. And we all know that my credit card—

Hey, wait a minute. That's it! How come I didn't think of this before? Skydiving costs hundreds of euros. When I go to pay for it, my credit card is going to be declined. The perfect reason to bow out of jumping out of a plane. Sure, Giselle and all her snooty friends will snicker about how poor I am, but isn't it better to be poor than dead?

Pierre pulls up in the circular driveway in front of the hotel. He's driving a sleek sports car today, instead of being chauffeured around in a town car. A valet opens the passenger door for me and I slip in.

"Sorry I'm late," Pierre says. "I've been on a conference call all morning. And I have a few more calls to make on the way to the airport." Then he hands me a steaming cup of coffee, his fingers brushing against mine. "I thought you might need this. When you texted this morning, you said that you didn't sleep well. Nerves?"

I picture Giselle, the skydiving daredevil supermodel in my head, and lie. "No, not at all."

"Really? You're afraid of flying. You know, you can always change your mind. No one will think less of you."

"Honestly, I'll be fine. The fear of flying is probably an advantage. I'll want to get off the plane so badly that I'll happily jump out of it."

He rubs his jaw. "Wow, I'm amazed at how brave you are."

I smile brightly at him. It's easy to be brave when you know that your credit card is going to be declined. Once that transaction doesn't go through, I'm home free.

On the ride to the small airport in the north of France where the skydiving operation is located, I take in the scenery while Pierre makes several business-related calls. His father seems to be involving him more in the day-to-day management of the family's commercial empire. I wonder if his parents are going to put an end to his rotation through front-line hotel jobs and promote him to an executive position early.

I glance over at Pierre and frown. The stubble on his chin and the dark circles under his eyes are signs that he's burning the candle at both ends of the stick. When he stops at an intersection, he stretches his arms above his head and yawns, before taking another call. This time it's to his lawyer, who he agrees to meet briefly at the airport to go through some important papers.

I shake my head. Only billionaires have their lawyers come running to them, fitting in business deals around skydiving, polo, and charity balls. The rest of us make appointments and wait patiently in the reception area until the lawyer has time to see us. And when we deal with lawyers, it's usually for some unpleasant reason, like the reading of a will or a divorce, not because we're brokering some multi-million dollar property acquisition or company merger.

When we arrive at the airport, we're greeted by Giselle. She squeals loudly when she sees Pierre. I roll my eyes as she attempts to lock lips with him again. Despite her efforts, Pierre simply gives her a couple of brief air kisses, then steps back and puts his arm around my shoulders. For once, I'm not upset about a public display of affection. The look on Giselle's face is totally worth it.

"You remember Mia, don't you?" Pierre asks.

Giselle gives an indifferent nod in my direction, then points at a group of people standing by a sign that says, *Skydive Beaumont.* "Everyone's here. Come, say hello."

Pierre squeezes my shoulder before he leads me over. There's a lot of kissing of cheeks, gossip about a rumored royal abdication, arrangements for a birthday party on a private island in the Caribbean, and plans to go to a nightclub later that night.

I stand awkwardly to the side, wondering if this group of self-absorbed people would have even noticed if a crash test dummy was standing here instead of me.

After a few minutes, a man with an uncanny resemblance to Bruce Willis takes pity on me. "You're, Mia, right? I'm Stefan, owner of Skydive Beaumont. Pierre told me that this will be your first time skydiving. You're our only beginner today, so while everyone else has some coffee, I'm going to take you through a short orientation session."

I pull my wallet out of my purse. For once in my life, I'm glad my credit rating sucks. Not that I actually knew what a credit rating was until Isabelle explained it to me a few weeks ago. "Uh, sure, but first I need to pay for it."

Stefan shakes his head. "No need to worry about that. Pierre's taken care of everything. It's his treat. The only thing you have to concern yourself with is jumping out of the plane."

12 - All the Shades of Green

Thirty-two minutes, five seconds later, I walk out of Stefan's office. I've watched a video about skydiving, produced a medical certificate, signed release papers, and quickly done a search on my phone to see if I can get a rush delivery of a crash test dummy to the airport.

"Are you okay?" Giselle asks. This is the most she's said to me since we've met, so I'm immediately suspicious.

"Yes, why?"

"Well, you do look a bit green." She waves her friends over. "Girls, take a look at Mia. Doesn't her complexion look green? I think she's using the wrong foundation."

The girls pepper me with questions while inspecting my skin. "Do you use primer?" "What kind of moisturizer are you using?" "Are your pores always this large?"

Then a fervent discussion breaks out about what a massive job doing a makeover on me would entail. A twenty-four carat gold facial enriched with Mongolian yak butter is mentioned. Someone suggests that Botox needs to be seriously considered. A Russian reality show star scoffs at the Botox idea. Apparently that isn't enough to deal with the tragic mess that is my face. "Sweetheart," she says in a husky voice, "I give you name of plastic surgeon. He do good job on you."

Meanwhile, Pierre, Stefan and the other guys are standing by the coffee station chatting about rugby. While normally I wouldn't gravitate toward a discussion about conversion kicks, it has to be better than listening to these girls.

I slip away unnoticed—they've moved on from discussing my facial shortcomings and are now talking about the new rutabaga diet fad—and sit on a couch next to the coffee station. Listening with half an ear to the guys, I leaf through a celebrity magazine. I do a double take when I realize that the woman on the cover is the same one who recommended plastic surgery to me.

Pierre turns to refill his coffee cup. I start to say hi to him, but Stefan comes over and slaps him on the back. "I hear wedding bells are on the horizon."

Pierre glances over at where the girls are standing and shushes him. "It's meant to be a surprise."

"Relax, they can't hear you," Stefan says. "From what you tell me though, I think she's going to be shocked. A proposal so soon after meeting? But I suppose with a diamond that big, she's hardly going to say no."

I burrow into the couch and hide behind my magazine. I don't think Pierre and Stefan realize that they've been overheard. My mind is whirring. Who is going to propose to whom? Then I stifle a giggle when I realize that I've said "whom" with a British accent. Granted, I said it inside my mind, not out loud, but I'd never normally talk like that. I'd say, "Who is going to propose to who?" And I'd say it with my flat, American accent.

The pilot walks into the reception area. "We're ready to take you up. Grab your gear and head over to the plane."

Pierre grabs Stefan's arm. "My lawyer was supposed to be here by now, and I really need to see him today. Can you give me a few minutes? I'll give him a call and see where he's at."

"Oh, yeah. That's part of the surprise you have planned, right?" Stefan waves the pilot over, then turns back to Pierre. "No problem. I'll take care of it."

As Pierre pulls out his phone, a harried-looking man rushes in. Oblivious to my presence, the two of them confer in hushed tones, while the lawyer sets his briefcase down next to the coffeemaker. He opens it, pulls out a stack of file folders, and shuffles through them. Pierre frowns and taps his fingers on the table. The lawyer mutters to himself while he looks through his briefcase again. Finally, he finds the right folder, and hands it to Pierre, along with a fountain pen. Pierre flips through the document, then signs his name on the last page with a flourish.

After he hands it back to the lawyer, Pierre rushes out of the reception area toward the airplane. I consider my options—do I stay here and continue to read my magazine, or do I join the others on the plane? Except for the discussion of my face, I've gone pretty much unnoticed by everyone. They might not even realize that I haven't boarded.

But, on the other hand, something is going on with Pierre, and I'm curious to find out what this urgent meeting with the lawyer was really about.

Nosiness wins out. As I stand and go to set the magazine on the table, the lawyer turns and bumps into me. His briefcase tumbles to the ground, and the file folders and papers fly out. I bend down to help him retrieve them. The documents all seem pretty dry and boring, full of lawyerly stuff. That is, until I get to one with the heading, "Accord Prénuptial." My online French refresher course has really been paying off because I know that this translates to "Prenuptial Agreement."

The lawyer snatches it from my hand and sticks it in a folder labeled, "Toussaint." Toussaint as in Pierre Toussaint.

Whoa, wait a minute. Why is Pierre signing a prenuptial agreement? Is he going to pull a diamond engagement ring out of the pocket of his jumpsuit and propose to Giselle on board the plane? Stefan mentioned that there were wedding bells in the air. I knew there was something weird going on between Pierre and Giselle. They must have had a fight and broken up. I bet he was only using me to make her jealous. He knew she would be at Auberge du Canard that night. That's why he asked me to go to dinner with him, so that she'd see him with another woman. He played it cool when Giselle showed up, but it was all for show. He's in love with her. He's always been in love with her. And now he's going to ask her to be his wife.

The pilot walks into the reception area. "Mia, we're waiting for you."

"Just give me a few minutes." I go into the ladies' room and splash cold water on my face. After taking a few deep breaths, I look at myself in the mirror. Wow, my complexion really does look green. But is it green from the anxiety of having to jump out of a plane, or is it green from envy?

My phone beeps. The timer reads zero. Turns out the countdown wasn't for the hours, minutes and seconds until I went skydiving. It was to count down the time until my heart was broken.

* * *

"There you are," Pierre says as I board the plane. "I was beginning to think you were going to stand me up."

Around a dozen people are seated on jump seats arranged against the sides of the aircraft. Like me, they're all wearing jumpsuits, helmets, and goggles. Unlike me, they all look thrilled to be here. Giselle especially. Little does she know her day is about to get even better.

Pierre taps the empty seat next to him. "I saved you a spot."

I gulp as I fasten my seatbelt. "I can't go through with this."

Pierre squeezes my hand. "It's okay, you can do this. Think of it like that scene on the Death Star when Stormtroopers are shooting at Luke and Leia and they have to do that Tarzan-like swing across that giant chasm."

"Are you saying people are going to be shooting at us when we jump out of the airplane?"

He laughs. "No, there won't be any shooting."

"Are we going to be swinging on vines?"

"Nope, no vines."

"And Planet Earth isn't in danger of being destroyed by a Death Star?"

"Not that I'm aware of."

"Then why are you bringing up *Star Wars*?"

He pinches my nose playfully. "Because I thought it would distract you from the fact that the plane is about to take off."

Giselle leans across the aisle. "If she doesn't want to do it, don't make her."

"I'm not making her do anything," Pierre says. "Mia knows that."

Giselle shakes her head. "Look at her. She's turning green again."

Pierre puts his finger under my chin and tips my face up. "You do look a little green."

"Must be all that pea soup I had earlier. I'm totally on board with jumping out of this plane. But I don't feel right that you paid for it."

"Is that what's bothering you?" He adjusts his goggles. "Don't be silly. It's my pleasure."

"Remember the first time we went skydiving, Pierre?" Giselle asks. "It was right after you came back from your gap year in Africa."

The discussion of their first skydiving adventure leaves me puzzled. I'd scratch my head if I wasn't wearing a helmet. Let's see, Stefan said that the girl Pierre was going to propose to would be surprised because they had only known each other for a short time. But Pierre went to boarding school with Giselle's brother. That means he's known her for ages. So it can't be Giselle who he's going to ask to marry him. But if it isn't Giselle, who does he want to be his bride?

Pierre smiles at me in a way that gives me butterflies in my stomach. Or maybe not. It could just be nerves making my tummy queasy. He leans in and whispers in my ear, "I have a surprise for you when we land."

My eyes widen. A surprise? Hang on. I've only known Pierre for a short time. Is it *me* he's going to propose to?

"Wow, I didn't think it was possible to turn any greener," Giselle says as the plane taxis to the runway.

The engines rumble, and I feel a vibration as we speed up for takeoff. As the plane lifts off the ground, I clutch my stomach.

"Don't worry, Mia," Pierre says. "I'll take care of you."

Take care of me? I narrow my eyes. I don't need to be taken care of. This is exactly the way my ex treated me. Like a china doll he had to protect. Like a little girl he had to help learn how to walk. Like a charity case he had to assist by paying for everything.

I'm so angry that I barely notice we're in the air. It isn't until I glance out the window and see clouds that I realize I'm flying in an airplane.

Pierre taps me on the shoulder. "Come on, let's double check your harness."

After making sure everything is securely connected, Pierre and I walk toward the airplane door. By this point, I'm ready to jump. The sooner this ordeal is over with, the better. All I want to do is get to the ground as quickly as possible, then escape from this French billionaire before he proposes.

"Ready?" Pierre asks.

As we step off the plane, I yell, "There's no way I'd ever get married again, especially not to you!"

* * *

This is terrifying! No, this is exhilarating! Terrifying! Exhilarating! It's a terrifying exhilaration!

Can you tell that I don't have a clue what I'm feeling as Pierre and I plummet toward certain death? Stefan told me that I'd experience thirty seconds of free-fall before Pierre pulls the ripcord and deploys the parachute. But this feels like it's been going on for way longer than half a minute.

I scream as we continue to free-fall. Something must have happened. Is the parachute broken? Did Pierre lose consciousness? We're going to die.

"But at least you'll die in Pierre's arms," a tiny voice whispers. "It's so romantic."

That must be my heart speaking. The only thing my stomach has been saying since we jumped out of the plane is, "I'm going to throw up."

"Seriously, heart, zip it," I say. "There's nothing romantic about dying in someone's arms. This isn't *Romeo and Juliet.*"

Before my heart can argue with me, I feel the parachute deploying. Our speed decreases dramatically. We're gently soaring through the air like birds. It's actually a pleasant feeling, slowly gliding down toward the ground. When we near our landing site, I remember Stefan's instructions and lift my legs. I feel a huge grin spread across my face as Pierre and I slide onto the ground. I survived!

Someone from Skydive Beaumont rushes over and unhooks the parachute and our harnesses.

Pierre unstraps his helmet and places it in the crook of his arm. He steps toward me, his lips pressed tightly together. After a beat, he asks, "Are you okay?"

I glance down. All my limbs still seem to be attached to my body. I don't see any blood. I have a ringing in my ears, but that's probably from all the screaming I did on the way down. All in all, I probably fared better than a crash test dummy would have.

"I'm okay."

His eyes turn steely. Tossing his helmet on the ground, he grabs me by my arms and pulls me toward him. For a moment, I think he's going to kiss me. Then I realize that's the furthest thing from his mind. "Why didn't you tell me you had been married before?" he asks, the tone in his voice icy.

I pull away from him and take a step back. "Because it was none of your business, that's why."

"It's very much my business."

"Your business?" I clench my fists. "Are you delusional? Just because your family owns half of France doesn't mean you're entitled to know everything. To have everything you want. To have everyone you want."

He folds his arms across his chest. "My family does not own half of France. Much of our holdings are overseas."

"Seriously, that's the part of this conversation you're focusing on?"

"It's the only semi-rational thing you've said." He paces for a few moments, then points back and forth between the two us. "I thought we had something here. I thought you understood me. I thought you saw beyond my family's wealth. But, no, you assume that just because I was lucky enough to be born into money, that I'm a jerk."

"I've known a lot of guys like you," I say. "Maybe they're not as rich as you are, but they're rich enough, and each and every single one has been a jerk."

Pierre's shoulders slump. "Is that what you really think of me?"

"I don't know what to think anymore, to be honest." I chew on my lip. "When I first met you, you were a waiter. I thought you were just a normal guy, trying to make a living. I liked you. We had fun together. Then I got to Paris and discovered that you're not just some ordinary guy, you're the heir to the Toussaint fortune. And that's when things changed."

"How did things change? I was the same guy you met on the cruise ship."

I put my hands on my hips. "No, you weren't. You tried to buy me off. You tried to control me. The free room at the hotel. The job at the art gallery. You wanted to prove how much better you were than me. How little old me from Small Town, USA could never survive in Paris without you."

"If that's what you thought, why did you accept my help?"

I'm at a loss for words. Why did I accept his help? I didn't want to. Isabelle, Ginny, and Celeste all convinced me that I was reading too much into everything. That he was just being nice. That he was just being my friend. Was that why I said yes to his assistance?

When I don't respond, he mutters, "She was right. You're a gold digger, just like the rest of them."

"She? Who? Your mother?"

Pierre furrows his brow. "My mother?"

"I've seen how she looks at me. Like I'm something you find on your shoe. Like I'm beneath her."

"You don't know my mother very well," he says.

"I know enough. I've dealt with women like her before. They don't want their sons to marry girls from the wrong side of the tracks. My mother-in-law was just like her."

"Your mother-in-law. Yeah, let's get back to the original topic. Why didn't you tell me you were married before? Was that because you ran out on your husband? Did you abandon him?" He narrows his eyes. "Who else did you abandon?"

I throw my hands up in the air. "I didn't abandon anyone."

"Sure. And why should I believe you?" He starts to walk away from me, then doubles back. Jabbing his finger into my chest, he says, "I'm glad I found out about the real you before it was too late."

"You mean before you asked me to marry you?"

"Marry you? Talk about delusional. Why do you think I wanted to marry you?"

"Stefan mentioned something about wedding bells. I saw the prenuptial agreement your lawyer brought to the airport for you to sign."

He arches an eyebrow. "A prenuptial? Trust me, that's not what he was there to discuss with me. You do realize that lawyers have more than one client, don't you? Honestly, did you really think I was going to propose to you? That talk about wedding bells had to do with a friend of ours who is going to propose to his girlfriend. It had absolutely nothing to do with you. Nothing."

I feel my face grow warm. The lawyer was flustered when he was picking up the papers. He probably put the prenuptial agreement back into the wrong folder. It didn't have anything to do with Pierre. How could I have been so stupid?

"What he brought for me to look at was something entirely different." Pierre gives me a scathing look. "Something that's completely irrelevant now."

As he strides away from me, I feel my chest tightening. Unzipping the top of my jumpsuit so that I can breathe, I think about what's happened today. I don't think I'm afraid of flying anymore, but I am afraid of something far worse—losing Pierre.

13 - Going Blue

After Pierre storms off, Stefan graciously offers to drive me back to the hotel. The ride back is quiet. At first, Stefan tries to engage me in conversation, but when my responses continue to consist of one-word answers, he gives up.

I go to my suite at the hotel and pack my bags. I have no idea where I'm going to sleep tonight, but I know it won't be here. I'm tempted to tuck a few bottles of the begonia-scented shampoo and conditioner in my purse, but I resist. I don't want to be beholden to Pierre any longer, not even for floral-scented hair.

Gathering up the last of my personal belongings, I take one last look at my home for the past few months. The large claw-foot bathtub, the comfortable king-size bed, the marmot painting over the fireplace, and the Louis the Sixteenth furniture in the living room all try to tempt me to stay. I need to get out of here quickly before I succumb to temptation. I've gotten way too accustomed to living in luxurious surroundings. This isn't who I am. I'm a simple girl, used to sleeping on a futon in a studio apartment.

I scoot out the door before I change my mind. It makes an oddly satisfying clicking noise as it closes behind me. The sound of something ending. Something that never should have started.

Once I'm in the elevator, I take a deep breath. The next thing I'm planning to do is going to be much harder. I have to tell Amélie that I can't work at the art gallery anymore.

As I walk through the lobby, I smile at the rubber duckies floating in the reflecting pool. Visions of Pierre carrying a velvet pillow as part of the daily duck parade flash through my head. He looked so goofy in that bellboy uniform of his, but it didn't seem to faze him. He seemed genuinely happy to wear it, performing the most mundane tasks for hotel guests. To look at him, you'd never realize that his family owned the hotel. He was at ease with all the rest of the staff, making them feel like he was just one of the gang.

Shaking my head, I push open the door to the art gallery. Amélie is at the sales counter with some customers. She raises her eyebrows when she sees my bags and motions for me to wait. While she rings up their purchase, I stroll around looking at the artwork on display. There's a new collection of miniature paintings in the corner—each one depicting a field mouse next to a different kind of flower. It's the type of thing my mom would love. I snap a photo with my phone. Considering how much they're selling for, it's the closest she's going to get to having one.

"What's going on?" Amélie says after she escorts the customers out of the gallery. "Why do you have your bags?"

"I'm leaving Hôtel de la Marmotte," I say.

"Oh, have you found an apartment?" She knows that I've been looking for one in what little spare time I've had. But finding something halfway decent in my price range had been a challenge, and Pierre kept insisting it wasn't a problem for me to stay at the hotel, so my search had been half-hearted at best.

"Not exactly." I feel my eyes welling up, and I pull a tissue out of my purse.

"Then why are you leaving?"

I dab my eyes and sniffle. "Because I have to."

Amélie leads me over to the seating area by the window, then walks briskly to the door and flips the sign from "ouvert" to "fermé."

"No, you can't close the gallery on my account," I protest.

"Nonsense. You're upset." She sits next to me and pats my knee. "Tell me what's happened."

I spill my guts, telling her how I had mistakenly thought Pierre was going to propose to me. "I made a fool out of myself."

"No, not a fool, *cherié.* It is not foolish to be in love."

"But, I'm not in love."

She smiles gently at me. "Are you sure about that?"

"Absolutely. I could never love Pierre and . . ." I crumple up the tissue in my hand as my voice trails off.

"And what?"

I walk over to the trash can and throw the tissue away. Turning back to Amélie, I say firmly, "And Pierre could never love me."

Amélie stands and smooths down her skirt. She looks as elegant as ever—the epitome of a chic Parisian woman. I'm still wearing my skydiving jumpsuit, my hair is a tangled mess, and one of my sneakers is untied. The contrast between the two of us couldn't be starker.

This is just one of the many reasons why Pierre and I aren't suited for each other. I lack the poise and fashion sense that women like Amélie, Giselle, and Pierre's mother have. Pierre needs someone who he can proudly display on his arm at charity balls.

"Now, I suppose the next thing you were planning on telling me is that you can't work here anymore." When I start to protest, she says, "Let me speak. I have seen girls like you before. Girls who don't believe in themselves."

"That's not true. I believe in myself."

"You think the only reason you got this job is because Pierre told me to hire you, *non?*" When I nod my head, she says, "You are wrong. I *considered* you for the job because Pierre sent me your resume and suggested that you might be a good fit."

I spread my hands. "Exactly."

"But it is I," Amélie taps her chest, "*moi*, who hired you, not Pierre. I am the one who read your articles in *Art Girl Moderne* and recognized how knowledgeable you were about art. I am the one who spoke with the gentleman you did your apprenticeship with."

"You talked to Henry Tusk?"

"He spoke very highly about your dedication and eagerness to learn. I also spoke with your manager at the last tattoo parlor you were employed at. He told me what a hard worker you are. You always went above and beyond what was required. Both of them also mentioned something which is very important to me—your artistic talent."

Staring at the marble floor, I feel overwhelmed by what Amélie has said. "They think I'm talented?" I ask softly.

"Yes, *cherié*. So, now you understand why I hired you? Not because of Pierre. And I made a good decision, *non*? You work hard, you are good with customers, and you have done an excellent job organizing the tattoo photography exhibition. So, you will continue to work for me."

When I raise my eyes, Amélie is giving me a look that reminds me of my second-grade teacher, Mrs. Murphy. "*Oui, madame.* I'll continue to work here."

"But I do think you need some time away from all this." Amélie waves her arms around the gallery. "Take a few days off." She pulls her purse out from underneath the counter and hands me a set of keys. "You can stay with Jean-Paul and me."

"But, I can't," I say. "What about the exhibition? We have so much to do to be ready on time."

She tucks a strand of my hair behind my ear and makes soothing noises. I nearly break down at the gesture. It reminds me of how my mother would comfort me when I was upset. "Mia, everything will be fine with the exhibition. You've worked so hard on it. There isn't anything else that needs to be done that I or someone else can't handle."

"But I want it to be perfect," I say.

"It will be," she reassures me. After writing down the address to her and Jean-Paul's apartment, she ushers me out the door.

* * *

After I arrive at Amélie and Jean-Paul's, I instantly feel some of my stress melt away. As stunning as the suite at Hôtel de la Marmotte was, I prefer the homeyness of this apartment. The decor is stylish, but it's also comfortable. Deep couches you want to sink into, leather armchairs next to a cozy fireplace, and a large dining table that looks like it has been in the family for generations.

I set my bags down in the guest room, then lie on the bed. I didn't sleep a wink the previous night because I kept tossing, turning, and staring at the skydiving countdown timer on my phone. A nap would do me good, but I'm not sure I'll be able to fall asleep. Thoughts of how angry Pierre was with me keep flashing in my head. So what if he didn't know I had been married before? It's not like he didn't keep plenty of secrets from me either. In fact, there are still things I don't know about him, like how he got that scar on his back, what his relationship with Giselle is, and why he's obsessed with marmots.

I feel my eyes grow heavy. Turning on my side, I pull a blanket over me and drift off to sleep. At least I think I'm falling asleep. Maybe I'm already asleep. I really hope this all is just a bad dream. I pray that when I wake up, I'll find myself on my futon in my old apartment back home.

* * *

"Wake up, *cherié*." I feel someone tap my shoulder. "Mia, we're going to have dinner soon. Time to get up."

I rub my eyes. This can't be my apartment. Instead of framed *Star Wars* posters on the walls, there's floral wallpaper. And this isn't a futon I'm lying on. It's a queen-size bed with a wrought iron headboard. The white chest of drawers looks antique, not like it came from a flat pack. Where am I?

"*Cherié*, are you okay?"

I sit up, propping a pillow behind my back. Someone just called me *cherié*. I know exactly where I am—Paris. It wasn't a dream. It all happened. From meeting Pierre on the cruise ship, getting a job at the art gallery, staying at the suite at Hôtel Marmot, going to a fancy charity ball, kissing Pierre, to jumping out of a plane with him.

I run my hands through the snarls in my hair, then smile faintly at Amélie. "I'm okay. Nothing a shower wouldn't help."

She opens up an armoire and hands me a stack of fluffy towels. "The bathroom is down the hall. Come join us when you're ready. We'll have an apéritif, then I thought you might want to help us make dinner. I remember you saying how much you wanted to learn how to cook steak frites properly."

I open my suitcase to pull out my toiletry bag. Lying next to it is a plastic bag. Ooh, I forgot I had bought hair dye. Time to say goodbye to the old Mia and hello to a new and improved Mia.

After mixing up the solution, applying it to my hair, and wrapping it in a plastic cap, I perch on the edge of the bathtub and check my phone. Pierre hasn't called or texted. No surprise there. I don't expect I'll ever be hearing from him again. I do have a cryptic voicemail from Celeste, though.

I dial her number, hoping her message doesn't mean what I think it means.

When she answers the phone, she sounds chirpy, but I have no idea what she's saying.

"That's how you say hello in Greek, dear," she explains.

"It sounds like a really hard language to pronounce," I say. "The only thing I can say in Greek is 'baklava.'"

"That's a good start," Celeste says. "My niece, Olivia, makes wonderful baklava. She had a great teacher. I think I told you about Xander, didn't I?"

"The guy that owns the taverna on the island where you're staying?"

"Uh-huh. He showed her his family's secret baklava recipe. I know you rave about the croissants in Paris, but seriously, the baklava here is to die for. Honey-soaked pastry with nuts. Absolutely delicious. Ginny had some when she was here. She loved it."

"Maybe someday I'll get to Greece," I say. "But right now, I have a lot going on in Paris."

"And how is Pierre?"

"Hang on a minute." I set the phone down and check my hair. A little bit of dye is dripping down my neck. After dabbing it off with a tissue, I pick the phone back up. "Remember the photography exhibition I was telling you about? The opening night is next week. Tons to do for it."

"That's nice, dear, but I didn't ask you about work. I asked you about Pierre."

"Um, well, honestly, things aren't great."

"Don't tell me you broke up."

"Broke up? That's a good question. It's not like we were seriously dating. Can you break up with someone if you've only been out with them a few times?" Then I furrow my brow. Exactly how many times did Pierre and I go out? Was it a few times or less than that? I press the phone to my head with my shoulder while I count on my fingers.

First, there was the *Star Wars* convention. I'm not sure that qualifies as a date. It might have simply been two friends attending an event where they can geek out over spaceships, lightsabers, and alien life forms. I suspect that the people Pierre normally hangs out with aren't sci-fi fans.

Second, there was the charity ball. That had to have been our first official date. I'm not the kind of girl to drag a guy out to a patio and make-out with him unless we're dating.

Third up was the dinner at Auberge du Canard. Was that a date? Or was that just a dinner between two colleagues who happened to be in the same city at the same time for work? Giselle's sudden appearance at the restaurant and Pierre's reaction to her makes it hard to categorize that one.

When I get to my ring finger, I sigh. The fourth pseudo-date Pierre and I had was today when we went skydiving. And we all know how that ended.

"Earth to Mia," Celeste says. "Something's obviously happened between the two of you."

"It did," I say simply. "And I promise to tell you all about it later. But right now, I have to go wash my hair."

Celeste hums a familiar-sounding show tune, then chuckles. "Are you going to wash that man right out of your hair too?"

"Uh, no. Just hair dye."

"Sometimes, I forget how young you are. I don't suppose you ever saw *South Pacific*. One day, I'll have to tell you about the time I was in an off-Broadway production of it. Anyway, go wash your hair."

"Hey before you hang up, Celeste, you need to explain your voicemail to me. Did you really get a tattoo on your—"

Darn it. My phone's died. I remind myself to dig the charger out of my backpack later, then get busy washing the hair dye . . . not to mention that Frenchman . . . right out of my hair.

* * *

When I walk into the kitchen, I catch Jean-Paul and Amélie mid-kiss. It's both awkward and sweet. I don't mean that they're awkward. They're adorable. Married for so long and still obviously in love. That part is sweet. I'm the one that feels awkward, interrupting their affectionate moment.

Before I can tiptoe out, Amélie spots me. She motions at the kitchen table. "Come sit and have an apéritif while I finish chopping the vegetables. Jean-Paul, go get her a drink."

Jean-Paul pours some pastis into a glass, then adds water, which changes the color of the anise-flavored liqueur from yellow to a milky-white. When he hands the glass to me, he does a double take. "Your hair is blue."

Amélie smiles at me. "It looks lovely. *Très chic.*"

Twisting my hair into a knot, I look at her uncertainly. "I'm not sure it's *chic.*"

"Oh, yes, it's very *chic*," she says. "You have a natural sense of style. Madame Toussaint was saying as much the other day."

"Pierre's mother thinks I'm stylish?"

"Yes. That surprises you?" She places a bowl of potatoes in front of me to peel. "You need to believe in yourself more, *chérie.*"

I take a sip of my pastis, then get to work on the potatoes.

Jean-Paul looks at me thoughtfully. "How did you react when Pierre told you that you were beautiful?"

I snort. "Beautiful? Me? Pierre? None of those things go together in a sentence."

"But he thinks you're beautiful. He told me that."

"Well, he never said that to me." I take another sip of my drink, savoring the intense licorice flavor.

"Hmm . . . I thought he had," Jean-Paul says.

While the three of us work quietly preparing the ingredients for our dinner, I think back to the night of the charity ball. Pierre had tried to kiss me in front of everyone. When I tried to stop him, he said something about there being nothing wrong with kissing a beautiful woman in public. Am I remembering that right? Did he call *me* beautiful?

"Okay, I'll show you how to make the Béarnaise sauce now," Amélie says.

While she demonstrates how to emulsify egg yolks and butter with vinegar, Jean-Paul inquires about whether Pierre asked me to be on the Board of Trustees for his charity yet.

I nearly drop the sprig of tarragon I'm holding. "Excuse me?"

"Yes, he was going to ask you once he got the paperwork back from his lawyer."

"Paperwork . . . lawyer . . ." I splutter, feeling my face grow warm as I remember the prenuptial fiasco.

Amélie takes the herbs out of my hand. "Pierre was very impressed with the charity work you did in the States. Imagine, helping former gang members like that by covering up their tattoos."

"Pierre said that you take symbols of hate and turn them into something else," Jean-Paul says. "How exactly do you do that?"

I shrug. "It just takes some creativity, I guess. I talk with the guys, ask them for their ideas, and draw some designs for them to consider. Then I get to work."

"But it's not work, is it?" Jean-Paul asks. "You do it for free."

"Well, sure. These guys are trying to make a fresh start in life. All it takes on my part is time. It's really no big deal."

Amélie shakes her head. "It is a big deal. Not everyone would work with people like that.”

“Everyone needs a second chance,” I say.

Jean-Paul seasons some steaks, then places them on a hot cast iron grill. “Pierre said that you do more than tattoo cover-ups. You also work with communities and raise money to help ex-convicts get a fresh start.”

“You know, I need to go make a call.” I tug at my collar while I inch toward the door. “Can you let me know when dinner is ready?”

Amélie calls after me. “Remember what you said about everyone deserving a second chance? Maybe you should call Pierre.”

14 - Yellow-Bellied Marmots

Birds chirping outside my bedroom window wake me the next morning. A light breeze makes the lace curtains flutter, and sunlight dances around the room. Stretching my arms above my head, I'm tempted to crawl back under the covers, but my stomach has other ideas, namely to be fed.

I'm surprised at how hungry I am, especially after the huge dinner I had. The French have managed to take a simple meal of steak and fries and elevate it to an art form. Add in red wine, salad, and chocolate mousse for dessert, and you can see why people who visit Paris never want to leave.

Do I want to leave Paris, especially after everything that's happened with Pierre? I'm really going to need to figure out the answer to that question. Last night, Amélie made me promise that I would stay and work at the art gallery until the end of summer. After that, the tourist season will wind down and the tattoo photography exhibition will be over. Then, I'll be free to leave Paris . . . if that's what I really want.

My stomach growls so loudly that the birds on the windowsill startle and fly away. When I check the time on my phone, I'm surprised that it's after ten. I can't remember the last time I slept in so late. No wonder I'm hungry.

Before setting my phone back on the nightstand, I check my texts, emails, and voice messages. Nothing from Pierre. Did he check his phone as well this morning to see if I had tried to contact him? Amélie had told me that I should give him a second chance and reach out to him, but I can't. Not yet. What would I say? There's so much I need to figure out first, on my own, starting with whether I want to make a life in Paris long-term. Besides, don't second chances work both ways? Does he want to give me one too?

The sound of my stomach growling drowns out my thoughts about Pierre. Giving in to hunger, I get dressed and head into the kitchen. While the coffee brews, I read the note Jean-Paul left for me on the table. "There's more to life than work. Go enjoy all that Paris has to offer."

Underneath the note is a large envelope with my name scrawled on it. When I open it, I find a walking map of the city and a guidebook, along with complimentary tickets to the Eiffel Tower and a boat ride on the Seine. I smile. Jean-Paul knows that, despite having lived in Paris for a few months, I've actually seen very little of the city. When I haven't been working, I've been sleeping. And when I haven't been sleeping, I've been working. Today, things are going to change. It's time to experience the City of Lights like a tourist.

After a quick breakfast of yogurt and fruit—I promise my stomach I'll feed it more later—I grab my map and head to my first stop, the Arc de Triomphe. When I get there, I'm struck by the grandeur of the memorial arch that honors soldiers who fought and died for France. I pause for a moment at the eternal flame near the tomb of an unknown soldier from World War I and give a moment of silent thanks for people who make the ultimate sacrifice serving their country.

Next, I stroll down the famed Avenue des Champs-Élysées toward the Place de la Concorde. The trees which line the avenue remind me of rectangular lollipops, the luxury clothing shops remind me of Giselle and her friends, and the cafes remind me that it's almost lunchtime. Waiters try to entice me to sit at one of the outdoor tables and enjoy a meal, but given my financial situation, I'm going to have to settle for a sandwich from a food stand instead.

An Egyptian obelisk stands at the center of the Place de la Concorde. Munching on a crusty baguette filled with ham and cheese, I examine the hieroglyphics on the large granite column. The Toussaint family owns a hotel in Cairo, a place I've always wanted to visit. Seeing the pyramids, exploring the Egyptian Museum, and shopping in a souq—these are all things on my bucket list. Maybe traveling to Egypt is what I should do next with my life. Obviously, I could never afford to stay at Pierre's family's hotel there, but I'm sure there are nice hostels in my price range.

The Louvre isn't far from the Place de la Concorde, but I decide to skip a return visit. It would remind me too much of Pierre. Instead, I walk down to the Seine and board one of the hop on and off tourist boats. The next hour passes by quickly. I learn a few interesting tidbits along the way, including the fact that there's only one stop sign in the entire city. I wonder if that's why the traffic is so crazy here. If I were a billionaire like Pierre, I'd definitely have a chauffeur drive me around everywhere. That would be a perk of being rich that I'd definitely enjoy.

As the boat nears the Eiffel Tower, I snap a few pictures of the most recognizable landmark in Paris. The line for tickets snakes around the block. Thankfully, the ticket Jean-Paul gave me gives me VIP access to the elevators to the top. I suppose one of the perks of being a concierge is getting complimentary tickets like these, and it was sweet of him to pass it along to me.

The elevator takes me to the second level. The views of Paris are amazing from here, and I even dare to walk out on the glass floor, which is eighteen stories above street level. Looking down, I experience a bit of vertigo, but nothing like I would have felt in the past. Skydiving seems to have cured me of not only a fear of flying but also a fear of heights.

Next, I board another elevator for the top of the tower. The views are even more stunning. I lean against the railing and try to make out famous landmarks.

"Hello, Mia," I hear an American woman say behind me. I turn around in dread, expecting to see one of the snobby ladies from the country club back home. Instead, I find myself face to face with Pierre's mother. She's impeccably dressed as ever—a sheath dress with an abstract floral print, pink stilettos, and amethysts dangling from her ears.

I'm having a hard time reconciling her fashionable Parisian attire with her flat American accent. Shouldn't she have a posh British accent like Pierre?

"Madame Toussaint," I splutter.

"Please, call me Gladys."

"Gladys? That's not a very French name," I blurt out.

"That's probably because I'm not French," she says, her eyes crinkling with amusement. "I'm American. Born and bred in North Dakota."

* * *

I blink rapidly, trying to recover my power of speech. The elegant woman standing in front of me is Gladys of North Dakota. Or, as they would say in France, Gladys de Dakota du Nord.

"Okay, let me see if I have this straight," I say. "You're originally from one of those rectangular states in the middle of the country."

She smiles, an expression I'm not used to seeing on her. "Yes, the rectangular state near the Canadian border."

"But, how . . . how . . ." My voice trails off. I don't even know where to begin. How did Gladys end up in France? How did she end up married to Pierre's father? Is it really so cold in North Dakota that people have to plug their cars in?

"My dad had a block heater on one of his cars," she says. "He'd plug it in before he started it in the winter. It helped."

"Oh, I guess I asked those questions out loud." Pierre's mother nods, and I press my fingers to my temples. I really need to get better at keeping my internal monologues inside my head where they belong. This whole talking out loud thing keeps getting me in trouble.

"Why don't we have a drink and I'll answer the rest of your questions?"

As she points at the entrance to the Bar à Champagne, I look around expecting her poodle to come barreling around the corner any minute and growl at me. "Where's your dog?"

"Lyonette? She's at home, tuckered out from playing in the park earlier."

"I suppose she's from North Dakota too."

"No, she's from the south of France. I adopted her from a dog rescue organization near Carcossonne. It's the same place we're raising money for with the photography exhibition that you're working on."

"She's a rescue dog?"

"Yes, poor thing was abused, then abandoned by her previous owner. She's come a long way since we've had her, but she still gets skittish at times. And when she gets overexcited, she sometimes plays too roughly. Like she did with you that day in the art gallery. I still feel terrible about how she ripped your blouse."

I chew on my lip. Not only have I made assumptions about Pierre's mother that weren't right, I've also misjudged her dog. Lyonette isn't some snooty, high-strung poodle. She's been abused and abandoned, and is having to learn how to trust humans again.

"Come on, you look like you could use that drink," Gladys says.

I follow her into the bar and wince when I see the prices. "I'm not really thirsty."

"Nonsense. You can't pass up bubbles at the top of the Eiffel Tower." She orders two glasses of pink champagne, paying for them before I can protest. "It's my treat."

"Really," I say. "I can buy my own drink."

I unzip my backpack and pull my wallet out. She shakes her head, the stern look on her face reminding me that this isn't just Gladys from North Dakota. This is also Madame Toussaint, the directrice d'Hôtel de la Marmotte. "Pierre told me that you feel uncomfortable when people buy things for you."

"He did?"

"I used to feel the same way with Pierre's father. When we first started dating, he was constantly showering me with gifts." Her expression softens. "He swept into my life, and swept me off my feet."

"How did you meet? Was it in North Dakota?"

"No, by the time we met, I was living in Montana, working at a hotel near Yellowstone National Park."

"The hotel was owned by the Toussaint family?"

"It is now. That's why he was there, to acquire it. Initially, he traveled back and forth from France, but once the deal was complete, he moved to

Montana to take over the day-to-day management of the hotel." She takes a sip of her champagne, then fiddles with her wedding band. "That was a wonderful time in our lives. We'd both work hard during the week, then the three of us would go hiking in the park on the weekends."

"The three of you? Pierre was there too?"

"Oh, yes. Pierre had been attending boarding school in Britain, but his father thought having him spend time in the States would be a good opportunity for him. He arranged for a private tutor for him so that he could keep up with his studies, but, between you and me, I think Pierre learned almost as much through his time exploring the outdoors and nature."

She asks the waiter to bring us some more champagne. "Would you like some caviar too?"

I wrinkle my nose. "Fish eggs?"

"Never had it?"

I shake my head.

"I'll order some. If you don't think about the fact that its salmon roe, I think you'll be pleasantly surprised at how good it tastes."

"Really?"

"Absolutely. I remember the first time Pierre tried caviar. I think he was nine or ten at the time. He wasn't convinced either, but now he loves it."

"Tell me more about what he was like as a kid," I say.

She spoons caviar onto a toast point and hands it to me. "The first time he saw a yellow-bellied marmot, he was so excited. He became obsessed with them, begging his father to get him one as a pet. He kept trying to explain to Pierre that they were wild animals who needed to live freely in nature. Pierre was despondent. So, I made him his own stuffed marmot."

"What are we talking about? Taxidermy? I guess that's the type of thing you do in North Dakota and Montana during the long winters."

She laughs. "No, I sewed one for him out of felt. He loved it. He would take it everywhere with him. He even tried to take it into the tub with him at bath time until we explained that Frank didn't like to swim."

"Frank?"

"Yes, Frank the Marmot. Don't ask me where he got the name Frank from." She glances at the plate in front of me. "You haven't tried your caviar yet. Go on, give it a chance."

I slowly lift the toast point to my mouth and nibble the edge of it. I feel tiny ocean-flavored bubbles pop on my tongue. It tastes slightly salty, slightly fishy, and a hundred percent delicious. "You're right, it is good."

"I'm not right about everything, but when it comes to caviar, I do know what I'm talking about." She hands me another toast point, which I quickly devour. "I knew someone like you would love the taste of fish eggs."

The taste of caviar turns sour in my mouth. "Someone like me? You think I'm a gold digger, don't you?"

Gladys frowns. "A gold digger? Not at all. Some of the more obnoxious people in Pierre's circle might call a woman a gold-digger if they thought she was after his money. But that'd be the last thing I'd ever say about anyone. Especially not after what I experienced after I married Pierre's father."

I lean forward. "What happened?"

"Listen, I'm a girl like you. I grew up in a small town. My parents worked hard, but we didn't have a lot of money growing up. I couldn't have told you the difference between a fish fork and a salad fork. And I certainly had never eaten fish eggs before." She pauses to sample the caviar, sighing in appreciation. "Anyway, after I married Pierre's father, we moved back to France. That's when I discovered that many members of Parisian high society considered me to be some sort of upstart country bumpkin who was only after his money."

"Oh, my gosh, that's awful. What did you do?"

She narrows her eyes. "I adapted. I learned how to speak French fluently, doing my best to lose all traces of my American accent. In fact, I rarely speak English these days. This is the first time in a long time."

"That can't have been easy."

She shrugs. "I was determined to be the perfect French wife. The clothes, the hair and make-up; things like that were easy. But getting people to accept me, that took time." When she fixes her gaze on me, I notice that her eyes are hazel, just like Pierre's. "So, you see, I'd be the last person to accuse you of being a gold-digger. No, that's not what I was worried about with you."

"What were you worried about?" I ask, not sure that I want to know the answer.

"My close friends call me a lioness. I'll do anything to protect the people I love. Pierre had been terribly hurt by another woman, and I didn't want to see that happen to him again."

"Let me guess, Giselle?"

She taps the side of her nose. "Correct. She's a piece of work. A liar and a cheater. I kept telling Pierre that he shouldn't trust her, but he didn't believe me. You know Giselle was married before, don't you?"

I shake my head.

"Pierre didn't, either. Turns out she had met some guy when she was traveling in Brazil, took a fancy to him, and married him. I guess he was gorgeous, but dumb as a rock."

"Are you saying she had a boytoy?"

"That's one way of putting it. Her secret boytoy. She never told any of her friends and family that she had gotten married. Eventually, she got bored with him, and came back to France for a while. Pierre had just come back from Africa and the two of them starting spending time together. Then one day, a gossip magazine discovered Giselle's secret husband. It's the kind of juicy scandal they love to print. Pierre was furious when the article came out. She laughed it off, saying that the Brazilian guy didn't mean anything to her."

"I can see how Pierre would be upset that Giselle was cheating on her husband."

"But it was more than that," Gladys says. "It was also the fact that Giselle abandoned the poor guy, like a dog abandons a toy they've tired of. When it came time to do his rotation as a waiter, he decided he needed to get out of Paris and away from Giselle."

"That explains a lot." I twirl a lock of my hair, then stifle a laugh. I had forgotten that I had dyed it blue. Earlier today, I would have been worried about what Pierre's mother would think of my hair color, but now that I've gotten to know Gladys de Dakota du Nord, things are different. I take a deep breath, then say, "I was married once. When Pierre found out about it, well . . ."

"He was angry," she says quietly.

"He told you?"

"No, he hasn't said anything to me. Amélie told me what happened." She cocks her head to one side. "I had an impulse to visit the Eiffel Tower today. It's not normally something I would do, but I was drawn here for some reason. And I think that reason was you. It was a chance to get to know you."

I raise my glass and clink it against hers. "And for me to get to know you too."

15 - A Star Wars Tangent

I tell Gladys everything about my short-lived marriage. She listens intently. There's no judgment, only understanding. Eventually, I run out of steam and out of stories. The experience has left me feeling lighter and deeply relaxed, almost like I've had a gentle massage at a spa.

As we part ways at the bottom of the Eiffel Tower, Gladys tells me that Pierre can be stubborn. "You'll have to be the one to reach out to him. After what happened with Giselle, he'll be skittish about trusting you."

I take her hands and squeeze them. "I do care for your son, but I'm not sure that's enough. I know you were able to adapt to this world, but I can't do that. I don't *want* to do that. Pierre and I weren't meant to be together. We need different things out of life."

"Nonsense. You two are perfect for each other. Once you and my son have a heart-to-heart, you'll see that too." She kisses me on the cheek, then gets into her car. Before the chauffeur closes the door, she adds, "You just have to believe, Mia."

As her car speeds away, I pull my phone out. So much has happened that I can't process it. I feel like my head is going to explode. It's time for a debrief with the girls.

Isabelle is the first to dial into the video chat. I turn my phone around so she can see the Eiffel Tower.

"What was it like at the top?" she asks.

"Full of fish eggs and bubbles," I say.

She laughs. "You say the weirdest things."

Ginny pops on. "What did I miss?"

"Mia is at the Eiffel Tower," Isabelle says.

"Did you know that a man cycled down the stairs in 1923 for a bet?" Ginny asks. "He won the bet, but the police arrested him at the bottom."

"How do you keep all those random history tidbits in your brain?" I ask.

Before Ginny can answer, I hear Celeste say, "How do I get this to work again?"

"You're pointing your phone at the floor, Celeste," I say. "Turn it around . . . there you go."

Celeste waves at us once she gets into view. "Hello, girls. Ooh, Mia, I love your hair. Blue really suits you."

"It suits my mood," I say.

"You still haven't patched things up with Pierre?" Celeste asks. "You really should."

"You sound just like his mother."

Ginny arches an eyebrow. "His mother? You mean the Ice Queen of France?"

"Turns out she's not as icy as I thought."

After I fill them in on my tête-à-tête with Gladys, Isabelle asks me what I'm going to do about Pierre. "Do you think his mom is right about the two of you belonging together?"

"Look, I'll be the first to admit that there's something between the two of us—"

Celeste chortles. "Something? A little something called love, that's what it is." Then she starts humming a show tune.

"*South Pacific?*" I ask.

"No, *Oklahoma*," she says.

I shake my head. "Never seen it."

"Well, here's what we're going to do, dear. I'm going to send you a ticket to Greece. You come visit, we'll watch *Oklahoma*, and we'll sort out your love life. It worked for Ginny. She had some baklava, we watched *To Catch a Thief*, and now she's with the guy she was always meant to be with."

"That's sweet, Celeste, but I can't go to Greece. The photography exhibition opens next week, and I promised Amélie that I'd work at the art gallery until the end of the summer."

"Well, I'll pop a ticket in the mail, just in case you change your mind."

"No, really, even if I could come to Greece, I would never let you buy my ticket."

Isabelle pipes up. "Mia has a hard time accepting gifts from people."

"My, oh my, if that isn't the craziest thing I ever heard," Celeste says. "What do you do on Christmas? Sit in the corner and play with crumpled up wrapping paper like a cat while everyone else opens up their presents?"

"No, that's different," I say.

"How so?"

"Um, I spend Christmas with my family and friends."

Celeste gives me a mischievous smile. "So gifts from friends are okay?"

Realizing I've been trapped in a corner, I quickly end the call, promising to touch base again with them after the photography exhibition.

* * *

A couple of days later, I get a cryptic phone call from Dominic de Santis asking if I can meet him at Voodoo Hoodoo that evening. The timing works well for me. I start work back at the art gallery tomorrow, and it'll be crazy busy putting the finishing touches on the photography exhibition. There will be little enough time to eat and sleep, let alone to visit the coolest tattoo parlor in Paris.

I spend the day puttering around Jean-Paul and Amélie's apartment, then grab my backpack and walk to the Métro. Some people turn up their nose at public transportation, but I enjoy it. The buskers playing music outside the station, the eccentric characters sitting next to you on the train, the diversity of languages being spoken—it all adds to the vibe that is Paris.

When I get to the tattoo parlor, Dominic greets me enthusiastically. "Your hair is fabulous. And your outfit is to die for. Now, come along. I want to get your advice about something."

"Me? My advice?"

"Yes, of course. That's why I asked you to come here." Snapping his fingers, he instructs his assistant to pour us some sparkling water, then grabs my hand. As he leads me toward the rear of the tattoo parlor, he tells me that everyone who is everyone is going to be at the opening night of the exhibition. "You will raise lots of money for those poor abandoned dogs. I'm thinking of adopting one. I have my eye on the most adorable Chihuahua."

When he pushes open the door to the back room, I gasp. Lying on the table is a man with a very familiar-looking back. Gazing at the elephant tattoo at the base of his neck and the yellow-bellied marmot tattoo on his right shoulder, I put my hands on my hips. "What exactly is going on here, Dominic?"

"I thought that would have been obvious." He points at the rock that the marmot is sitting on. "I need to finish this portion of the tattoo, and I want to get your advice on how to do the shading."

Yeah, right. A world-renown celebrity tattoo artist wants my advice on something as basic as shading? Not very likely. "This is a set-up. Who put you up to this?"

Pierre rolls over on his side, giving me a view of his sculpted abs. He fixes his eyes on Dominic. "Please tell me my mother didn't have anything to do with this."

Dominic puts his hand to his chest in mock horror. "I don't know what you two think is going on here. I simply wanted to get the advice of a colleague on your tattoo."

"I bet it was Amélie," I say.

"Where is that girl with the sparkling water? I'm dying of thirst. I'm going to track her down." Dominic waves his hand at us. "I'll leave the two of you to discuss the marmot tattoo."

Pierre sits up on the table and runs his fingers through his hair. I want nothing more than to rush over and run my own fingers through his sandy-brown locks. The last time I touched his hair, it was incredibly soft. I'm dying to find out what conditioning product he uses, but that would seem like a weird question to ask in this particular moment.

Instead, I lean against the wall, maintaining a safe distance between the two of us. "Do you think he's coming back with water?"

Pierre suppresses a smile. "I highly doubt it."

"Do you really think your mother arranged for us to run into each other here?" I ask.

"I hope not," he says. "She still doesn't know that I have tattoos."

"Do you really think she'd be upset by them?"

"Yeah." He sighs. "Ever since I can remember, she told me that people with tattoos lack class. She can be a real snob sometimes. I've tried to tell her a million times that tattoos are mainstream now, but she's got a real hang-up about it. I don't know why."

"It probably has to do with what she experienced when she moved to Paris."

"Why do you think that?" Pierre asks, his brow furrowed.

"It couldn't have been easy being an American from a small town, suddenly finding herself thrown into French high society. She told me about—"

Pierre pushes himself off the table and takes a step toward me. "You spoke with my mother?"

"Uh, yeah . . ."

He narrows his eyes. "When?"

"A few days ago." I fold my arms across my chest, unsure why he's so agitated. "I ran into her at the top of the Eiffel Tower. Gladys and I had a good chat over champagne and caviar."

Pierre scrubs a hand across his chin, then bursts out laughing. "She told you her real name is Gladys? Wow, I think you're the first person outside of me and my father who knows that. She insists on being called Juliette."

"Like I said, we had a good chat. Turns out we have a lot in common. We're both from small towns, grew up on the wrong side of the tracks, and . . ."

Pierre takes another step forward, closing the gap between the two of us. "And what?"

"Nothing," I mumble, lowering my gaze and squeezing my arms tighter around my chest.

"Tell me," he says as he softly strokes my cheek. When I don't respond, he gently kisses the top of my head, then trails kisses down my face, pausing to nibble on my earlobe. He slips his fingers underneath the collar of my blouse and pulls it back slightly. I gasp as he brushes his lips against my neck. He draws back and looks intently at me, his hazel eyes sparkling in the overhead light. "Tell me."

Snaking my fingers through the belt loops of his jeans, I pull him back toward me. I run my hands up his bare chest, then loop them around the back of his neck. As he bends his head down to kiss me, I whisper, "And we both fell in love with French guys."

"Love," he murmurs, his lips brushing against mine. "You love me?"

"Yes, I love you." Then I start giggling. Totally inappropriate for the moment, I know.

When Pierre looks at me quizzically, I explain. "Sorry. That scene from *The Empire Strikes Back* is playing in my head. The one where Princess Leia tells Han Solo that she loves him right before he's about to be encased in carbonite and he replies, 'I know.'"

Pierre gives me a cocky grin. "Despite the fact that I own a Han Solo costume, I'm no Han Solo—"

"You don't have to tell me that," I say with a teasing tone. "You're not nearly as good of a spaceship pilot as he is."

He puts a finger on my lips. "Let me finish. What I was going to say is that you should tell me you love me again and wait for my reply without going off on some *Star Wars* tangent."

"*Star Wars* tangent? Me? Never." I hold my hands up in a mocking surrender fashion. My mouth grows dry as he grabs my wrists and presses me against the wall. As his lips near mine, I groan before uttering the words, "I love you."

"I love you too," he says, then kisses the side of my mouth.

As his kisses become more intense, the door flies open. Dominic's assistant is standing there with a tray. "Monsieur de Santis said that you two wanted some water."

* * *

I'm mortified at being caught doing the smoochy-face thing. I grab the tray from Dominic's assistant and practically run into the reception area. After setting the tray on the coffee table, I sink onto the red velvet couch.

Pierre sits next to me and takes a sip of water. "That tastes good. It was getting hot in there, don't you think?"

My face feels flushed. I grab a glass and gulp down its contents. Then I burp. So ladylike, I know. But when you drink water that's carbonated really quickly, well, sometimes things go terribly wrong.

Pierre laughs, and I smack him playfully. He pours me some more water, which I sip more slowly this time.

"So, we should probably talk," I say.

"Talk. That sounds serious. Wouldn't you rather go back into that room and talk about my tattoo some more?" He winks. "And by 'talk about my tattoo,' I mean—"

I hold my hand up. "I know exactly what you mean. But I think we've had enough tattoo talk for right now. Although, there is one tattoo-related question I have."

Pierre points toward the back room. "Shall we?"

"I think we can discuss it out here," I say with a smile.

"Okay, shoot." Pierre leans back in the couch.

"It has to do with your scar. Dominic has done an amazing job incorporating it into the marmot tattoo. So naturally, I want to know how you got the scar."

He quirks an eyebrow. "Naturally."

"Jean-Paul told me that you had an injury which put an end to playing rugby in college. I assume this scar has something to do with it?" When he nods, I add, "I've figured out most of your secrets, but I still don't know the story behind this one."

"Secrets? I don't have any secrets from you."

"Hah. When I met you, you were a waiter. You never told me you were a billionaire. That's a pretty big secret."

Pierre runs his fingers around the rim of his glass. After a beat, he takes my hand in his. "Listen, I get that the fact that I come from money is a big deal to you, but it's not what defines me. I wasn't drawn to you because of your financial status. When I first met you, I was attracted to the fact that you were a *Star Wars* geek like me."

"You weren't attracted to me because of how gorgeous I am?" I say in a mocking tone.

His expression grows serious. "Mia, that goes without saying. You are incredibly beautiful."

"As beautiful as Giselle?" As I utter those words, I realize how pathetic I sound.

"Sure, Giselle is pretty, if you like that kind of thing. But you're . . . you're . . . beautiful inside and out." He runs his fingers through his hair. "You'll have to excuse me. I'm not very good with this kind of thing. My parents are both really reserved. We never really talk about feelings and—"

Now Pierre looks like the one who's mortified. As his face reddens, I take pity on him and try to lighten the mood. "Wow, this is really getting sappy, mister. Sorry, I was just having an insecure moment because I know about you and Giselle's history."

He cocks his head to one side. "You do?"

"Yep, Gladys told me all about it."

"I'm going to have to have a word with her." He shakes his head, then says, "Just believe me when I say that you're beautiful, okay? And we'll leave it at that."

"Believe," I say softly.

Pierre claps his hands together. "Okay, what else do you want to know? What other secrets do you think I'm hiding from you?"

"Well, there's the Board of Trustees thing. What was that all about?"

"Oh, that." Pierre purses his lips. "There were a lot of misunderstandings the day we went skydiving, weren't there? You thought I was going to propose, when what I was planning on doing was asking you to join the board of my charity. I really think we can benefit from your experience with grassroots fundraising, and you'd bring a fresh perspective to the work we do."

"Yeah, that whole prenuptial thing was pretty embarrassing."

He takes a deep breath. "And I'm embarrassed about how I reacted when I found out you had been married before. Amélie told me all about your ex and what a jerk he and his family were to you. I shouldn't have jumped to conclusions."

"Hmm, so Amélie told you about my ex and your mother filled me in on Giselle? They're a couple of busybodies, aren't they?"

"The best kind of busybodies, don't you think? If it hadn't been for them, we wouldn't be here right now." He reaches for my hand and gently kisses the back of it. "Was that okay? I know you're not a big fan of public displays of affection."

I rub my thumb on the palm of his hand. "I'm starting to get used to them. Now, about that scar."

He laughs. "Not everything is a juicy secret. Some are just embarrassing. When I was in college, I went to a panel at a *Star Wars* convention. Some really big cast members were on stage. I was standing on a wobbly chair, trying to take pictures of them. This die-hard fan wearing a Wookie costume rushed the stage. Security was running after him, and I got knocked down."

"Ouch," I say. "You must have landed on something sharp."

"Yep. I had a replica of the knife Han Solo used in the original *Star Wars* movie. Turns out those things aren't made out of plastic. I ended up needing surgery, so I was out of rugby for the rest of the season."

I squeeze his hand. "Oh, you poor thing."

"You want to kiss it and make it better?" he asks with a wink.

I pour him some more water instead, and we spend the rest of the evening talking about marmots, *Star Wars*, and skydiving.

16 - Believe

"Everything looks wonderful, *chérie*," Amélie says.

I look around the art gallery with a critical eye. It's the night of the opening reception for the photography exhibition. There's nothing more I can do. The photographs have been hung, the catalog has been printed, and the catering is set up. Now, all that remains is to open the doors and let the guests in.

I spend the evening making sure glasses are filled with champagne, answering questions about the work on display, and handing out brochures about the animal shelter that we're raising funds for. I even arrange for some dogs to be adopted. Dominic will be providing a home to not one, but two Chihuahuas, and Pierre's mother has taken a liking to a German Shepard-Beauceron cross.

Giselle is there too. She shows an interest in the picture of a bichon frise puppy, but I tell her the dog isn't available. He is, but Giselle is the type of person who has pets because they look cute in her handbag, not because she has a genuine interest in their well being.

I can tell that she's annoyed with me because I hear her tell her friends that my unsophisticated American palate could never appreciate escargot. Giving her a haughty look, I snatch one of the slimy snails from a tray and pop it into my mouth. I'm prepared to smile my way through this disgusting morsel when, to my surprise, I discover that escargot are delicious. Garlic and butter—what's not to love?

I grab a few more and put them on a plate along with some other hors d'oeuvres. Roaming around the gallery, I see Pierre standing with his mother in front of the photographs that were taken at the Voodoo Hoodoo the day Dominic was inking a marmot on Pierre's shoulder.

I have to confess that I eavesdrop on their conversation. Gladys recognizes Pierre's back. At first, she's taken aback that he had gotten a tattoo of an elephant without telling her. He explains to her that it was a reminder of the work that he does with African orphanages. She purses her lips, then her expression softens when he tells her that the yellow-bellied marmot is in her honor, of the day she said yes to his father's proposal and became not only his dad's wife but also Pierre's mother.

Slipping away unnoticed, I mingle among the guests. As a couple from Sri Lanka tell me that they want to buy the photographs which were taken at the Voodoo Hoodoo, a woman asks for everyone's attention.

"Mia, Mia, where are you?" Amélie calls out. I raise my hand meekly. "Come up here, please."

As I make my way to join her, Jean-Paul congratulates me on the success of the reception

When I get to the front of the art gallery, Amélie hands me a glass of champagne. She raises her own glass and makes a toast. "I want to thank Mia, the talented young woman from America, who is responsible for this evening. This exhibition wouldn't have happened without her. The Galérie d'Art Animalier are lucky to have her."

As I take a sip of champagne, Pierre's mother makes her way through the crowd.

When she reaches me, she says in English, "It's not just the Galérie d'Art Animalier who are fortunate to have Mia. It is also everyone at the Hôtel de la Marmotte who are grateful to have her in our midst. And now I would like to present her with a small token of our gratitude."

As a bellboy presents me with a yellow duckie, I grin at Gladys de Dakota du Nord.

* * *

Pierre grabs my hand. "Come with me."

As he leads me toward the back room, I laugh. "No, I don't think so, mister. We can't go play smoochy-face while there's a reception happening out here."

"Making out with you?" He shakes his head. "That is the last thing I had on my mind."

"Yeah, sure," I say. Then I do a double take. "Wait a minute, are you saying you don't want to kiss me? What? Do I have escargot between my teeth?"

He laughs. "This has nothing to do with snails. No, I have something for you back here."

"Okay," I say dubiously.

"Sit here," he says, pointing at a stool in the corner. Then he reaches behind the canvases stacked in the corner and pulls out a large box.

"What's that?"

"It's called a present. Can't you tell from the awesome gift wrapping?"

He places the box on the table behind me. I swivel my stool around and smile when I see the R2-D2 and C-3PO pattern on the wrapping paper. "What is it?"

"You don't seem to be very familiar with how presents work." He taps the large gold bow on top of the box. "You remove the ribbon, tear the paper off, and rip the box open to reveal its contents."

I do as he recommends—untying ribbon, tearing paper, and ripping the box open. My eyes widen when I see what's inside. "Is this what I think it is?"

"Again, confused about how this process works. After opening the box, you remove the object inside and inspect it."

I chew on my lip, undecided about what to do.

Pierre leans down and whispers in my ear. "It's just a present. It doesn't mean anything other than the fact that I love you. I'm not trying to control you or buy you off. Although, if you like it, a thank-you kiss wouldn't go amiss."

As I gingerly pull Pierre's gift out of the box, a huge smile creeps across my face. "This is a custom-made lightsaber."

"Don't forget the titanium handle," he says. "Do you like it?"

"Like it? I love it." I hop down from the stool and swing the lightsaber back and forth. "Oh, my gosh, it feels fantastic."

"I'm glad you like it." Pierre grins and taps his cheek. "Does it deserve a kiss?"

"Let me think about it." I twirl around, sweeping the lightsaber in circles around me. Mesmerized by the way the light glistens off the blade, I'm oblivious to where I'm pointing my lightsaber. A crashing noise startles me, and I yelp as a ceramic statue tumbles off the table.

Pierre dives, sliding across the floor, and catching it just inches before it would have been smashed into smithereens. After he places it back on the table, I set my lightsaber against the stool. Standing on my tiptoes, I plant a kiss on his cheek. "Thank you, I love it."

He turns my head toward me and brushes his lips gently against mine. "And I love you."

After a few minutes of toe-curling kisses, I say, "There's something I wanted to show you." He winks as I unbutton the sleeve of my blouse. "No, silly, it's not that. It's this."

He lifts my wrist and smiles. "Is that what I think it is? A tattoo?"

"Uh-huh. Dominic did it for me the other night. See what it says?"

Pierre traces his fingers gently around the tattoo. "Believe."

"That word means a lot to me," I say. "Believe in myself, believe in my dreams, and believe in—"

Pierre finishes my sentence for me. "Believe in love."

Then we play smoochy-face.

Epilogue - Pierre

I furrow my brow as Mia adjusts the straps on her parachute. "Make sure they're tight."

Mia smiles at me. "Stop fussing. I know what I'm doing. It's been almost a year since I did my first tandem jump with you, and I've had plenty of training and practice since then."

"It's been *exactly* one year since that first time we went skydiving together," I say. "This is our skydiving anniversary."

"I don't know if that's a day we want to celebrate." Mia frowns. "That fight we had was horrible."

"It was all my fault," I say. "I overreacted when you told me you had been married before."

"No, it was my fault. I shouldn't have sprung it on you like that." She squeezes my arm. "At least you didn't have an embarrassing misunderstanding like I did. Can you believe I thought you were going to propose to me when we landed?"

I suppress a smile. "Yeah. What a crazy idea, huh?"

"Enough rehashing of the past," Mia says. "It's time to jump out of a plane."

The door opens, cold air rushes in, and I feel goosebumps all over my body. The goosebumps aren't a new sensation—I feel them every time I'm about to skydive. But this time, they're a reminder of how nervous I am for this particular jump. This is the jump that could change everything.

I watch as Mia steps out of the plane. It's hard to believe that only a year ago she was afraid of flying. Now she can't wait to get back up in the air and go skydiving. As I follow her, a huge grin spreads across my face. Sharing my passion for skydiving with the woman I love is more than I could have ever hoped for.

After we land and remove our gear, Stefan walks toward us with a spaniel-mix puppy bounding alongside him.

"Who is this cutie-pie?" Mia asks.

"His name is Yoda," Stefan says.

"Yoda? I didn't think you were a *Star Wars* fan," Mia says.

Stefan shakes his head. "I'm not."

Mia cocks her head to one side. "Then why did you name your dog after a *Star Wars* character?"

"I didn't," Stefan says, giving me a sideways glance.

I clear my throat. "I named him. He came from the animal shelter."

"He's adorable," Mia says. "It's great that you're going to give him a good home."

"Um . . . I was hoping *we* would give him a good home." I nod at Stefan and he unclips Yoda's leash.

Mia gives me a quizzical look as the puppy runs toward her. She bends down and grins as he licks her repeatedly on the face. As she scratches Yoda's head, she asks, "What's this attached to his collar?"

"Why don't you have a look?" I take a deep breath while she unties the small velvet pouch from Yoda's collar. As she opens it, I kneel on the ground next to her. She gasps as she peeks inside.

"Is this what I think it is?" she asks.

Her hands are trembling, so I take the pouch from her and pull out a diamond ring. "Will you do me the honor of becoming my wife, Mia?"

She looks up at me, her eyes glistening with tears, and nods.

While I slip the ring onto her finger, Yoda runs in circles around the two of us, barking excitedly.

Mia laughs, then pulls the dog into her lap. "You didn't have to bribe me with a puppy. I would have said yes, anyway."

"But it didn't hurt, did it?" I rub the dog's silky ears. "He was one of a litter of three who were abandoned."

"You mean there are two other puppies who need homes? We should adopt them." When I raise my eyebrows, she quickly adds, "What should we name them? Leia and Luke? Or should we go with Han and Lando? Maybe Rey—"

I silence her with a gentle kiss. "Enough *Star Wars* talk."

She kisses me back, then says, "You know we're going to have a *Star Wars*-themed wedding, don't you?"

"I'd expect nothing less," I say dryly.

Then we play smoochy-face again.

III

Smitten with Strudel

1 - The Problem with Marshmallows

There are three things I can't stand more than anything in the world—marshmallows, nylons, and secretive men.

I'll apologize in advance if you're one of those people whose eyes light up at the thought of s'mores or rice krispie treats, or if you have a drawer full of hosiery. But I think we can all agree that guys who are closed books, who never tell you the whole truth, those are the worst.

Given my recent run of bad luck, I'm not surprised that I'm having to deal with two of my pet peeves on the first day at my new job, namely marshmallows and nylons. Fortunately, since I've sworn off guys, cryptic, cagey men won't be a problem I have to deal with. Right?

Please tell me I'm right.

I really need to be right about this. I'm nervous enough starting this new job. The last thing I need is another guy barging his way into my life and turning everything upside down.

Take deep breaths, Isabelle. In, out. In, out.

I repeat this mantra to myself for a few moments. After my last exhale, I feel better. It's okay to feel anxious, I tell myself. It's okay to have these feelings.

Then I remind myself what a great opportunity this job is. An American girl like me working on a European riverboat cruise line. What's not to love? Sailing to exciting ports of call. Exploring quaint towns and bustling cities. Learning about new cultures. Meeting interesting people. Eating delicious food. Who wouldn't be thrilled?

I straighten my shoulders and look around the reception area of the

Abenteuer, the riverboat that will be my home for the next four months. We're currently docked in Mainz, a German city on the Rhine River. The boat has just undergone some renovations, and everything sparkles and gleams. Unfortunately, the maintenance crew is still working on the air-conditioning system—a necessity for these warm summer days—so I'm dripping with sweat, which isn't a good look when you're hoping to impress your new manager and colleagues.

After wiping my brow, my eyes light on Sophia Papadapolous, the bubbly Greek front desk receptionist assigned to conduct my new employee orientation.

She's still brandishing a tray of marshmallows. "Isabelle, are you sure you won't try one? It's a new recipe that the executive chef created. They're amazing."

Did I mention the marshmallows are green? Not an attractive shade of green either. More like something you'd see in a petri dish in a lab experiment.

I shake my head. "No, really. I'm not hungry. I just—"

I can't finish my sentence because Sophia has shoved a marshmallow into my mouth.

Did I mention that they're enormous? Seriously, who needs marshmallows this big?

I try desperately not to gag, but it's hard not to. I feel like I'm choking on a sugary ball of cotton. I try to swallow it, but the spongy texture freaks me out. I can't do it. I really can't.

I frantically try to find a tissue in my purse to spit it out into, but all I come up with is a crumpled up twenty Euro bill. If I spit the marshmallow into it, I doubt that anyone's going to accept it as legal tender after that. Would you take money covered in marshmallow? No, of course you wouldn't.

While I'm pondering my options, Sophia prattles on about the executive chef's other dessert creations.

There's no box of tissues in sight. I have no idea where the restrooms are, and I'm starting to freak out.

Someone clears their throat behind me. I turn and see a man wearing a gray suit. He's not wearing a tie, and his black shirt is unbuttoned at the collar. I catch a glimpse of gold chain before my gaze drifts upward past a jawline with the perfect amount of stubble to a pair of icy-blue eyes framed by hair so blond it looks like a whiteout in a snowstorm. Normally, I'm attracted to men with dark hair and eyes, but there's something about this guy that's making me rethink that.

Not that I'm thinking about this stranger in that way. Definitely not. Sure, he's handsome, but I can tell from the look on his face that he knows women fall for him left and right. And that smugness . . . that's definitely not my type.

His eyes sweep over me before focusing on Sophia. "Excuse me, miss. Is this where I check in?" he asks with a crisp German accent.

"You must be Erich Zimmerman. We were told you would be boarding the boat a day early." Sophia presents the tray to him and smiles brightly. "Marshmallow?"

"No," he growls.

Sophia's hands tremble slightly when she sets the tray down. As she prints out his registration form, Erich gazes at me intently. Pointing at the left side of my face, he says, "Your cheek is swollen."

Why yes, it is swollen. Swollen because there's a giant inedible marshmallow pressing my cheek out like I'm some sort of hamster.

Of course, I'm thinking this, not saying it out loud. I was raised not to talk with my mouth full, thank you very much.

Erich cocks his head to one side, waiting for a response. When I don't reply, he turns his attention back to Sophia.

I gently stroke my cheek. Is it possible this marshmallow is burrowing through my tooth enamel? Are cavities already forming? Is a huge dental bill looming in my future? What's the world record for keeping a marshmallow in your mouth without swallowing it?

As these questions swirl around in my head, I spot a crisp white handkerchief tucked in the pocket of Erich's suit jacket. He must have seen me staring at it, because he hands it to me. I immediately spit the disgusting, gooey marshmallow into it.

Then I do the unthinkable—I hand the handkerchief back to Erich.

Why? I don't know. Maybe because my mom always told me to return things promptly after borrowing them?

Erich eyes the sticky handkerchief in his hand, then thrusts it back at me. "Keep it."

As he asks Sophia where he can wash his hands, I feel my face grow warm. I'm mortified. Beyond mortified. Within seconds of meeting this suave debonair European guy, I've embarrassed myself beyond belief. I'm sure my face is almost as red as my legs.

Oh, yeah, I forgot to tell you why I hate nylons so much. Every time I wear them, my legs break out into a rash. And when I'm nervous, like I am now, my rash breaks out with its own rash.

I haven't worn nylons since my days in the Air Force. Back then, nylons were required when wearing a skirt. That's why I usually opted to wear pants with my dress blues. But here on the *Abenteuer*, pants are not an option with my uniform. The HR department was very clear—no skirt, no nylons, no job.

In hindsight, I should have opted for "no job." I should have stayed back home in Texas. I should have kept my dead-end job working at the mini-mart. I should have . . .

Enough with the "should-haves," Isabelle. Deep breath. In, out. In, out.

My breath hitches in my chest when I realize Erich is looking me up and down. Why is he so handsome? No one should be this good-looking. Especially not a guy whose handkerchief I just spit a marshmallow into.

Erich's eyes widen ever so slightly when his gaze reaches my legs. I'm pretty sure it's not because they're long and shapely. No, if I had to hazard a guess, he's horrified by the red, blotchy hives covering them.

"You really should get that looked at, Isabelle," he says. "You wouldn't want it to interfere with your morning run."

He nods briskly at Sophia and me, then turns toward the restroom. As he walks away, I crumple his handkerchief in my hands and try to resist the urge to scratch my legs.

Then I do a double-take. How does he know my name? I'm not wearing a name tag, and I'm positive he didn't overhear Sophia say my name. I'm certain that we've never met before. I furrow my brow as another thought sinks in—and exactly how does he know I go running every morning?

* * *

While I'm pondering how Erich Zimmermann knows who I am, a beefy hand clamps down on my shoulder.

"I should have you fired for what you just did," a gravely voice hisses in my ear. "Spitting into the handkerchief of a VIP guest—that is *verboten*."

I spin around and find a stocky woman in her early sixties glaring at me. Her beady eyes narrow as she cracks her knuckles, one by one. My stomach twists into knots and I feel the hives on my legs multiplying. This woman is seriously scary, like a villain out of a James Bond movie.

Sophia nudges me and whispers, "You should apologize to Frau Albrecht. Otherwise . . ." Her voice trails off, leaving me to fill in the blanks as to what fate awaits me if I don't immediately express my contrition.

I startle, recognizing the woman's name from the paperwork the cruise line sent me. Frau Albrecht is the Director of Guest Services. In other words, my new manager.

"Um, I'm sorry, ma'am," I splutter. "It's just that marshmallows—"

She holds one of her beefy hands up, cutting me off. Her knuckles look swollen. I'm guessing she won't be able to get her gold signet ring off easily.

"Do not make excuses," she says slowly, emphasizing each word.

Frau Albrecht's German accent sounds harsh, unlike Erich's, which sounded smoky and sexy. His voice was the kind that makes you feel all tingly from your toes all the way up to your—

Whoa, Isabelle. Stop thinking about that man's accent. You swore off men, remember?

As usual, my inner voice is way more rational than the rest of me. I shove all thoughts of Erich out of my mind.

"You're not going to fire her?" Sophia asks Frau Albrecht.

My new manager purses her lips. "Unfortunately, Head Office won't let me."

The way she says "Head Office" makes it sound like the ultimate authority, one that cannot be defied.

Sophia furrows her brow. "But I thought you made all the hiring decisions on board the boat."

"Normally I do," Frau Albrecht says. "But for some reason, Head Office is earmarking Isabelle Martinez for special treatment. They think she is an exceptional hire. Goodness knows why. She's never worked aboard a cruise ship of any kind, and her only customer service experience comes from working at a mini-mart." She spits out "mini-mart," like it has left a foul taste in her mouth.

Sophia turns to me. "A mini-mart? You mean like one of those stores at a gas station?"

"It wasn't located at a gas station. It was next to a dry cleaners," I say, as if that makes my former dead-end job so much classier.

"Huh." Sophia cocks her head to one side. I can't tell if she's trying to figure out what "dry cleaners" means in Greek or if she's trying to find something polite to say about mini-marts.

"Ah, Herr Zimmermann." Frau Albrecht oozes charm as she gives the VIP guest a wave.

Chewing on my bottom lip, I watch Erich walk toward us from the restroom. His hands look marshmallow-free. I can't say the same about mine. Awkwardly clutching his handkerchief in my fist, I look down at the floor.

Frau Albrecht starts to speak in German to Erich, but he interrupts. "English, please."

"My deepest apologies for your treatment earlier by a member of my staff." I can feel Frau Albrecht's beady eyes boring into me. She grabs the handkerchief from me, probably instantly regretting that choice given how sticky it is, then says to Erich, "We will have this dry cleaned for you immediately."

"That's unnecessary," he says. "Isabelle can keep it. For allergy sufferers, a handkerchief can come in handy."

My eyes widen. I take a step toward Erich. "How do you know I have allergies? What are you, some kind of stalker?"

"Isabelle, don't be rude," Frau Albrecht says sharply. "Herr Zimmermann is a personal friend of the owner of the cruise line and our VIP guest. You must treat him with respect."

"It's fine. Isabelle and I are just bantering," Erich says in a soothing tone. Then he turns to me, "Isn't that right?"

"Uh, yes," I say hastily. "Bantering. That's what it is."

No, that's not what it is. This is not bantering. This is just plain weirdness. What kind of stranger drops in facts that he shouldn't know about you into casual conversation? I need to get to the bottom of this.

Erich bows slightly. "Now, if you'll excuse me, ladies, I will get settled in my stateroom."

As he walks up the staircase that leads from the reception area to the deck above, Sophia whispers to me, "I'm glad you're not getting fired. I have a feeling things are going to be interesting with you on board."

Frau Albrecht clears her throat, then gingerly hands me back the handkerchief. "I believe this is yours. Now, about your duties."

As she explains what's expected of me as a desk receptionist, I notice that Erich's handkerchief is monogrammed. Except the initials aren't "EZ" for Erich Zimmermann. Instead they're "STW." Why is he carrying someone else's handkerchief?

Frau Albrecht's cell phone rings, mercifully stopping her lengthy description of the proper use of a three-hole punch. Apparently, the secret is in how you apply pressure. While she listens to the person on the other end of the line, she hands me a stapler and motions for me to practice using it. This office equipment tutorial is almost making me miss my days working at the mini-mart.

Sophia and I exchange glances when Frau Albrecht screeches into the phone, "What? Head Office wants me to do what?"

She listens for a few more moments—enough time to crack her knuckles several times over—before hanging up. Turning to me, she says through gritted teeth, "You're no longer a desk receptionist."

Sophia squeezes my hand. "You're firing Isabelle? I thought you couldn't do that?"

"No, I'm not firing her. I'm . . ." Frau Albrecht pauses to take a deep breath, grimaces at me, then continues. "I'm promoting her."

"Promoting me?" I ask. "Promoting me to what?"

"Congratulations," Frau Albrecht says flatly. "You're our new tour manager."

"Tour manager?" Sophia abruptly releases my hand. "But she can't be. That's Maria's job."

"Head Office has transferred Maria to another role. She'll be based in London."

"No, that's not possible," Sophia says. "Maria is my best friend. She would have told me if she was being transferred."

"It was very sudden," Frau Albrecht says.

Sophia pulls her phone out of her pocket, but before she can dial her friend, Frau Albrecht stops her. "You won't be able to reach her. Her flight has already taken off."

"Fine. I'll speak with her later," Sophia says. "But why Isabelle? If anyone should be promoted, it should be me. I've been working on this boat for three years, and Maria was training me to take over her role one day."

"Yes, you would be much better suited to the role." Frau Albrecht turns and glowers at me. "But Head Office instructed me to give the job to Isabelle."

I hold my hands up. "I don't want it. Give it to Sophia. Besides, I don't even know what a Tour Manager does."

Frau Albrecht ignores me and goes into the small office behind the front desk. She returns a moment later and thrusts a large binder in my hands. "Everything you need to know is in here. We have passengers boarding tomorrow for a weeklong Rhine River cruise. I hope you're a quick study."

Before I can ask any other questions, Frau Albrecht tells Sophia to join her in the office. I stare at the binder and gulp. I'd give anything to be back at the mini-mart right now.

I'm about to push open the office door and insist that Frau Albrecht give Sophia the job when I overhear the two of them talking.

"But that job should have been mine," Sophia says.

"Don't worry," Frau Albrecht says. "She will fail. I guarantee that by this time tomorrow complaints will be so numerous that Head Office will have no choice but to fire her and give you the job."

"Are you sure?"

"Absolutely," Frau Albrecht says. "She is completely unsuited for the position. One way or another, I'm going to make sure she leaves here in disgrace."

I straighten my shoulders and hug the binder to my chest. Challenge accepted, lady. The only one who's going to be disgraced is you.

Then reality sinks in and I slump against the wall. How in the world am I going to pull this off?

* * *

The clock is ticking. I have less than twenty-four hours before the passengers begin boarding the *Abenteuer*. They'll be expecting their tour manager to greet them, answer any questions they may have about the cruise, and brief them about the itinerary and ports of calls. And they'll expect that their tour manager is knowledgeable about the history and culture of the areas they'll be visiting.

Boy, are they in for a surprise.

As of right now, all I know about the cruise is that we start in Mainz. From here, we'll sail north, first stopping at Rudesheim, Koblenz, and Cologne in Germany, then onward to Amsterdam in the Netherlands, where the trip will end and the passengers will disembark.

And that's pretty much the extent of what I know. Detailed knowledge of each port? History and culture of the region? What time dinner is served? I don't have a clue.

I shift the binder in my arms. Time to get cracking. I've got a lot to learn.

The reception area is bustling with activity as crew members get the boat ready for departure, so I decide to head to the library, where I can hopefully get some peace and quiet.

I race up the stairs, then through the opulent lounge, where passengers can gather for drinks, play card games, or just sit quietly and look out the windows, taking in the sights. The entrance to the library is next to the sleek wooden bar.

Pushing open the door, I breathe a sigh of relief. The small room is deserted. I kick off my heels, and my feet sink into the plush carpet. I set the binder on a coffee table, then inspect my legs. The itchiness is unbearable, but I remind myself for the millionth time not to scratch them.

It's not easy. What's the point of having an itch that you can't scratch? There are some mysteries about the design of the human body that I'll never understand—Why in the world do our ears keep growing? What's up with having an appendix since it serves no purpose? Itchy skin is right up there.

I plop onto the couch and stare at the binder. I know my therapist and I have talked about the importance of embracing change, but this is ridiculous.

I should quit. There's no shame in quitting, right?

Okay, there's a little shame, but I can live with shame. It wouldn't be the first time. But there's the little matter of my bank account balance. Usually, I'm very careful with my finances. But I've spent more than I planned on this European adventure. Now all I have left is that crumpled up twenty Euro note in my purse. Since I won't get my first paycheck until next month, I was counting on free room and board to get by.

I look down at the amethyst ring on my right hand, and my eyes tear up. Memories of my grandmother's funeral flood back. "She wanted you to have this," my mom had said to me. "She was a strong woman, just like you are." That was right before I joined the Air Force. I thought I was a strong woman at the time. But so much has happened since then. Nowadays, I'm scared of my own shadow and panic when there's any change to my routine.

After wiping my eyes, I grab my phone and send a text to my mom. It's time to swallow my pride and ask for help. I know she'll be happy to loan me some money, but I hate being in this position.

While I wait for her to respond, I absent-mindedly scratch my legs. When I realize that I've drawn blood, I shake my head. Why am I still wearing these ridiculous nylons? If I'm quitting this job, it's time to take these babies off.

I walk out of the library and head to the restrooms at the far end of the lounge. Of course they're closed for cleaning. Just my luck. I could go to the restrooms on the deck below, but I don't want to run into Frau Albrecht until I'm sure my mom can help me out financially.

The itching is insane. I rush back to the library. There's no one inside, so I close the door and hitch up my skirt. I strip the nylons off one leg, then as I'm tugging the other side over my other ankle, I hear a familiar German voice ask, "Do you need assistance?"

Startled, I try to pull the nylons back on and straighten my skirt. Things don't go as planned, and I end up on the ground with my nylons twisted in a ball in my hands and my skirt turned around so that the zipper is in front. It's a good look . . . not.

I squeeze my eyes shut. If I can't see who's talking to me, they can't see me, right?

"May I assist you?" the man asks again.

Hoping it's not who I think it is, I crack open one eye. Then I groan. It's him. Or at least it's his shoes. Why I recognize Erich Zimmermann's shoes, I have no idea. It's not like I'm into men's shoes. Now men's suits, those I notice. Especially ones that emphasize their broad shoulders. Like the gray suit Erich had on earlier.

I crack open my other eye. Is he still wearing that suit?

Stop thinking about what Erich's wearing, Isabelle. You're lying on the floor clutching a pair of nylons in your hands. Is now the time to be thinking about menswear?

I squeeze my eyes shut again. Maybe he'll take the hint and go away.

"Here, let me help you up," Erich says, oblivious to my hint.

Taking a deep breath, I open my eyes and see his outstretched hand. I extend mine, but he frowns.

Of course. That's the hand with the nylons in it. He probably thinks I'm trying to give them to him, like I tried to give him back his marshmallow-encrusted handkerchief. He's smart, I'll give him that. Too smart to accept anything I try to hand to him.

I extend my other arm, and he pulls me to my feet.

"Thanks," I mutter.

"Your leg is bleeding," he says matter-of-factly.

I gasp when I see the bloodstain on the carpet. Why couldn't I have resisted the urge to scratch my legs?

As I try to blot it out with my nylons, Erich walks over to a small buffet table by the window and pours a glass of water.

Really? Is he going to watch me try to clean this up while having a refreshing drink?

"Try this instead," he says, pulling a fresh handkerchief out of his pocket and dipping it in the water. After he hands it to me, he leans back against the wall.

Okay, he was helpful with the wet handkerchief, but it's really annoying how he's calmly standing there watching me.

I finally manage to get the blood out, then Erich helps me to my feet again.

Glancing at the handkerchief in my hand, I say, "I don't suppose you want this one back either."

He shakes his head. "No, you can keep that one as well. Although, it isn't as fascinating as the first one I gave you."

Since when did handkerchiefs become fascinating? "Okay, thanks. It'll make uh, an interesting souvenir."

"Souvenir of what?"

I shrug. "My short-lived tour manager job."

Erich furrows his brow. "Short-lived?"

"Yeah, I'm going to quit. I'm not cut out for this."

"Quit? No, you're not quitting," he says firmly.

"Uh, yes, I am." I shove the handkerchief in one of my jacket pockets and the nylons in the other. "Not that it's any of your business."

"Oh, but it is my business." Erich's eyes grow steely. "There's no way you're quitting. Not after all the trouble I went to arranging for you to get this job."

I arch an eyebrow. "You got me this job? I don't think so. I never even met you until today, mister."

Erich folds his arms across his chest. "We may not have met before, but I can assure you that the reason you have this job is because of me. It's the perfect cover for our mission."

I arch an eyebrow. "Our mission?"

"Yes, we've been tasked with stopping an international arms deal."

2 - The Third Street Thugs

I double over with laughter, not caring that I'm making snorting sounds. Stopping an international arms deal? Is this guy for real?

As I wipe tears away from my eyes, Erich asks coolly, "Do you think letting terrorists get a hold of weapons is a laughing matter?"

The expression on his face is so serious that it sends me into another round of uncontrollable laughter. When I finally catch my breath, I ask, "Did my friend Mia set this up? I've warned her about her practical jokes."

Erich frowns. "You can't tell Mia about this. You can't tell anyone. This is top secret."

"Top secret, of course." I try not to smile as I pretend to be zipping my lips.

"You're not what I expected," Erich says after a beat.

"We just met. How could you have expected anything?" Then my eyes widen and I start to edge toward the door. "Hey, wait a minute. You knew what my name was, that I'm a runner, and that I suffer from allergies. Have you been following me?"

Erich holds up his hands. "No, I haven't been following you. It was in your file."

I stop in my tracks. "My file? What file?"

Erich looks at me as though I'm stupid. "Your Air Force file."

"How did you get a hold of my file? You realize it's a serious crime to hack into a government database."

"Of course, I didn't hack into anything." Erich shrugs. "Not that I couldn't have if I wanted to. Piece of cake."

Wow, not only is he an oddball, but he also has a huge ego. This situation is getting stranger by the moment. There's no way some random German dude could have gotten a hold of my file. To be honest, I don't know whether to flee or stay and find out how he knows so much personal information about me. And this thing about terrorists? Someone has seen too many spy movies. He probably likes to look at himself in the mirror and say, "Bond, James Bond," out loud while pretending to fire a gun.

The obvious conclusion is that he's some sort of stalker. Time to make my exit. I edge toward the door.

Erich lets out an exasperated sigh. "Isabelle, what is wrong with you? Stop playing around. We have serious work to do. The organization is counting on you. I need to begin your briefing."

The way Erich emphasizes "the organization" and the tone of his voice makes my body tense. And his use of the term "briefing"—I haven't heard that since I was in the Air Force.

"Wait a minute, is this . . ." My voice trails off as I realize there's more going on here than I initially thought. This isn't a practical joke, and this mysterious stranger is no stalker.

Erich grabs my arm and pulls me toward him. Then he whispers in my ear, "Does 'the third street thugs' ring a bell?"

The minute Erich utters that code phrase, I know for certain that this is real. When I left the Air Force, my commanding officer told me that if anyone ever approached me saying, "the third street thugs," it would be a sign that they needed to reactivate me for duty.

My breathing becomes shallow and my pulse races. Feeling faint, I press my hands against Erich's chest to steady myself. "The initials on your handkerchief—STW," I say faintly. "It was a signal."

"That's right, Isabelle," he says. "A signal that the organization needs you. You know what STW stands for—save the world—and we need your help to do it."

"So what you said about stopping an international arms deal is real?"

Erich tips my face up so that I'm staring into his icy-blue eyes. "Yes. I need you. We need you."

"Why me?" I cringe as I hear my voice squeak.

"Because of your particular talents."

"Talents? Me?" Could my voice get any squeakier?

Erich lowers his face so that his lips are brushing against my earlobe, sending tingles down my spine. "Well, you were the Youth Scrabble Champion when you were fifteen and you took third place in the National Scrabble Tournament in your freshman year of college. Undaunted, you came back the following year and took the championship," he says softly.

I can't help myself. I start laughing again. This time it's a slightly maniacal laugh. I step backwards and press my hands to my mouth. Taking a few deep breaths, I shake my head. "Scrabble is going to stop an international arms deal? What's next? Bringing down the Mafia with Candyland?"

A slight smile plays on Erich's lips. "Ah, Candyland, the kids game. I'll suggest that to my superiors."

"And who exactly are your superiors?"

Before Erich can answer, I hear Frau Albrecht's voice over the loudspeaker. "Isabelle Martinez, report to the dining room. I repeat, Isabelle Martinez, report to the dining room."

Erich points to the doorway. "You better get going. Frau Albrecht doesn't seem like a woman you want to keep waiting."

I wring my hands together. "But Scrabble, an international arms deal . . ."

"I'll explain over dinner. Meet me at eight in the reception area. I know a place in Mainz that makes great pfälzer saumagen. You'll love it." Erich gives me a warning look. "Be on time. I don't like to be kept waiting either."

Can you believe it? After Erich dropped that huge bombshell, my stomach grumbles at the sound of pfälzer saumagen. I have no idea what it is, but considering I missed lunch, and breakfast was ages ago, anything sounds good.

"Hungry?" Erich asks.

"Famished." My phone buzzes. "That's my mom. I texted her about quitting."

"Text her back and tell her it was a mistake. We need you in this tour manager role." He holds up his hand, forestalling my questions. "Like I said, I'll explain over dinner tonight."

"Fine," I mutter as I type a response. When I look back up, Erich has vanished.

Frau Albrecht's voice booms over the loudspeaker again. "Isabelle Martinez, report to the dining room immediately."

I slip my shoes back on and grab the binder from the coffee table. I guess there's no harm in playing along for now. Time to report for duty. But you better believe I'm going to get some answers from Erich before I decide whether to stick with this "Scrabble-playing tour manager save the world from terrorists" gig.

* * *

When I reach the entrance to the dining room, I see Frau Albrecht standing in front of the double doors, tapping her foot while she stares pointedly at her watch.

"You're late," she barks.

"Sorry. I was . . ." I shift uneasily as I try to figure out what to say.

"You were what?"

Realizing that I can't exactly explain to her that I've spent the past thirty minutes with her VIP guest talking about a top-secret mission, I tap my binder. "I was studying."

"Good," she says. "Then you know how long the Rhine River is."

"Uh, not exactly."

"It's 1,230 kilometers long. That's 765 miles for you Americans. These are the types of facts that you need to have at your fingertips," she huffs.

I sigh. I'm not sure what's going to be harder—pulling off the tour manager role or stopping an international arms deal.

"Now, hurry along," Frau Albrecht says. "Sophia needs to finish your new employee orientation. It's important that you're familiar with how the meal procedures work."

When I walk into the dining room, I spot Sophia putting a chef's hat on her head.

"How do I look?" she says playfully to a man wearing kitchen whites.

He rubs his bare head, then reaches for his hat. Sophia tries to dart away, but he grabs her by her waist and tickles her. She finally yields and gives his hat back to him.

As he places it back on his head, he says, "You look better without a hat."

Sophia tucks some stray hair back into her bun and grins at him.

Then he motions at her uniform, adding, "You'd look even better without that on too."

Okay, I really don't want to see how far they take this, so I clear my throat.

Sophia frowns when she sees me. "Oh, you're here."

I smile and restate the obvious. "Yep, I'm here."

Extending my hand, I start to introduce myself to Sophia's companion, but she interrupts. "Isabelle is the girl I was telling you about who spit out your marshmallow."

The man purses his lips. "You spit out Auguste Renoir's marshmallow? Auguste Renoir will not forget this."

"Who's Auguste Renoir?" I ask.

Sophia strokes the man's arm. "*This* is Auguste Renoir. The executive chef aboard the *Abenteuer*. He's a genius."

Since the man talks about himself in the third person, I'd have to say that the jury's out about whether he's a genius. Narcissist, sure. But genius? I have my doubts.

Naturally, I don't say this out loud. Instead, I apologize. "Sorry, I'm allergic to marshmallows." A slight fib, but the last thing I need is to get on the wrong side of Auguste Renoir. I wouldn't want him to poison my food.

The chef looks at me with disdain. "Peanut allergies, seafood allergies, now marshmallow allergies. What's next? Are people going to start claiming they're allergic to water?" Then he storms into the kitchen, yelling at a sous-chef who didn't peel the carrots to his master's liking.

"Well, shall we get started?" Sophia asks. She spends the next hour explaining the menus, the wine selection, seating arrangements, and table settings. When she starts to show me how the salt and pepper shakers are refilled, I stop her.

"Do you mind if we finish this later?" I check the time on my phone and gulp. "I have less than twenty-one hours to memorize everything in this binder."

"Don't forget the welcome presentation you have to give tomorrow evening," Sophia says.

"Welcome presentation?"

"Yes, after dinner, the tour manager gives a two-hour presentation to the passengers. It's considered one of the highlights of the cruise." Sophia smiles bitterly. "Or at least it was when Maria had the job."

I put my head in my hands and groan. "I hate public speaking."

"Maria loved it."

"Of course she did," I say. "It probably helped that she knew what she was talking about. I don't have a clue."

Sophia's expression softens. "Maria and I shared a cabin. I think she may have left her flash drive behind. It might have the presentation she used for the welcome session on it. I'll check when I get off duty."

"I'd really appreciate that," I say.

"No problem." Sophia walks to the kitchen and pushes on the swinging door with her hip. She motions at my legs. "Better make sure you're wearing nylons next time Frau Albrecht sees you. I wouldn't want you to get fired."

As she walks into the kitchen and calls out for Auguste Renoir, I wonder why Sophia is suddenly being so helpful. One minute she's angry that I got the tour manager job instead of her. Now she wants to make sure I don't get fired? Something fishy is going on aboard this boat, and it's not just the salmon they're serving for dinner.

* * *

As Erich and I walk through the old town of Mainz to the restaurant later that night, he refuses to explain the mission until after we eat.

"You'll be able to think more clearly on a full stomach," he says to me. "You know how you get when your blood sugar levels drop."

I stop in the middle of the picturesque market square and put my hands on my hips. "Exactly how do I get?"

Erich waves a hand in my direction. "Like this. Cranky."

"I'm not cranky."

"If you say so."

I step forward and jab my finger in Erich's chest. "I *do* say so. Besides, how would you know anything about my blood sugar levels, anyway?"

"Your file was very extensive." Erich gives me a sly smile. "Do you want me to tell you what it says about what you talk about in your sleep?"

My jaw drops. "Please tell me you're kidding."

"I am. The only person who would know if you talk in your sleep or not is your boyfriend."

"I don't have a boyfriend," I say. "But I suppose you already knew that."

Instead of responding, Erich grabs my hand and leads me across the square to a pedestrian street lined with rustic half-timbered buildings. "The restaurant is down here."

I pepper him with more questions about the arms deal, but he limits his responses to historical tidbits about Mainz.

"Did you know that you're walking through over two thousand years of history? This area dates back to Roman times," Erich says. "And remember the medieval tower we passed by earlier? It's called the Eisenturm, or Iron Tower. It used to be a watchtower and gate on the old city walls."

I'm finding it hard to concentrate on what Erich is saying. And no, it's not because my blood sugar levels are low. Or because Erich is holding my hand.

No, frankly, it's because Erich's history lesson is boring. While my friend, Ginny, would be thrilled to learn that Mainz is where Johannes Gutenberg invented the movable type press, I can't stop yawning.

But when Erich mentions Mainz is the wine capital of Germany, my ears perk up.

"Wine? Yes, please," I say.

As Erich ushers me inside the restaurant, he promises to order us a bottle of his favorite riesling.

The minute I walk into the cozy dining room, I feel like I'm transported back in time. Beeswax candles flicker against the plastered walls, pottery is displayed along wood shelves running the length of the room, and the trestle tables and benches look as though they've been here since the Middle Ages.

A woman wearing a moss green skirt and bodice paired with a white lace blouse and apron seats us in a booth in a secluded alcove. Before I can stop him, Erich orders pfälzer saumagen for both of us.

"I would have preferred to choose for myself," I say. "Maybe I would have liked something else."

"Trust me, you'll love the pfälzer saumagen."

I take a sip of the crisp riesling, then say, "Trust is something you'll have to earn."

"If we're going to work together, you're going to have to trust me." He takes a sip of wine, then leans back against the booth and stares at me, almost as though he's daring me to challenge him.

So I do. "You said 'if' we work together. That means I can walk away from all this and you."

He laughs, which annoys me. "You could, but I suggest you wait, try the pfälzer saumagen, and hear what I have to say first."

I give him my fiercest stare. "Okay, I'm waiting."

"First, we eat. Then we talk."

When the waitress brings our entrees, I ask her what pfälzer saumagen is.

"Pfälzer refers to the region and saumagen means 'sow's stomach' in English," she says. "The stuffing consists of pork, potatoes, onions, and spices."

"Did she say 'stomach'?" I ask after the waitress leaves. "I'm pretty sure any file of mine would have pointed out that I don't eat organ meat."

"Ronald Reagan sampled saumagen when he visited Germany," Erich says.

"And that's supposed to be a selling point?"

Eventually, Erich persuades me to try it, and, between you and me, it is delicious. And the side dishes of mashed potatoes and sauerkraut are so good that I want to lick my plate clean.

When we're finished, Erich asks if I want some strudel for dessert.

"It's not made with kidney or liver is it?"

"No, just apples . . . although if you prefer kidneys and liver, I'm sure that could be arranged."

"Let's stick with apples."

When the strudel arrives, Erich is finally ready to tell me about the mission. I don't know why he had to wait until dessert to spill the beans. Must be some kind of control thing. I've met men like him before—emotionally detached, secretive, and always having to be in charge. In fact, I've dated a guy like that before. Huge mistake.

"So exactly what kind of mission is this?" I ask in between bites of flaky, buttery pastry and juicy, spiced apples.

"The kind where we save the world," Erich says.

"That's a bit overly dramatic, don't you think?"

"I don't do drama. I only do truth."

I roll my eyes. "Slap that slogan on a t-shirt and some coffee mugs, and you'll make a fortune."

"I have no interest in making money. I'm interested in—"

"Yeah, yeah. I know. You're all about saving the world." I push my empty dessert plate aside. "How about some details about this world-saving mission?"

"We have intelligence that an international arms deal is going to take place in Basel, Switzerland."

"You do realize that we're in Mainz, Germany, right? Basel is what, like two hundred miles away?"

Erich smiles. "Someone's been studying their binder."

"I wish you hadn't mentioned the binder," I say. "I've wasted over two hours here with you, hours that I could have used to study."

"Isabelle, your IQ is off the charts and you have a photographic memory. All you have to do is skim through the binder and you'll be all set."

"It's not quite that simple." I look longingly at Erich's unfinished strudel, and he pushes his plate toward me. "Tell me more about the mission. All I know is that the deal takes place in Basel."

"See, you are a quick study. I said that five seconds ago and you've retained that information like that." Erich snaps his fingers.

I ignore his barb. "But on this cruise, we're not headed to Basel. We're headed north to Amsterdam."

"That's true."

"Then why am I involved?"

"Because a jewel thief is going to be one of your passengers."

I arch an eyebrow. "I thought this was about illegal weapons, not jewelry."

Erich takes a sip of his espresso, then says, "It's about both. The jewel thief has a stolen emerald necklace—"

"Obviously it's stolen," I point out. "You're talking about a jewel thief."

"See, what did I say about you being smart?" Erich represses a smile, then adds, "The jewel thief is going to sell the necklace to a fence in Amsterdam. The fence will then sell the necklace to the head of the Nouveau Rouge Order."

I gasp. "The Nouveau Rouge Order is involved? But they're responsible for . . ." I can't bear to utter out loud the atrocities they've committed.

"Now you see why it's important that this deal is stopped?" Erich fills my wine glass. "Well, the head of the Nouveau Rouge Order is going to, in turn, sell the necklace to a sheikh in exchange for the weapons. That transaction will take place in Basel."

"But no one knows what the head of the Nouveau Rouge Order looks like," I say. "We don't even know if it's a man or a woman. At least that's what they report in the press. Maybe the organization knows more?"

"Well, fortunately, that's not something you have to worry about. You only need to help us with the operation in Amsterdam."

I take a sip of wine and consider what Erich has told me. This riesling really is good. After another sip, I ask, "Why doesn't the jewel thief take a plane to Amsterdam? It seems odd to vacation with a stolen necklace."

"Possibly because security checks aren't as stringent on a riverboat. Or maybe he's afraid of flying," Erich suggests.

"I can relate to the fear of flying." I rub my temples. "I'm starting to get a headache. Do you have any painkillers?"

"You should be careful who you accept pills from," Erich says.

"Why? Because they could be poisoned?"

"It's been known to happen."

"I really hope you're not serious."

Erich reaches across the table and takes my hand in his. "I won't let anything happen to you. That's why I'm on this cruise, to watch out for you."

"So if you're on the cruise, why don't you do all this super secret spy stuff? Not that you've told me what I need to do yet."

"I don't have the necessary skill-set. But you do. Don't worry, what you have to do is simple." Erich squeezes my hand, then releases it. "Just get close to the jewel thief. Make him trust you, gain his confidence, and then . . . well, I'll fill you in on the rest of the details later."

I shake my head. "Later? You can't be serious."

"It's for your own protection," Erich says. "The less you know right now, the better."

"Fine," I say through clenched teeth. "But you can at least tell me why you picked me for this."

"Three reasons. First, your background as an intelligence analyst in the Air Force means you have all the necessary clearances. Second, you already were working on the riverboat the jewel thief will be on. It was a simple matter of pulling strings to get you promoted to a job where you'll have close contact with the jewel thief."

"You might want to explain that to Sophia," I mutter.

Erich taps his finger on the table. "And third, and perhaps most important, you play Scrabble at a championship level."

As if all that wasn't enough to digest, Erich then presents me with a jewelry box. Yeah, cause that's what you do when you're enlisting someone to help save the world—you give them jewelry.

3 - Rash Cream Disasters

The next morning, I get ready for work. After tucking my hair into its regulation bun, I put on my uniform—black skirt and jacket, white blouse, and those dreaded nylons. My legs instantly react, sending signals to my brain that scream, "Scratch us! Now!"

I ignore my legs' demands while I open the velvet box that Erich gave me last night. Ordinarily, I wouldn't accept jewelry from a stranger, but I made an exception in this case. After all, it's for the mission. The fact that I love charm bracelets doesn't hurt either.

Pulling the bracelet out of the box, I marvel at the gold charms—each one is a replica of a Scrabble tile with the various letters and point values etched on them.

I run my fingers over the "E" tile. Funny how it's right next to the "I" tile. "E" for Erich and "I" for Isabelle. When Erich clasped the bracelet on my wrist after dinner, I made a joke about how I can't seem to escape him, not even metaphorically on a charm bracelet. I thought it was funny, but he didn't crack a smile.

"Focus on the mission. The jewel thief is a Scotsman named Hamish MacDougall." Erich showed me a picture of a man in his late sixties or early seventies. His hair is white, but his beard still has a touch of russet. The man had probably been a full-blown redhead when he was younger.

Erich told me that Hamish has been responsible for some of the most notorious jewelry heists in Europe, but that no one has ever been able to prove it. Then he added, "Make sure Hamish notices your bracelet and then you can use it as a way to build rapport with him."

"Why? Is he going to want to steal it?" I asked.

Erich shook his head. "No, this isn't valuable enough for someone like him."

"Then why the bracelet?"

"Because he's obsessed with Scrabble," Erich explained. "When he finds out you're a Scrabble champion, he'll want to play with you. Prove that you're a worthy opponent, someone who can compete at an international level. Then, when the time is right, he'll ask you to be on his team at the Scrabble tournament in Amsterdam."

"That's it? Play Scrabble?"

"Yes. That's it . . . for now," he said as adjusted the bracelet, his fingers stroking the inside of my wrist and sending shivers down my spine.

As I recall the sensation of Erich's touch on my skin, my breath hitches in my chest.

Snap out of it, Isabelle. There wasn't anything romantic about his touch. This is just a job for him.

I tuck some wayward strands of hair back into my bun, then grab my binder. Time to head to the library and get some more studying done before the passengers embark this afternoon.

"You're late, again," Frau Albrecht barks as I walk through the reception area.

I glance at the clock on the wall. "But it's only eight. I don't have to be at the check-in desk until one."

"Correct. But you were supposed to be in the dining room thirty minutes ago."

"Oh, thanks, but I'm not hungry," I reply. "I had a big dinner last night."

"Your lack of appetite isn't my concern," she says. "Your dereliction of duty is."

"Dereliction of duty?" I splutter. "I was awake until three this morning reading about Heidelberg Castle, the Gutenberg Museum, and how riesling wine is made."

"Humph. That explains those dark circles under your eyes. You know they have concealer for that kind of thing." The older woman presses her lips together as she examines my legs. "Wear some dark-colored nylons to hide that rash."

"The nylons are what's causing the rash," I point out. "If you could make an exception so that I don't have to wear them, then—"

Frau Albrecht slams her hand on the desk. "No more exceptions. It's bad enough that Head Office sent an email saying you should be allowed to wear non-regulation jewelry. All the other women who work aboard this boat are content with a pair of simple stud earrings, but no, you have to wear a gaudy bracelet too."

I take a quick step backwards, conscious of the gold charms swaying back and forth on my wrist. "I'm sorry. I didn't realize they would do that," I say, trying to appease her.

She points toward the hallway leading off the reception area. "Go."

Figuring flight is the better option in this situation, I rush into the dining room.

"Finally." Sophia motions for me to join her at one of the tables. She hands me a stack of napkins. "Fold these."

As I try to follow along while Sophia transforms a napkin into a flower, I ask her why we're doing this.

"This isn't a large ocean-going cruise ship with staff dedicated to certain departments," she says. "There are only thirty crew members aboard the *Abenteuer*. We all have to pitch in."

"I hope they don't expect me to cook. Unless the passengers like burnt toast, then I'm your girl," I joke.

Sophia narrows her eyes. "I doubt the executive chef would let you in his kitchen. Not after how you insulted his marshmallows. Now hurry up and fold those napkins. We still have to help get cabins ready."

"How long is that going to take? I need to get ready for my welcome presentation."

"Oh, you don't have to worry about that. I found Maria's presentation on her thumb drive." Sophia smiles, but it's one of those smiles that doesn't quite reach the eyes. "All you'll have to do is click through the slides and read off the talking points."

"Wow, really? Thanks a million. You're saving my butt." I continue to work on the napkins, but mine look more like mushrooms than flowers. After trying to fold a few more, Sophia shakes her head and tells me to place wine glasses on each table instead.

Auguste Renoir hovers behind me with a ruler, making sure each glass is placed at the appropriate distance from the edge of the table.

"No, no, no!" The chef throws his hands in the air. "If the table is not set correctly, it will reflect poorly on Auguste Renoir."

After he shouts at me for setting a red wine glass down instead of a white wine glass, I stamp my foot. "Isabelle Martinez cannot work in these conditions." I shake my head when I realize I've started referring to myself in the third person, too.

The chef puts his hands on his hips. "Then perhaps Isabelle Martinez should quit."

I thrust the wine glass I'm holding at him. "Fine, I will."

"You're going to quit?" Sophia asks hopefully from across the room.

"I am . . ." I pause when I see my charm bracelet reflected in the windowpane. I take a deep breath and continue, "I am *not* going to quit."

Darn that Erich. He's managed to convince me that I'm essential to this mission. If I quit, then the terrorists would win. No matter how much I want to flounce off this riverboat, I can't.

The chef hands me back the wine glass. "Continue. Auguste Renoir doesn't have all day."

After another hour getting the dining room ready, and then another three hours cleaning cabins—turns out my strong suit is cleaning toilet bowls—Sophia and I head down to the reception desk.

"You sit here," she says, motioning at one of the stools. "After I check in each passenger, hand them a welcome packet, make sure they know where their cabin is, and answer any questions they have."

My hands shake as the first people board the boat. What if they ask me difficult questions, like "Which direction does the Rhine River flow?" Or "Do I need an electrical adapter for my hairdryer?"

I'm so nervous that I'm worried that the hives on my legs are going to start spreading to my arms and face. That would not be a good look. But what would be worse is if Hamish MacDougall rebuffs my attempts to bond with him.

I listen carefully to people's accents as Sophia checks them in. There are plenty of German, Swedish, and French accents, but no one speaks with a Scottish lilt. One couple converses rapidly with Sophia in Greek. I wonder what she's said to them about me because when I hand them their welcome packets, they look at me like I have the plague.

My ears perk up when I hear fellow Americans. "Hello there, darling," a middle-aged woman says to Sophia. "We're the Sinclairs. Emma and Hank Sinclair."

"I'm Hank and she's Emma," her husband points out.

Emma playfully slaps Hank's arm. "She can figure that out, silly. Why would a gal as good-looking as me be named Hank?"

I lean forward. "Where are you from?"

"Alabama," Emma says.

"Greenville, Alabama," Hank adds.

I grin. "That's near where *Sweet Home Alabama* took place, right? I loved that movie."

"Me too." Emma smiles. "Do I sense a little southern in that accent of yours?"

"Yes, ma'am," I say. "Texas born and bred."

Emma looks at Hank. "And you thought there wouldn't be any Americans aboard this cruise."

Sophia kicks my leg under the desk, causing my hives to cry out again to be scratched. "Stop chitchatting," she says in an undertone. "There's a line of people waiting to check in."

After telling the Sinclairs that I'll see them later, Sophia and I continue working. We have two hundred passengers on this cruise, which is significantly smaller than what you'll find on a big ocean-going cruise ship. It means that we can get to know the passengers on a more personal level, and more importantly for the mission, I can keep a close eye on Hamish. That is, if he ever shows up.

After an hour has passed and there's no one else waiting in line, Sophia says, "Looks like that's everyone accounted for."

"Are you sure?" I furrow my brow. "Where's the—" I stop myself just in time. Can you imagine if I had asked Sophia where the jewel thief was?

"Where's the what?" Sophia asks without looking up from her keyboard.

"The maps of the boat," I say to cover my tracks. "I seem to have misplaced them."

Before Sophia can answer, an older gentleman shuffles toward the check-in desk. He's leaning heavily on an intricately carved cane, and each step he takes looks painful. "Good afternoon, lassies," he calls out cheerfully.

I mentally pull up Hamish MacDougall's picture in my head. Yep, this is him. The notorious jewel thief. The man who is going to be indirectly responsible for terrorists getting their hands on illegal weapons.

Extending my hand so that he'll notice my Scrabble charm bracelet, I start to say hello, but Sophia bats my arm away. "You're out of welcome packets," she says. "Go grab another one from the back."

By the time I find the spare packets—they were hidden underneath Frau Albrecht's enormous purse—Sophia is already directing Hamish to the elevator. "Just take that up one flight to your cabin," she says.

I try to rush after him to give his welcome packet, but Sophia tells me not to bother. "I found one already."

My shoulders slump. I missed my opportunity to connect with Hamish. It's only day one of the cruise and I've already botched the mission.

* * *

After finishing my shift, I head to my quarters, grateful that I have a single room. Sophia had cattily pointed out that this was unusual for someone at my job level.

"The only reason I have my own room right now is because Maria used to be my roommate," she told me. "And now Maria is gone. Transferred because of you."

Did Erich arrange for me to get my own room? He's pulled strings already—engineering my tour manager promotion and getting an exception to the dress code so that I can wear this charm bracelet—maybe the single cabin is also his work. Now, if only he could get Frau Albrecht to drop the nylons requirement.

Earlier this afternoon, she gave me a pair of black nylons to hide my rash. They're even itchier than my previous ones. I have a couple of hours before I'm back on duty, so I strip off my uniform and take a cool shower, hoping that will soothe my legs.

It doesn't help. My legs are wet, but they still feel like they're on fire. I slip on my robe, comb my hair, then perch on the edge of the lower bunk. After sending my friend Ginny a quick text, I slather rash cream on my legs.

While I'm screwing the lid back on the rash cream container, a knock on the door startles me. When I drop the container, I utter a naughty word, possibly two. All of my rash cream is on the floor. Who knows when I'll be able to get more.

I sigh. Please let the person who knocked be a rash cream salesperson. I stand and walk over to the door, but before I can open it, Erich walks in.

"Uh, hello," I say sarcastically. "Most people wait to be invited into someone's cabin before they enter."

"Didn't you say come in?" Erich asks.

"No, I said . . . never mind." I grab a towel from the bathroom and start to clean up the rash cream from the floor.

"Sorry," he says. "Good thing I'm not a vampire."

"Huh?"

"Vampires can't enter someone's home unless they're invited. Didn't you see *Twilight*?"

"I'm sure my file was very clear about the fact that I can't stand sci-fi and fantasy movies." As I wipe up the rest of the rash cream, I say, "But it's a relief to know that you don't sleep in a coffin at night."

"No, coffins are too constraining. I toss and turn when I'm sleeping."

My face grows warm as I imagine what Erich looks like tossing and turning in bed. Is he the type of guy who wears a t-shirt and shorts to sleep in? Or pajamas? In the buff?

Oh my gosh, I have to stop thinking about Erich in this way. I turn to him and snap, "What are you doing here, anyway?"

"I'm here for your debriefing. Standard operating procedure after an agent makes contact with a target." Erich unbuttons his jacket and sits down on my bunk. "So what did you find out about our Hamish MacDougall?"

"Nothing. Sophia didn't give me a chance to speak with him." I tuck my hair behind my ears, then groan. "Great. Now I have rash cream in my hair."

Erich looks at my legs. "You really should see a doctor about that."

"Better yet, why don't you get Frau Albrecht to drop the nylons requirement?"

"I tried, believe me, but my contact in Head Office can only do so much. If he asks for too many exceptions, people would become suspicious."

I walk into the bathroom, saying over my shoulder, "Oh, come on, nylons are the least suspicious thing you could request. Promoting someone like me on the spot to a tour manager position? That's what sends up red flags."

After I wash the rash cream out of my hair, I run a brush through it. When I come back out, Erich says, "You look nice with your hair down."

"Yeah, that's another thing your guy could work on—getting rid of the bun requirement. The pins hurt my head."

Erich holds my gaze for a moment, then clears his throat. "We should get back to the debrief."

"I told you, I don't have any information to share," I say. "I didn't speak with the jewel thief."

"That doesn't mean you don't have any intel." Erich stands and crosses the short distance in the room to face me. Placing his hands on my shoulders, he says, "You'll have learned something about Hamish MacDougall without realizing it. Somewhere in that subconscious of yours is valuable information."

I gasp when Erich spins me around and places his hands over my eyes, messing up my hair in the process. "Relax, take a few deep breaths, and cast your mind back to when you first saw the jewel thief."

Exactly how am I supposed to relax in this situation? Erich is inches away from me. When I squirm, he whispers, "Keep your eyes closed. It will help you recall important details. Think back. Shutting off your vision will help awaken your memories. What are your other senses telling you?"

This is torture. Complete and utter torture. The only thing I can sense is Erich. The feel of his hands on my face, the smell of his cologne, the taste of his lips.

Whoa, hang on there, buttercup. It's not like you've kissed Erich. How would you know how his lips taste?

"This is ridiculous," I mutter.

"Humor me, Isabelle. Just relax and tell me the first thing that comes to mind."

"If I do, will you leave me in peace?"

"Of course," he says. "Now, deep breaths in, deep breaths out."

As I inhale and exhale slowly, I feel him doing the same. Soon we're breathing in sync, like it's the most natural thing in the world.

"The jewel thief," Erich prompts.

"His cane looks like an antique, but it's a fake. There's a slight groove where the ivory handle meets the ebony wood. He's originally from Aberdeenshire, but currently lives in Glasgow. He has a small scar on his left earlobe. Likely from having an earring torn out of his ear. And he recently petted a miniature poodle."

I feel like Sherlock Holmes gleaning all this information from careful observation of Hamish's appearance and listening to his accent.

"Excellent," Erich says crisply. He drops his hands and steps away from me. My senses are shaken from the abrupt way he took his hands off my shoulders. Even though I know he's only a few feet away from me, it feels like he's a million miles away.

When I spin around, he has his hand on the door handle.

"You're leaving?"

"Of course. We finished the debriefing."

"But I . . ." I wring my hands as my voice trails off. I can't very well say that I want him to stay.

Misinterpreting my hesitation, Erich says, "Don't worry. You're doing fine. You're a natural at this. You're going to be a very effective agent for the organization." Then he bows his head slightly before closing the door behind him.

* * *

I rush into the corridor after Erich. "What do you mean by that?" I yell at his retreating back. His only response is a brief wave over his shoulder.

I clench my fists and stomp my feet. Very mature, I know.

I spin around, realizing the door across the hall from me is open. Sophia pokes her head out and asks, "What is going on out here?"

Cinching my robe tightly around my waist, I turn and apologize. "Sorry, I didn't realize I was speaking so loud."

"Is that who I think it is?" Sophia points toward the end of the corridor where Erich is pushing open the door that leads to the stairwell. She gasps. "If Frau Albrecht finds out you're having an affair with a passenger, she'll fire you."

"An affair? Hah. You'd have to pay me to sleep with that man."

"He's paying you for sex?" Sophia gasps. "That would make you a—"

My eyes widen. "What? No way. I'm not a . . ." I can't bring myself to say the word. I hold up my hands, take a deep breath, then say, "There's nothing going on between the two of us."

Sophia smirks. "Do you always receive male company in your cabin wearing a robe? And your hair looks like the very definition of bed-head."

"Erich showed up unannounced and barged into my cabin. If I had known he was coming—which I didn't—I would have been dressed."

"Erich? Is that what you're calling him?" Sophia cocks her head to one side. "You're on a first-name basis with a VIP passenger and you have the audacity to claim that there's nothing going on."

"Really, there isn't," I say.

"Then why was he in your cabin?"

"Um . . . to give me some rash cream for my legs?"

"Right. Herr Zimmermann just happens to carry around rash cream in his suitcase. Totally believable."

"I think he's a pharmaceutical sales representative. It's a new product that they're doing a clinical trial for." As the words rush out, I realize how unbelievable it all sounds.

"You realize that most clinical trials are done at doctors' offices or hospitals," Sophia points out. "People don't take riverboat cruises to find test subjects."

"They don't?"

"You're a really bad liar. If you're going to have an affair with a passenger, then you should come up with a better cover story." Sophia shakes her head. "Well, I guess it doesn't matter. Once I tell Frau Albrecht about you and Herr Zimmermann, you'll be history. She'll march you off the boat so fast your head will spin."

And I'll have your tour manager job. She leaves this last bit unsaid, but we all know that's what she's thinking.

Sophia startles when a voice says behind us, "Where are the towels, cherie? Auguste Renoir is dripping water all over the floor."

When I spin around, I bite back a smile. The executive chef is standing in Sophia's doorway, buck naked except for his chef's hat and a washcloth that he's holding over his private parts.

"Hmm . . . I seem to recall that as part of my new employee orientation, Frau Albrecht was very clear that the staff is not to engage in, um, what did she call it? Oh, yeah, inappropriate relations with each other." I point at the chef. "Do you think she would consider this inappropriate?"

Sophia grits her teeth. "Fine, let's call a truce. You don't tell her about Auguste and I won't tell her about Herr Zimmermann."

"It's a deal."

Sophia mutters something to the executive chef about being more discreet, then slams the door in my face. After a moment, she opens it back up and hisses. "Better not count on getting Maria's presentation from me. You'll have to wing it."

4 - An Unexpected Phone Call

I have a serious situation on my hands. I was counting on having Maria's presentation. I'd click through her slides, read off her talking points, and try to avoid any detailed questions. Easy peasy. Now I have less than an hour before I'm supposed to be in the lounge to welcome the passengers.

Why did I blackmail Sophia into keeping my supposed affair with Erich a secret? Who cares if she had told Frau Albrecht that I was sleeping with a passenger. Frau Albrecht would have fired me and then I would have been off the hook for this presentation.

Well, there's a perfectly good explanation for that. Two actually. First off, I care about my reputation. The last thing I want is for people to think I was fired because I was having "inappropriate relations" with a VIP passenger. Second, I'm still broke. After telling my mom that I didn't need her financial help after all, I can't really go back and ask for money now.

I let out a huge sigh. Then I leaf through my binder, scrawling notes down furiously while keeping an eye on the time. With only ten minutes to spare, I quickly get dressed and fix my hair and make-up. I run up the two flights of stairs that lead from the lower deck, where the crew cabins are located, up to the reception area. As I'm rounding the corner, ready to dart up the next set of stairs to the lounge, I spot Frau Albrecht at the reception desk. She's cracking her knuckles while barking orders at a hapless desk clerk.

Not wanting to be her next victim, I spin around. I creep backwards out the door onto the outer deck.

"Hey, watch where you're going," someone says, but it's too late. I trip over a coiled rope. As I land on my hands and knees, my binder goes flying out of my arms. It bounces off the deck, sending all my handwritten notes up into the air. I scramble to catch them, but they float off in the breeze and land in the water.

I watch in horror as the pages float off down the Rhine River. Perhaps the passengers would be interested in seeing me do magic tricks instead of giving a welcome presentation? I sigh, then scoop up what's left of my binder. When I walk back into the reception area, Frau Albrecht frowns.

"You're always late," she says. "The passengers will be getting impatient."

I nod, then slowly march up the stairs to my impending doom. The good news is that I scraped my legs when I fell, so the pain from the cuts on my calves is distracting me from the itchiness of my rash. It's important to be able to look on the positive side of things, right?

When I walk into the lounge, I gulp. So many people, all waiting for me. Contrary to what Frau Albrecht said, they don't seem to be waiting impatiently. They're happily sipping on after-dinner drinks, taking selfies, and chatting with their fellow passengers. The room is buzzing with energy. Maybe they won't notice if I silently disappear.

I inch out of the room, being careful this time to look behind me, when someone calls out my name. Emma from Alabama waves at me, then tugs on her husband's sleeve to alert him to my presence. When Hank sees me, he beams.

"Quiet down, folks," he says. "Miss Isabelle is here to give us her presentation."

I look down at my grandmother's amethyst ring. *She was a strong woman. You're a strong woman. You can do this.*

I walk up to the front of the room and grip the sides of the podium. "Good evening, everyone."

"We can't hear you," someone yells from the back.

"Speak up, lassie," another man says.

I look up sharply, recognizing that Scottish accent. Hamish MacDougall is seated at a table in the back of the room. He gives me an encouraging thumbs up.

One of the bartenders rushes up and clips a microphone on the lapel of my jacket. "Is that better?" I ask, checking the sound level with the crowd.

When they murmur their approval, I take a few deep breaths. *You can do this, Isabelle. You've read the binder front to back. The information is in your brain. You just have to let it out.*

I decide to be honest with the audience. "I'm not very good at public speaking," I confess. "In fact, I'm a bundle of nerves."

Being vulnerable seems to work. I can feel supportive energy emanating from the audience. Feeling encouraged, I state the obvious. "You're on board the *Abenteuer*. It's a riverboat."

"I think you mean *she's* a riverboat," someone says. "Boats are always female."

"Yeah, that's true," an older man standing by the bar says. "Like women, ships are unpredictable."

After the crowd good-naturedly boos him, I continue with some other obvious facts. "We're going to sail on the Rhine River and see lots of interesting stuff. There will be delicious food. Did you enjoy your dinner tonight?"

A few of the passengers nod. Others look confused, like I'm a stand-up comedian who can't seem to deliver a funny punch line.

"Better get on with it, dear," Hank says in a stage whisper. "The crowd is getting restless."

"Um . . . who likes cuckoo clocks?" I ask.

A few people raise their hands.

"There's a place that sells them in, um . . ." I wipe sweat off my brow as I struggle to remember the name of the German town where the shop is.

When I pause to take a sip of water, Sophia approaches the podium. She hands me a laptop. "Here's Maria's presentation," she whispers.

I furrow my brow. "Why the change of heart?"

"It's not about you," she says. "It's about the passengers. They deserve a first-class presentation, not whatever this is that you're doing."

She hooks up the laptop, and I breathe a sigh of relief when Maria's opening slide displays on the screen. I click to the next slide and practically do a fist pump when a map of the Rhine River appears. It triggers my memory, and I point at the screen. "That's Rudesheim. That's where you can buy a cuckoo clock."

"Just read out the talking points on each slide and you'll be fine," Sophia says in an undertone. "Do not ad-lib."

So I do. I talk through the itinerary and explain the optional excursions in each port. The information flows freely. I even start to add in detail to augment Maria's talking points. I've got this. When I get to a slide titled, "Entertainment on Board," I get a little cocky. I can recite all the activities planned for the passengers from heart. So I simply click to the next slide but don't bother to turn around to look at it.

I start to tell the passengers about the traditional dance troupe who will be performing later in the week when a woman points at the screen and screams.

"What is that?" someone asks.

"It looks like a laboratory experiment," a man says. "Something you'd see in a petri dish."

Other people start to chime in, clearly horrified by what's behind me. When I spin around to see what's so disgusting, I'm confronted with a close-up of a red, blistering rash. A very familiar rash. The very same rash that's on my legs. How do I know it's my rash? Because it says so in big letters right on the slide.

* * *

Could I be any more mortified? I want nothing more than to run out of this room as fast as I can. But for some reason, my feet feel like they're super-glued to the floor. I can't seem to budge.

This is one of those times that I wished alien abduction was real. If little green men beamed me up to their spaceship right now, I'd be thrilled. Who cares if they do some weird experiments on me? It'd be better than being here in a room full of people staring at a picture of the horrifying rash on my legs.

The aliens aren't coming to save the day, are they? My therapist had suggested using humor to manage my anxiety in stressful situation. I clear my throat, then tell a joke. "A friend of mine made so many rash decisions, he became a dermatologist."

I don't know what the bartender is putting in people's drinks, but it must be pretty potent because everyone cracks up. Then, before I know it, people are shouting out their own bad jokes.

When Hank yells out, "How do you spot a secret agent? Give him measles," I look around the room. Is Erich here? Would he laugh at a joke about secret agents? I doubt it.

After a few more minutes of audience participation, I finally manage to wrap things up, telling the passengers to be ready bright and early the next morning for our excursion to Heidelberg Castle.

Several people come up afterwards. Some ask questions about the itinerary, some want to know if the marshmallows are gluten-free. But a surprising number share their own skin condition stories. It's amazing how people can bond over their dermatological issues.

"Honey, my nephew is a dermatologist in Boulder," one lady says. "Why don't I send him pictures of your rash? Then you can do one of those video calls so that you can get his professional opinion. He's single, you know."

I politely thank her, but decline the offer for both the consultation and fix-up. Spotting Hamish at the bar, I rush over to see if I can strike up a conversation with him, but he leaves before I get a chance.

Frau Albrecht's voice booms over the loudspeakers. "Isabelle Martinez, please report to reception."

This should be fun. When I reach the bottom of the stairs, Frau Albrecht is standing there, her arms folded across her chest.

"Head Office phoned," she says. "About you. Again."

"Listen, I can explain," I say. "Sophia gave me those slides. You can't possibly think that I'd show pictures like that."

The older woman furrows her brow. "Pictures of what?"

"Oh, isn't that why Head Office called you?"

"No, they called to say that you don't need to wear nylons anymore." She cracks a couple knuckles, then adds, "Yet another exception is being made for you. Curious, isn't it? What makes you so special?"

Sophia walks out of the back room. "Oh, Isabelle, how did your presentation go?" she asks innocently.

"I think you know exactly how it went," I say. "You sabotaged it."

Sophia holds a hand to her chest. "Me? Never."

Frau Albrecht looks back and forth between the two of us. "What exactly happened during the presentation?"

"I have no idea," Sophia says. "I was in the back room filling out paperwork."

I fling my hands in the air. I've had enough of this. Erich can nab the jewel thief on his own. "Tell you what, Frau Albrecht, why don't I make things easier and resign. It's obvious I'm not wanted here."

At my announcement that I'm quitting, Frau Albrecht gives me a self-satisfied smile. The way she licks her sharp, pointy teeth reminds me of a lioness who is about to devour her kill.

"I'll be sure to inform Head Office of your resignation," she says. "No need to work your two-week notice period. Sophia can take over your job immediately. Why don't you go pack your bags? I'll call for a taxi to collect you."

I sense Erich behind me, and my whole body tenses. He places his hands lightly on my shoulders, then says to Frau Albrecht, "Isabelle isn't resigning."

The older woman presses her lips together. She's obviously in a difficult situation. Contradicting a VIP passenger and personal friend of the cruise ship line owner would be frowned upon by Head Office. But she desperately wants to be rid of me.

What to do, what to do, she seems to be thinking. Her eyes flicker back and forth.

Erich doesn't give her a chance to decide. "Like I said, Isabelle isn't resigning."

He presses his fingers into my shoulders and says in an undertone that only I can hear, "That was a foolish thing to do."

"What was foolish was agreeing to your ridiculous plan in the first place," I whisper.

There's no response from him. The only sound I can hear is my heart beating. Or is that his heart beating?

Erich suddenly releases me, then says brightly to Frau Albrecht, "I'm glad we cleared that up. Have a good evening."

"Good evening, sir," the older woman says, her voice choking back rage.

"Come along." Erich grabs my elbow and steers me up to the sun deck. The deck chairs are deserted. The passengers are probably all still in the lounge, telling each other jokes and comparing eczema treatments.

Erich comes to a halt at the stern of the boat. He pulls his phone out and places a call. "It's me," he says. "Isabelle needs to be convinced about her importance to this mission. I think it's time we told her everything."

Erich listens intently for a few moments, then brusquely hands me the phone. When I press it to my ear, a familiar voice says gruffly, "Hello, Isabelle."

I'm so startled that I almost drop the phone. The last person I expected to hear on the other end of the line was my former commanding officer. "General Taylor," I splutter, instantly feeling my posture straightening. I resist the urge to salute.

"It's time you were read in," the general says. "Erich can explain the details more fully, but suffice it to say, this mission is critical. The terrorists' target is the United Nations in New York. If you don't help, there will be a tremendous loss of life. In order for this mission to be successful, Erich needs you. Your country needs you. The world needs you. You need to step up."

The general continues talking, but all I hear repeating over and over through my head is, "Erich needs you." As I stare into his icy-blue eyes, I wonder what it would be like to be truly needed by this man.

5 - A Semi-Naked Man

The next morning, I wake up with an excruciating headache. This sort of thing happens to me when I'm stressed. Considering the fact that I agreed to help Erich and the general save the world, you could say that I'm feeling a bit of pressure.

I squeeze my eyes shut and rub my temples. This can't be real, right? I must be having one of those waking dreams. A dream so vivid that it seems real. Cause there's no way that the United States government has asked me to go undercover and help the German equivalent of James Bond stop an arms deal and prevent a terrorist attack on the United Nations. Sure, that's totally believable.

Nope, here's what's going to happen. I'll open my eyes and find myself lying in bed in my cramped studio apartment in Texas. I'll pop a couple of painkillers, take a shower, put on jeans and a t-shirt, and head to the mini-mart for my shift. I definitely won't be on a riverboat docked on the Rhine River.

I pry my eyes open and . . . whoa, this isn't my apartment. Am I still dreaming? I sit up on the edge of my bed.

Wait a minute, not my bed. My bed is a fold-out couch from Lou's second-hand store. But I appear to be perched on the bottom bunk in a ship's cabin.

The pressure in my head intensifies. You don't feel pain in your dreams, do you? Oh, my gosh, this *is* real. I am working undercover on a riverboat. And that German James Bond? He's real too.

Memories of last night flood back. Erich calling my former commanding officer, General Taylor. The general convincing me that my government needs me. Me reluctantly agreeing to help Erich save the world. Then Erich telling me I should be grateful to him because I don't have to wear nylons anymore.

Okay, time to stop thinking about Erich. Gotta get up and do this tour manager thing. I get ready in record time, probably because I'm not having to spend ten minutes applying rash cream and gingerly pulling nylons on. Actually, I'm tempted to wear nylons just so Erich doesn't have a reason to smugly tell me how he pulled strings and "saved" me from them.

There you go. I'm thinking about him again. Why is that man always on my mind? He's everything I can't stand—secretive, unemotional, and way too sure of himself.

I check the time. Yikes, I'm late. A quick glance in the mirror to make sure all my hair is tucked into a tight bun, then I dash up to the reception area. I spend the next twenty minutes making sure all the passengers who signed up for the excursion to Heidelberg Castle are on the tour bus. Just as I'm about to tell the driver to close the door, Sophia barges on the bus.

"You're not coming with us, are you?" I ask her. "I thought you were working at the reception desk today."

Sophia ignores me—she's still irritated that her plan to sabotage my presentation last night backfired. Instead of the passengers complaining about me, they're talking about how refreshing it is to have a tour manager who is self-effacing and has a sense of humor.

My nemesis looks around the bus, then says to someone standing outside, "No problem, there's an empty seat." Then she gives me an evil look and says, "Last minute addition to the tour."

Then Erich boards the bus. Super. Just when I thought I was going to get a day away from him.

"Where's Hamish?" he whispers as he sits next to me.

"He canceled at the last minute. Something about not feeling well."

Erich shoots me a look. "But this tour is supposed to be an opportunity for you to bond with him."

"What was I supposed to do? Tell Frau Albrecht that I can't escort the group to Heidelberg Castle, then barge into Hamish's cabin and force feed him chicken noodle soup until he feels better?"

Erich shakes his head, then stares out the window at the passing scenery.

When the bus pulls up to the historic site, the group oohs and aahs over the picturesque red sandstone edifice. Situated on the forested slopes of the Königstuhl hill, the castle towers over the city of Heidelberg. Over a million people visit this area each year. Fortunately, I'm only responsible for the thirty-two passengers who signed up for this excursion. My duties today consist primarily of babysitting the group. A professional tour guide is going to show them the castle, which is great, because I haven't had a lot of time to study up on the history of the area.

After I hand my group off to the tour guide, a blonde woman in her mid-twenties intercepts me. "You must be Isabelle," she says. "I'm Zoe."

I cock my head to one side, trying to place her. I don't recognize her from the riverboat. Maybe she works at the castle.

"You know, Zoe Randolph," she says. "From the magazine?"

"The magazine?"

"Uh-huh. We're here for the photo shoot. Didn't Sophia tell you we'd be meeting you at the castle?"

"Ah, that explains it." I smile. "Let's just say that Sophia's not great with communication. You're going to have to fill me in."

"No problem. Let me get my colleague over here first." She waves at a man who's standing by the entrance. As he saunters over, he pauses to take a picture of some passengers from the *Abenteuer* who are inspecting the German Renaissance architecture.

Zoe introduces us. "This is Max Guerrero, the magazine's photographer."

Max takes my hand in his and kisses the back of it in a show of exaggerated gallantry. "Pleasure to meet you, Isabelle."

Zoe rolls her eyes. "Max, knock it off. We're here to do a job, not find you a girlfriend."

Max grins. "Who says I can't do both?"

"Just ignore him. I find it works better that way," Zoe says to me. "Anyway, we were sent here by a travel magazine to do a story on the riverboat cruise."

Max holds up his camera. "I'm in charge of the pictures. Zoe takes care of the words."

"That's because you can barely string a sentence together," Zoe says to him. "Taking photos is the easy part. All you have to do is point and click."

"There's way more to it than that. You have to consider the lighting and camera angles. Then there's the post-production editing." Max turns to me and pretends to frame up a shot. "In the case of Isabelle, she's so gorgeous that I wouldn't need to worry about lighting or do any editing."

Zoe makes a gagging motion. "Enough already, Casanova. Why don't you go take some photos while Isabelle and I talk logistics."

Max gives her a playful salute, then goes off to join the tour group.

"Sorry about my colleague. He's a compulsive flirter." Her smile fades for a moment, then she says brightly, "Fortunately, he doesn't behave that way with me. We keep things professional."

We talk for a while about arranging interviews with some of the passengers, then Zoe says, "Who's that guy? He keeps staring at you."

I look over in the direction she's indicating and see Erich. His arms are folded across his chest, a sour expression is on his face, and his gaze fixed firmly on me. The total opposite of fun-loving, flirtatious Max. "Oh, him. He's a VIP passenger."

"Is there anything between you two?" Zoe asks. "He's got that possessive vibe going on. You should have seen the look on his face when Max was flirting with you."

I press my lips together. "Nope, nothing going on. It's strictly professional."

"If you say so." Zoe looks dubious. "I better go check on Max and make sure he's taking photos, not chatting up girls."

After she walks off, I turn to look back at Erich. We engage in a staring contest for a few moments. Man, could he look any crankier? I take a photo of him to send to one of my friends. I had sent her a text earlier about meeting a mysterious stranger and she wants to see what he looks like.

While I'm checking to see how the picture turned out, Erich grabs my phone. "No photos of me."

"Hey, that's personal property," I say, yanking it back.

"I don't like having my picture taken," Erich says.

"I don't like marshmallows, but that doesn't mean I can stop other people from eating them."

"A picture is different."

"How?"

"A marshmallow is just . . ."

"A disgusting, sugary treat?" I suggest.

He nods. "They really are disgusting, aren't they? How can people eat them?"

I shrug. "No accounting for taste. But why do you care if I take your picture? Are you worried I'm going to steal your image and do some voodoo over it?"

Erich furrows his brow. "Voodoo?"

"You know, a magic spell to make you do something you don't want to do."

"Like kiss you?"

My mouth drops open. "Where did that come from?"

"Just seeing if it would get a reaction out of you."

There's zero emotion in his voice, which infuriates me for some reason. "I definitely do not want you to kiss me."

"I see," he says calmly.

"I think we should change the subject." I tug at my jacket. "Why do you hate having your picture taken? It's not like you're hideous looking."

"You think I'm good-looking?"

"I didn't say that. I said you're *not* hideous looking. That's the bottom of the scale. The next step up is 'horrible,' followed by 'ugly.' Good-looking is near the top of the scale."

"So, which one am I? Horrible or ugly?"

"Let me take another picture and we'll see."

"No pictures," he says intently. "In my line of work, we avoid pictures."

I wave my hands at the crowd of tourists milling about. "You don't think you're in a million people's pictures already in the background?"

"Probably," he says. "But their phones are less likely to be monitored. You're part of this mission. You have to be careful."

"So is it okay if I look at cute kitten videos?" I ask sarcastically.

"I'm not really a fan of kittens," Erich says. "Puppies would be okay."

"Hmm, and here's me thinking pythons were more your thing."

Max comes over and interrupts us. "Sorry, man, I just need to ask Isabelle something." He turns to me and drapes his arm over my shoulders. "Would you be able to show me around the ship later today as part of my photo shoot?"

"The ship isn't that big," Erich says. "You can find your way around on your own."

Max steps away from me and turns to face Erich straight on. As the two guys square off I notice that, although Max is taller, Erich's shoulders are broader. Not that broad shoulders are a thing for me. They aren't. Really.

Trying to calm things down, I put my hand on Erich's arm and give it a gentle squeeze. Then I turn to Max. "No problem. I'll meet you after dinner?"

Max gives Erich a cocky grin, then rejoins the tour group.

Erich looks down at my hand, and I quickly remove it. "You need to stay focused on the mission," he says. "You can flirt with guys once it's over."

"I wasn't flirting with Max."

"Yes, you were. You batted your eyes at him."

"Batted my eyes? What era are you from?" I laugh while I do an exaggerated batting of my eyes. "Like this? Sounds like you're jealous."

"Jealous? No. I'm a professional. The only reason I'm interested in your love life is because of the mission."

Man, is this guy tense. He takes everything so seriously. When I ask him if he ever relaxes, he says, "Sure, in between missions."

"When's the last time you were between missions?"

Erich considers this for a moment, then says quietly, "I can't remember."

"Pretend you had a day off from saving the world. What would you do?"

Erich frowns. "That's a silly question."

I put my hand back on his arm and, this time, he doesn't seem to care.

"Just humor me. What would you do if you had twenty-four hours of uninterrupted time where you didn't have to worry about anything but you?"

"I'd go horseback riding."

"You like horses? I grew up with them. We have a ranch and I . . ." I hold up my hand. "Why am I telling you that? Of course, you already know about my family's ranch. You know, it really sucks knowing everything about me is in some file."

"That's not true, Isabelle." Erich's gaze softens. "All your thoughts are secret. No one knows what you're thinking except you."

He excuses himself, and as he walks away, I chew on my lip. Thank goodness he doesn't know what goes on in my head. Cause if he did, he'd know that I can't stop thinking about kissing him.

* * *

By the time I get all the passengers back to the boat from Heidelberg Castle, I'm exhausted. Who knew that babysitting a group of tourists was so tiring? Erich disappeared halfway through the tour, telling me he'd find his own way back to the boat. I was having a hard time being around him without thinking extremely unprofessional thoughts, so I was grateful that he left.

I head to the kitchen to grab a sandwich for dinner, planning to eat in my room and study up on our next destination.

"There you are," the executive chef says when I walk through the door. "Herr Zimmermann has requested room service, and he wants you to bring it to his stateroom."

"Me?" I gulp, not wanting to face Erich again today.

"Auguste Renoir does not like that tone of voice." He slams a steak on the counter and glares at me. "Everyone is busy getting the dining room dinner ready for the first seating."

A waitress bustles into the kitchen to grab some glasses. "She thinks she's

365

better than the rest of us," she says. "Gallivants around all day sightseeing, then wants to take the rest of the night off and have a bubble bath while everyone else works."

"Did you know that she doesn't have to wear nylons?" a dishwasher informs the room. "Special exception from Head Office."

The waitress scowls. "Lucky girl. I can't stand wearing nylons."

I hold up my hands. "First, I wasn't sightseeing. Second, I don't have a bathtub. And third . . . well, I agree. Nylons suck. Maybe if all the women banded together and stopped wearing them, Head Office would change the policy."

The chef points to the corner of the kitchen. "Wait there while I finish grilling Herr Zimmermann's steaks."

I furrow my brow. "Steaks? Plural?"

"One of them is probably for you," the waitress says cattily. "He also ordered caviar and champagne."

"Voilà," the chef says as he plates Erich's dinner. "Now go. You are disrupting Auguste Renoir's kitchen."

I grumble the entire time I wheel the cart to Erich's stateroom. The grumbling turns into shallow breathing when Erich opens the door. The man is completely naked. His skin glistens with droplets of water, and he's holding a razor in one hand.

Okay, he's not *completely* naked. There is a towel wrapped around his waist, but I'm pretty sure there's nothing on underneath that. So, yeah, naked.

I push the cart toward him. "Here's your dinner."

Erich steps back and points at the table by the window. "Go ahead and set it up there."

"Um, I think I'll pass." Yep, no way I'm going to go in there with a naked man. "You can leave the cart outside your door when you're done and someone will be by to pick it up."

A couple walks by Erich's stateroom at that very moment, and stops to say hello to him. Erich points at the table again. "Go on," he says to me. "This is room service, isn't it? If I wanted self-service, I would have gone to a fast-food restaurant."

Not wanting the other passengers to witness me flinging a steak at him, I wheel the cart inside. I set the plates and glasses on the table, then set the champagne bucket next to them.

"Go on and sit down," Erich says as he closes the door behind him. "I'll just be a minute."

"Sit?"

"Yes, you know how to sit, don't you? You lower yourself down onto a chair. For someone with an IQ off the charts, you'd think you'd be familiar with the concept."

"Someone's cranky," I say. "Sounds like you might have low blood sugar. Is that why you ordered two steaks?"

"No, I ordered two steaks because there's going to be two people dining."

"Oh . . ." It dawns on me that he probably invited another woman to his stateroom for dinner. I try to recall who among the passengers he might be interested in and all I can come up with is a woman from Luxembourg who I saw him talking with earlier. "Then why do you want me to sit down?"

He shakes his head. "Because you're the woman I'm dining with. Now sit."

I perch on the edge of the chair. Why do I feel relieved that it's me the other steak is for, not the lady from Luxembourg?

A few minutes later, Erich comes out of the bathroom, dressed in gray slacks and a black t-shirt. His hair is still damp, and he's freshly shaven. As he fills up the champagne flutes, he says, "I thought it might be a good idea if we got to know each other better so that we can work more effectively as a team."

"Team-building? Over steak and caviar?"

"Can you think of a better way?"

"Well, at the mini-mart, team-building usually consisted of seeing who could restock the shelves quicker. Whoever lost had to clean the men's room."

Erich smiles briefly, then raises his glass. "How about a toast? Here's to—"

Before he can finish, there's a knock on his door. When Erich opens it, I hear Frau Albrecht greet him. "Good evening, Herr Zimmermann. Since you're a VIP passenger, I wanted to check in and make sure everything is to your satisfaction."

I try to maneuver my chair so that she won't see me, but I'm not quick enough.

"Isabelle, is that you?" Frau Albrecht frowns. "What are you doing in a passenger's cabin?"

Erich comes to my rescue . . . kind of. "I asked Isabelle to have dinner with me. I want her to give me a personal history lesson of the region."

"Personal?" Frau Albrecht arches an eyebrow at me. "Exactly how personal?"

Before I can answer, Erich says, "Thanks for checking in. Have a good evening." Then he quickly closes the door before she can ask any more questions.

I push back my chair. "I don't think this is a good idea. I think from now on, we should meet in public places. This is ruining my reputation."

"Do you really care what people think of you?" Erich asks.

"Of course I do, don't you?"

"Not really."

"I find that hard to believe."

Erich looks out the window at the water and says slowly, "Maybe there is one person whose opinion I care about."

Could he be talking about me? I rub my grandmother's ring, hoping it will give me some guidance as to how to handle this situation. The answer comes to me with blinding clarity—*Run as fast as you can before you kiss him or he kisses you. You must avoid kissing. Kissing this man would be very, very dangerous.*

"I need to go." I push past Erich and race to the door. Then I say something stupid. "I'm supposed to meet Max."

Erich's eyes turn steely. "We wouldn't want you to be late, would we?"

6 - Mystery Meat

The next day, after an early breakfast, the ship sets sail for Rudesheim, a major tourist attraction in the region. We'll be there until mid-afternoon when we set sail again, traveling through the Rhine Gorge to Koblenz.

Luckily for me, it's a semi-free day. The passengers have a choice of two organized excursions led by professional guides, or they can explore the town on their own. For those folks who are going to do their own thing, I'm responsible for shepherding them from the boat to the center of town. From there, they'll go off and enjoy the shops, restaurants, and historical attractions. Then I'll meet back up with them in the afternoon to make sure they get back before the *Abenteuer* departs.

Hamish didn't sign up for any of the excursions, so I assume he's going to explore the town and I'll finally get my opportunity to speak with him. But when he doesn't appear, I'm at a loss as to what to do. Frau Albrecht is tapping her watch, making it clear I should have left with the group fifteen minutes ago.

"Alright, everyone, let's head into town." Holding up an umbrella so they don't lose sight of me, I lead the passengers from the dock to Drosselgasse, a quaint street in the heart of the old town.

Everyone wanders off except Erich. He's acting like nothing happened last night. No more talk of team building. No more innuendos. He's back to being aloof and business-like. I'm surprised that he isn't giving me a hard time for Hamish being a no-show.

"Don't worry," he says to me. "I heard one of the desk clerks say that he's planning on coming into town a bit later. They've arranged a taxi for him."

"This isn't a huge town, but it's still not going to be easy to track him down," I say.

Erich rubs his hands together. "You're in luck. I know exactly where he'll be. We know that he's a cuckoo clock collector. There's a famous shop that sells them near here that he's bound to visit. All we have to do is stake out the shop. Then you can follow him in and start up a conversation."

When he leads me through town to a restaurant, I'm surprised. "Is this where they sell the clocks?"

"No, that's across the street. See it over there? I thought we'd wait here until Hamish shows. Hungry?"

"Not really. But I guess I could have some coffee while we wait."

"You'll need more than coffee," he says to me. Then he speaks in rapid-fire German to the server and orders for me.

"I said I wasn't hungry."

"You can't visit Rudesheim and not try the leberknödel."

"Please tell me it's not made with stomach parts," I say. "Once was enough for me."

"No stomach," Erich says. "I promise you'll love the leberknödel. I order it every time I'm in Rudesheim."

"What is lubberknuckle?"

When I stumble over the German pronunciation, Erich smiles. "Leberknödel," he repeats slowly. "Knödel means dumpling."

"Oh, I love dumplings," I say.

The waiter deposits two steins of beer on the table, and Erich makes a toast. "Here's to an efficient partnership."

"An *efficient* partnership?" This must be business-like Erich's new take on team building. Beer instead of champagne. I take a sip of my beer, then add, "You Germans do love efficiency, don't you? What is it they say about Germany—the trains always run on time?"

"I can assure you that the trains do not always run on time," Erich says. "Just last week, my train was twenty seconds behind schedule."

"Was that a joke? No, I take that back. You're not the joking type."

"That's not true. I have a sense of humor." Erich says something in German, then chuckles. When I stare at him pointedly, he translates, "Can a kangaroo jump higher than a house? Yes, because a house can't jump."

I roll my eyes. "Like I said, you're not the joking type."

"Ah, here it is." Erich motions for the waiter to set a plate in front of me. "Your leberknödel."

"It looks good." I take a cautious bite of the dumpling, then nod approvingly. "It's tasty. What did you get?"

"Blutwurst." Erich slices off a piece of sausage and spreads coarse mustard on it before popping it into his mouth.

After taking a bite of sauerkraut and mashed potatoes, I ask, "Is that like bratwurst?"

"Kind of, except it's made with blood."

I shudder. "Gross. I'd never eat that, or anything made with organ meats."

"Organ meats?"

"Yeah, you know, like heart, kidney, liver," I say. "My mom used to make liver and onions every Thursday night. It was revolting, so one week my sister and I went on a hunger strike and refused to eat it. She tried to serve it to us again for breakfast the next day. But turns out we could out-stubborn my mother, so it went off the menu."

Erich points at my plate. "So, you like the leberknödel?"

"So good." I devour the rest of the dumplings, then dab my napkin to my lips. "I'd definitely order them again. How do you pronounce it again?"

"Leberknödel."

"You said that 'Knödel' means dumplings, right?" After Erich nods, I ask, "So what does 'leber' mean?"

"Promise you won't get mad." Erich bites back a smile. "It means liver."

My eyes widen, and I make a choking sound. "Liver? I ate liver dumplings?"

"Yes, and you enjoyed them."

I gulp down my beer to wash the taste of liver out of my mouth. "No more ordering for me. Understood?"

Erich points at his plate. "Want to try some of my blutwurst?"

"No, I do not want to eat your blood sausage. Next thing I know you're going to tell me that the mashed potatoes were made with marshmallows."

"No, I would never do that to anyone. Marshmallows are horrible."

"Well, at least there's one thing we can agree on." I take another sip of beer, then say, "You said that you order leberknödel whenever you're in Rudesheim. Is this where you were raised?"

Erich averts his eyes and fiddles with his silverware. "Um—"

An oompah band marches down the street, and the sound of the tuba drowns Erich out. I'm fascinated by the lederhosen that the men wear. When they finally depart, the waiter asks Erich something in German.

I hold my hand up, "Do not let him order dessert for me."

The waiter laughs, then says in English, "No, I was asking your boyfriend if you wanted any coffee."

I feel my face grow warm. "My boyfriend?"

Erich folds his arms across his chest and shakes his head. "She is not my girlfriend."

"And he is not my boyfriend," I say.

"Sorry. It seemed like you were a couple," the waiter says apologetically. "Would either of you like dessert? Coffee?"

"We would like some . . ." Erich's voice trails off when I glare at him. "Sorry, you go ahead and order for yourself."

"I'd like some strudel, please."

"Make that two," Erich says.

After the waiter departs, I say, "I can't believe he thought we were a couple."

"Yes, it's obvious that we don't have feelings for each other," Erich says.

"True, the only feelings I have for you are as a partner. An efficient partner."

Erich looks across the street, then says, "I don't think you'll have time to have your strudel. Hamish just went into the cuckoo clock shop."

* * *

"Can you get my strudel to go?" I yell over my shoulder as I dash toward the cuckoo clock shop. Then I halt in my tracks, spin around and say, "Make sure it's made with apples, not liver."

Erich nods, but I'm not quite sure I believe him. He'll probably tell the waiter to make my strudel with a variety of organ meats. If you can't trust a guy to order food for you, can you really trust him with anything?

General Taylor did vouch for him, though. So I'm sure Erich's good at what he does. He can be trusted with spy stuff, but nothing else. Not my food, not my heart, not my—

I slam the door firmly on that train of thought and enter the shop. The sound of cuckoos signaling that it's two o'clock greets me. If you've never been in a room full of hundreds of cuckoo clocks all going off at the same time, I don't recommend it unless you have earplugs.

Okay, let see. The cuckoos are telling me that it's two. That means I have an hour before I'm supposed to escort the passengers back to the boat. That gives me about forty-five minutes before I have to leave the shop and get to the meeting point on time. Can I engage Hamish in conversation and bond with him over Scrabble by then? I really don't have a choice. We'll be in Amsterdam in less than a week, and if Hamish doesn't ask me to be on his Scrabble team, the mission is toast.

Before I even open my mouth, the shop owner greets me in English and asks me what state I'm from. Why is it that Europeans can tell an American from a mile away? After telling him that I'm from the great state of Texas, I wander through a series of small, interconnected rooms, each one full of clocks. I can see why a collector like Hamish would come here.

I'm starting to wonder if Hamish has sneaked out the back door when I spot him inspecting a display of jewelry in a glass case. Each piece features cuckoo clocks, and some of them even look like they're functional. Hamish seems drawn to a charm bracelet. This is the perfect opening. I extend my arm so that my Scrabble charm bracelet is on full display, point at the one he's examining and say, "That's gorgeous."

Oblivious to my jewelry, he says absentmindedly, "When I was younger, I used to have a girlfriend who loved charm bracelets. She was a fine lassie."

"What happened to her?"

Hamish strokes his beard and stares off into the distance. "I did something I knew she wouldn't approve of, so I broke up with her. She ended up marrying another man. Lucky bloke."

"I'm sorry," I say, still waving my charm bracelet around like a mad-woman.

"She's a widow now." Hamish gives a heavy sigh.

"Maybe the two of you can get back together. You always hear about second-chance romances. Couples who broke up only to get back together later in life."

"No, you can't go back in time," he says decisively. "I've learned that the hard way."

Noticing that Hamish's cane is propped up against the display cabinet, I pick it up. "This is stunning." I run my fingers along the wood, making note of the faint groove by the handle. "My grandfather would love one of these. Where did you get it?"

Hamish's face darkens. "It's a one-of-a-kind."

He goes to grab the cane from me and stumbles. I steady him and help him sit on a nearby chair. "Are you okay?"

He grips his cane tightly in his hands, then his gaze drifts to my wrist. "Are those Scrabble tiles?"

I resist the urge to do a fist pump in the air. "They are. I got this bracelet when I won the Nationals."

"You're a Scrabble champion?" Hamish asks.

"Uh-huh. Do you play?"

"I dabble in the game," he says, downplaying his abilities.

I smile brightly at Hamish. "It's been so long since I've played. Would you be interested in a match tonight after dinner?"

Hamish gets to his feet. "I'd be delighted to, young lady."

After we make arrangements to meet later, Hamish excuses himself to go talk about winding mechanisms with the shop owner.

I make my way back to the restaurant and give Erich a big thumbs up.

* * *

I wake up the next morning with a spring in my step, still riding on the high of winning three games of Scrabble in a row last night.

After a three-year hiatus from the word game, it felt so good to play again. The excitement of drawing for first play, the feel of the wooden tiles against my fingers, the thrill of placing 'Q' on the triple-letter score square, and the rush when I played all of my seven tiles in a single turn. I was in heaven.

Hamish looked at me appreciatively when I won our final game with 'zaxes.' And I have to confess, I might have even gloated a little. I'm counting the hours until our rematch tonight. It's going to be hard to concentrate on my tour manager duties today because all my brain wants to focus on are obscure two and three-letter words.

I practically skip to breakfast—skip is worth ten points, by the way—and greet Auguste Renoir cheerfully when I enter the kitchen.

"Silence. Auguste Renoir does not like to be disturbed when he is making omelets." The chef lobs an egg at me and it narrowly misses me. "Out of his kitchen."

"Hey, you could have hurt me," I say.

"That was the idea," he snarls. "Clean that mess up, then get out."

"Mind if I grab a piece of toast first?" I ask tentatively.

"Out!"

As I run out of the kitchen, I hear several eggs splatter against the wall.

I walk through the dining room, saying good morning to everyone. I suggest that they may want to consider something other than omelets. "I think the chef might be short of eggs," I explain. "Perhaps some toast and bacon instead?"

Emma and Hank are seated at a table by the window, and they motion me over. "There's our fellow southerner," Emma says. "We haven't seen you since yesterday morning."

After chatting about our favorite southern dishes, I ask them how their excursion yesterday was. "You went on the wine tasting tour, right?"

Hank grins. "Emma got a little tipsy."

Emma bats her husband's hand and says, "They shouldn't give you all that free wine if they don't expect you to drink it. Have you tried the local riesling yet, dear?"

"I tried some in Mainz, but not in Rudesheim," I say. "But I did have a nice beer yesterday."

"Oh, you should have had a glass. I liked the sweet ones. Hank liked his 'trocken.' That means 'dry' in German.

"You certainly seemed to have learned a lot about wine."

"She was the teacher's pet." Hank beams at his wife. "Of course, it comes naturally to her, seeing as she was an elementary teacher before she retired."

"What grade did you teach?" I ask.

"Second," she said. "Such a sweet age."

I turn to Hank. "What line of work were you in?"

"I had a security firm," he says.

"Oh, like bodyguards?"

Hank shakes his head. "No, more along the lines of securing company property during transport. Making sure it gets from one destination to another."

"That sounds interesting." I stand and excuse myself. "I have to get going. See you later for the excursion to the Ehrenbreitstein Fortress?"

"Yes, dear, see you then," Emma says.

Rather than risk running into Frau Albrecht in the reception area, I exit onto the deck and take the back stairs down to the crew quarters. Whistling the theme song from *Jeopardy*, I open the door to my cabin. When I see Erich sitting on my bunk eating a piece of toast, my good mood evaporates.

I don't even bother to ask how he got into my cabin. I just hope that Sophia or any of the other crewmembers didn't see him. There are already enough rumors floating around this ship about my supposed affair with Erich.

"Your breakfast is over there. There's black coffee and I took the liberty of ordering you dry toast. That way, you'll know that there's nothing in your breakfast but bread. No kidney, liver or the like. Scout's honor."

"You're German. What do you know about the Boy Scouts?"

"We have Boy Scouts in Germany. They're called . . ." Erich frowns, then says, "Never mind. Eat your breakfast quickly. We have work to do."

"We? I think you mean I have work to do," I say. "In forty-five minutes, I'm leading an excursion. Will you be joining? Or are you going to stay here?" I ask sarcastically.

"I think I'll stay here," he says. "I have an activity planned."

"What? Lying on a lounge chair on the sun deck?"

"No, more of an exploratory activity."

"Exploratory . . . oh, my gosh. You're going to break into Hamish's room, aren't you?"

Erich holds up a card key. "Is it really 'breaking in' if you have a master key? Now, I need you to text me once the group is at Ehrenbreitstein Fortress and confirm that Hamish is with you. Can you do that?"

"I think I know how to text," I say in between bites of dry toast.

"You're missing something critical."

"Yeah, I know. Butter."

"No, if you're going to text me you need . . ." He pauses as though we're in a game show.

I channel my inner *Jeopardy* contestant. "What's a phone? Don't worry, it's in my purse." I take a sip of black coffee and wince. There's a reason why cows were created, namely for their cream.

"You need my number." Erich reaches into my purse and pulls out my phone. This man has no sense of privacy. He types in his phone number, somehow managing to circumvent my password protection. "While I'm here, I'm going to clear your search history."

"Uh, no you're not."

"Yes, I am. What do you think would happen if your phone fell into the wrong hands? What would people think if they saw your search history?"

"It's not like I'm looking at porn sites," I say. "Just some shopping sites and social media."

"Oh, Isabelle, do you think I'm stupid? You've been doing searches on how to be a spy. It sent off alarm bells at headquarters. If you want to know how to be a spy, all you have to do is ask. I'll be happy to teach you."

Erich clicks a few buttons, then hands my phone back to me. "Are you going to finish that?" he asks, pointing at the lone piece of toast on the plate.

"No, take it. Without butter, it tastes like cardboard."

He leaves my cabin, munching on his dry toast, and I sink onto my bed. If Erich knows what I'm searching for on the Internet, does he know about the texts to my friends? The texts where I talk about the mysterious hot guy I met?

7 - Werewolf Side Effects

Later that night, Hamish and I have a Scrabble rematch in the lounge. I feel nervous, not because of the large crowd that has gathered around to watch, but because of Erich. He's sitting at the bar, sipping on scotch, looking at me. Not at the Scrabble board like everyone else, but directly at me.

Is he trying to communicate something telepathically to me? If so, what? An update on what he found when he searched Hamish's room earlier today? A word that I can make with a "Q," but no "U"? How he really feels about me?

Ignoring Erich's uncomfortable stare, I lay down my tiles. One of the people watching says, "Qapik? That's not a real word."

"It sure is a real word. It's Azerbaijanian money," Hank tells the man. Then he pats me on the shoulder. "Well played, Isabelle."

Hamish ignores the chatter and inspects the tiles on his rack. When a smile creeps across his face, I steel myself. He's a worthy opponent. His ability to recognize word-building opportunities is impressive. This is one of those times, and I groan as he builds off my "Q" to spell "quixotic."

Quixotic—the unrealistic and impractical pursuit of something. That's what this mission feels like to me. Erich is hoping for the impossible from me, that I'll be able to stop Hamish from selling the stolen emerald to the bad guys. His faith in my abilities is idealistic at best. Foolish at worst.

I can't believe I let General Taylor talk me into helping Erich. The general pushed all of my buttons, appealing to my sense of duty and desire to stop the unthinkable from happening. But his faith in me is misplaced. Not too long ago, I was working at a mini-mart.

Hamish interrupts my thoughts, laying down the rest of his tiles. "I think I won this one, lassie."

After we total up our points, I concede the game.

"Should we go again?" he asks.

I waver. "I'm not sure. It's getting late. Maybe we should call it a night."

Hank leans forward. "You gotta play one more game, sweetheart. I've got money riding on you."

I turn to look at him. "You're betting on Scrabble?"

"Sure thing." He grins. "It's like betting on *Jeopardy.* Even if you lose your shirt, you feel smart doing it."

Emma confides, "I could never get Hank to sit still long enough to play Scrabble. It's a real treat to see him so interested in it."

I nod at Hamish. "Okay, one more game."

"You won't regret it, lassie. Well, that is unless you lose again." Hamish winks at me, then suggests we take a fifteen-minute break first. While he goes off to the restroom, Max approaches the table.

"I'd like to get some pictures of you playing Scrabble," he says. "Zoe thinks it might be a nice addition to the article. Two champions playing each other on a riverboat is a unique angle."

"Okay," I say. "Hamish will be back soon."

"In the meantime, let's take some pictures of just you posing with the Scrabble board." Max shows me where he wants me to sit, then touches the side of my head. "How about if you take your hair down?"

"Oh, I can't. If you have long hair, you're required to wear it in a tight bun."

Max makes a show of looking around the lounge. "I don't think anyone here is going to rat you out."

The hairpins are pressing painfully on my scalp, so I let Max convince me. After I pull my hair loose, I run my fingers through it to untangle it.

"So much better," Max says appreciatively. Then he pushes a lock of my hair behind my ear. "Gorgeous."

"Thinking of becoming a hair stylist?" Zoe has her hands on her hips and she's glaring at her colleague. "Because if you're looking for a career change, I'd be more than happy to call our manager and tell her to send another photographer out to replace you."

"She's just jealous," Max says in a stage whisper.

"Photographs," Zoe snarls. "Any day now."

"Someone's touchy." Max grins at Zoe, but gets to work, taking several photos of me from various angles.

When Hamish returns to the table, he politely refuses to have his picture taken. "No thanks, young man. This ugly face might break your camera. Focus on the bonnie lass instead."

My phone beeps. It's a text from Erich: *More focus on the mission. Less focus on flirting.*

Oh, boy, he hasn't seen flirting yet. I slip my hand through Max's arm. "Can I see the pictures you took?"

While Max shows them to me, I make sure to lean in closer. I glance back at Erich, curious to see his reaction. But all I see is a vacant barstool and an empty glass.

* * *

Erich avoided me for the rest of the night. The following day, I thought I might see him on the excursion to Cologne, but he didn't make an appearance. His loss, really, as the rest of the passengers had a great time. I think I'm getting the hang of being a tour manager. The key is to make sure you know where the restrooms are located—that's the number one question I get from the passengers—and keep everyone hydrated in the warm summer weather.

"Wasn't the Chocolate Museum amazing?" Zoe asks me.

We're sitting on the sun deck, enjoying an after-dinner drink while the boat makes its way from Cologne to the Netherlands.

"I noticed Max got you some hazelnut pralines," I say to her.

"Oh, he didn't buy them for me," Zoe says. "He tried to give them to that

Australian girl, but when she told him she had a boyfriend back in Sydney, he handed them to me. Like some sort of consolation prize."

I cock my head to one side. "I'm not so sure that's what was going on. I think he did that to make you jealous. He always intended to give you those chocolates."

"I've worked with Max for years. If he liked me romantically, I'd know by now. All we do is fight like cats and dogs." Zoe gives me a sideways look. "If anyone's jealous, it's Erich. Every time he sees Max talking to you, he's got daggers in his eyes."

I sit up straight. "Do you really think he's jealous?"

Zoe grins. "You like Erich, don't you?"

"No, of course not. Besides, the crew aren't allowed to become romantically involved with the passengers."

"Yeah, that's what's holding you back," she says dryly.

"Even if I liked him," I hold up my hand, "and that's a big 'if,' I still wouldn't want to get involved with him."

"Why? Because he'll be getting off the boat once we get to Amsterdam?" Zoe asks.

Oh, wow, once the mission is over, I'll never see Erich again. I chew on my lip as that sinks in.

"Earth to Isabelle," Zoe says. "That's what it is, isn't it? You don't want to lose your heart to someone you won't see again."

I take a deep breath, then let it out slowly. "I guess so."

"Hah, you admitted it," Zoe says triumphantly. "You're sweet on him."

I smile. "My friends would say that I'm smitten with him."

"Smitten. That's cute," Zoe says. "I love old-fashioned sayings like that. Isabelle is smitten with Erich," she says in a sing-songy voice. "First comes love, then comes marriage, then comes Isabelle pushing the baby carriage."

I laugh despite myself. "Erich is the last person who would ever settle down and get married, let alone have kids. It wouldn't be possible in his line of work."

"What does he do?" Zoe asks.

"Uh, he's a pharmaceutical sales representative."

"That doesn't seem like the type of career that's incompatible with getting married and starting a family," Zoe points out.

I try to come up with a plausible rationale for Erich remaining single. "I think the drugs he sells have some serious side-effects."

"Like infertility? There's always adoption."

"No, it's not that he can't have children," I say. "The drugs cause hair to grow out of inappropriate places."

"You realize that happens to everyone as they get older." Zoe taps the space between her upper lip and her nose. "Women grow mustaches and men have hair coming out of their ears."

"No, I'm talking about hair in thick patches all over his body. Fur, really." I realize I'm digging myself in further, so I go for broke. "Like a werewolf. He has to shave ten times a day."

"You're making that up," Zoe says.

I shrug. "This is silly. I met Erich a few days ago. It's not like I'm even thinking about a serious relationship with him. But . . ."

"But you are thinking about something with him." Zoe gives me a sympathetic look. "Maybe you should let that something happen and see what it leads to."

"Well, nothing is going to happen if he thinks Max is interested in me."

Zoe cocks her head to one side. "Really? Most guys like that sort of challenge."

"I can't see Erich fighting for me."

"Okay, I have a crazy idea," Zoe says. "What if I make it seem like Max and I are a couple? Then Erich would think that he has a clear field."

"How would you do that?"

Zoe stares off into space for a moment, then looks back at me. "I could kiss him," she says shyly. "All you have to do is arrange for Erich to see me plant one on Max."

"Really? You want to kiss your arch-enemy?"

"We ladies have to stick together," she jokes. "Besides, it's for a good cause."

"I'm not sure this is a smart idea."

"Because he's a passenger?"

"Right now my manager suspects I'm having an affair with Erich, but if she ever had proof that I actually was having inappropriate relations with him, she'd fire me and I'd end up back at the mini-mart."

Zoe interrupts my thoughts. "I can't picture you working at a mini-mart."

"Yeah, me neither," I say wryly. "It was meant to be a temporary gig, but ended up lasting for three years. Thankfully, my friend Mia convinced me to come to Europe with her. We were about to book airplane tickets when I won a free cruise for the two of us from the States to Europe. It seemed like a sign. Then I saw an advertisement for this job, and the rest is history."

"Yay for Mia," Zoe says. Then she grabs my hand. "Hey, there's Max. Why don't you go track down Erich and lure him up here? Give me a sign and then I'll fake kiss Max."

* * *

Somehow Zoe has convinced me this is a good idea. I find Erich sitting in the lounge, leafing through a magazine. "How come you're not playing Scrabble with Hamish?" he asks.

"He wanted a night off. Said the arthritis in his knee is acting up." I furrow my brow. "Although I'm not sure how you can be a jewel thief if you need a cane to walk."

"Or things aren't what they appear to be."

"Are you saying that he's faking it?" When Erich shrugs, I jab a finger in his direction. "Oh, come on. You'd know if he's faking it. You have a file on him."

"I'm not in the mood to play games with you tonight," Erich says. "Why don't you go find your boyfriend, Max? I'm sure he'd be happy to entertain you."

"He's not my boyfriend, and don't you go starting that rumor. His girlfriend would be livid if you did."

"What girlfriend?"

"Zoe."

"The two of them are a couple?" Erich looks puzzled. "But then why does he keep flirting with you?"

"They had a fight. I think he was trying to make Zoe jealous." I take the magazine from Erich and close it. "I need to talk with you about something."

"We can talk here," he says.

"No, someplace more private. Let's go up to the sun deck."

When we walk out on deck, I see Max and Zoe standing at the railing. Max's back is to me, so I give Zoe a covert signal.

Zoe grabs Max's hand, then pulls him toward her. As she kisses him, I nudge Erich. "See, they're a couple."

Erich looks at them, then gives me an appraising look. "It's funny, but sometimes the people you least expect to get together do."

Wow, those two are getting pretty passionate. For a fake kiss, there sure are some sparks. I give Zoe a covert thumbs up, then clear my throat. "Maybe we should go someplace else," I suggest to Erich.

Erich nods. "We'll go to my stateroom."

He heads down the stairs, and I hurry to catch up with him. "I don't think that's a good idea."

"You were the one who wanted to talk with me privately."

"Yeah, but Frau Albrecht saw me in your room the other night. What will she think if I'm seen there a second time?"

"It doesn't matter what she thinks," Erich says as we walk down the corridor. "What matters is what the passengers think, and they're singing your praises."

When we reach his cabin, I double check to make sure no one is watching before I slip inside. He motions for me to sit, then continues. "You're a natural problem-solver and you think quickly on your feet. You were wasted working in that mini-mart."

"I'm coming to realize that too," I say. "My contract on the riverboat runs until November. So I guess I have between now and then to figure out what I want to do."

"Why not go back into intelligence? General Taylor won't say what happened to you in the Air Force and why you left. But I do know the issue is about confidence, not ability."

"Stop pretending you don't know," I snap. "I'm sure it's in my file."

"Not the copy I have." Erich runs his fingers through his hair. "You probably don't believe me though."

I chew on my lip. "It doesn't matter. It's in the past."

"Well, if you ever want to talk about it, I'm here for you," he says earnestly.

"Thanks," I say. "Listen, I'm beat. I'm going to head off."

As I walk toward the door, Erich asks, "Wait, before you go, what is it you wanted to talk with me about?"

"Oh, um . . . if anyone asks, you're a pharmaceutical sales representative."

"I am?"

"Yeah, that's the cover story I gave Zoe and Sophia."

"Look at you, creating cover stories for me," he says, smiling despite himself.

"And another thing, the reason you're single is because the drugs you sell have side-effects."

"Really? What kind of side effects?"

"Let's just say you're very hairy underneath those clothes. Like werewolf-hairy."

"So you think about what I look like without my clothes on?"

My face grows warm and I stare down at the carpet. "No, I don't have to think about it. I saw you in a towel the other day."

"And I resembled a werewolf?"

"No, not at all. I just panicked when I was talking with Zoe about you and that's what I came up with."

"So exactly why were you talking about my relationship status with Zoe, anyway?"

I rub my temples. This is not my best conversational moment. Fearing what the next words out of my mouth might be, I yank Erich's door open. "Is that the fire alarm? I better go investigate." Then I rush down the corridor, praying that he doesn't come after me.

8 - Is Normal Overrated?

No, there wasn't a fire. Erich knew that, but he let me go. Upon reflection, I realized that General Taylor probably didn't share the details of what happened in the Air Force—he had agreed to keep what happened between the two of us. Erich had been genuinely concerned and was sincere in offering to listen if I wanted to talk. Is it possible for a guy to be secretive and not be a jerk? I'm beginning to think it might just be.

I slept fitfully last night, haunted by strange dreams of Erich turning into a werewolf. So when I board the tour bus that will take us to the Rijksmuseum in Amsterdam, I'm carrying an extra large coffee with lots of cream and sugar.

I finish caffeinating my system when the bus pulls up in front of the museum. After tossing my cup in the trashcan, I hold an umbrella over my head. "Alright, everyone, this way to see masterpieces by the Dutch masters, Rembrandt and Vermeer."

As I lead the group into the atrium, Erich suddenly appears. "I didn't see you on the bus," I say, trying to adopt a casual tone.

"I had an early meeting in Amsterdam," he says. "So I took a taxi here."

The sunlight flooding through the glass roof illuminates dark circles under Erich's eyes, circles I haven't seen before. "Is everything okay?"

"Of course," he says. "We're on track for the mission."

"No, I meant you. Are you okay?"

Erich points at a man holding a clipboard. "I think that's your tour guide."

As I walk over to introduce myself, I wonder why Erich is avoiding my question. I chat for a few moments with the tour guide, then he introduces himself to the group. After an overview of the Rijksmuseum, we head to the Gallery of Honour where some of the most famous works are housed. When we pause in front of *A Mother's Duty* by Pieter de Hooch, the group laughs when the guide explains it depicts a woman delousing her child.

The tone becomes more serious when we view Rembrandt's *The Jewish Bride.* "Some people believe this painting depicts Isaac and Rebecca disguising themselves as brother and sister so that they could escape King Abimelech," the guide explains. "However, see how Isaac has his arm around Rebecca? Unable to hide their love for each other, they are sharing a tender moment."

"Aw, isn't that sweet," Emma says to her husband.

Hank puts his arm around Emma, unconsciously mimicking the pose from the painting. "Sure is. You can't hide what you feel for someone."

Erich and my eyes meet and we hold each other's gaze for a very long moment, almost as though we're playing chicken. I lose, but only because someone jostles me.

As the group traipses to the next alcove in the gallery, Erich lingers, looking at *The Jewish Bride.*

"There's something wrong," I say to him. "What is it?"

He shakes his head. "I don't want to worry you."

"Well, I'm already worried, so you might as well spill the beans."

Erich paces back and forth for a moment, then says, "Headquarters hasn't been able to eliminate Hamish's partner for the Scrabble tournament."

I wring my hands. "Please tell me you don't mean what I think you mean when you say 'eliminate.'"

"What?" Erich takes a step back. "No. Poor choice of words. He's not going to be harmed."

"That's a relief." I glance over at the tour group to make sure they haven't moved on. "What happens if you can't 'eliminate' him, so to speak?"

"It *will* happen," Erich says. "I just thought it would have happened by now. Carry on as normal with Hamish, playing Scrabble."

"But the tournament is tomorrow," I point out.

"I'm well aware of that, Isabelle," he says sharply.

I clutch my stomach as waves of anxiety roll over me. Sitting on a nearby bench, I put my head in my hands.

Erich sits next to me and puts his arm around my shoulders. "Hey, I'm sorry. I didn't mean to snap at you."

"It's not that. It's the mission. I'm one of those people who compartmentalizes things. Always have. I put things into separate rooms in my brain, and that's how I stay in control. Except sometimes, those things escape from their separate rooms and collide in my brain. And then I panic."

Erich squeezes me tightly without saying a word. His quiet strength makes me feel safe.

"I'm a liability to this mission. There has to be some other way to shadow Hamish at the Scrabble tournament."

"I'm sorry," Erich says softly. "If there was another way, we would have done it. You're our only hope."

I twist my grandmother's ring around my finger, then take a deep breath. "It's fine. I can do it. Just promise me that after the tournament is over, my job is finished and I can go back to my normal life."

Erich nods. "I promise. Your life will go back to normal by the time tomorrow night rolls around."

Okay, that's settled, but I'm left with one nagging question—is a normal life what I want?

* * *

"Do you mind if we play in the library tonight instead of in the lounge?" Hamish asks me.

Hamish looks tired tonight. The way he's leaning so heavily on his cane, I wonder if he should be on his feet at all.

"Of course not."

"Thanks," he says as we walk slowly toward the library. "Do you ever have those days when you crave peace and quiet? On larger cruise ships, you can lose yourself in a crowd. But here on a riverboat when there's only two hundred passengers, it's hard to escape. Getting a cup of coffee takes at least a half hour because everyone knows you and wants to chat."

I hold open the door for him. "You sound like an introvert."

"Aye, lassie. I do need my alone time."

I hesitate before setting the Scrabble board on the table. "We don't have to play tonight."

"Ach, no, being with you is like being by myself, but better." He slowly sits in one of the armchairs. "You're a solace to my soul."

Hamish draws the low tile, so he gets to go first. He places his first word—snath.

As he marks down his score, I ask, "The handle of a scythe?"

"That's correct. We Scrabble players are word freaks, aren't we? Our vocabulary is odd, to say the least."

I study the tiles on my rack. If I played off Hamish's "S," I could spell out "secret." It seems like a sign from the universe. Everyone has secrets—Hamish, Erich, and me. Flustered, I end up playing "set," earning myself a whopping three points in the process.

"That the best you can do, lassie?" Hamish asks. "You seem distracted tonight. Boyfriend troubles?"

I snort. "I don't have a boyfriend."

"What about that good-looking man I saw you talking to the other night?"

"I talk to all the men, good-looking or not. It's part of my job."

"No, this was different. There was definitely chemistry between the two of you."

I frown. Has everyone seen the sparks between Erich and me? Trying to misdirect him, I say, "I'm not sure who you mean."

"That German fellow."

"There are several Germans on the cruise." I point at the board. "It's your turn."

"Point taken. I shouldn't butt into your love life." Hamish strokes his beard. "Remember that woman I told you about in the cuckoo clock shop?"

"The one that got away?"

"That's the one. She was always interfering in other people's love lives. She enjoyed nothing more than to set people up. Or better, helping get them back together if they had broken up." Hamish's smile fades and he goes back to studying his tiles.

"What are your plans after you disembark tomorrow?" I ask, trying to lighten the mood. "Are you going to spend some time in Amsterdam?"

"Oh, I thought you knew. I'm playing in the second annual European Scrabble team tournament this weekend."

"I have to confess, it seems odd to play Scrabble as part of a team," I say. "That's more common for school tournaments, isn't it?"

Hamish nods. "It is an unusual format. But it's a lot of fun. My partner and I complement each other."

I glance at the clock. It's already ten, and Hamish is still talking about playing with his partner. It doesn't look like headquarters has managed to "eliminate" Hamish's teammate. The mission has already failed before it began properly.

We continue to play, and I resign myself to spending tomorrow here on the riverboat, not at a Scrabble tournament helping to stop an international arms deal. Just when I'm about to excuse myself for the night, Sophia enters the room.

She hands Hamish a folded piece of paper. "I have a message for you, Mr. MacDougall."

Hamish reads it, then groans.

"Bad news?"

"Yes, my partner is stuck in Istanbul. He won't be back in time for the tournament tomorrow." Hamish folds the note and sticks it in his pocket. "Funny. I didn't even know he was going to Turkey."

"Oh, that's too bad. I know how much you were looking forward to playing Scrabble with him."

Hamish gives me a considered look. "You wouldn't want to . . ." He shakes his head. "No, I shouldn't ask."

"Ask what?"

"Would you consider playing in the tournament with me tomorrow? You'd be doing me a real favor."

"Actually, I'd love to," I say with a huge grin on my face.

Hamish grins back. "What are the odds my partner would have to withdraw at the last minute and I happen to make the acquaintance of a Scrabble champion on this cruise?"

"It's quite the coincidence." That's what I say, but we all know I don't believe that. If a covert organization is pulling the strings, then it's amazing how dramatically your odds increase.

* * *

I text Erich the good news and he tells me to meet him on the sun deck. When I come up the stairs, I'm relieved to see that he's the only one up there. He rushes toward me and scoops me up in his arms. With his hands cinched around my waist, he twirls us around. "You did it, Isabelle. You got him to ask you to be his Scrabble partner," he says in my ear. "You're incredible."

With each spin, he presses my body tighter against his. His muscles are taut. His breath is hot against my skin. His lips whisper my name.

I wrap my hands around his neck and brush my cheek against his. He trembles and just when I think he's going to kiss me, he abruptly sets me down.

"Sorry, I got carried away," he says.

"Yeah, I think you might have let your self-control slip a bit there." I try to say it with a light, teasing tone, but my voice cracks as I wrestle with my own self-control.

"Are you okay?" Erich starts to reach for me, but stops himself and shoves his hands in his pockets. "You seem a little . . . um, tense."

"Tense? Me? You're the one whose eyes are dilated," I say.

"Of course, they're dilated. It's nighttime."

"Oh, is that the reason why?"

Erich takes a step back, re-establishing a respectable amount of space between us. "Your eyes dilate to let in more light. It's a scientific fact," he says.

His self-discipline is back. I hate it. Something needs to be done about it. I want to kiss him until he loses control.

"Isabelle, what are you doing?" Erich asks as I close the gap between us.

I run my hands up his arms, my fingers tracing his biceps before resting on his broad shoulders. "I think I liked you better when you got carried away."

Erich's breathing becomes shallow. "We can't get carried away."

I nibble on his earlobe. "Speak for yourself."

"*I* can't get carried away," Erich says. His voice is husky. His control is slipping.

"Why?" I stroke Erich's neck with my fingernails.

"The mission . . ." His voice trails off as he places his hands on the small of my back.

I turn my head so that my lips hover a fraction from his. "Do you want me to kiss you, Erich? Or do you want to talk about the mission?"

He doesn't use words to answer me. He uses his mouth, pressing his lips against mine. Our first kiss is tentative, but any gentleness quickly dissipates. We can't get enough of each other.

My head is spinning, my heart is pounding, my skin feels flushed. I don't know what self-control is anymore. This goes on for an eternity. Then a tiny voice in my head makes itself known.

Remember what happened in the Air Force, Isabelle.

And just like that, my self-control is back. I push Erich away, take a deep breath, then say coolly, "You're right, Erich. We can't do this. The mission comes first."

9 - The Dog Ate My Homework

Frau Albrecht frowns when I walk into the reception area the next morning. "That outfit is unacceptable. Where's your uniform?"

Personally, I think my outfit is totally acceptable. Say goodbye to that ill-fitting suit and scratchy polyester blouse. The floaty sundress and sandals I have on are far more my style. And wearing my hair loose over my shoulders is such a relief after having it pinned back in that awful bun.

Sophia looks up from the computer and her face lights up. "Does this mean you're quitting?"

"No, I just have the day off," I say.

"The day off? Are you kidding me? You only started working here a week ago. I haven't had a day off in three months." Sophia turns to Frau Albrecht. "How come she gets time off and I don't?"

"Isabelle most certainly does not have the day off." Frau Albrecht taps her pen on the counter. "Unless you are planning on resigning, then we need you here at the front desk. The current passengers are disembarking, and then we have a four-hour window to get the boat ready for the next set of passengers. Now go back to your cabin and change into your uniform. The alternative is handing in your letter of resignation."

"But, um . . ."

"Um, what?" the older woman says.

Last night Erich had promised that he would arrange for me to have the day off so I can play in the Scrabble tournament. Did he finally find some strings he couldn't pull?

"Well?" Frau Albrecht asks impatiently. Then her phone rings. She grunts hello, listens for a few moments while cracking her knuckles. Then she gives me a full on glare. "Apparently, Isabelle does have the day off."

Sophia looks like she wants to roast me on a spit.

"I'll be back this evening," I say, rushing to get off the boat before Sophia hurls a stapler at me.

When I walk onto the dock, Erich is leaning against a car.

I'm not sure what to say to him or what to do. After what happened last night, I foolishly hoped we'd be able to avoid each other. But we have a mission to do. Together.

Erich is wearing his game face. Just another day at the office for him. When I ended the kiss last night, he looked stunned, but only for an instant. He quickly regained his composure and agreed that getting involved romantically was a bad idea.

"Hi," I say. "I didn't expect to see you today."

"Really? I told you I'd drive you to the tournament." He opens the passenger door. "Hop in."

I slip into the car, clutching my purse on my lap. We drive to the venue in an uncomfortable silence. To pass the time, I review the tournament rules.

Unlike the tournaments I've played in before, where one player is pitted against another player, this is a tag-team event. Each team has two people. Each player in a team has their own rack of tiles, one playing right after the other one before the next team takes over. This works out great for me. Because Hamish will be sitting next to me the entire tournament, I can keep a close eye on him.

Teams are seeded according to their ratings from their players' associations. Hamish and his former partner were the number two seed. But because I haven't played Scrabble competitively in several years, and don't have a current rating, Hamish has gone in early to the tournament to discuss the situation with the officials. Part of me feels guilty that, because Hamish's partner was "eliminated" and I've taken his place, we may end up seeded near the bottom. It would be an embarrassing ranking for someone of Hamish's caliber.

"We're here," Erich says, as he pulls up in front of a hotel in the heart of Amsterdam. He puts the car in park. "Let's go over the plan one more time."

His tone is businesslike. I shift my body to face him and adopt a neutral expression. "Go ahead."

"Stick close to Hamish. According to our intel, he's supposed to make the exchange with the fence during the tournament."

"How's he going to do it? It's not like you can casually hand over an emerald necklace."

"We don't know, and before you ask, we don't know what the fence looks like either. That's why you're there, to observe everything that's going on. Take pictures of everyone he talks to, everyone he looks at, everyone he nods to, everyone—"

"Yeah, I think I got it. Take pictures of everyone." I pull my phone out of my purse. "I better make sure this is fully charged. Yikes, it's down to twenty percent."

Erich reaches across me and opens the glove box. "Don't worry, I've got you covered. Use this one instead."

As he passes me a new phone, his fingers brush against the back of my hand. We both look at each other, conscious of the electricity between us.

I avert my eyes and rummage through my purse again. "You know what? I think I have a charger in here somewhere. Yep, there it is." Holding his phone gingerly with the tips of my fingers so that we don't have to make contact, I try to give it back to him. "Here you go."

He shakes his head. "No, you have to use the phone I gave you. The photos you take will automatically upload to our servers. We'll be able to match them against our files so that we can identify the fence."

"Hmm . . . you've already been monitoring my phone—a total invasion of privacy which I'd like to mention again for the record—so I assumed you'd be able to see what photos I took on it already."

Avoiding my invasion of privacy point, he says, "This phone has certain special features that yours doesn't."

"Ooh, like a James Bond phone? Can it shoot bullets or bake bread?"

Erich gives me a slight smile. "Bake bread?"

"I missed breakfast," I say. "I was busy studying my Scrabble word lists. Anyway, what does it do?"

"See this red button on the side? Push that to zoom in when you're taking photos. And, if at any point you feel like you're in danger or you need urgent help, press the star button on the keypad."

I look at the phone incredulously. "That's it? Those are the special features? Don't you guys have your own Q? Even if this thing can't make sourdough bread, I expected something more impressive."

"You do realize that James Bond and Q are fictional characters, don't you? You need to take this seriously, Isabelle. If anything were to happen to you . . ." Erich grips the steering wheel and mutters something under his breath. Then he turns to me and says, "Back to the plan. Don't interfere with Hamish making the exchange. We want him to pass the necklace to the fence. Your job is to get the photos so that we can identify him or her. Then we'll take over from there. Your part of the mission will be over."

"Understood." I tuck the phone Erich gave me into my purse. "So I meet you after the tournament for a debrief?"

"Correct." He points at the passenger door. "You better get going. Hamish will be waiting for you."

I try to find something else we need to discuss, something we need to cover, just so that I can put off going into the tournament. The role I play in the mission sounds easy on the face of it, but what if things don't go to plan? Actually, if I'm being honest with myself, there's another reason I don't want to get out of the car, and that has to do with Erich. Spending time with him has been exhilarating. Yes, there was that amazing kiss, but it's more than that.

"You don't have much time," Erich reminds me.

I reluctantly step out of the car. As I watch Erich drive away, I fiddle with the Scrabble charms dangling from my wrist. I used to love this bracelet. Now it will just be a bittersweet reminder of falling for someone I could never be with.

* * *

When I walk into the hotel ballroom, memories of my competitive Scrabble-playing days flood back. A sign hanging from the ceiling reads: *Welcome to the Second Annual European Scrabble Team Tournament.* There are fifty small tables dotted around the room, each with a Scrabble board, and a timer. At the front, several people are clustered around a large whiteboard. One of them is brandishing a dictionary while the others are arguing about something. Scrabble players always find things to debate—should certain words be banned, should there be a penalty for challenging valid words, and whether boards with a built-in Lazy Susan are a sacrilege.

Hamish is sitting on a small couch next to a buffet table. As I walk over to join him, I snatch a cheese and ham pastry. "Good news, bad news," he says. "Which one do you want first?"

"Good news, I guess."

"We're still the number two seed," Hamish says as he brushes some lint off his shirt.

"That is good news," I say. "How did that happen?"

"The officials are taking your previous championship status into account, but . . ." Hamish pauses to take a sip of coffee.

"I guess this is where the bad news comes in?"

"It's a provisional ranking. They're going to assess you during the warm-up round," Hamish says. "Before the tournament kicks off, there's a round of regular Scrabble games—one person against one person. Basically, it's a way for everyone to loosen up. The officials want to see how you perform. If you do well, then we'll keep our number two seed position."

"So no pressure, then," I say.

"Scrabblers, can I have your attention, please?" One of the officials calls the room to order. "My colleague is going to come around the room with a container. Please place your phones, tablets, and other electronic devices in it. They'll be returned to you after the tournament."

"He's kidding, right?" I ask Hamish.

"Sorry, lassie, but those are the rules due to a cheating scandal last year. There was this guy who had one of those fancy watches. You know, the kind that tracks your steps and heartbeat. Well, he had his girlfriend stand behind his competitors during matches. She would send coded messages to her boyfriend on his watch, telling him what tiles his opponents had. He would pretend to be looking at his watch to monitor his pulse, but in reality he was using the information his girlfriend sent to cheat."

"That's pretty clever," I said.

"Scrabble is serious business," Hamish says. "Especially when there's big prize money up for grabs."

"Phones, please." A man wearing a sweater vest two sizes too small for him thrusts a plastic container in front of me. His eyes are magnified by the oversized hot pink glasses perched on the end of his nose. He shakes the box, this time inches away from my face. "Phones."

I gulp. The success of my mission depends upon the phone Erich gave me. "But I'm expecting an important phone call."

Sweater vest man sighs. "Let me guess. Your grandmother is in the hospital on her deathbed."

"Well, um . . ."

He looks bored. "No, wait, I've got it. Your dog ate your homework. Maybe your backpack was stolen."

Not entirely sure what dogs and backpacks have to do with Scrabble, I venture a guess. "Are you by any chance a schoolteacher?"

"You're a clever one, aren't you?" He adjusts his glasses, which makes him look even more bug-eyed. "I've heard all the excuses. I know that your generation can't bear to be without your devices, but if you want to play Scrabble, you're going to have to say goodbye to it."

"Go on, lassie," Hamish urges.

I send Erich a quick text letting him know his phone has been confiscated, then reluctantly deposit it in the box. After the schoolteacher finishes his collection, he locks the container in a storage closet on the far side of the room.

Great. Lock-picking doesn't feature on my resume. Without the phone, all I can do is concentrate hard on what everyone looks like, then hope a sketch artist can turn my descriptions into something useful.

"Scrabblers, please take your assigned places for the warm-up round," the official announces.

"Your table is over there." Hamish points to the far end of the room.

I furrow my brow. "Where are you going to be?"

"Lucky for me, I don't have to go far."

"But I thought we'd be sitting together." I wring my hands. How am I supposed to keep a close eye on Hamish if we're on opposite sides of the room?

Hamish mistakes my concern for nerves for the match. "Don't worry, lassie. You'll do fine. I have every faith in you."

When I get to my table, my opponent is waiting for me. I extend my hand and introduce myself. Before she shakes my hand, she puts on a pair of pink furry mittens. When I ask her what her name is, she says, "I don't have a name."

"Everyone has a name," I say. "You would have needed a name to register for the tournament."

"Oh, *that* name." She removes her mittens, applies hand sanitizer, then puts them back on. "That name is Bob."

"Nice to meet you, uh, Bob."

There are two chairs at the table. One is facing the wall. The other is facing the direction where Hamish is sitting. Naturally, Bob sits in the seat facing Hamish. The very same seat I need to be in if I'm going to keep an eye on the Scotsman.

Bob does not want to switch chairs. I plead, I beg, I whine. Nothing works. Then I pull out the twenty Euro note from my purse—the only money I have, the one I almost spit a marshmallow into—and Bob is suddenly happy to cooperate.

I empty the bag of tiles onto the table so we can both confirm all hundred tiles are present and accounted for. "Ready to get started?"

"Just a minute." Bob reaches into her backpack and pulls out a roll of tinfoil. She fashions a hat out of it and places it on her head. "Ready."

You know, I'd like to say that's the strangest thing I've seen at a Scrabble tournament, but I'd be lying. Besides, Bob's hat is pretty jaunty—a cross between a beret and a Stetson. You wouldn't think you could combine those two styles of hats, but then again, who thought breeding a pit bull and a Chihuahua was a good idea? Turns out pithuahuas are adorable.

I struggle through the match, mostly because I spend more time trying to watch Hamish than I do looking at my tiles and maximizing my points. The only reason I end up winning is because Bob thinks that the colored spots on the board are bad luck, and avoids them at all costs. When I try to explain to her that she can earn double and triple scores using them, Bob puts her hands over her ears.

After the game is over, Bob removes her hat, taking care not to crumple it, and scurries off to the buffet table. I go find Hamish, making mental notes of all the people I pass.

"How was your match?" Hamish asks.

"I'm going to go with interesting."

"Those are the best kind," Hamish says. "Listen, I need to run to the gents. I'll meet you back here."

My eyes widen. "You're going to the bathroom?"

Hamish laughs. "That's what happens when you become old. The coffee runs right through you."

Erich and his stupid plan. Stick with Hamish. Follow Hamish. Don't lose sight of Hamish. Exactly how is this plan supposed to work if Hamish goes to the men's room?

10 - Scrabble Nerds

Time to get stealthy. Erich told me to keep Hamish in my sights, so I'm going to have to follow him to the men's room without him noticing me.

As part of my mission briefing, Erich showed me a map of the hotel. I know the ballroom is located in a separate wing. There's only one entrance into the ballroom from the hotel. Because of the cheating scandal last year, tournament officials guard that entrance, only admitting properly credentialed competitors inside. No family, friends, reporters, or secret agents allowed.

At the rear of the ballroom, a set of double doors opens up to a large corridor. The men's room is at one end of the corridor, the ladies' at the other end. You see how this is going to get tricky? Hamish will go in one direction, and as a woman, I should theoretically be going the other way.

Casually standing by the buffet table, I watch as Hamish traverses the ballroom. He moves slowly, pausing every few feet to catch his breath. Once he walks through the door to the corridor, I spring into action. I set my coffee cup down, then dart through the crowd. When I reach the door, I push it open slowly and poke my head around. As predicted, Hamish is still walking toward the men's room.

Fortunately, there's a group of Scrabble players huddled in the middle of the corridor, having an animated discussion about strategy. I use them as camouflage while Hamish makes his way to the restroom. While I'm standing there, I'm tempted to offer my own opinion about whether you should sacrifice your turn in order to exchange your tiles in the hopes of getting better ones. The answer is yes, by the way. From a short-term perspective, it seems foolhardy, but if you adopt a long-term perspective, it can be advantageous.

It's easier to think strategically when it comes to Scrabble. So much harder with relationships. With Scrabble, if you sacrifice your turn, you'll get zero points for that round, but you could end up winning the game. When it comes to love, if you make a grand gesture and sacrifice something important to you, there are two possible outcomes: live happily ever after or lose your heart. Losing a Scrabble game is one thing, but losing your heart . . . well, that's something else entirely. When that happens, you might just find yourself working in a mini-mart.

What should have been, is, I remind myself. *Acknowledge and accept the past. Time to move forward.*

It really is time to move forward. Forward past this group of Scrabblers. Hamish just went into the men's room. And now I need to . . . actually, I have no idea what to do next. Wait outside the men's room? That seems kind of stalky. Follow him into the men's room? Even stalkier. But when you're trying to save the world, you do what you got to do.

I open the door to the men's room a crack and peek in. On one side of the room are urinals. Fortunately, no one is doing his thing, if you know what I mean. Three stalls line the other side of the room. They have doors that run floor to ceiling, so I can't tell if they're occupied. Hamish is obviously in one of them, but I don't know which one.

As I creep inside, my sandals creak on the tiled floor. Slipping them off, I close the door quietly, then tiptoe over to the sinks. Leaning against them, I stare at the stalls. It feels a bit like a game show—what's behind door number one? Is it an older Scottish man who suffers from arthritis? Or is it an all-expense paid trip to Disneyland?

Turns out it's a young guy sporting a Scrabble t-shirt. The shirt is really cute, and I'm tempted to ask him if it comes in women's sizes. He looks surprised to see me. "Long line at the ladies' room," I whisper to him so that Hamish won't hear me. He motions to the stall he just exited, then leaves without washing his hands. Gross.

Okay, we know stall number one is empty now. That means Hamish is behind door number two or door number three. I check my hair in the mirror while I wait. It looks so much better loose than tied back in a bun.

I see door number two open out of the corner of my eye, and panic because I still haven't come up with a cover story to explain why I'm stalking Hamish in the men's room.

Phew. It's not Hamish. This time it's a middle-aged man. He's wearing a top hat, tuxedo, and bow tie. One of those people who treats Scrabble tournaments as formal events. I pretend to be a cleaner, scrubbing the sink with a paper towel. He seems nonplussed by my presence. He washes his hands. I give him an approving nod. Then he pulls a bottle of hand sanitizer out of his pocket and applies some. I'm impressed and mentally award him double points for personal hygiene.

Then he tosses his paper towel at the trashcan. He misses, but doesn't bother to pick it up off the floor. He knows it's on the floor, but deliberately chooses to leave it there for the custodial staff. Sure, his hands might be clean, but he's a jerk. I pick the towel up and throw it away. Then I spy what looks like a gum wrapper on the floor and toss that, too. You owe me, buddy.

That leaves door number three. I've decided what my cover story is when Hamish comes out—"This isn't this the women's room? But I could have sworn the icon on the door was wearing a skirt."

Totally believable, right? Such an easy mistake to make. It looks like a bathroom; it smells like a bathroom. Of course, there is the pesky matter of the urinals, which kind of give away the fact that this isn't the ladies' room. Anyway, I'll cross that bridge when I get to it.

I wait for what seems like an eternity. Then I begin to worry. It can't possibly take that long to go to the bathroom. Did Hamish have a heart attack or a stroke? Should I open the stall door and make sure he's okay? Do I break the door down?

Hamish might be a jewel thief, but he's still a nice guy. I have to do something. I knock gently on the door. "Hamish, are you okay?" When he doesn't answer, I knock more loudly. The door creaks open, apparently not latched properly.

When the door opens fully, I gasp. The stall is empty. Well, almost empty. Leaning against the tiled wall is Hamish's cane.

I run my fingers through my hair. Where did he go? Then, feeling a breeze, my eyes drift upward and I see an open window. It looks like my elderly, arthritic jewel thief has done a runner.

* * *

How does a senior citizen who needs a cane to get around pull himself up eight feet in order to crawl out a small window?

Well, duh, obviously he was faking the whole thing. Who knows if he's even Scottish.

I set my sandals down, climb onto the toilet seat, and peer out the window. It opens up to an alleyway. A dumpster is conveniently located underneath the window. There's no sign of Hamish, but that's not surprising as I spent nearly five minutes waiting in the men's room for him to appear. Plenty of time for him to shimmy out the window and disappear.

I scoop up Hamish's cane and hoist myself up to the windowsill. As I leap on top of the dumpster, I wonder if this is what it feels like to be a cat thief. I survey the alleyway, then startle when a rat runs across my feet. My bare feet. Why did I leave my sandals on the bathroom floor?

A debate rages inside me—climb back inside and retrieve my shoes or run down the alley in the hopes of spotting Hamish. I shake my head. Hamish is probably long gone by now. Get your shoes and retrieve Erich's phone. That's the sensible plan. But just as I reach up to grab hold of the windowsill, someone slams the window shut.

Time for another plan. Jump off the dumpster, walk down the alleyway dodging broken glass, rats, and garbage, then hope you can find a taxi on the main road. Sure, that will totally work cause taxis love picking up people who aren't wearing shoes and don't have any money on them. Sigh.

Not coming up with any better alternatives, I hop down from the dumpster. Fortunately, I make it through the alleyway unscathed. I'm now standing on a busy road. Hamish is nowhere to be seen, and taxis are non-existent. Turning right, I head back to the hotel, wincing when a woman runs over my toes with her baby stroller.

I hop up and down on one leg while waving the cane around wildly. "Son of a—"

"Isabelle, what in the world are you doing here?" a familiar voice says.

Erich is sitting at a cafe table, a pastry halfway to his mouth. He pushes back his chair and comes over to help me. "Here, sit down."

"Having a little coffee break?" I ask sarcastically.

He frowns. "Shouldn't you be playing Scrabble?"

"Yes, I should be, but things happened." I snatch up his pastry and take a bite.

"What things happened?"

"Hamish had to take a pee," I say, covering my mouth because it's full of the most delicious raspberry filling.

"I'm sorry, I'm not seeing the connection between going to the bathroom and playing Scrabble."

"Hamish went into the men's room, the ordinary way through a door. Then he left the men's room, more unconventionally, through a window. So you see, there's no more Hamish and no more Scrabble." I polish off the pastry, then take a sip of Erich's coffee while he processes this.

"Why didn't you press the star key to let us know you needed urgent help?"

"Because the phone was confiscated. New tournament rules—no devices. How did you guys not know that was going to happen?"

Erich furrows his brow. He grabs his tablet and furiously taps on it. "That explains why, according to this tracker, you're still inside the hotel."

"Didn't you get my text? I sent you one when they took away the phone."

"No, nothing came through."

"And didn't you wonder why you hadn't received any pictures from me? That's what I was supposed to be doing during the tournament, snapping pictures."

"Between you and me, we've been having some technical difficulties on our end. They told me it was just a glitch and that your pictures were saved somewhere on the system. They promised a fix so we could access them." Erich scowls. "When I get my hands on the systems team—"

"Okay, enough hating on IT right now," I interject. "First things first. What are our next steps?"

Erich rubs the stubble on his jaw, then stares at the cane. "Can I see that?"

"He left it in the bathroom," I say as I hand it to him. "Speaking of which, we need to go back there to get my sandals."

"I was wondering about the bare feet." Erich runs his fingers along the length of the cane, then presses his fingernails on the groove near the handle. When the top of the cane opens and reveals an empty compartment, we both say "ooh" at the same time. "Looks like he kept the necklace in here. That's why I didn't find it when I searched his cabin."

"Do you think he gave the necklace to the fence in the men's room? He was in there for a few minutes before I worked up the nerve to go in."

"Did you see anyone else in there?" Erich asks.

"There were two men. The first was a young guy who didn't wash his hands. The second man was wearing a tux..." My eyes widen as I remember something. "Wait a minute, I think that was Bob wearing the tux."

"Who's Bob?"

"A woman I played against in the warm-up round."

Erich cocks his head to one side. "A woman named Bob in the men's room?"

Remembering the technique Erich taught me, I close my eyes and let the memories flood back. "That wasn't a gum wrapper I picked up. It was tin foil. Bob had a tinfoil hat. The man in the bathroom used hand sanitizer. So did Bob. There was pink lint on the tux. Bob wore pink mittens."

I take a deep breath and open my eyes. "Tuxedo man and Bob are the same person."

"Interesting," Erich says. "But how does it connect with Hamish?"

"I noticed Hamish brushing some lint off his shirt at the beginning of the tournament. I didn't pay much attention at the time, but I'm certain it was pink. Just like Bob's mittens. I think Bob and Hamish connected that morning, then made arrangements to do the exchange in the men's room during the break."

Erich gives me a huge smile, then kisses me on the cheek. "You're brilliant."

I'm startled by the sudden affection, but now's not the time to figure out what that's all about. Instead, I grab Erich's hand. "Come on, let's see if Bob is still at the hotel."

* * *

While we run around the block to the hotel entrance, I fill Erich in on what else I remember about Bob. He phones in a report to headquarters as we dash through the lobby. When we get to the ballroom, we're stopped by the obnoxious sweater vest-wearing official. He folds his arms across his chest. "Competitors only."

"I am a competitor." I reach up to show him the lanyard around my neck, only to realize it's missing. "My badge must have fallen off."

The official shifts his position so that he's completely blocking the entrance to the ballroom. "Sure. Aliens abducted you and when they were beaming you on board, it fell off."

I fold my hands into a prayer position and implore him. "But I have to get inside."

"Sorry. No badge. No entry."

Fury boils up in me. Doesn't this guy know that global security is at stake? I try to push him aside, but there's a surprising amount of muscle underneath that sweater vest.

"Erich, want to give me a hand?" I snap.

Instead of answering, he walks away.

"Hey, where are you going?" I shout at him.

Without turning around, he crooks his finger behind him, motioning for me to follow him. I release my hands from the official's meaty arms. "Next time, buddy," I tell him, but he doesn't seem fazed by my idle threat.

Trailing behind Erich as he races through one hallway to the next, I fume. "Bob is going to get away and you think now is the time to explore the hotel?"

"Did you think there was only one way into the ballroom?" He holds open a door and ushers me inside the hotel's kitchen. "Follow me."

"If you can get in here so easily, why didn't you or one of the organization's other agents pose as a cook or waiter? Wouldn't that have been an easier way to infiltrate the tournament?"

Erich stops so that someone carrying a heavy pot can get by. "We thought of that, but the kitchen staff can't spend all their time in the ballroom without raising suspicion."

If anyone is surprised to see us wander past their workstations, they don't show it. One of them even offers us an hors d'oeuvre. Of course, Erich carries himself with confidence and assurance. Maybe they think he's part of management, inspecting operations.

Erich pushes open a swinging door at the far end of the kitchen. "Ta da," he says when I see the ballroom on the other side.

The ballroom is quiet except for the rattle of Scrabble tiles. Everyone is focused on their boards, scouring their brains for high-scoring letter combinations. I search the room for Bob, but there's no sign of anyone in a tuxedo. "I don't see her. But maybe she has a new disguise."

Erich shakes his head. "No, Bob is long gone. Once she got the necklace, there wouldn't have been any reason for her to stick around."

I cock my head to one side. "Then why did you agree to come back here?"

He points at my feet. "You can't keep walking around like that. Come on, let's go find your shoes."

* * *

I make Erich go into the bathroom to retrieve my sandals. I've had enough of men's rooms to last me a lifetime. As I'm slipping them back on my feet, Erich steadies me. "Let's grab some lunch."

"How can you be thinking about food right now? And don't say it's because of my blood sugar levels."

"Okay, we'll pretend that's not why. Anyway, I know this place that makes the best—"

"It better not be balkenbrij," I say.

"You've heard of it?"

"Before we got to Amsterdam, I looked up all the names of foods I won't eat in Dutch. That way, I won't end up getting something like balkenbrij. Animal heads? No, thank you."

As we walk back into the ballroom, Erich says, "Don't worry, this place we're going to serves German food. The strudel is out of this world."

"You come to the Netherlands and eat German food?"

"Well, the place is run by my aunt. I kind of have to stop by when I'm in town."

I halt in my tracks. "You're going to take me to meet your family?"

"In a way," Erich says. "Now, where's the phone?"

"In there." I jerk a finger at the storage closet. "But it's locked."

Erich pulls a lock pick out of his pocket and grins. "Not a problem. Can you create a distraction?"

"Sure." I walk over to a table on the other side of the room and stand behind one of the competitors. I whistle, then say in a loud voice that carries across the ballroom, "Would you look at that. This woman has ten tiles on her rack."

The uproar that ensues is predictable. Having more than seven tiles is the most blatant form of cheating there is in Scrabble. I feel horrible about what I did to the woman. She only had the regulation amount of tiles, but Erich did say to create a distraction, and I couldn't think of anything else in the spur of the moment.

I push my way through the angry mob that's forming around the poor lady and rush back to Erich. "Grab Hamish's phone too," I say. "It's the one with the tartan cover."

We quickly exit the ballroom, much to the sweater vest official's surprise. "How did you get in there?" he yells at our retreating backs.

During the car ride to the restaurant, I can't stop laughing about our escape. "James Bond has nothing on us."

"James Bond probably has a better IT department," Erich grumbles as he pulls up in front of a nondescript building. There's a small German flag stuck in a planter by the door and a tattered poster of Berlin taped on the inside of one of the windows. When we enter the restaurant, the lights are off, and the place is deserted.

"I guess German food isn't that popular in the Netherlands," I say.

"That's the way we like it," a woman's voice says.

I squint in the darkness, trying to make out who's speaking, but all I can see are cobwebs.

"Bring your friend back to the kitchen," she says.

Her voice is deep and raspy. It sends chills down my spine. Am I about to be eliminated because it's my fault that the mission failed?

Erich puts his hand on the small of my back. "It's okay," he says in a soft, reassuring voice.

As he guides me into the kitchen, the lights suddenly come on, blinding me. I put my hands over my eyes and let out a tiny whimper. The bright lights. I know what that means—they're going to interrogate me before I'm eliminated.

"For goodness' sake, dim those lights," the woman barks at someone. "The girl can't see."

Once the lights are adjusted, I can make out a woman standing behind a metal food prep counter. She's the spitting image of Frau Albrecht, from her beady eyes down to her incessant knuckle cracking.

"Is that who I think it is?" I whisper to Erich.

He murmurs in my ear, "No, but I think they might have been twins separated at birth."

"Silence!" Frau Albrecht's doppelganger slams a meat cleaver on the counter, sending reverberations through the room.

Erich calmly introduces us. "Isabelle, this is Aunt C."

"This is your aunt?" I ask.

"No, this is Aunt C. 'C' as in chief. That's her official designation," Erich explains.

"Sit down." Aunt C points at two wooden stools, then gives me an appraising look. "So this is the girl I've heard so much about."

"I think you mean woman," I mumble.

Erich puts his fingers to his lips. I probably should keep quiet, but my grandmother's ring glints in the light. I feel courage flowing through me. I lean across the counter and glare at the older woman. "What exactly have you heard about me?"

She turns to stir a pot on the stove, ignoring my question.

"Oh, I get it. You've read my file. You think you know everything there is to know about me." I tap my chest. "But you'll never know everything. You'll never know what's in my mind and heart."

Aunt C cackles. She looks at Erich and says, "You were right. She is feisty." Then she sets a bowl of soup in front of me. "Eat."

"I'm not hungry."

She chuckles. "Don't worry. There isn't any organ meat in there. Just chicken thighs."

"Try it," Erich urges.

"It's good," I say begrudgingly after sampling a small spoonful.

"Good. I'm glad you like it, especially considering it's your last meal."

I spit out my soup. "You really are going to kill me."

"Feisty and imaginative," Aunt C says as she wipes off the counter. She looks at me and her expression softens. "I meant that this is your last meal with Erich. You won't see him again after today."

I look over at Erich, but he's concentrating on his soup. Aunt says something to him in German. He nods, then carries his empty bowl to the sink. He walks back to me and kisses my forehead. "Take care of yourself, Isabelle."

Then he walks out of the door, and he's gone. Gone forever.

11 - Potato Allergies

It's hard to believe it's been a month since the Scrabble tournament. A month since the mission failed because Hamish had to go to the men's room. A month since I said goodbye to Erich at that strange German restaurant.

Since then, we've had four cruises up and down the Rhine River, and I've really gotten into the groove of being a tour manager. Even Frau Albrecht grudgingly admitted that I was doing a satisfactory job. Okay, she didn't say "satisfactory." She said, "You're not utterly disappointing," but that's close enough for me. Sophia and I have even come to a semi-truce. In fact, she's seemed to really warm up to me after I told her I wasn't planning on renewing my contract. The job she's had her heart set on will be all hers next season.

Admittedly, the week I spent with Erich was chaotic and I was anxious much of the time, but I felt so alive. It made me realize that being a tour manager isn't what my future holds. I'm not sure what the universe has in store for me, but it's certainly not working on a riverboat or at a mini-mart.

Erich reminded me that there are positive attributes to anxiety. People who constantly worry about what could go wrong are better at responding to threats because their brain processes danger more efficiently. Given his German love of efficiency, I can see why he liked that particular fact. He also pointed out that if you spend a lot of time ruminating about things, you tend to be more intelligent. There are days where I'd happily trade some IQ points for not constantly obsessing about things, but I'm learning to find peace with how my brain is wired.

We're currently in Amsterdam, at the start of a seven-day cruise to Basel,

Switzerland. The latest group of passengers is waiting for me in the lounge, ready to hear my welcome presentation. I calmly walk up to the podium, attach the mike on my lapel, and greet them warmly. "How's everyone doing tonight? We're delighted to have you aboard the *Abenteuer*. I met most of you when you checked in, but for those who don't know me, my name is Isabelle Martinez and I'll be your tour manager on this cruise."

Sophia pipes up from the back of the room. "There isn't anything about this cruise that Isabelle doesn't know. You're lucky to have her."

I smile at her, then click through the slides. The presentation goes smoothly. No embarrassing photos, no questions I can't answer.

When the session is over, several passengers approach me to ask about excursions near Breisach—should they go on the cycling trip through the Black Forest or explore the medieval village of Colmar? They're delighted when I tell them they can do both.

I notice an older gentleman standing off by himself at the edge of the group, presumably waiting to speak with me. His jet-black hair is pulled back into a ponytail, and he's dressed in dark jeans and an oversized houndstooth jacket. The curled tips of his handlebar mustache are impressive. How exactly do guys do that? Do they use tiny curling irons? Special styling products?

The group asks a few more questions about the best desserts to order once we get to Germany. "The strudel, without a doubt," I tell them. "It's my absolute favorite."

When they wander off, I turn to the mustached man. "Can I help you, sir?"

There's something familiar about him. He's wearing dark sunglasses indoors at night, so maybe he's some sort of celebrity who thinks sunglasses can conceal his identity.

The man clears his throat, then says in a heavy Russian accent, "Ready for another adventure?"

"Oh, yes, there will be plenty or adventures on the cruise. I was just telling those folks about the cycling excursion. And if you're not afraid of heights, you can take the cable car in Koblenz."

"Those don't sound very exciting," he says. "I was thinking of an adventure of a different kind."

An adventure of another kind? Is he propositioning me? I did not sign up for this. Attempting to defuse the situation, I say, "You know what, sir, why don't I get you one of the brochures and you can have a look at the excursions we have available?"

As I turn to get a brochure from the table, he grabs my hand. What does this guy think he's doing? My adrenaline kicks in, and I get ready to stomp on his foot with my heel.

"I see that you're still feisty," he says as he removes his sunglasses.

I find myself staring into a pair of icy-blue eyes, and my heart flutters. "Erich? Is that you?"

* * *

Except for the eyes, the man standing in front of me looks completely different from the Erich I knew. But the way his fingers felt as he grabbed my hand, that was oh so familiar.

"What are you doing here, Erich?" I put my hand on my stomach, trying to quiet the butterflies in it. "And why are you in disguise?"

"Shush, don't use that name. It's Andrei Petrov now." He put his sunglasses back on. "A Russian businessman on vacation."

"This is crazy. Next thing you know, you'll be telling me you're here on a mission."

"I'm always on a mission. You know that," he says. "Why don't we go somewhere more private and I'll explain."

I follow Erich to his cabin in a daze. I was getting into a stable routine aboard the boat. Boring, but stable. I thought I wanted more excitement in my life, but now I'm not sure. When Erich opens the door, I'm so out of sorts that I don't even care if anyone notices that I'm going into a passenger's room.

Reminding myself to breathe slowly, I survey his accommodations. "I see you got a stateroom again."

"I'm not sure I could cope with a budget cabin after I've experienced this," Erich says wryly.

After motioning for me to sit on the small settee, he proceeds to take off his disguise. First, he removes his sunglasses, then peels off his fake beard and mustache. Next, he takes off his wig, revealing his natural blond hair. Hair I'm longing to run my fingers through.

As soon as Erich hangs up his suit jacket and unbuttons the top of his shirt, his posture transforms. Gone is the stooped over Russian businessman. In his place is the German equivalent of James Bond—confident, sexy, and dangerous.

"Are you hungry? I could order room service," he says.

"I'm fine." I cock my head to one side. "Why are you still talking with a Russian accent?"

"It helps to stay in character."

I hug one of the throw cushions to my chest. "Were you playing a character on the last cruise? Are you even German?"

Erich—if that's even his name—doesn't answer. "Well, I'm hungry." He picks up the phone and orders grilled fish. Not steak like before. Did he even like steak or did he eat it because his fake German persona was supposed to? What do I really know about this man standing in front of me?

I guess I said that last bit out loud, because Erich says, "You knew more about me than most people." The tone of his voice is harsh, bitter almost. He pours himself a shot of vodka and downs it. "I started to care for you and . . ."

He pauses to refill his glass. His hand is grasping the bottle so tightly that I'm scared it's going to shatter. "What a mistake that night was. I should have never let that happen."

Before he can down his drink, I walk over and place my hand on his arm. "You don't think I regret that night, too? But it happened. We kissed, and it was incredible."

Erich sets his glass down so quickly that I jump back. He grabs hold of me, pulling me into his arms. His hands run up and down my back. "It was incredible, wasn't it?" he murmurs in my ear.

My breath hitches in my chest as I breathe in his familiar scent. He lowers his mouth and his lips brush against mine. I twine my fingers through his hair, pulling him closer to me. My heartbeat quickens as I wait for him to kiss me again.

"Room service," a voice calls out.

Erich turns his face from mine, and says loudly, "Leave it by the door, please."

"How could they grill a fish so fast?" I wonder out loud.

Erich releases me, then sits on the edge of the bed and puts his head in his hands. "I told Aunt C that it was a bad idea to have us work together again."

Not knowing what to say, I go to the door to get the room service. Checking to make sure no one is in the hall first, I grab the cart and wheel it into the room. I set his fish on the table, then pour myself my own shot of vodka. Then I remind myself that I don't normally drink shots, and set the glass aside.

Erich looks up at me. "I'm sorry, but this is what you do to me. You cause me to lose control of my emotions. And that's a liability in my line of work."

I sit on the bed next to him and take his hand in mine. "When I was working in intelligence, I dated someone who was a field operative. We both had to keep so many secrets from each other that it destroyed our relationship."

"So you understand." He caresses my hand gently. "Whatever this is between us, we can't pursue it."

"Agreed. That's why I pulled away from you that night on deck. Believe me, I didn't want to, but I knew it was for the best." I take a deep breath, then point at the table. "Your fish is getting cold. You should eat."

He nods. "Okay, then I'll tell you about our mission."

"*Our* mission?" I shake my head. "After I botched the last mission—"

Erich interrupts me. "You didn't botch anything. We had bad intel. If we had known they were going to confiscate your phone, we would have come up with a different plan. Not to mention how our IT department screwed up. What a disaster."

"But the men's room," I say. "I was standing outside while Hamish made the exchange with Bob."

"Again, bad intel on our part. We were operating under the assumption that the exchange would be done during the Scrabble match, not in the bathroom."

"Well, when you put it that way . . ."

Erich walks over to the table and uncovers his plate. "Do you want to hear about our new mission?"

"Sure." I rub my hands together, eager to hear the details.

He takes a bite of his meal, then frowns. "I hate fish."

"The mission," I prompt.

"Oh, yeah, I think you're going to like this one. We need you to pretend to be my fiancée."

* * *

"You want me to be your fake fiancée?" I burst out laughing. "That's the most ridiculous thing I've ever heard."

"That's not what Aunt C thinks," Erich says. "She believes that the mission has the best chance of success if you go undercover as my fiancée."

"Perhaps she's pulling your leg?"

Erich shakes his head. "Aunt C wouldn't joke about something like that."

"Yeah, no kidding," I say. "She didn't strike me as someone who has a sense of humor. But I suppose people who work for the organization don't. I guess it comes with the territory."

Erich protests. "I have a sense of humor."

"You've told me one bad joke since I've known you. That does *not* constitute a sense of humor." I shake my head. "The few times I've heard you laugh, your eyes don't light up. It's like you're laughing because you think you're supposed to, not because you're actually having a light-hearted moment."

"That's not true."

"Really? When's the last time you laughed so hard you couldn't stop? Not just a brief chuckle, but a full-on belly laugh."

Erich lowers his eyes and his shoulders slump ever so slightly. "I haven't had much to laugh about lately," he says quietly.

"I'm sorry," I say gently, feeling awful that I started this line of conversation. Like the rest of us, Erich probably has his own history full of painful memories.

"Nonsense," he says crisply, fixing his icy-blue eyes on mine. "Nothing to be sorry about. Now, shall we talk about the mission?"

You can't make someone talk about something they don't want to. And, to be honest, I'm not sure I want to know what's happened to Erich in the past. Could I handle it?

I fold my hands in my lap and adopt an attentive pose. "Sure, go ahead. I'm all ears."

He pushes his plate away. He's only taken a couple of bites of his fish. I guess the real Erich is more of a red meat guy. Or is the real Erich a lover of seafood and he's only pretending not to enjoy his meal? My head is swimming, trying to discern what's real and what's not.

"There will be a black-tie party at a historic mansion in Basel," Erich says, interrupting my thoughts. "It's being held to raise money for endangered animals. I'll be attending, posing as Andrei Petrov, an eccentric and reclusive Russian businessman. He hasn't been seen in public in over twenty years, which makes pretending to be him easier."

"What kind of business is Andrei in?" I ask.

"Potato peelers," Erich says.

I cock my head to the side. "So not a rich businessman then?"

"There's a lot of money in potato peelers."

"Are they encrusted in diamonds? Plated in twenty-four carat gold?"

"No, just ordinary metal." He shrugs. "What can I say? People eat a lot of potatoes in Russia. They need peelers."

"Okay, so how does a fiancée fit in?"

"Well, Andrei recently became engaged to a beautiful, young Russian woman. Fortunately, she's also a recluse. They met on a dating app. It's really a classic 'opposites attract' love story. His fortune is based on potatoes. She's allergic to them."

"How do I fit in?"

"You're similar in looks to Andrei's fiancée."

"But you said she's beautiful." Yeah, I admit it, I'm fishing for compliments.

Erich gives me an appreciative look. "You definitely check that box."

I repress a smile and try not to let my thoughts stray too far from the mission at hand. "But I'm not allergic to potatoes. I eat them all the time. In fact, I had French fries for lunch."

"Were they the shoestring ones? I had those the last time I was on board the *Abenteuer.* I love the seasoning salt the chef puts on them."

"Uh-huh. The salt is what makes them so addictive. I have them practically every day." I pat my stomach. "It feels like I've gained a lot of weight since I started this job."

"Doesn't look like it to me," he says as his eyes sweep over me.

"It's the suit," I say. "The material is stretchy. That's the only good thing I can say about this uniform, really. What I wouldn't give to wear normal clothes again."

"You'll get to wear an evening gown to the party," Erich says.

"Ooh . . . what does it look like? What color? Is it strapless?" Then I mentally slap myself. I'm not in a boutique shopping for dresses. I'm sitting here with a spy who's concocted the most bizarre cover story for an undercover mission that he wants me to be part of. "Never mind, let's get back to the fiancée potato allergy thing. Exactly how does this all fit into your latest save-the-world plan?"

"Okay, so when Andrei fell madly in love with Svetlana—"

"Svetlana, huh?" I repeat her name a few times. "Okay, I can live with that."

"Anyway, he asked her to marry him and she agreed on one condition—that he sell his potato peeler business."

"Wow, that's asking a lot," I say. "Quite a sacrifice our Andrei is making for love."

"He probably thinks he doesn't deserve her." Erich clears his throat. "Anyway, at the party, Andrei is going to the party to meet with a sheikh who wants to buy the potato peeler business."

"They have a lot of unpeeled potatoes in the Middle East?"

"You'd be surprised. It's a real problem."

"If I didn't know better, I'd almost think that was a joke," I say.

"Maybe it is," Erich says with a faint twinkle in his eye. "Anyway, the sheikh also happens to be an arms dealer."

"You mean *the* arms dealer? The one who is going to give Nouveau Rouge Order weapons in exchange for the necklace that Hamish stole? The same terrorist group who is going to be responsible for the attack on the United Nations?"

Erich nods. "That's the one."

I rub my temples. "Let me see if I've got this straight. Hamish stole an emerald necklace. Hamish put the emerald in a secret compartment in his cane. Hamish then sold the necklace to the fence, Bob, in the men's room at a Scrabble tournament."

"You're a hundred for a hundred so far," Erich says. "Keep going."

"Okay, Bob then passed the necklace to the terrorists. Now a member of the Nouveau Rouge Order is going to this party to exchange the necklace for the weapons."

Erich nods. "That's correct."

I run my fingers through my hair, then grumble when I remember it's still pinned up in a bun. "So what is the sheikh going to do with the necklace?"

"Give it to Andrei in exchange for the potato peeler business."

"Hasn't anyone ever heard of cashier's checks?" I muse. Then I look at Erich. "But if you're hanging around for the sheikh to give you this necklace, isn't it too late? Won't the terrorists already have their hands on the weapons?"

"Tell you what, why don't we save that part of the plan for another day," he says. "I haven't slept in thirty-seven hours and I need to get some shut-eye."

As Erich escorts me to the door, I say, "Aren't there other agents who could pose as Svetlana? Surely someone else has to resemble her. Someone with actual field experience. Why in the world would you want to involve me?"

"Well, you speak Russian fluently, which is critical. You score high on agility tests and you can run fast." When I furrow my brow, he says, "It will make sense when I tell you more about the plan."

"I still think there have to be other people who can speak Russian and are athletic."

"There are. We do have a back-up plan in place," he admits. "But . . ."

"But what?"

"We have chemistry together. People will believe that we're in love." Erich pauses, then adds, "At least, that's what Aunt C thinks."

"What do you think?"

Erich shoves his hands in his pockets. I think we make a good team."

"Andrei and Svetlana," I say. "That has a nice ring to it."

"So, you'll do it?" Erich asks.

"Da," I say, answering him in Russian.

12 - Crawling through Cardboard Boxes

Why in the world did I say yes to Erich's latest hare-brained scheme? Me, posing as a Russian billionaire's fiancée—ridiculous, right?

There are three big issues with his plan. First of all, it's been ages since I've spoken Russian. I'm pretty rusty, but Erich is convinced that it'll come back to me.

Second, I have to pretend to be allergic to potatoes. Erich told me I should avoid all potato products until the mission is over. That way it'll be second nature to me to say no to all things potato, because, heaven forbid, they serve potato puffs at the party and I snarf them down, blowing my cover. It seemed logical when Erich explained to me, but giving up my daily shoestring French fries from now until the mission? That's a big ask.

The third issue, and the most terrifying one, is having to fake being attracted to Erich. How am I supposed to do that?

Okay, I know what you're thinking—Isabelle, this isn't something you're going to have to fake. You're totally attracted to him. Everything about him drives you crazy. Whenever you're in the same room with him, you want to brush your lips against his, feel his strong arms enveloping you in an embrace . . .

Okay, enough of that train of thought. You're right. I'm attracted to Erich. End of story. But we're going to have to be physically affectionate with each other during this party, standing close to each other, holding hands, and the occasional kiss. One little peck on the cheek and it's going to be hard to rein in my desire for him.

So why did I agree to this? Is it because I want more excitement in my life? Or is it because I want to spend more time with Erich? Or both?

I push these thoughts out of my head. I have guests waiting for me in the reception area, eager to head out on this morning's excursion. As I pass Erich on the way to the dining room to grab a to-go coffee, he says quietly in Russian, "My cabin tonight."

"Da," I reply, wishing it was already this evening.

It was a rough day at Kinderdijk, a UNESCO World Heritage Site south of Amsterdam. As we toured the open-air windmill museum, two of the guests decided it would be a good idea to take a picture with some goats. They bent down to pose with the animals. One of the goats decided that the woman's long brown hair looked like it would make a good snack. When he started chomping on it, she yelped.

That might have been the end of the story, but she was wearing a wig and when she tried to extricate herself, there was a struggle. The goat won. He placidly continued to chew on the wig while she screamed and threatened to sue the cruise line. By the time we recovered her wig, rinsed it out in the bathroom sink, and calmed everyone down, we were two hours late boarding the boat. Naturally, Frau Albrecht blamed me.

We finally get underway for the overnight sail to our next destination, and I head to Erich's cabin. As usual, I make sure the coast is clear before I enter. The last thing I need is for people to think I'm having inappropriate relations with a passenger. The rumors about me having an affair with Erich were bad enough. Imagine what it would be like if they started talking about Andrei and me.

"She's slept with two different passengers," they'd say.

Concerned that they'd think I was a complete hussy, I'd want to correct them—"It's only one passenger. Erich and Andrei are the same guy. And I didn't sleep with him." Of course, that wouldn't fly. I can't break Erich's latest cover. So it's better if the rumors don't get started in the first place.

When I walk into Erich's cabin, he pulls me toward him and kisses me on both cheeks.

"I thought we weren't doing this," I say, squirming out of his arms.

"We're not doing it for real," he says. "Just practicing so that we look natural at the party."

"Why don't we focus on the mission details?" I suggest.

"Fine." He pulls a folder out of the desk drawer. "This is a dossier on Svetlana. While she hasn't been seen in public in a few years, you need to be prepared in case there's anyone at the party who knows her. If they notice any differences in appearance, you'll need to attribute it to cosmetic surgery. Despite being a young woman, she has her plastic surgeon on speed dial."

I flip through the pages in the folder. "She's a pet groomer?"

"Uh-huh, specializes in hamsters."

"I didn't know hamsters needed to be groomed."

Erich leans against the desk. "The rich and famous have their hamsters flown to her on their private planes for blowouts. Hamsters with sleek, shiny fur are the latest thing among the one percent."

"I can't imagine they enjoy that. I hope she uses a cool setting." Erich gives me a look and I hold up my hand. "Don't worry, I'll disguise my feelings about blow drying hamsters when the time comes."

"The other thing you need to do is practice your Russian. That's all we should speak with one another from this point forward." He switches to Russian, saying, "Then there's your agility training."

"I've been wondering about that. What kind of training are you talking about?"

"You need to practice squeezing into small spaces and maneuvering around in them."

I raise my eyebrows. "And here I thought my job was to look pretty on your arm and talk about hamsters."

"Yes, and crawling through an air-conditioning duct." Erich unrolls a blueprint. "See this here? This is in a small office off the reception hall. It won't be in use during the event. There's a vent in the ceiling where you can access the ductwork. You'll follow the ducting from here to a vent in the library. Once you're in position, you'll record the meeting between the sheikh and the terrorist. That will give us the evidence we need to bring the Nouveau Rouge Order down."

"Why can't you do this?" I ask as I study the blueprint.

"My shoulders are too broad to fit through the ducting."

I pause for a moment to take in his physique. I do like those shoulders of his, but right now I wish they were a lot narrower. "Okay, well, it sounds easy enough," I say. "It looks like a straight shot from the office to the library."

Erich purses his lips. "Well, not exactly. When the owner of the building decided to have the air-conditioning system updated, he awarded the contract to his nephew."

"I don't follow."

"Well, the nephew was in the midst of making a career change. He used to have a company that designed rat mazes."

"That's a thing?"

"Sure, but not very lucrative, hence the move into air conditioning." Erich traces a zigzag line on the blueprint with his finger. "He installed the ducting to resemble a maze. There are lots of tight twists and turns, not to mention dead ends. Extremely inefficient."

"So basically, I have to pretend I'm a rat," I say. "And here I thought being a spy was such a glamorous job."

"Glamorous? Hah. You'd be surprised how much paperwork there is."

I walk over to the settee and sit down. Patting the spot next to me, I ask, "How did you become a spy, anyway?"

"I filled out an application. It's pretty much like any job."

"Being a spy is definitely not like any other job," I say. "I worked at a mini-mart. They were so desperate for workers that, if you so much as glanced at the application, they hired you on the spot."

"Admittedly, the secret agent recruitment process is a bit more in-depth. You attend an assessment center where they put you through a series of personality assessments, role-playing exercises, and simulations."

"Did any of the simulations cover crawling through air-conditioning ducts?"

When Erich laughs, I notice that it seems less forced. "Not exactly."

"So that's it. You take a few tests, and presto, you're a spy?"

"No, if you pass the assessment center, then there are extensive back-ground checks. I'm sure you went through something similar to get security clearance when you worked in intelligence."

"Yeah, it was really thorough," I say. "They talked to my family and friends, checked out my bank accounts, and asked me about my overseas travels."

"One of the last things they do is have a stranger approach you on a bus or train, something like that." Erich rubs his jaw. It looks raw, and I wonder if he's having a reaction to the adhesive he uses for his fake beard. "They engage you in conversation and see how much personal information you disclose."

"Let me guess, you aced that test. No one could accuse you of blabbing too much about yourself."

"True," he says. "In my line of work, it's an asset."

"That must be harder in your personal life," I muse.

Erich gives me a wry look. "It's easy when you don't have a personal life."

* * *

"So, this is it," Erich says. It's the last evening of the cruise. We've just docked in Basel. Erich and I are on the sun deck, leaning against the railing and watching the water lap against the side of the boat. "I'll be disembarking with the rest of the passengers tomorrow morning. Then I'll meet you back here in two weeks' time for the black–tie event."

"After spending each night with you training for the mission, it's going to be strange to go back to normal for two weeks," I say.

"You'll still need to prepare," Erich says. "Practice your Russian, avoid potatoes, and keep crawling through cardboard boxes."

I laugh as he reminds me of the simulations he set up in his cabin. Somehow, he managed to procure boxes that are the exact dimensions of the air-conditioning duct I'll be climbing through, and set up a mini-maze on the floor of his cabin. Housekeeping thought it was very strange, but he explained that he was a cat in a past life and had an affinity for boxes. They still thought it was odd, but at least they decided he was a harmless eccentric.

"You only have two weeks before the mission," he cautions me. "You sail back up to Amsterdam, then return here to Basel. You need to keep focused."

I gaze into the distance, watching the sunset. It's not going to be the same without Erich on board. It's amazing how quickly I've become accustomed to spending every hour I'm not working with him.

Erich clears his throat, then pulls a small velvet box out of his jacket pocket. The last time he gave me jewelry, it was the Scrabble charm bracelet. This one is smaller; the size of box that would normally contain a ring. When he bends down, for a moment, I think he's going to propose. Where did that crazy thought come from? But instead he picks up a napkin that the breeze has blown our way.

He gets back to his feet and thrusts the box into my hands. "This is for when I see you next."

When I open it, I gasp. "I hope this is fake."

Erich removes the ring and slips it on my finger. "Don't worry, it's not a real diamond. It's what's inside the diamond that's really valuable." He shows me how to press the band so that the diamond and its setting pop open, revealing a miniature recording device.

That's when the reality of what I'm supposed to do hits me. Up until now, it's seemed like a game. I mean, I've been crawling around in cardboard boxes, for goodness' sake. Something kids or cats do. Not something people do if they're about to embark on a mission to stop the Nouveau Rouge Order.

Are you kidding? Me stopping terrorists?

I begin to feel that sense of overwhelming doom that signals the start of a massive anxiety attack. My heart pounds, my skin grows clammy, and I feel faint. I clutch the railing while repeating every mantra I can think of to calm my breathing. Nothing works.

"Isabelle, are you okay?" Erich catches me by the waist when I start to collapse. "What's going on? Talk to me."

His touch calms me, and after a while, I feel able to speak again.

"I can't do this, Erich. I'm sorry."

"Of course you can," he says.

I pull away from him. "Look at me. I'm already panicking. Imagine what would happen if I had an anxiety attack while crawling through the ductwork."

Erich cradles my face. "What can I do to help?"

"Nothing." I remove the ring and hand it back to him. "There's nothing you can do. You're going to have to go with the back-up plan. I'm sorry."

"You have nothing to be sorry about." Just like in the German restaurant, he kisses my forehead. "Take care of yourself, Isabelle."

As he walks away, my eyes tear up. This is the second time I've said goodbye to Erich. I thought the first time was bad, but I think this one might just break me.

13 - The Undercover Passenger

It's been a week since Erich and I said goodbye. I can't tell you how many times I wanted to call him and tell him I changed my mind. Sure, they had another agent ready to step in and take my place, but Erich and I had trained for a week for this mission. Was she as prepared as I am? Would people believe that she and Erich were in love? Do they have chemistry together? When he kisses her, will he forget all about me?

Wow, am I ever self-centered. All I seem to care about is Erich being with another woman, not the actual mission. This is supposed to be about stopping terrorists. My personal feelings about Erich are irrelevant in the larger scheme of things. I have to keep reminding myself of that.

Sophia nudges me. "Are you okay? You seem distracted."

I snap out of my self-indulgent daydreaming and smile at her. "Yeah, I'm fine."

"If you ever need to talk . . ." she says tentatively.

"Thanks, but I'm not sure talking will help," I say, fidgeting with my charm bracelet.

"Well, if you change your mind, you know where I am."

Now that she knows she's getting the tour manager job for sure next season, Sophia has been so much fun to work with. She jokes around and shares stories about the crew. My favorites are the ones about Frau Albrecht's background. Who knew the woman had such an interesting life before working aboard a riverboat. The fact that Frau Albrecht was on the German national synchronized swimming team when she was younger amazes me. But her dreams of turning pro were brought to a halt when she developed a terrible allergy to chlorine. Just touching a drop of pool water caused her to break out in a terrible rash. Kind of makes you wonder why she wasn't more sympathetic to my allergy to nylons. Was it because her hopes for the future were crushed? Is that why she likes to see other people suffer?

As if she can sense me thinking about her, Frau Albrecht comes out of the back room and inspects the reception desk. "Isabelle, straighten up those welcome packs. We're ready to begin boarding."

Sophia prints out the passenger manifest while I stack the welcome packs.

Frau Albrecht signals for the doors to be opened. "Let's make sure check-in goes quickly and efficiently." Then she lowers her voice and adds, "Someone may be undercover on this cruise."

Sophia scowls. "Again? It wasn't that long ago we had someone undercover. That guy was a real nightmare to please."

I startle, knocking a stapler and pen holder on the floor. They knew about Erich being an undercover agent? And now there's going to be another spy on board?

"Clean that up, Isabelle. Everything needs to look shipshape," Frau Albrecht says. "We can't afford a bad rating."

As I'm scooping up the pens, I look up at the older woman and ask, "Why would an undercover agent rate you?"

"Because that's their job." She shakes her head. "Get your head out of the clouds. You need to be sharp. My bonus depends on it."

Now I'm really lost. The organization is giving out bonuses? Does this mean that Frau Albrecht is also an agent? Is Sophia one too? My head is spinning. I sit down and fan myself with a piece of paper.

"Did your source in Head Office give you any idea what they look like?" Sophia asks Frau Albrecht.

"All I know is that it's an American woman who will be traveling with a relative. Her last assignment was on a cruise from Miami to Italy. This will be her first time on a riverboat."

"How old is she?" Sophia asks.

"Retirement age," Frau Albrecht says. "Oh, and one other thing, apparently she loves to dance. But I don't know if she'll be on board this cruise or the next one."

"I hate not knowing." Sophia smooths down her skirt. "But I guess that's the point. You never know which passenger Head Office has sent undercover to evaluate the crew's performance, so you have to make sure you give excellent service to everyone."

"Wait a minute," I say. "This woman you're talking about—she's like a mystery shopper in a store?"

"Correct. Haven't you been paying attention?" Frau Albrecht snaps. "Just be on the lookout for someone who fits the description, then make sure to give her the VIP treatment."

Relieved that Frau Albrecht and Sophia aren't talking about secret spy agents—and feeling slightly stupid that I didn't figure it out before—I relax into welcoming the guests on board. Sophia and I even make a bit of a game out of it as we try to identify who the undercover passenger is.

During a lull, I go into the back to print out more handouts. Naturally, the copier jams and I spend ten minutes pulling paper out of the feeder tray. While I'm trying to get toner off my fingers, Sophia rushes in.

"Hurry up and get out front. I think the undercover passenger is here." Sophia hands me a wet wipe, then ticks items off on her fingers. "She's American. She's traveling with her niece. She arrived in Italy in May on a cruise ship from Miami."

Sophia is practically jumping up and down by this point. She grabs my hand and squeezes it, getting toner on herself. "And get this—she asked me if there was a dance floor. She wants to practice her tango."

"Clean up and let's go give her the VIP treatment," I say, tossing her the pack of wet wipes.

When I see who's standing at the reception desk, I do a double take. "Celeste? I thought you were in Greece."

The woman beams at me. "Surprise!" Then she scoots around the desk and envelops me in a hug.

"You two know each other?" Sophia asks.

"Remember how I was telling you I won tickets for a transatlantic cruise?

That's how my friend Mia and I got to Europe," I say to Sophia. "Well, that's when I met Celeste. She kind of adopted us, along with Ginny, this other girl we met on board."

Celeste pinches my cheeks. "I like to think of myself as you girls' fairy godmother. Whenever one of you has troubles with your love life, I'm there to help out."

I smile warmly at Celeste. She's like a surrogate mother and eccentric Dear Abby rolled into one. Her advice is often a bit strange, but always heartfelt.

"Now, come meet my niece, Olivia. She's been staying with me in Greece." Celeste leads me over to a woman about my age who has a bemused look on her face. Her tousled black bob, perfectly applied make-up, and stylish clothes make me feel positively frumpy with my tight bun and ill-fitting uniform.

"Olivia met a wonderful guy—he owns a taverna near my villa," Celeste says after she introduces us. "He makes the most divine baklava. But his mother . . . well, let's just say that I thought it would be good for Olivia to get away for a while."

Olivia rolls her eyes at her aunt. "Do we need to tell everyone my life story within two minutes of meeting them?" She turns to me and says, "You should have heard what she told the taxi driver. Did he really need to know how old I was when I learned to walk?"

"It's such a coincidence that you would go on a cruise on the same boat I'm working on," I say to them.

"It's no coincidence, dear. The universe told me your love life is at a crossroads." Celeste loops her hand through my arm. "I'm here to help."

* * *

When I walk into the lounge later that evening, Celeste is perched atop the baby grand piano, belting out show tunes. Frau Albrecht is convinced that Celeste is the undercover passenger, so she's ordered the staff to give her the VIP treatment. That includes having the bartender ready to refill Celeste's water glass should she look even the slightest bit parched and a waiter holding a tray of chocolate-covered marshmallows in case hunger strikes her.

I think the executive chef was smart to coat his marshmallows in chocolate—it disguises their unpleasant green color. You still couldn't pay me to eat one of them, though. But the passengers seem to love them and the kitchen can barely keep up with demand.

Olivia is sitting at the table where Hamish and I used to have our Scrabble matches. Seeing her there makes me wonder what the Scotsman is up to now. After making his escape from the hotel bathroom at the Scrabble tournament, he hasn't been seen since. There were reports that he had turned up in the Maldives, but those turned out to be false.

How do I know all this? Well, I did something cringe-worthy this afternoon. I phoned the German restaurant that Erich took me to in Amsterdam. When a woman answered the phone, I panicked. What was I thinking—that Erich would answer the phone himself?

"Hello," the woman had barked into the phone again. "Is anyone there?"

I pretended I was calling to place a takeout order, then hemmed and hawed.

"I don't have all day," she said. "What do you want to order?"

I said the first thing that popped into my head. "Could I have some pfälzer saumagen, please?"

"Hmm, pfälzer saumagen," the woman said dryly. "But I thought you didn't eat organ meat, Isabelle."

Feeling like a prank phone caller who's been caught out, I asked tentatively, "Is that you, Aunt C?"

"Of course it is, you silly girl," she snapped. "Who else did you think would answer the phone?"

"I think I dialed you by mistake," I said, wondering if running to the restroom and flushing my phone down the toilet would be a good idea. Anything to make this call end.

"Considering this number is classified, that seems highly unlikely." Aunt C let out an exasperated sigh. "Did Erich give it to you?"

I stalled, not wanting to get Erich in trouble. "Well, you see . . ."

"Just answer the question."

"Yes, he gave it to me," I confessed. "But it was only in case there was an emergency."

"And is this an emergency?" she asked.

I paced back and forth in my cabin, not sure how to answer. I eventually responded. The high-pitched squeak in my voice made me cringe. "I guess it depends on your definition of an emergency."

For some reason, this made Aunt C chuckle. Then she took pity on me, filling me in on Hamish's vanishing act and Erich's new partner. By the time the call was finished, I felt sick to my stomach, not just because Erich was working with some other woman, but because Aunt C hinted at concerns over my replacement's abilities.

While I'm obsessing over Erich and his new fake-fiancée, Olivia waves me over. I resolve to stop thinking about anything related to Erich. How long do we think this particular resolution will last?

"See that guy at the bar? The one with the red hair?" Olivia asks as I sit down. "He keeps trying to hit on me. I've told him repeatedly that I'm not interested, but the message doesn't seem to be getting through."

When I glance over at the bar, the redheaded man raises his glass at Olivia. She frowns. "Switch places with me, will you?"

Once she's seated with her back to her would-be suitor, I ask, "Did you tell him you have a boyfriend?"

"I shouldn't need to mention a boyfriend. If you tell a guy that you're not interested, that should be enough. There shouldn't have to be another man in the picture to get him to back off." She takes a sip of her wine, then adds, "Besides, I'm not sure if I have a boyfriend anymore."

"Your aunt mentioned something about his mother. What's going on?"

"Did you ever see *My Big Fat Greek Wedding*? This is kind of like that, but without the wedding. Definitely not the wedding." Olivia stares vacantly out the window. "Xander's mother always envisioned her son marrying a

Greek woman. She's constantly playing matchmaker, bringing different girls to his taverna all the time."

"Even when you're there?" I ask.

"Yep. My presence doesn't stop her at all. An American woman, especially one who doesn't even have Greek ancestry, is not what she had planned for her son." Olivia leans forward. "I went to all this trouble of learning how to make her favorite dish, but she spent the entire meal pointing out what I did wrong."

"That sounds awful," I say. "What did Xander do?"

"He had a big argument with his mom, but it was in Greek, so I don't know what was said." Her eyes well up. "Afterward, he pretended like nothing was wrong, but he became so distant."

I make sympathetic noises, and she wipes away a tear. "Anyway, that's when Aunt Celeste suggested this cruise. She thought it would be good for me to get some time away from Xander."

"He'll realize what he's missing," I say, squeezing her hand. "Absence makes the heart grow fonder."

"But it's not just him. It's like I'm also dating his family," she says. "Have you ever been in that situation?"

I shake my head. My problems with Erich have nothing to do with his family. In some ways, family might be an easier issue to deal with. You know what you're up against. Everything is out in the open. But with Erich, it's the secrets that are keeping us apart.

Our conversation drifts off as Celeste sings "Bali Ha'i." Her voice is low and husky and she sways slowly in time to the music.

Olivia smiles. "When she was younger, my aunt was in an off-Broadway production of *South Pacific*. It's good to see her so happy. It was hard for her when Uncle Ernie passed away."

We listen to Celeste sing for a while. When she finishes, Olivia turns to me. "I love that song. A mysterious island calling to you to come to it—it's so romantic."

I furrow my brow. "Romantic? How so?"

"Did you ever meet someone you fell in love with right away, before you even knew that much about them? That's what it reminds me of—falling for a mysterious stranger and taking a chance on love." She blushes, then toys with her wineglass. "I know, I'm being silly. You can't fall in love with someone you know nothing about, right?"

I nod in agreement, but honestly, I'm wondering if she's wrong. Is it possible that I'm in love with Erich, a man I know nothing about?

* * *

"What are you two girls talking about?" Celeste sits at the table and a waiter instantly rushes up with a bottle of champagne for her.

As he pours her a glass, he asks what else he can do to make her stay aboard the *Abenteuer* more enjoyable. "Anything you want, madame, it is yours."

"Well, there was this tattoo I was thinking of getting," Celeste says. "But I keep changing my mind about the design."

The waiter looks flummoxed. This is probably the first time a passenger has asked his opinion on what kind of tattoo to get. "What are you considering?" he asks.

"I was originally thinking of something that says, 'Floss.' Dental hygiene is important, don't you think?"

The waiter unconsciously runs his tongue across his front teeth, and I realize I've done the same thing. Funny how a mere mention of flossing can make you worry that you have something stuck between your teeth.

"Yes, dental hygiene is important, madame," he says.

Celeste takes a sip of her champagne. "Lately, I've been thinking of getting a tattoo of a cat."

The waiter smiles. Probably thinking—crazy cat lady, I've seen this kind before. "Yes, a kitten tattoo would be nice. Perhaps a calico or Siamese?"

She waves a hand in the air. "No, not that kind of cat. I was thinking about one of those scanning devices."

Olivia furrows her brow. "Do you mean a CAT scan?" She turns to me. "My dad was just telling us about the CAT scan he had done. I bet that's what put it in her head."

"Yes, that's it." Celeste turns back to the waiter. "Don't you think that would make a nice tattoo?"

He shifts the bottle of champagne from one arm to another. "Um . . ."

Olivia pats her aunt's arm. "We should let him get back to work, don't you think?"

"Of course," Celeste says. "But first, can you get Olivia and Isabelle some champagne glasses? Bubbles are meant to be shared."

The waiter shoots me a look. The champagne is reserved for passengers, not the staff. Especially the premium stuff he's serving Celeste. Not wanting to ruffle feathers, I ask for a glass of sparkling water instead.

"Are you sure, dear?" Celeste asks. "After that wonderful welcome presentation of yours, you deserve to celebrate."

"Water's fine," I say.

As the waiter rushes off to put in the order, Celeste looks at me. "Now, time to tell me about this mystery man of yours. What does he look like? Any birthmarks? What does he do for a living? Does he like chocolate? What's his star sign? What movie can you see him starring in?"

Celeste's random string of questions makes me smile. I answer the easy ones first. "He has blond hair and blue eyes. From what I've seen, he doesn't have any birthmarks."

"From what you've seen?" Celeste arches an eyebrow. "We'll come back to that later."

My face flushes as I remember how Erich opened the door to his cabin wearing nothing but a towel. Trying to distract myself, I plow on with answering Celeste's question. "Um, I think he likes chocolate. Doesn't everyone? I can totally see him as James Bond."

"Ooh, James Bond," Olivia says. "Sounds like he's dangerous and sexy."

I groan. That James Bond answer slipped out so naturally, but the last thing I need is for anyone to have the slightest reason to connect Erich with secret spies.

"Did I say James Bond? I meant James T. Kirk."

"From *Star Trek*?" Olivia asks.

"Yeah, that's the one," I say, feigning a confidence that I don't have. Maybe it's *Star Trek*. Maybe it's *Star Wars*. I always get them mixed up.

"Anyway, he's a pharmaceutical sales representative. . ." My voice trails off as the waiter serves Olivia and me our drinks. I don't want him to hear me talk about Erich. Half the crew still believes I had an affair with him. When the waiter leaves, I say, "Erich says it's a pretty boring job. About as far away from a secret spy as you can get."

"If you say so, dear." Celeste leans forward, her eyes sparkling. "Now, let's get to the heart of the matter. Last time I heard from you, you were head-over-heels for this guy."

I cock my head to one side. "I was?"

"You might not have said that explicitly," Celeste admits. "I could tell that's how you felt though. But something happened. What was it?"

"It wasn't meant to be, that's all." Then I try to change the subject. "I'd love to hear about your days performing off-Broadway."

Celeste sees right through me. "Another time, dear. Now, there are four major reasons why relationships don't work. Different backgrounds. That's a barrier that can be overcome. It's not always easy, but it can be done. You said that your fellow is German. Could that be the issue?"

Not waiting for me to answer, she shakes her head. "No, that's not it. Then there's betrayal. That can be hard to move past as well. But that's not the problem either, is it?"

"No," I say, wishing this conversation was over.

Olivia pipes up. "Okay, so if it's not betrayal or different backgrounds, what is it?"

Celeste looks at me thoughtfully. "It's a matter of trust. Isabelle doesn't know if she can trust him."

I avert my eyes and study my water glass. "Erich is a consummate professional. I'd trust him with my life."

"How often to you put your life on the line with a pharmaceutical sales representative?" Olivia asks.

I bite back a smile. If only she knew what Erich really did for a living.

"You don't trust him personally," Celeste says. "Is that it?"

"Trust is predicated on being completely open with one another, don't you think?" I ask.

"Ah, he's the secretive type." Celeste's smile fades. "The very first man I fell in love with was the same way. He was evasive about what he did for a living. For a while I thought he was an insurance agent, but when I found out what he really did, well . . ."

Olivia leans forward. "I didn't know there was anyone before Uncle Ernie. What happened?"

"He broke up with me. I was devastated at first. But it was for the best." She pats Olivia's hand. "And then I met your uncle. The most wonderful man in the world."

"Did you ever wonder what happened to that first guy?" I ask.

"Sometimes. But, we're talking about you, remember?" She motions at me. "Go on."

"I understand why Erich's secretive," I say. "It's critical in his line of work."

"I can see that," Olivia says. "The pharmaceutical industry is cut-throat. Companies don't want their competitors to steal their trade secrets. But he's keeping other secrets from you, is that it?"

I shrug. "It doesn't really matter. The chances of our paths crossing again are next to nothing."

"Sometimes, it's easier to make a fresh start," Olivia says. "Love shouldn't be this hard."

"Don't make any hasty decisions, dear," Celeste says to her niece. Then she turns to me. "And you shouldn't write your fellow off so easily, either. After all, you have secrets of your own, don't you? Maybe the two of you are destined to become each other's secret-keepers."

"Secret-keepers," I say softly to myself. That has a nice ring to it.

Celeste fights back a yawn. "Well, girls, it's bedtime for this old broad."

As we say goodnight, I remember something. "You said there were four reasons why relationships didn't work out, but you only mentioned three.

What was the fourth?"

"Oh, that one can be a real deal-breaker," Celeste says. "Watch out if one of you is a cat person and the other one is a dog person."

* * *

It's been fun having Celeste and Olivia aboard. They've been a great distraction. Between keeping busy with work, then spending time with the two of them when I'm not on duty, I've managed to stop thinking about Erich.

Okay, that's a lie. I have dark circles under my eyes because I can't sleep. I've tried everything—counting sheep, listening to a meditation app, even avoiding caffeine—but nothing works. Memories of Erich play through my head until the early hours of the morning.

But the time with them has flown by and now it's the night before we dock in Basel. The night before Erich undertakes the mission with my replacement.

Celeste, Olivia, and I are sitting on the sun deck, not far from the spot where Erich and I had that amazing kiss. Celeste is leafing through a travel magazine while Olivia texts someone. From the expression on her face, I think it's Xander.

"There's a piece in there about this riverboat," I tell Celeste. "There's even a picture of me playing Scrabble."

She flips to the article, then smiles. "Don't you look pretty with your hair down. Why don't you wear it that way more often?"

"The bun is regulation." I adjust one of the hairpins so it isn't jabbing into my scalp. "I could cut my hair short so that I don't have to tie it back, but I don't really want to do that. I only have a few more months left working aboard the boat, so I'm trying to put up with it."

Celeste nods, then looks back at the magazine. Then she gasps, causing Olivia and I both to stare at her.

"Is that who I think it is?" Celeste pulls a pair of reading glasses out of her purse and examines the magazine more closely. Then she points at one of the pictures. "Who's that man there?" she asks me. "The one in the background. Do you remember his name?"

"Oh, that's Hamish MacDougall," I say. "He was my Scrabble partner."

Celeste looks ashen. Her hands are shaking and she nearly drops the magazine.

"What is it, Aunt Celeste?" Olivia asks. "What's wrong?"

"It's nothing. I thought I recognized someone, but I was mistaken." Celeste hands me the magazine, then stands. "I think I'm going to turn in. I'll see you girls in the morning."

As she walks away, Olivia turns to me. "What do you think that was about?"

"I don't know," I say. "Something spooked her."

"I've never seen her react that way before," Olivia says. "I better go check on her."

She gives me a quick hug, then rushes after her aunt. I flip through the magazine, trying to figure out what it was that made Celeste leave so abruptly. Something nags me at the back of my brain that I can't put my finger on. Something about my friend Ginny.

Then it hits me. When Ginny went to visit Celeste in Greece, Celeste told her about the first man she fell in love with. It was the same story that Celeste had told Olivia and I earlier, but with one critical difference. The reason she broke up with her first love is because she couldn't accept his career choice, so to speak. A career that involved stealing jewelry.

I turn to the article that Zoe wrote and look at the picture Celeste had been examining. Is it possible that the jewel thief Celeste used to be in love with is the very same man as Hamish MacDougall?

14 - A Surprise Delivery

When we dock in Basel the next morning, I say a teary goodbye to Celeste and Olivia. They're both heading back to Greece. Celeste has decided to spend what's left of the summer at her villa there, and Olivia is going to see if she can work things out with Xander. I try to talk to Celeste about Hamish before she leaves, but she clams up.

Celeste envelops me in a hug. "I have a feeling things are about to take a mysterious turn for you, Isabelle," she says. "Stay in touch, dear, and let me know what happens."

After they leave, I go back to helping Sophia with checkout.

"Do you think your friend was the undercover passenger?" Sophia asks once we say goodbye to the final passenger. "If so, I hope she gives us a good report to Head Office."

"I don't think she was," I say. "She did leave a glowing review on social media though."

"I guess that's something." Sophia sighs. "But that means we're still on pins and needles wondering who the undercover passenger is."

While we're filling out paperwork, a man walks into the reception area bearing a large paper bag.

"Sorry, sir," Sophia says. "We don't begin boarding for another four hours."

"I have a delivery for Isabelle Martinez," he says.

Sophia points at me, and he deposits the bag on the counter.

"What's this?" I ask.

He shrugs. "I don't get paid to ask questions."

I open it up and pull out a Styrofoam container. My jaw drops when I see what's inside. "Pfälzer saumagen? What the heck?"

Sophia peers over my shoulder. "You got lunch?"

"Hey, wait a minute," I yell after the deliveryman as he's walking out the door. "Where did you get this?"

"I picked it up at the airport," he says over his shoulder. "It came on a private plane from Amsterdam."

Before I can rush after him to ask him more questions, Frau Albrecht marches into the reception area and glares at me. "How many times do I have to tell you—no eating while on duty."

"But I'm not eating," I say. "I didn't even order this."

She snorts and picks up the paper bag. "It says Isabelle Martinez right here."

"But—"

Frau Albrecht holds up her hand. "Eat on your own time. Now, if you need me, I'll be inspecting the cabins." As she sets the bag back on the counter, a card falls out.

Sophia picks it up and discretely hands it to me. Once the older woman leaves, I open it up. When I read what it says, I'm in even more shock.

The organization needs you. Our mutual acquaintance has grave concerns about your replacement's ability to carry out the task in question. He refuses to ask you to help, so I'm forced to do so on his behalf. It's not too late to reconsider your decision. Without you, lives could be in jeopardy.

PS Enjoy the pfälzer saumagen. Our mutual acquaintance told me about the time he introduced you to it.

As I tuck the card back into the envelope, I notice my hands are shaking. It's obvious who the note is from—Aunt C. She must have had the food flown from her restaurant in Amsterdam to Basel. And the "mutual acquaintance" she refers to is obviously Erich. I can't believe he told Aunt C about the time he ordered me a dish in Mainz made with organ meat, a dish I ended up enjoying.

This is blackmail in its most blatant form. If I don't help Erich, then the unthinkable could happen.

"You look white as a ghost. Is it bad news?" Sophia asks.

"It's the worst kind of news," I say. "The kind that means you have to do something that terrifies you in order to help someone you love."

* * *

Yes, that's right. I said the L-word out loud. This isn't something theoretical anymore. I love Erich. I might not know any details about his background, I may not know what shaped him into the man he is today, but I know the essence of him. And that's what I love—the part of him that's true yesterday, today, and tomorrow.

Okay, that's enough cheesiness, Isabelle. You've got a party to get to.

"Remember Erich Zimmermann?" I ask Sophia.

"The hot VIP from Germany? Sure," Sophia says while she prints out the list of passengers who will be boarding the boat later today. She glances down at my legs. "That rash cream he gave you did wonders."

"It was actually the nylons," I say. "Once Frau Albrecht told me I didn't have to wear them anymore, the rash cleared up."

"That was Head Office's doing," Sophia says. "Frau Albrecht was furious that she had to make so many exceptions for you. I just wish they'd make an exception for me."

"What do you mean?"

Sophia sets the stack of papers to one side. "I'm dying to tell someone. Can you keep a secret?"

"Of course." If only Sophia knew how good I am at keeping secrets.

Sophia looks around to make sure we won't be overheard, then whispers, "Auguste Renoir proposed."

"Oh, my gosh, that's wonderful." I give her a hug, then say, "Let me see the ring."

Sophia pulls a delicate gold chain out of her blouse. Dangling from it is a gorgeous diamond ring.

"That's stunning," I tell her. "But why aren't you wearing it on your hand?"

She frowns as she slips the necklace back inside her blouse. "Employees aren't allowed to date. If we want to be together, one of us is going to have to resign. Since Auguste has a more senior role, it makes sense for me to find another job."

"But if he stays aboard the *Abenteuer*, that would mean the two of you wouldn't see each other very often," I say.

"I know. He's offered to quit, but I told him no. He has good career prospects with the cruise line." Sophia wipes away a tear, then plasters on her usual smile. "Anyway, enough of that."

"But you and Auguste . . . I wish there was something I could do."

"Do you mind if we don't talk about it anymore?" Sophia adjusts the collar of her blouse. "Now, why did you mention Herr Zimmermann?"

"Well, you were right in a way about us," I say.

She claps her hands together. "I knew it. The two of you were having an affair."

"No, we weren't," I say. "Well, we kissed once, but that was it."

"Uh-huh." She looks dubious. "So what happened?"

"We decided that a relationship wasn't workable."

"But he's not a passenger anymore," Sophia points out. "The two of you can date now."

"That's what I wanted to talk to you about. He's here in Basel. I have a chance to see him, but I'm on duty tonight. I'm supposed to give the welcome presentation."

Sophia smiles. "Go on. I'll cover for you."

"Are you sure?"

"I'll tell Frau Albrecht that you're sick. Just make sure you're back here by tomorrow morning when we set sail."

After thanking her a million times, I rush to my cabin to grab everything I'll need for this mission. As I pack the evening gown Erich had arranged for me to wear to the party, I make a mental note to see if he can pull one last string with Head Office and get an exception made for Sophia.

* * *

I'm standing outside Erich's hotel suite, but can't bring myself to knock on the door. What am I supposed to say when he answers? It's not like I'm going to tell him that I love him. I barely admitted that to myself. The last thing I'm going to do is confess that to him.

After stalling for a few minutes, I finally summon up the courage and rap on the door. Steeling myself for an awkward encounter with Erich, I clasp my hands in front of me and try to project an air of confidence.

When the door opens, I'm confronted with something I should have anticipated if I had been thinking clearly—a gorgeous woman wearing a stunning black beaded evening gown. Of course, Erich's new partner would be here in his suite. She's posing as Svetlana, the fake fiancée.

The woman greets me in Russian, and, even though I understand what she's saying, I stand there with my jaw open, unable to speak.

She repeats her greeting in German, French, English, and even Cantonese. I finally manage to respond, saying, "Room service."

She arches an eyebrow, taking in my obvious lack of hotel uniform and tray.

"Who is it?" a man calls out in Russian.

My heart flutters at the sound of Erich's voice. Feeling like I might collapse any minute, I brace myself against the doorjamb.

"A woman talking nonsense. I think she is drunk."

I jab a finger in Fake Svetlana's direction. "I'm not drunk. I'm just . . ." My voice trails off when Erich walks up behind her.

"Isabelle?" he asks. Then he smiles at me. The hugest smile I've ever seen on him. One that lights up his eyes. "What are you doing here?"

"You know this woman?" Fake Svetlana shoots me a look that sends shivers down my spine. She could rival Aunt C in the intimidation department.

Before Erich can answer, his phone rings. He puts it to his ear, and his expression sobers. He listens for a few moments, then hands it to Fake Svetlana.

After a one-way conversation, she thrusts the phone back at Erich and glares at him. "That was Aunt C. She says that I've been replaced." She turns her icy stare in my direction. "Replaced by her."

Every word she utters is dripping with venom and I take a few steps back. I look around the hallway for the security cameras. Ah, there's one, right across from Erich's hotel suite. Aunt C must have tapped into it. That's the only explanation for how she knew I was standing at Erich's door at this very moment.

"Well, perhaps that's for the best," Erich says placidly.

"The best?" She spins around and grabs Erich by his arms. "I'll tell you what's for the best. And it's not this—"

Erich's phone rings again. He looks in the direction of the security camera and nods. Then he hands the phone to Fake Svetlana without answering it. "I think it's for you."

As she listens to the person on the other end of the line, I stare at the carpet wishing this awkward moment would be over. Fake Svetlana has basically been fired because I showed up. There are some weird parallels with how Maria, the original tour manager aboard the *Abenteuer*, was replaced by me. And now this woman.

The phone call over, Fake Svetlana storms past Erich into the suite. Erich sighs, then motions for me to follow him inside. While I wait in the living room, I listen to Fake Svetlana yell at Erich. The woman has an impressive knowledge of Russian curse words.

She flounces back out, a wheeled suitcase in tow behind her. As she barrels past me toward the door, she jams her elbow into my side. "Sorry," she says sarcastically.

"Wait," Erich calls out.

Fake Svetlana spins around, a hopeful look on her face. "Have you changed your mind?"

Erich shakes his head, then points at her hand. "I need the ring back."

She pulls it off her finger and flings it at him. He makes an impressive catch, and I wonder if he played baseball as a kid.

After the door slams behind her, Erich turns to me. "Sorry, you had to go through that."

"She's kind of scary," I say, half-joking, half-not. "Were you worried she might knife you in your sleep?"

"That was the least of my worries," he says. "She wasn't up to the mission. I was fearful she would get us killed."

"Aunt C said you had grave concerns about her."

"She wasn't supposed to tell you that." Erich takes my hands in his and squeezes them. "I told her not to drag you into this."

"It was my decision," I say firmly. "I'm ready to face my fears. The mission is a go."

We talk for a few minutes, and I finally convince Erich that I'm up for it.

"If you're absolutely sure," he says holding up engagement ring. "Then would you do the honor of being my fake fiancée again?"

I grin as he slips the ring on my finger. It feels good to be back working with Erich. Whether we have a future as anything more . . . well, I can't think about that now. I need to focus on the mission.

15 - Hamster Brushes

As we walk up the marble stairs to the entrance of the historic mansion where the party is taking place, Erich turns to me and says, "You look gorgeous."

"It's the dress," I say, running my hands down the silver sequined evening gown I'm wearing. "Anyone would look good in this."

"It's not the dress. It's you," he says. "You'd look good in a sack of potatoes."

"Please don't talk about potatoes. I haven't had any for ages."

"But after you pulled out of the mission, didn't you start eating them again?"

"No, I didn't. I don't know why. Maybe some part of me knew that I would end up playing the role of a Russian woman with a potato allergy after all?"

Erich points at the charm bracelet on my wrist. "You better let me hang onto that. Scrabble isn't really the real Svetlana's thing." He helps me unclasp it, then slips it in his pocket.

When we walk into the grand ballroom, the sheikh greets us. He extends his hand to Erich. "I'm honored that you would break your self-imposed exile to attend this event, Mr. Petrov."

My eyes widen slightly at the use of the Russian name. Then I check myself. Tonight, we're not Erich and Isabelle. We're Andrei Petrov and Svetlana Sidirov. Two eccentric Russian recluses. One a billionaire who made his fortune in potato peelers and the other, his fiancée, a famous hamster groomer.

Potato peelers and hamster groomers. That sounds absurd, doesn't it? If I hadn't personally seen the files on Andrei and Svetlana, I'd think it was a joke. But, nope, they're real people.

Erich clasps the sheikh's shoulder. "For a deal this important, I felt I had no choice. I built my company from the ground up. I can't sell it without looking the buyer directly in the eye."

"There is wisdom in this," the sheikh says. "My father always said that there is no substitute for conducting business face-to-face."

Erich puts his arm around my shoulders. "May I introduce my fiancée?"

"Miss Sidirov, what a delightful pleasure," the sheikh says. "My daughter will be thrilled to hear that I met you. She has one of those longhaired hamsters. What are they called?"

"An Angora?" I ask.

"Yes, that is the breed. But its fur is constantly getting tangled and matted. What would you suggest?"

"Well, I'm introducing a new line of hamster brushes. Each one is carved from organic ebony and the bristles are handcrafted by Tibetan monks. They're guaranteed to keep your hamster's hair silky smooth and free of tangles."

The sheikh nods slowly, then summons one of his assistants over. When he has an intense conversation with him in Arabic, Erich shoots me a warning look. I twist my fake engagement ring around my finger. Was the bit about the hamster brushes over the top? Have I blown our cover already?

"I will buy two hundred of them," the sheikh says to me. "I have instructed my assistant to place the order."

I breathe a sigh of relief. We make some more small talk about hamster wheels, then the sheikh excuses himself so that he can greet some new arrivals.

"Hamster brushes?" Erich whispers to me. "Where did that come from?"

"I don't know. It popped into my head. I got nervous, and I improvised." I grip Erich's hand. "Oh, my gosh, the minute the assistant tries to place the order on Svetlana's website, he's going to realize that I'm a fraud. She doesn't sell hamster brushes."

"She does now," Erich says, tapping out a text on his phone. "I've got our IT department on it. They'll create a cloned version of her site, making sure hamster brushes are featured prominently."

"Right, your IT department," I say dryly. "The same ones whose systems failed during the Scrabble tournament? We're trusting those guys?"

"Aunt C has made some organizational changes," Erich says. "I'm sure it will be fine."

He sounds confident, but from the way his brow is furrowed, I think he's worried.

"Okay, let's focus on what we can control," I say. "What does the point person for the Nouveau Rouge Order look like?"

"All we know is that it's a woman and that she'll be wearing a red dress and a cat brooch," Erich says.

"Why a cat brooch?"

"Our intel wasn't that specific."

A waiter passes by with a tray of hors d'oeuvres. I snake out a hand to snag a potato puff, but Erich stops me. He grabs my hand and raises it to his lips. "Remember, you're allergic to potatoes," he says before kissing the back of my hand.

"So that's all you have to go on—red dress and a cat brooch," I say, trying to ignore the sensation of his lips on my skin.

"Our source didn't want to give too much away," Erich says.

"Well, they definitely succeeded." As another waiter presents us with a tantalizing display of food, I sigh. "Why is everything made out of potatoes?"

"I suspect it's in celebration of my business deal with the sheikh." Erich motions for the waiter to move on to the next group of guests. "I promise that when this mission is over, I'll get you the biggest baked potato you've ever seen."

"I'll hold you to that." Then I point toward the other side of the room. "Look at that woman talking with the sheikh. She's wearing a red dress."

"There are a number of women wearing red tonight. We need her to turn around so that we can see if she has a cat brooch. Once we confirm that it's her, we'll execute the plan." Erich strokes his fake beard and looks at me thoughtfully. "Are you absolutely sure you're okay with going through with this?"

I pull his hand away from his chin. "Be careful with that. It looks like it might come off."

"You didn't answer my question."

"I'm absolutely, one hundred percent certain that I'm okay to go through with this," I say, emphasizing every word. "The plan is straightforward. We go to the office. You hoist me up to an air-conditioning vent. I climb through the ductwork until I get to the library. Then I turn this sparkly ring into a recording device, capture everything that's said, make my way back to the office, and presto—we've captured ourselves some terrorists. What could possibly go wrong?"

"She's turning around." Erich tugs on my arm.

I look at the woman's dress. "There's the cat brooch. The target has been identified and confirmed." Then my gaze travels upward and I see her face. "You've got to be kidding me."

"What is it?" Erich asks.

"That's Bob," I say.

"Bob from the Scrabble tournament?" Erich squints in the woman's direction. "Are you sure?"

"Positive." Then I pull Erich toward me and plant a kiss on his lips.

* * *

"What was that for?" Erich asks.

"Shush." I shift our position slightly so that Erich's back is facing Bob. Burrowing my head into Erich's chest so that I'm hidden from view, I whisper, "I don't want Bob to see us."

"And kissing creates an invisibility cloak?" Erich asks in an undertone.

"I was afraid you would say something too loudly and draw attention to us."

"Uh-huh." Erich twists his head and looks behind him. "She's turned back around. Let's make a break for it."

We move quickly through the ballroom, keeping clusters of other guests between us and Bob. Once we're in the clear, we dash to the office. I ask Erich why Bob is here. "I thought Bob was a fence, but if she's here, that means she's also a member of the Nouveau Rouge Order."

Erich closes and locks the office door, then turns to face me. "It's possible that our intel was faulty."

"IT problems, faulty intel—does anything in the organization work?" I ask.

"Aunt C makes a mean apple strudel. And we do have an excellent dental plan." After reaching up and removing the grating from the ceiling, he glances back at me. "Ready?"

"Just a sec." I slip off my heels, then detach the skirt from my dress, revealing a pair of form-fitting shorts. They're covered in silver sequins, like my dress, but far more practical for crawling through ductwork.

Erich whistles. "You're the sexiest hamster groomer I've ever worked with."

"Enough staring at my legs, mister. Hoist me up."

Once I'm inside the air-conditioning duct, I hear Erich's voice in my ear. "Testing, testing."

"You're coming in loud and clear. I hope you can hear me because my mike is sewn into the neckline of my dress, and adjusting it would be a challenge," I say. "It's more cramped in here than it was in the cardboard boxes."

"You're fine," Erich says. "Remember not to speak unless you absolutely have to. Sound carries through this ducting."

"It's pitch-black up here," I say. "You're going to tell me when to turn left and right, correct?"

"Yes, don't worry. There's an app on my phone with a map of the ductwork. Your position is overlaid on it. I'll be tracking you the entire time." He pauses for a beat, then says, "Are you sure you're okay?"

Actually, I'm not okay. My heart is racing and my skin is clammy. But I can't tell Erich that or he'll call a halt to the mission. So I lie. "Couldn't be better."

"Okay, the sheikh starts his meetings promptly. That means you only have four minutes to get to the library." Erich gulps audibly. "Forward seven feet, then right."

I inch through the ductwork while he calls out directions, banging my head a few times, and scraping my knees on the sharp corners.

"Three minutes, twenty-two seconds remaining," Erich says. He continues guiding me through the ductwork, then finally says, "One more left turn and you should be there."

As I round the corner, I see light ahead. That must be coming through the grating in the library. Erich confirms that I'm in position. "Time to turn on the recorder," he says. "Once the meeting is finished, and the library is clear, I'll guide you back to the office."

I press the hidden latch on the engagement ring and the diamond pops open, revealing the high-tech equipment inside. According to Erich, this thing is capable of picking up even the faintest of conversations.

When the door to the library opens, I suck in my breath. Peering through the vent, I watch as Bob enters the room, followed by the sheikh. He offers her a drink, but she refuses.

"Let's get down to business," she says in a clipped British accent.

"As you wish," the sheikh says. "Let me see the necklace."

Bob hitches up her skirt. Strapped to one of her legs is a gun, and on the other is a small velvet bag. The sheikh eyes her cautiously, then relaxes when she removes the bag and presents it to him.

"Ah, it's even more beautiful in person." The sheikh holds up the necklace and the diamonds and emeralds sparkle in the light from the chandelier. Then he examines it more closely using a jeweler's loupe.

"Satisfactory?" Bob asks.

The sheikh slips the necklace back into the bag. "Yes, I'm satisfied."

"Excellent," Bob says. "Now the location of the weapons."

While the sheikh reels off a set of coordinates, I feel something crawling on my right leg. Something cold and slimy. What kinds of creatures live in air-conditioning ducts? It continues up my leg and when it reaches the bottom of my shorts and bites me, I yelp.

Bob looks directly at the vent. Then she grabs the necklace back from the sheikh. "You set me up."

The sheikh holds his hands up. "I didn't. I swear."

"Liar," Bob shrieks.

I don't wait to see what happens next, inching backward as fast as I can. The creature isn't crawling on my leg anymore. That's because it's now in my hair. I've seen this exact same scenario in a horror movie. It didn't end well for the heroine.

"Erich," I hiss. "I need directions."

There's no response. Of course, there isn't. This is the perfect timing for another technology snafu. Yes, that's sarcasm. Do you know how hard it is to crawl backwards through ductwork, especially when it's shaped like a rat maze? Add in the slimy creature in my hair and it's no wonder I'm having an anxiety attack.

After a few wrong turns and dead-ends, I finally make it back to the office. I slip down through the vent, landing with a thud on my hands and knees. I shake my head vigorously. When something jumps out and slithers away, I shudder.

"Erich, where are you?" The mission has been blown," I say as I get to my feet and turn around. "We need to . . ."

My voice trails off as I see who's in the room—Bob, and she's holding a gun to Erich's head.

"Fancy a game of Scrabble?" she asks me. Then she cracks Erich across his temple and he crumples to the floor.

16 - The Undervalued Letter Opener

I scream Erich's name, but before I can rush over to him, Bob waves her gun at me.

"Stay where you are," she says.

I clasp my hands behind my back and press the diamond back into position, then look around the room to get my bearings. In front of me is a large oak desk. File folders and pens are strewn across the top of the desk, but there's nothing I can use as a weapon. Off to the side are built-in bookshelves. Perhaps I could hurl one of those thick leather-bound encyclopedias at Bob and knock her off balance?

As I edge slowly in that direction, Bob aims her gun in my direction. "I told you to stay where you were. Let me see your hands."

I hold my hands in front of me. "See, they're empty."

"I bet you wish that was a real engagement ring, don't you?" She snorts, then kicks Erich's shoulder. "Hank told me that you were gaga over this one."

My jaw drops. "Hank? Hank Sinclair from Alabama? The guy who was on my first cruise?"

"The Nouveau Rouge Order is everywhere," Bob says. "I wanted one of my agents on board to keep an eye on Hamish. I needed that necklace to make a deal with the sheikh."

I'm having a hard time reconciling the woman in front of me with the woman I played Scrabble against in the tournament. This Bob has an elegant hairdo and is dressed in a chic evening gown. Her eyes are cold, and she handles the gun in her hand like a pro. The other Bob wore a tinfoil hat and pink mittens. She seemed harmless at the time, but now I know how deeply I was deceived.

"Hank is one of your agents?" I twist the engagement ring around my finger. "That would mean you're one of the Nouveau Rouge Order leaders."

"I'm *the* leader," she says, waving the gun around for emphasis.

"So she wasn't an ordinary fence," I mumble to myself. "I played Scrabble with the leader of the Nouveau Rouge Order and let her slip through my fingers."

"Speak up," Bob says. "I can't stand people who don't enunciate the words."

"I didn't say anything."

"You're lying. I hate people that lie to me." She takes a step toward me. "Do you want to know what happened to the last person who lied to me?"

"You mean the sheikh?"

Bob grabs me by the throat with one hand. "Of course, I mean the sheikh. You're even stupider than you look."

As I struggle to breathe, I cast my eyes across the room to where Erich is lying. Is this how it ends? Bob kills us both before I have a chance to tell Erich how I feel about him?

Then I see something glinting in the light of the desk lamp. What looks like a piece of metal is peeking out from underneath one of the file folders. I reach for it, grasping it with the tips of my fingers. As it slides out, I give a mental shout of triumph when I see that it's a letter opener.

When it comes to office supplies, I had always undervalued the run-of-the-mill letter opener. Honestly, how hard is it to rip an envelope open? But after tonight, I'm going to be singing the letter opener's praises because now it's going to double as a very effective weapon.

The look of surprise on Bob's face when I use the letter opener on her is priceless. But it doesn't compare to Erich's expression when he opens his eyes and sees Bob lying on the floor clutching her side.

* * *

Erich gets to his feet and retrieves the gun and the letter opener from the floor. He sets them on a table in the far corner of the room, then points at Bob. "Did you do this?"

"Forget about her," I say, rushing to his side. "Are you okay?"

"I'll be fine." Erich rubs his temple and winces. Then he hands me his phone. "Press the star key. That will connect you with headquarters. Tell them to send in the strike team."

While I tell headquarters what happened, as well as alert them to the fact that Hank is also a member of the terrorist group, Erich checks to make sure Bob's wounds aren't life-threatening. Using a throw from an armchair, he applies a makeshift bandage. Then he pulls some zip ties out of his pocket and secures her.

"There, that should hold her." The look he gives her is full of contempt, but when he turns his expression softens. "What about you? Are you okay?"

After reassuring him that I'm fine, I tell him that the strike team is on their way. I glance over at the door to the office. "You locked that. How did she get in here?"

Erich walks over to Bob and yanks the cat brooch off her dress. He turns it around and inspects the back. "Yep, thought as much. This is a multipurpose tool disguised as jewelry. There's a screwdriver, corkscrew, pliers, and even a lock pick. I should show this to the team back at headquarters."

He shoves it in his pocket, then pulls the charm bracelet out. "I almost forgot I had this in here."

The door swings open and two heavily armed agents rush into the room. "Everything okay, sir?" one of them asks.

"We're fine, thanks to Isabelle." Erich removes his wig, then pulls his fake beard off. "Where are we at with the sheikh?"

"We have him in custody. We're screening the rest of the guests to make sure no one affiliated with the sheikh or the Nouveau Rouge Order slips through." The agent looks at Bob. "After we make a final sweep through the mansion, we'll come back for this one."

Erich nods. "Any report from IT? My comms link with Isabelle went down.

Do we know if they got the feed from the recorder?"

The agent rolls his eyes. "They're giving us their usual song and dance about restoring communications, but they assure us that the data is secure."

Erich sighs. "James Bond never has these issues."

"At least you have a good dental plan," I quip. "So what if you have a few computer glitches here and there."

The agents chuckle, then excuse themselves to continue the sweep of the building.

I pull the fake engagement ring off my finger. "I suppose you'll be needing this back."

As I hand it to Erich, he mutters something. It sounds like he said, "Next time I give you a ring, it will be for real," but that's ridiculous, right? We have the head of a terrorist organization lying on the floor. Who could possibly be thinking about marriage at time like this?

Erich holds up the charm bracelet. "Do you want to keep this as a memento?"

I take the bracelet from his hand. "A memento? A souvenir of our time together. That sounds so final."

Bob groans. I glance over to make sure she hasn't bit through her zip ties. When I look back at Erich, his icy-blue eyes are glistening. Are those tears?

He clears his throat. "I don't want this to be final. We work well together. We're a very, um, efficient team."

"Oh," I say, suddenly deflated. "You're talking about our working relationship."

"No, that's not what I mean." He starts to run his fingers through his hair, then grimaces when he touches the side of his head where Bob struck him. "She did a number on me."

I close the gap between us, and hold out the bracelet. "Can you help me put this on?"

Erich takes the bracelet from me and nods. He strokes my wrist gently after he fastens the clasp, and we both start to speak at the same time.

"Ladies first," he says.

"I want you to be my secret-keeper," I say quietly. "I want you to know everything about me, not because you read it in a file, but because I told it to you."

I shiver as he trails his fingers down my neck. "Secret-keeper. I like the sound of that." His lips follow his fingers, lightly brushing the skin on my neck. "There's a secret I don't share with anyone . . . until now."

Erich pulls back and leans against the desk. He moves a pile of file folders to one side and pats the spot next to him. I sit by his side and listen as he tells me his story. It takes me a moment to realize that he's speaking English with an American accent, not the German one I had grown used to.

"You asked me once where I was from in Germany. I don't know if you noticed, but I avoided answering."

"Oh, I noticed," I say gently.

"The truth is that I grew up in Iowa." When I turn my head to look at him, he adds, "I was born in Germany, but my parents died in a car accident when I was a baby. I was sent to live with my great-aunt and great uncle in the States. They did their best bringing me up, but I always knew that I was a burden to them."

I squeeze his hand. "No, that can't be true."

"It is," he says simply. "They never had children of their own, and to be saddled with an infant in their golden years was something they didn't sign up for. They always made sure my basic needs were provided for, but a child need something more."

"A child needs love," I say.

Erich takes a deep breath, then continues. "I graduated high school at sixteen, then ran off to Europe. At first, I traveled around, but eventually found myself in Germany where I went to college. The other students were friendly, but I was a loner, preferring to keep my distance . . ."

Erich's voice trails off, and I scoot closer to him. He puts his arm around my shoulders and I lean into him. "Go on."

"Well, after college, I joined the organization—you know that part. It was great at first. Smart people, committed people, people who believed in something. I worked my way up through the ranks. Can you believe my first assignment was to the IT department?"

"Sounds like they've gone downhill ever since you left," I say.

He briefly chuckles, then turns more serious. "I was eventually assigned to work as a field agent. My partner was an experienced agent. She showed me the ropes. There isn't anything that woman didn't know about creating a convincing cover story. She was a pretty special lady."

"Was?" I ask.

Erich gets up and paces back and forth, pausing briefly to check on Bob's restraints. "She died during an operation."

"Oh, I'm sorry," I say, knowing how inadequate those words are. After a beat, I venture a guess. "Was she more than a colleague?"

"Yes." Erich sits back on the desk, and puts his head in his hands for a moment, then looks directly at me. "When she was killed, I swore that I'd never get close to anyone again. Especially not someone I work with. My feelings for her distracted me." Erich's voice cracks slightly. He clenches his fists, then slowly relaxes them. "If I had been more focused on the mission, maybe I could have prevented her death."

I want to reassure Erich that he's wrong, but I can't. Because I've experienced something so similar, that it's eerie. The only thing I can think to do is share my own secret.

"You know much of this already from my file," I say. "When I was in the Air Force, I worked as an intelligence analyst, which you know. Toward the end of my term of service I became involved in a relationship with a foreign officer. He was a member of an ally nation's defense forces on special assignment to our unit. I was so head over heels in love, that I wasn't focused on my work and I missed something . . . something important."

Erich leans over. "Hey, I already know all of this, and it wasn't your fault. A lot of people missed something that day."

"But if I hadn't been so caught up in daydreaming about this guy, I wouldn't have missed it. I was good at my job."

"I know that too," Erich says. "Why else do you think the organization wanted you for this mission?"

I chew on my lip for a moment. "There's more, though. Something that's not in the file you've seen. Something that only a few people know. The officer I fell in love with . . . he was a double agent. An operative for a hostile nation, and I didn't recognize the signs. If I had, maybe he could have been stopped. But I didn't, and I can't even begin to tell you how badly he compromised our systems."

I look sideways at Erich. He looks stunned, but after a moment he takes my hand and kisses the back of it.

"Thank you for trusting me with your secret," he says. "For the record, I doubt if you would have known if he was a double agent or not. But I can see how you feel like you should have."

"That's why this has been so hard for me," I say. "Never quite knowing if someone is who or what they say they are. That's when the anxiety attacks began. When my term of service was up, I walked away from the Air Force and straight into a glamorous career at the mini-mart. I became a shell of my original self."

"But you're not that woman anymore," Erich says. "You're strong, determined, and smart."

"Just like my grandmother," I say, glancing down at the ring of hers on my right hand. I look back at Erich. "I have one last secret to share with you."

Erich smiles. "Me too."

"Gentlemen first this time."

Erich cups my face with his hands. "I love you, Isabelle. And I can't imagine a future without you, my secret-keeper."

"You stole my secret," I say.

"You mean you . . ." His voice trails off, waiting for me to finish the sentence.

"Yes, I love you too, Erich," I say as he leans down to kiss me. Then I realize I have one more important question, and I pull back. "Is your name even Erich or is that a cover?"

Erich grins. "Funnily enough, Erich is my real name. For some reason, I felt compelled to use it for the mission aboard the *Abenteuer*. Maybe something inside me knew that I would be meeting you."

We both stare into each other's eyes for what seems like an eternity. Then

Bob grunts, and we both look over at her.

"This is worse than a soap opera," she says. "Would you just kiss her already and put us all out of our misery?"

* * *

As Erich and I are coming up for air, an agent pokes her head into the office. "Aunt C would like to speak with the two of you, sir," she says. "And we're ready to take the prisoner into custody."

The agent sets a metal case on the desk. She unlocks it and a screen pops up. She points at a large red button. "The secure line is activated. Press that to speak with headquarters."

After she wrestles Bob to her feet and ushers her out of the office, Erich initiates the call.

"Congratulations," Aunt C says to us. "Thanks to your efforts, the mission was a success. You captured the head of the Noveau Rouge Order, and we have stopped the terrorists from getting their hands on the weapons."

She pauses to listen to someone out of view. Turning back to us, she says, "Someone else wants to join the call."

I grin when I see General Taylor sit next to Aunt C. She doesn't look pleased to be crowded out.

"I understand you've been a busy lady, Isabelle," the general says. "You've done an exceptional job. The reports I've received have been glowing. I'd like you to consider coming back to work in intelligence for me."

Aunt C leans across the general so that her face fills the screen. "Don't answer until you hear our offer?"

I furrow my brow. "Your offer?"

The general tries to maneuver his face back into the picture, but Aunt C is too nimble for him. "Isabelle," he says in a muffled voice. "Ours is the better offer."

Erich and I exchange glances while the two of them bicker.

"What do you want to do? It looks like you have options," he says to me. "Of course, there's always the mini-mart."

I elbow him in the ribs. "Do not ever mention the mini-mart again."

He holds up his hands. "I promise. So then which option are you going to choose—Air Force intelligence or a career with the organization?"

"It's an easy decision," I say. "The organization."

"Is that because you want to work with me?" Erich asks with a cocky grin on his face.

"Well, there's that," I say. "But I also heard you have a great dental plan."

Erich laughs, then points at Aunt C and the general continuing to argue about who I should work with. "Do you think they'd notice if we disconnected?"

"Not at all," I say, pressing the red button.

Erich closes the case, then pulls me into his arms. "Now about that dental plan . . ."

But before he can go into the details of whether root canals are covered, I silence him with a kiss.

Epilogue – Erich

Isabelle is sitting at the kitchen counter looking at her laptop when I sneak up behind her. But before I can put my hands over her eyes, she launches herself off her stool, does a back flip, and then executes a martial arts move I've never seen before. The end result is that I'm lying on the floor. I'd move, but Isabelle is pinning me down.

"Someone's been training," I say.

Isabelle snorts. "Someone's been slacking off on his training."

"I'm on vacation," I say. "It's the first one I've had in a very long time. Can't a fellow relax a little?"

"Just don't go getting soft on me," she jokes.

I give her a stupid grin. It's an expression that seems to make a regular appearance on my face ever since Isabelle came into my life. Isabelle grins back, her dark eyes sparkling. Not only is this woman beautiful, she's also whip-smart and every bit my equal when it comes to working in covert intelligence.

Okay, let's be real, here. She's a million times better than me in the spy game. Something Aunt C doesn't hesitate to remind me of on a regular basis. I'm lucky she's my partner at work, not to mention my partner in everything else outside of work.

"Ready to say uncle?" Isabelle asks.

"Yes, but on one condition," I say.

Isabelle arches an eyebrow. "What's the condition?"

"That you give me a kiss."

"Hmm, isn't a kiss you give someone as a reward?" Isabelle asks. "I'm not sure you should be rewarded for slacking off on your training."

"Oh, no, it wouldn't be a reward. It'd be a punishment. You're an awful kisser."

When Isabelle bursts out laughing, I take advantage of her loss of focus. Using one of my tried-and-true moves, I free my hands from her grasp, then reverse our position so that she's now lying on her back. I lower my face so that my lips are brushing against hers. "Now, about that kiss."

The timer on the oven buzzes, interrupting us. "Dinner's ready," I say, getting to my feet, then helping Isabelle to hers.

Isabelle sits back on her stool. "What are we having?"

"Your favorite—baked potatoes," I say, peeking inside the oven. "I also made some schnitzel and there's strudel for dessert."

"Yum," Isabelle says as she pulls her laptop toward her.

"Your turn to cook tomorrow," I say.

"I have something special planned," Isabelle says. "Fondue. My friend in Switzerland sent me her recipe."

"Sounds good." I pull the potatoes out of the oven, the say, "It will be the last meal of our vacation. I heard from Aunt C. She has a new assignment for us. We're headed to South America. A terrorist group is threatening to sabotage a major cacao processing facility."

"That sounds serious," Isabelle says. "Interrupt the chocolate supply and you'll cause global chaos."

"That's why they're sending in the A-team." I set the plates on the counter. "Put your computer away, it's time to eat."

"Just a sec. I got an email from Sophia. She and Auguste Renoir set a wedding date." Isabelle looks up at me. "Thanks again for pulling strings so that Head Office made an exception and let them work on the riverboat together."

"It seemed like the right thing to do," I say. "After all, she covered for you the night of the mission in Basel."

While Isabelle replies to Sophia, I pour two glasses of riesling. As I take a sip, I reminisce about the first time Isabelle and I had riesling together. What a difference six months has made in her confidence. After the string of successful missions we've carried out over that period of time, I think Isabelle has realized what an asset she is to the organization. She believes in herself again.

After dinner, we do the dishes, then I tell Isabelle that I have a surprise for her in the other room "Go look at the coffee table."

As she walks through the archway that separates the kitchen from the living room, she laughs. "Is that a Scrabble board? But I thought you hated playing Scrabble."

"For you, I'll make an exception," I say, pulling her into my arms. After giving her a quick kiss, I motion for her to sit on the sofa. "Now, I can't exactly play at a championship level like you, so you'll have to be patient with me."

"First, we draw to see who goes first." Isabelle starts to grab for the bag of tiles, but I snatch it away from her.

"I'd like to go first, if you don't mind."

As I pull tiles out of the bag and arrange them on the board, Isabelle shakes her head. "That's not how you do it. We each draw seven tiles from the bag and place them on our racks."

"That's seven tiles." I spin the board around so that she can see it. "Go ahead, count them."

"No, you have to put them . . ." her voice trails off as she looks down at what I've spelled out.

"What's my score?" I ask as I point at each tile in turn. "Let's see, there's M, A, R, R, Y, M, and E. Don't I get double or triple points for that?"

"Does that mean what I think it means?" Isabelle asks in a shaky voice.

"It means I want you to be my wife." I hand her the tile bag. "There's something else in there."

As she pulls the velvet jewelry box out, I hold my breath. What if she says no? Why would a woman as amazing as Isabelle want to spend the rest of her life with me?

She opens the box and pulls out the ring. After a beat, she asks, "Are those amethysts on either side of the diamond?"

"I know how much you love the amethyst ring your grandmother left you.

I thought it would be nice if they coordinated." I take a deep breath. "You still haven't given me an answer. Will you marry me?"

Isabelle sets the engagement ring down on the board, then fishes through the bag of tiles. After a moment, she lays three letters down on the board—Y, E, and S. Then she slips the ring on her finger.

"You know, for a novice Scrabble player, you're actually pretty good at the game," she says, coming over and sitting on my lap. "Now, since you seem to have won that game, how about a reward?"

"Or is that a punishment?" I murmur in her ear before proceeding to kiss my new fiancée.

About the Author

Ellen Jacobson is a chocolate obsessed cat lover who writes cozy mysteries and romantic comedies. After working in Scotland and New Zealand for several years, she returned to the States, lived aboard a sailboat, traveled around in a tiny camper, and is now settled in a small town in northern Oregon with her husband and an imaginary cat named Simon.

Find out more at ellenjacobsonbooks.com

Also by Ellen Jacobson

The Smitten with Travel Romantic Comedy Series

Smitten with Ravioli
Smitten with Croissants
Smitten with Strudel
Smitten with Candy Canes
Smitten with Baklava
Smitten with Caviar

Smitten with Travel Collection: Books 1-3
Smitten with Travel Collection: Books 4-6

The Mollie McGhie Cozy Mystery Series

Robbery at the Roller Derby
Murder at the Marina
Bodies in the Boatyard
Poisoned by the Pier
Buried by the Beach
Dead in the Dinghy
Shooting by the Sea
Overboard on the Ocean
Murder aboard the Mistletoe

The Mollie McGhie Cozy Mystery Collection: Books 1-3
The Mollie McGhie Cozy Mystery Collection: Books 4-6

ALSO BY ELLEN JACOBSON

The Complete Mollie McGhie Cozy Mystery Collection

The North Dakota Library Mysteries

Planning for Murder
Murder at the Library
Poisoned by the Book

www.ingramcontent.com/pod-product-compliance
Lightning Source LLC
Chambersburg PA
CBHW060940190726
48286CB00005B/1358